Praise

Bus No. 7 is an action-packed ride filled with high-voltage suspense and characters who aren't always what they seem. The twists and turns in this edgy thriller had me riveted past my bedtime. Mary J. Nestor is a masterful storyteller, and I hope she's writing a sequel.

HELEN P. BRADLEY Author of the novel *Breach of Trust*, voted best new local book in Connect Savannah's "Best Of" contest

Nestor's *Bus No. 7* is a riveting tale of infidelity, betrayal, drug addiction and murder in the shady underbelly of society. An exciting read.

G.J. Journalist and bestselling author

Mary Nestor's debut novel introduces a collection of unsavory and dangerous characters that sweep the reader into a dark landscape of crime and addiction where even the savvy detective has to play catch-up. *Bus No. 7* has readers wondering—what awaits when they turn the next page?

KAREN DOVE BARR Author of *Burnt Pot Island* and the forthcoming *Night's a Shadow, Day's a Shine*

Buckle your seat belt—*Bus No. 7* is a ride you won't forget. In Nestor's debut, a lost phone and wallet set off a chain reaction hurtling a cast of strangers onto a collision course. Racing through a city's underbelly, motives unravel and alliances shift, they speed toward a shocking end no one sees coming. Compelling, captivating, and addictive— *Bus No. 7* is a high-stakes story with every page revealing another lie.

BRIAN THIEM Author of
The Mudflats Murder Club

Mary Nestor's amazing new book, *Bus No. 7*, is a thriller in the best meaning of the word—a chilling tale that will have you on the edge of your seat!

ROSEMARY DANIELL Award-winning
author of *Secrets of the Zona Rosa:
How Writing (and Sisterhood) Can Change
Women's Lives*, and nine other books of
poetry and prose

Bus No. 7

To Betty,

Take Your Seat...

Mary J McitBoe

BUS NO. 7

MARY J. NESTOR

BOLD
STORY
PRESS

CHEVY CHASE, MARYLAND

Bold Story Press, Chevy Chase, MD 20815
www.boldstorypress.com

First edition: June 2025
Library of Congress Control Number: 2025910832
ISBN: 978-1-954805-85-9 (paperback)
ISBN: 978-1-954805-86-6 (e-book)

Cover and interior design by KP Books

Printed in the United States of America
10 9 8 7 6 5 4 3 2 1

To muses, demons, and lovers

Acknowledgments

TO SISTER ALICE, of the Sisters of Saints Cyril and Methodius, who taught the English Seminar class my senior year at Andrean High School, Gary, Indiana, and insisted on taking out all the "ands" in my poem "Justified" that appeared on the first page of the Senior Class Literary Magazine. This was my first experience seeing my work in print.

To my sisters Barbara and Fran, who were the first readers of the finished manuscript and offered honest but loving feedback.

To my sister Veronica, who watched out for me, encouraged my writing, and masterminded a daring escape for me that would have been (and may be) a page-turner in a future novel.

To my cousin Elaine, who invited me to the Bear River Writer's Conference in 2016, where I had the good fortune to get the last open spot in the short story seminar, where *Bus No. 7* was born as a short story.

To my seminar leader at the same writer's conference and to the audience at the closing night's open mic session who encouraged me by listening in rapt silence at the edge of their seats as I read what would become the first three chapters of *Bus No. 7*.

To Rosemary Daniell, author and poet and founder of the Zona Rosa Writer's Group, who showed me boundless support, love, and guidance in the following years as I finished writing the novel.

To all the members of the Savannah, Georgia, Zona Rosa Writer's Group who inspired me with their enthusiasm for my new pages at each meeting.

To Charlene Rothkopf, my dear friend, mentor, and fellow author, who graciously introduced me to her publisher, Emily Barrosse of Bold Story Press and set in motion a contract and my dream of getting *Bus No. 7* into print.

To Emily Barrosse, Founder and CEO of Bold Story Press, for taking on a first-time fiction writer, and to Karen Gulliver, Editorial Director, my gracious and forgiving editor, for her patience and coaching and for not giving up on me through the many editing rounds.

For the time and space to write—the second floor of Foxy Loxy in Savannah, the public libraries in Savannah and Hilton Head Island, an uncomfortable chair by an electrical outlet at B&N, on the deck looking over the pond in Queens Grant, and for finishing this Acknowledgments section on the deck of the Sunrise Catcher, Harpswell, Maine, overlooking Casco Bay.

To my dear best friends Judy and Deleise, who never let me give up my dream of being a writer, and for sharing enough experiences and escapes to fill a series of romance novels and mystery/thrillers.

Note that the characters in *Bus No. 7* are purely fictional, but if you think you see yourself in a character or scenario, thanks for the inspiration and for being a "muse unaware."

1

———

THE DAMN BUS was late again. Annabelle shifted from one foot to the other, trying to reposition her bulging belly off her bloated bladder, which was screaming for relief. *I should have peed before I escaped the office, she thought. But I can't miss the four forty-five-Number 7 bus or I'll be standing on the plaza in the crush of the five-o'clockers.* She could see them coming, spreading like water from an unattended garden hose on a hot summer sidewalk—first a trickle and then a rush, spreading in a Rorschach pattern onto the city streets.

She felt a sharp tug in her belly as she stretched on tiptoe to lift herself over the crowd at the bus stop, hoping for a glimpse of Bus No. 7. *Two more weeks, and this will be all over.* Hallelujah! she whispered as she spied the bus over the crest of the hill.

I must get a seat, she thought, as she pushed belly first to the boarding sign.

"Baby coming!" someone called out.

Annabelle forced a smile, inwardly fuming that she was identified by the creature she was carrying instead of the professional, sexy, exciting woman that she was. Lately she felt she was just a big belly perched on top of two very tired legs. The same legs that Jake fell in love with and couldn't keep his hands off—legs partly responsible for her current uncomfortable condition. But at least for the next couple of weeks, she could use her belly like a wedge to get to the front of line, parting the crush of commuters like Moses at the Red Sea.

The bus coughed and sputtered to a stop; Annabelle was first in line. She didn't see the girl with the pink hair and earbuds coming fast on her right, foot poised to leap into the bus ahead of her. Just then, an arm shot out from behind, blocking Miss Pink Hair's approach. Startled, Annabelle looked back to see a young man in a fraternity blazer, hand firmly placed on the door opening, shielding her from the sneak attack.

"Are you OK, ma'am?" His voice was soft and concerned.

How polite, Annabelle thought, as she smiled a grateful, shy smile. *Those college boys have such nice manners.* "Yes, thanks."

The bus had already made half its stops along Market Street, but Annabelle found an empty seat midway up the aisle. From her vantage point near the window, she observed the race for the few remaining seats as the crowd outside funneled in.

Once loaded, the bus bounced down the old, cobbled street and over the trolley tracks, long unused but preserved as part of the city's historic charm. The bus brakes hissed at each stop, releasing its captives and welcoming new ones. Annabelle tried to relax, wondering whether Jake would be at the last stop to drive her the rest of the way home. He had left a voicemail—something about needing to work late . . . again. As she glanced out the window, a few dark clouds crowded out the late afternoon sunshine.

Stop, hiss. As the bus started up again, the nice young man with the fraternity blazer came from the back of the bus and sat down next to Annabelle.

"Just wanted to make sure you're OK, ma'am," her defender said, his eyes squinting with worry.

Annabelle found it both comforting and unnerving that he looked so concerned. For a moment she felt a tug—this time in her gut.

"That girl almost knocked you off your feet," he said, clasping and unclasping his shaking hands, shifting sideways to face her.

She felt another tug. "I'm fine, really."

"I'm David," said the young man, with a narrow smile.

"Annabelle. Really, I'm fine." She turned her head to avoid his gaze, only to see his reflection in the bus window, his eyes looking her up and down with that same stare.

Annabelle closed her eyes to rest, hoping the young man would get the hint. But she felt his heavy stare wrap around her as if to draw her closer. She opened her eyes to find him staring at her belly.

"Sorry, I don't mean to be rude," David said. "My dad's new wife is expecting, and I'm going to have a little brother soon. Babies are all we seem to talk about at our house. Yours coming soon?"

Annabelle smiled weakly at her new protector. "Yes, a couple of weeks."

"I thought so," he said. "Well, I'm glad that you're OK." He rose and returned to the back of the bus.

Hiss. Stop. Hiss. Stop.

Annabelle turned to look back, and he was gone.

2

EARLIER THAT DAY, David had gotten off the bus at Market Square as he did every Tuesday. In his navy blazer, khaki pants, and button-down shirt and tie, he blended with the professional crowd working in the glass and steel towers surrounding the square. The five-dollar blazer from Goodwill with the fraternity honor society crest on the breast pocket was a nice touch. East Side Community College Honor Society was known for attracting the best and brightest young men, thought to be charming and gracious, well-schooled in business and social graces. Privileged young men were also known to push the legal limits but not regarded as sinister or dangerous. Just what David needed—a cover for his late-afternoon appointment with his dealer.

His former boss and dealer, Darcy Grover, had a nice cover as well; a C-Suite office on Market Square from which she ran a lucrative side business in cocaine, crystal meth, and opioids du jour. A year ago, David had been a bright student at East Side Community College and one of ten summer interns at West End Technologies. Darcy, CEO of West End Technologies, had a reputation for devouring companies and an occasional handsome male summer intern. Just a few weeks into his internship in her office, David was learning about more than balance sheets from this high-powered, voracious, and ruthless woman. Darcy liked her men young, hot, and unpredictable, fueled by drugs and shots of Don Luna Grand Reserve. But for Darcy, the attraction didn't last long. The feeling was mutual. When the summer internship and liaison ended, David had been glad to be rid of her demands but now was hooked on the drugs she continued to make available ... for a price.

David had made his way past the guard and up the elevator to Darcy's sixteenth floor office suite. She was usually civil, but today was different; Darcy had a new young intern, and David was now an awkward inconvenience. There would be no more meetings or transactions. She could pass along the name of another source for his drugs, but it would cost double.

He pleaded. She turned her back, picked up the phone, and told him to leave. Still, his craving for cocaine and oxycodone would not be denied, no matter what it cost or what he had to do. He could feel the aching begin.

Now David found himself on the street with a phone number for a new dealer scanning the crowd for a likely source of cash. He wiped his nose with the back of his shaky hand. He had to make something happen—and fast.

3

MARKET SQUARE WAS always full of people at the end of the workday. Lots of distracted people on cell phones, David observed, *I can lift a wallet and be gone before they know it.*

From the front of the crowd at the bus stop he saw a head slowly rise up like a submarine periscope, scanning for a bus. He had recognized her from previous Tuesdays—long blond hair, maybe thirty, and very pregnant. She tottered a bit on her tiptoes and then went periscope down into the crowd.

David had taken Bus 7 home a few times, getting off at a stop just before the end of the line. He recalled that she rode to the end of the line and was always alone. And now she was hardly likely to run very fast. He moved a little closer, threading his way through the crowd as the bus came to a stop in front of her. Standing behind her, David saw her expensive handbag, laptop bag, and iPhone. He could feel excitement rising in his gut, along with a craving for the dizzy rush of Oxy coursing through his body, soon to be satisfied. David's pleasure ache got stronger. His heart was racing, his body aching for the sweet relief he would get when this bit of business was over. The rush of pleasure was almost paralyzing, flowing through his veins again.

Their little chat on the bus had been enough to reassure him of his selection. She didn't notice when he slipped out the back door of the bus. Walking, then running, David replayed his bus-stop heroics in his head. It all happened so fast, as if orchestrated by a complicit puppet master with Miss Pink Hair, Annabelle, and David compelled to play their parts, unaware of the intended final act. Now as he sprinted down the darkened streets taking a shortcut to the last stop, he replayed the encounter as if written on the pages of a dark, foreboding script:

Bus hisses to a stop.

Doors open.

Pregnant woman moves to climb the bus stairs.

From Stage right, Miss Pink Hair runs over, foot in mid-air, elbow out to push pregnant woman out of the way.

From behind the pregnant woman, a handsome young man steps close to her and puts up his arm to the side of the open door, blocking Miss Pink Hair.

Handsome young man is a hero, the pregnant woman is grateful—open and an easy mark.

David smiled and quickened his step. He turned the last corner just as Bus 7 was coming around 5th Street, two blocks from the last stop. From a shadowy doorway across from the bus stop, he could see only two people left on the bus—the driver and the woman. Perfect.

Curtain up.

Stop. Hiss.

Act Two begins.

ANNABELLE TRIED TO relax in her seat, but it was hard, with thirty pounds of baby weight, placenta, and taco grande nachos balancing on her bladder. As she shifted, a pain began slowly, then intensified so quickly Annabelle could hardly catch her breath. She had dozed off after her bus seatmate got off and awoke feeling the sharp pains in her back and belly.

Jake had left a voicemail earlier, telling Annabelle that she should take the bus since he couldn't be at the plaza to pick her up.

Take the bus? What a loving, caring husband, she seethed. She leaned down to grab her cell phone from her bag. The pain seemed to be coming faster, and even her thumbs ached with every punch of the phone's keyboard.

She felt a warm, sticky ooze well up inside her sturdy, double-thickness underwear until it found an escape route to the bus seat and then down her leg. She let out a ragged scream, still groggy from her nap. Her doctor had already set up Shepherd Hospital for the delivery, and she was able to get one text out before the next contraction tried to split her in two.

"Jake not coming. On the bus. Something has happened. Please, Shepherd Hospital. Why am I texting you? *You* don't fucking care."

The bus took the corner wide around 45th Street and then corrected course, throwing her bag on the floor and tossing out her phone and wallet. She could barely see it over her belly, legs sprawled apart, instinctively avoiding the now cold, sticky, watery mess making its way down her leg over her shoes and puddling on the floor. Her feet and legs looked oddly swollen, spilling over the sides of her black Italian leather pumps. *Baby or not, I'm not going to waddle around in those sturdy orthopedic shoes the nurse so smugly showed me at my last doctor's visit. Not this sexy little soon-to-be mama.*

The first contraction followed the breaking water like an attentive soldier, with such force that she screamed again. The rest was a blur. Screams, pain, and people rushing in and out of her consciousness. Jake's car wasn't in the usual spot by the flagpole. Staring out at the deserted street, she felt a tug in her gut again.

Someone else was out there, but not for her comfort.

5

DAVID COULD BARELY focus in the dim street light. The figures on the bus looked more like shadows than humans—one shadow the driver, who would soon be gone, and the other an awkward, bulging woman, the main character in Act Two of a play under David's directorial command. *It's easier this way,* David thought, though he cared little for his unsuspecting cast.

The sliver of moon was hidden by gathering clouds. The lights over shop doors were too bright where David planned to approach Annabelle after she got off the bus. He pulled a Ravens baseball cap from inside his blazer, intended just for moments like this and pulled it low over his forehead.

"The eyes tell the story," his father had said to a young David as he delivered yet another merciless whipping. "Life is cruel, son, and I'm only helping you learn how to face its cruelty like a man."

David learned that well. "The eyes tell the story. No crying. No fear. No shame." *No clear view of my face, Dad. And no positive identification. You forgot that little benefit, you sick, cruel bastard!*

Stop. Hiss.

The bus pulled to the last stop. David played the scene in his head. *Pregnant woman gets off the bus, and it drives off, leaving her the perfect mark. As she walks past the darkened theater front, young hero snatches her laptop bag and purse and … then what? Hero runs away? Hero knocks woman down? Knocks her out? Strangles her with bag handles? Crushes her head with his boots?*

Lost for a delirious moment, David looked up to see the shadows moving on the bus, but not according to David's script. The woman looked like she was slumped over in her seat in the middle of the bus. The driver was standing by her side, then he turned and ran to the front of the bus and then back again. The woman didn't move. The bus doors swung open and expelled the driver, his hands clutching his head as if in agony as he frantically ran up and down the darkened street.

"Hey, you there," the driver called out to David. "You with the cap on."

Lost in the unexpected drama playing out on Bus 7, David had strayed out of the shadows, as if to get a better seat in a dark theater from which to watch the show.

"You! Come here," the driver commanded in panic, his words piercing the dark night. "I need help. She needs help! Oh, God, help us!"

How could I be so stupid—the driver can see me!

David steadied himself. If he kept his head down, the cap would hide his eyes. He put up a weak, trembling hand to wipe the wet stream beginning to run from his nose and walked toward the bus, redirecting the adrenaline conjured up for the imagined deed to just keep his hands and feet under control.

David pulled the cap lower over his eyes as he approached the bright lights of the bus.

"What happened?" David asked the bus driver, reluctantly switching his role from strung-out addict/robber/murderer to concerned hero.

The driver was alternately waving his hands in the air and gesturing to the bus.

"This is my last stop," the driver said, grabbing David's arm and propelling him towards the bus door. "One more passenger and I could get off this metal can and get a beer. I stop the bus and look back, and there she is, big as a whale, slumped over in the seat, something wet running down her leg and onto the floor! Three marriages and six kids. I know what that sticky mess is."

David did, too. Good old Dad, providing him with another life lesson on dealing with pain and the cruel world. David would have had that little brother that he had described to Annabelle on the bus, if his mother had just been stronger when her time came.

It's just a natural thing," his father told little David. "No need to rush to the hospital."

Even now he would sometimes be jolted from a deep sleep by his mother's agonizing screams, first from the birth pain, then from the still, lifeless body of her new baby boy.

"Stop staring and help me, will you?"

The driver shook David's arm and bolted up the bus steps. There she was as the driver described her. David felt no pity, only disgust and regret. *She's a weak one. It would have been so easy.*

David's gaze shifted to her laptop bag and open purse, now spilling its pricey contents all over the floor, about to be enveloped by the fast-moving, sticky pool.

I've called 911," the driver said, glancing over his shoulder from Annabelle to David, "but they aren't very quick this time of day. And I heard over the radio there's a big pileup near the Market Plaza. One last stop. Why couldn't she have just made it off the bus, and down the street?" the driver whined. "Not my responsibility anymore."

David smiled to himself. *Funny, I was thinking the same thing.*

"Let's get these things off the floor," David said in his most concerned voice.

The bus driver was back at the front of the bus, yelling something into his cell phone while scanning the dark streets for signs of the EMTs.

David bent over Annabelle's body, avoiding the sticky pool, and scooped up her phone and wallet just in time. "Mine now," he murmured as he slipped them into a hidden jacket pocket sewn into it for times like this.

The driver came running down the aisle just as David made a show of picking up the rest of Annabelle's belongings and put them into her bags, which he shoved into the seat across the aisle. *The laptop, iPad, and jewelry would have been mine too, if I had encountered Annabelle under cover of the darkened street,* David thought, angrily playing the scenario in his head. The driver stood over him, his hands waving in the air.

Annabelle started to stir, then moan, then started screaming. David cupped his hands over his ears, unconsciously that little boy again.

"Don't just stand there," the driver yelled at David. "Do something to make her shut up. I'm trying to listen for the ambulance."

David's script had changed. He'd been up to no good, but now he was supposed to be helpful and kind and a real hero in this disaster.

David put a trembling hand on Annabelle's shoulder. At first touch, Annabelle grabbed his hand, eyes closed, as if grabbing a lifeline on a stormy sea.

"It's OK, it's OK," he said, faking concern in his best soothing voice. She let out another scream, barely heard over the blare of the ambulance siren.

"Thank God!" the driver yelled. David watched him bolt out of the bus and run into the street, again alternately waving his arms and grasping his head, this time in relief.

Alone with Annabelle, who was as quiet as if asleep, he saw a new opportunity. Why hadn't he noticed it before? Around her neck was a slim gold chain with a very large diamond in a gold water lily setting, alternate petals curved to hold it tight. Struck more by its possible market value than beauty, David gently lifted Annabelle's head resting on the bus seat to reveal the oval clasp. With his other hand, he snapped it open and slid the chain across the back of her neck into his shaking palm and, in one seamless motion, into his jacket pocket.

Wouldn't have seen this in the dark street. Lucky me.

The rest happened quickly. David was again the observer, hardly noticed by the EMTs who followed their own well-rehearsed script. They approached in their uniforms, holding cases and talking into radio receivers. The bus driver, running behind, herded them like sheep into their pen. "She's in there," he pointed.

Annabelle stirred, opened her eyes, and moaned. David heard the driver's frantic voice inside the bus. "You're on the No. 7 bus, ma'am. I'm Gus, the driver. You're going to be OK," he said, as the EMTs—now the real heroes—took over.

David backed up as the EMTs stormed the bus; he was now trapped, forced to witness the scene unfold. The bus's back door, where he had made his earlier exit, was closed tight. He sat down in a back-row seat, head down. *Don't attract attention,* he thought. *As soon as they are gone, I can disappear into the dark street.*

The driver was now slumped in the front of the bus, happy to stay out of the way of the drama, dreading the mountains of paperwork he would have to file and, even more bitterly, thinking of the beer and buddies he would miss on this fucked-up night. From under the protection of his cap David listened as the EMTs grilled the driver for information. "Who was she, was she alone, what was her name?"

The driver responded with a string of I don't knows, followed by an exasperated, "I just drive the bus, I'm not a tour guide!"

David realized that only he knew her first name. *Better not to know too much*, he reasoned and slumped further in his seat, relieved that he remained unnoticed. He looked up to see the EMTs carefully descend the bus stairs with Annabelle and move toward the ambulance. He saw her handbag and laptop bag on the gurney at her feet.

He felt the bulge of her phone and wallet tucked in his secret pocket against his damp skin, that was soaked with sweat from excitement and withdrawal.

The EMTs slid the gurney into the ambulance and slammed the doors shut. David had to choose the right moment to slip off the bus and into the night. It was getting late, and he still had to call the new dealer that Darcy had pointed him to and make a score tonight. His body was beyond angry; its wrath like blows across his body from an unrelenting tormentor.

The EMTs and the bus driver huddled near the ambulance, engaged in a heated discussion. David slowly rose from his seat, hoping to escape unnoticed out the back door of the bus. Just then he heard shouting; the driver was waving his arm and pointing to the bus. As if standing center stage in the spotlight bathed in the bus's bright interior lights, David was again exposed. *Bad fucking timing*, he thought. The EMTs and the driver saw David in motion.

"Stop, wait!" he heard the driver call out as he rushed to the bus. Then looking over his shoulder at the EMTs, he heard the driver say, "That guy should go with her."

6

DAVID KEPT HIS head down and climbed obediently into the ambulance. It was better to keep his mouth shut and keep his now uncontrollably shaking hands out of sight.

"Make sure these go with her to the hospital," the driver said, flinging Annabelle's purse and computer bag at David's feet.

The doors slammed, and the ambulance raced off almost simultaneously. The blare of sirens pierced the dark, deserted streets, drowning out Annabelle's moans and screams.

The ambulance jolted to a stop. The bright lights of the emergency entrance blinded David for a moment. He watched the EMTs and waiting hospital staff go through their well-choreographed rescue routine, ignoring the slumped figure sitting in the back of the ambulance.

"Thanks, pal," said the driver as he grabbed Annabelle's bags.

David watched the parade of characters sprint into the hospital and disappear around the corner. Left behind, he was poised for escape, but then he had a cunning realization. Hospitals have lots of drugs. Hospitals are busy. People are distracted. Some things that go missing might not be missed at all.

It was easy to slip into the chaotic scene. Immediately after Annabelle's arrival, three gunshot victims rolled in, with doctors, nurses, and assorted staff running alongside gurneys and yelling out orders. The smell of blood, sweat, and night people living on the fringes almost sickened him. His eyes darted back and forth, looking for—he didn't even know what—when he spied him—Two Knuckles.

Damn!

He almost didn't recognize Two Knuckles in the green scrubs of a hospital aide, except for the scar on his nose and the distinctive tattoo on his left hand. Just to be sure, David edged closer. Two Knuckles got his name after he lost a bar fight and two fingers to a drunk and a broken beer bottle. As Two Knuckles reached for a gurney and started wheeling a patient down the hall, David saw the gap on his right hand. *That's him.*

David picked his way past a nurse trying to examine a screaming baby and her crying mother. He caught up with Two Knuckles as he turned the corner.

"Hey Two K," whispered David as he leaned in behind him.

"What the fuck?" Two Knuckles slowed down and cranked his neck to David's whisper.

"What are you doing here, man? And quit with the Two K. It's Dewain; here it's Dewain. Stop walking with me, and shut the fuck up! There's a loading dock around the side of this building. Meet me there in fifteen. Be cool."

David watched Two K head down the hall and into an elevator. The hallway was quiet, and he suddenly felt conspicuous. He turned, pulled his cap low over his eyes, and went back into the chaos of the emergency room lobby. He made his way out the door, past the ambulances disgorging humanity in distress, sprouting tubes and monitors and bags of life-giving liquids held aloft. *Wonder what's in those bags,* David wondered idly. *Probably nothing worth stealing.*

He wound his way around the building, past the parking lot to the loading docks. Even in the dark, he made out Two K's silhouette against the dim glow of the dock lights. A sign hanging by one corner above Two K's head read "Safety Is No Accident" in black block letters. A spiral of smoke rose from a cigarette in his hand as he flicked ash into the dark night.

"Two K, this is the last place I thought I'd find you. A junkie and felon working in a hospital? Around helpless sick people? A fucking pharmaceutical candy store! And *Dewain*? Jesus! Man, I'd really give a shit about how this came down, but right now I need some relief, you know. Has *Dewain* figured out the combination to the drug cabinets yet? Can *Dewain* fix his buddy David up?"

As David moved closer, Two K stepped back.

"Back off, junkie," Two K commanded. "How do you think I keep this gig? I'm not using, and I'm not stupid enough to carry while I'm working. They can pull me anytime to pee in the cup. Random testing. That doesn't mean I don't do a little business now and then. What do you want, junkie David? What you need, *baby*?" His voice turned into a snarl, drawing out the b-a-b-y with a sneer.

David loathed Two K, but especially since he was now in a pathetic, needy position. When they had been classmates in middle school, David was afraid of him and the bullies he hung out with. The last time he had seen Two K was five years ago at a dive bar on the edge of town. Two K had spotted David alone at the end of the bar and shook him down for some cash. He had still been the bully, and his pride in once gouging out an opponent's eye had made it reasonable to comply. Now David would again take the insults, the sneers, even the laughing. Hell, he'd take a beating—anything for a couple of Oxy or some coke or whatever it would take to make his raging aching go away. Two K leaned against the loading-dock platform and took a long drag off his cigarette, dropped it, and crushed it out.

"I got you covered, junkie. But it's gonna cost you. This is prime stuff—you know, for all the sick people in here. Not that street shit, but the best greedy drug companies can come up with."

David shoved his shaking hands into his pockets and came up with the two hundred dollars he had taken to Darcy's office for the buy that afternoon.

"Here," David said as he held out the folded cash. "Now what have you got?"

"Hold on, there. *Primo* stuff, junkie. You can swallow it, crush it, snort it, or cook you up some pleasure you've not even dreamed was this side of hell."

Two K turned, grabbed the damp bills from David's sweaty hands, leaned in close, and said slowly and deliberately, "What else you got for De-wain?"

Desperate, David stuffed his hands in his pockets again, and pulled out the necklace he had taken off Annabelle on the bus. The diamond caught the dim light and Two K's attention.

"Oh, now that's what I'm talking about," he cooed as he watched the diamond flashing, swinging from the delicate chain. "Where did you get this?"

"Belongs to a woman from the bus I was on. Pregnant, slow. Rode here with her in the ambulance. All I wanted was her wallet, but she started screaming about the baby, and there was so much water and blood, but I couldn't do anything and—"

David felt a blow to his head, and he was on the ground with Two K's knee on his chest and his hand over his mouth.

"Shut the fuck up! You're crazy, man. A crazy junkie thief. You stole this from some *pregnant woman* on the bus? And you came here with her? And you are talking to me? No, man. I don't want any part of this. Probably got this from her husband. Looks expensive, easy to trace, a bitch to sell or pawn. No good to me," he said, as he flung it next to David's sprawled body.

"Pathetic junkie," Two K repeated, shaking his head. "I happen to have $200 worth of some nice pills I just lifted from a little old lady in ICU who won't need them after tonight." Two K tossed two white capsules onto David's chest. "Your first and last buy from Dewain. And don't come back here."

David waited until Two K rounded the corner and disappeared into the dark. He carefully swept his hands over his chest, finally clutching the two pills in his fist as he got to his feet. He grabbed the necklace, picked his hat off the ground, and pulled it low over his eyes. He walked to the emergency room entrance, made his way to a water fountain, popped one capsule, and bent to take a long drink.

7

———

ANNABELLE'S DELICATE NECKLACE felt like a hundred-pound weight inside his blazer pocket. Probably an expensive gift from her husband, Two Knuckles had said. So, David can't hock it. If it's missing, they knew he was the last person with her. The stupid bus driver or one of the EMTs would be able to ID him. He had to get rid of it

"These things don't really amount to anything, except what they're worth, son," his father had said to him as they walked into the dusty, dim pawn shop on the west side of town. And when would you have time to roller skate, anyway? Skating is for sissies. Not a manly thing. More for girls in dresses. Now put them on the counter, son."

Eight-year-old David slowly lifted the roller skates he had gotten from an aunt for his birthday and put them on the counter. He had only been able to look at them in the box. The black leather shoes with the long laces, silver wheels that buzzed when he spun them, lying on their sides in the box. David looked away at the rows of plastic radios, musical instruments, and various guns in cases around the shop as his father completed the transaction.

"Not much of a gift," his father had said as he pocketed the five dollars. "Not worth much at all."

A gift. David had to return the necklace; people might remember he had been with her. He walked over to the hospital directory on the entry wall. Two K's capsule had eased his pain. He was feeling—what was it exactly? Not remorse. Not regret. No, he would have done anything to get what he needed, and that at once terrified and delighted him.

According to the directory, the birthing center was on the fifth floor. He reached out to punch the elevator button, then caught himself short. *Damn pill is making me feel safe, and stupid.* He pulled his cap lower, swung around, and disappeared through the exit door and took the stairs, two at a time, to the fifth floor.

He slowly pushed the stairwell door open and peered into the hallway. Not a person in sight. Anyone could walk up here unnoticed—at least that's what he hoped. *Hospital security. What an oxymoron,* David thought, smugly proud of his vocabulary. Underneath that cap of his, under the dirty blond hair curling at the base of his neck, was a nice little brain with an IQ that would put many to shame.

When people met David, they often made the mistake of taking in his detached demeanor, six-foot lanky frame with broad athletic shoulders and fitted button-down shirt as just another cute, awkward college boy. He used to object when approached that way, but quickly learned a twenty-five-year-old could use his youthful looks to his advantage. That wavy hair and slightly sexy, one-sided smile sometimes accompanied by a wink from his azure blue eyes got him through a lot of doors—office, bar, and bedroom, depending on the situation and his needs. *A blessing and a curse,* he thought, catching his reflection in the nursery window as he made his way down the quiet hallway.

"Such a pretty boy he is. You make too much of a fuss over him," David's father would taunt his mother when she brushed his curly hair or cupped his face in her hands before planting

a kiss on his cheek. "How is he supposed to be a man, with all the primping and coddling? May as well put a dress on him and silky ruffled panties."

How prophetic, he thought.

It had all started with a pair of silk boxers. It didn't take long for Darcy to move in on her new intern. Long, sultry looks from her dark eyes in an empty elevator or after the others had left a meeting. An innocent brush of her hip against his leg as they collided at the break room fridge. Her soft, breathless, whispered "So sorry!" accompanied by the touch of her hand on his forearm, lingering just a little too long. She knew her prey, and assessing the characteristics she desired was part of her interview process. Shy, smart, handsome. Lean and taut body and just the right promise under his khakis. She liked watching the nervous ones cross and uncross their legs. It made the interview so much more entertaining.

Internships had a timeline, and so did Darcy. Within two weeks, his work sessions with her ran late after everyone else had left the office. Who could turn down a shot of tequila from the boss after a hard day's work? And a line or two? Just a little extra perk from a successful, powerful mentor who was so generous and nurturing. Darcy was good at it, and so convincing. David was young, eager, and —well, a man. One late working day, after they finished a spreadsheet, two shots and a line of coke, Darcy walked over to her desk, pulled out a box, and slid it over to David.

"For you, my pretty, sexy man," she cooed, looking out at the city twinkling in the dark below.

"A gift? For me?" David asked, dazed.

The coo turned into a snarl. "Who else is here?" snapped Darcy, impatiently. Recovering her sweet demeanor, she whispered softly, "Just open it."

David fumbled with the ribbon and opened the box. Under the crisp tissue paper was a pair of Versace jet black, silk boxers—his size. He felt a sudden urge to vomit. Of course, he slid them on at her insistence and off again before his body could warm up the cold, soft silk against his skin.

5

———

THERE WAS AN issue at the nurses' station. A distraught father and six family members were talking and gesturing in hushed agitation. As David approached, he heard something about traveling all day crammed together in a minivan to see their "new grandbaby/cousin/uncle," and they all wanted to go in together to take a photo to send to the rest of the family. The nurse held her ground at three visitors at a time.

David smiled at his dumb luck and swiped a used visitor badge someone had left on the station counter as he passed by, proving his point about hospital security.

Each room was marked with the parents' names on a cute placard with bunnies and balloons in pink or blue for the baby, just like candy in a display case. David knew her first name only. His eyes darted back and forth under his cap as he walked down the hall, dodging nurses, orderlies, and an increasing number of visitors.

He turned the corner and saw "Annabelle and Jake" in two slightly lopsided hearts, surrounded by blue balloons and bunnies outside door 547C. A boy. He froze for a moment and couldn't breathe. His heart seized up. *A baby brother.*

Just short of the slightly open door, he could hear voices, low and then getting louder. Some rustling of covers while moving a tray table? Someone pouring water? It was hard to tell who might be in the room with Annabelle.

He reached inside his blazer and found the necklace, smooth and cool in his sweaty fingers. *Got to get rid of this fast,* David thought, as he heard a sudden loud ruckus behind him. Coming down the hallway was the family from the desk, all seven of them, looking at each door they passed and pointing, almost chanting in unison, "Room 545, Room 545" as they all squeezed into Room 545, laughing, and talking over each other. David hid behind a tall cart loaded with covered meal trays parked between the two rooms.

Stuck in his hiding place, David felt trapped. *Got to get out of here before someone can remember me.* Suddenly the red light above Room 547 started flashing, accompanied by short bursts of a muted buzzer. Within seconds, a cart followed by a doctor and two nurses careened around the far end of the hallway, racing towards the flashing buzzer. The cart fishtailed in front of the frantic emergency team, white coats flying, arms waving people out of the way. A dark-haired man about David's height poked his head outside Room 547, gesturing to the rescuers, and they all disappeared into the room.

Seizing his moment, David pulled the necklace out of his coat pocket, emerged from his hiding place, and quietly entered the room. The emergency team's eyes and hands were frantically attending to the convulsing body in the bed, which he recognized as his mark from the bus. He spied Annabelle's computer bag on the floor near the door. In one motion, David crouched down and slid the necklace into the open corner of the bag. He turned, still half crouching, out of the sightline of the emergency team and made his escape.

Outside the room, he heard the continued chaos and the doctor shouting orders. As he rounded the hallway corner, David stopped and looked back at the room. The dark-haired man was leaning up against the outside door frame, taking a call on his cell phone. David saw his head tilt back as he talked. Was he smiling? Laughing? *How strange.* The doctor summoned him back into the room. The dark-haired man gestured for the doctor to wait and turned, smiling as he directed his attention back to the caller, then pocketed his phone and stepped back in.

9

OUT ON THE street, away from the hospital's glare and crowds, David turned his mind back to his earlier quest. He had one more of the pills he'd gotten from Two Knuckles tucked away in an inside pocket, but that was not going to satisfy him for long. Already, he could feel a slight aching inside his gut—or was it hunger?

It was now hours since he had boarded Bus 7, and he hadn't eaten anything since the noontime greasy double burrito from the Totally Tostada Tornado food truck parked in the square near the park. He saw a neon sign in the distance flashing alternately "Bar" and "Eats" against the evening sky. It seemed like the right combination after a hard day's work. Neither the neighborhood nor the bar looked familiar, but he was drawn in by the flashing, persistent invitation above his head.

The bar was dim. He recognized the smell. Small, dark bars all smelled the same—a mixture of old, musty wood, deep-fry grease, spilt beer, after-five blue collar sweat, and just a faint hint of vomit from a good night gone bad. A large, curved wooden bar with cushioned bar stools took up the long side of the room. A mix of round and square wooden tables and chairs were scattered around the rest of the room like jacks tossed out on the ground to start a new game.

David made his way to the far end of the bar, sliding onto a barstool as the bar's curve made its way to the wall. From his vantage point, he imagined how the other patrons ended up here. The couple at the other end of the bar were gazing at each other, their eyes locked. The man's left arm curled around her neck and rested on her shoulder; fingers extended just far enough to gently stroke the skin just above her left breast. Her left arm was positioned on the bar—and her right hand? Deliberately out of sight, but actively engaged. They were definitely not married. A lucky date for him? A working girl plying her trade?

He shifted his attention to a few men seated at the bar, nursing their beers, blankly staring at the TV screen. One looked like he might have been married and was making that one beer last long enough so his wife would be asleep when he got home. And seated at a table near the window, a fifty-ish overdressed couple holding hands, both of them gazing transfixed at her left hand. A bouquet of flowers rested on the table next to a small, empty box with a satin lining, its top snapped open. Two losers hoping for a second chance? A match made on the internet? A dime-store novel with a cliché ending of happily-ever-after, traveling the world together in their RV?

"Pick your poison," the bartender sighed, tossing a bar menu on the counter. He aimed a frown at the clock on the wall behind David. "Just got here, and it's dead, dead, dead. Two a.m. can't come fast enough. The drinks are good, and tonight I'm feeling generous. He wiped his hands on a wrinkled towel tucked into his belt.

"The food—eat at your own risk. Sal back there in the kitchen had another knock-down with his ex-girlfriend before his shift. He's out for revenge, and customers, I'm afraid, are his victims for the night."

David ordered a double Makers Mark and the ribeye and settled back.

"Want to run a tab?" asked the bartender.

Tab? Shit! David remembered that Two Knuckles had all his cash. Instinctively, he shoved his hands in his jacket pockets and then inside and felt Annabelle's wallet and phone.

He slipped it out of its hiding place. It felt warm, birthed from deep inside his inner coat pocket. He pushed back from the bar just enough to open the wallet on his lap and make out the contents. Bus passes. Two banks of credit cards. A few faded pictures, receipts, and two concert tickets. Then David saw them. Ten crisp new $100 bills. The bartender refilled David's glass and tried to peer over the bar.

"Trouble?" he asked.

"No," David smiled, giving the bartender a quick wink. "No trouble at all."

David devoured the steak the bartender delivered, had another two fingers of Markers Mark, and leaned back on his barstool. He fished his phone out of his back pocket and felt for the crumpled note that Darcy had shoved in his hand with the number of her substitute dealer.

Thanks, Darcy, for providing a new supplier who doesn't require the added surcharge of sex and having to pretend to like it.

Darcy was powerful and successful. It had taken her time to earn that corner office. At forty, she rose to CEO with a six-figure income and a lucrative side gig supplying the best cocaine this side of the river to a list of prominent, discreet clients. David smoothed the note on the bar; the phone number was like the combination to the lock on a prison cell, and he felt like an innocent man pardoned by the judge, walking through the prison gates.

David punched in the dealer's number. Excitement began to build inside of him. He could almost feel the crisp hundred dollar bills straining to get out. No answer, but the voicemail kicked in.

"You called me, so leave a message or don't." Beep.

David turned away from the bartender's prying glance, spun his stool to face the back wall, and muttered a quick message into the phone. The guy sounded like a real jerk, but it didn't matter if he was the devil himself. David had the cash, and this dealer wasn't the first jerk he'd run into that night.

Now to wait. The bar was darker now, with only the faint glare of a streetlight penetrating the grimy front window. The middle-aged couple that had admired the ring had left, leaving behind the now-wilting flowers. Two empty beer glasses sat on the bar; their users had long disappeared into the dark streets. The lovers were now squeezed together in a back booth, locked in a heated discussion.

David opened Anabelle's wallet under the bar and slipped the bills into his pocket. He pulled out the photos. A smiling younger version of Annabelle and a good-looking athletic guy standing next to her, one arm around her waist. They both faced forward, but her face turned to look at him. He stared a perfect half-smile, unaware of her loving gaze. The other photo showed a cottage by a lake with two people in a canoe, ready to launch from a rickety dock. The figures were too small to distinguish. A faded memento from a happy vacation?

She wouldn't be needing the bus passes, so David put them in his pocket with the bills. The concert tickets were for the Annual Rock Festival in two days, $250 seats right up front. She wouldn't need those, either. David slipped the tickets into his shirt pocket, wiped off the wallet with his napkin, and slipped it back into his pocket just as another pocket started to vibrate. Annabelle's phone.

"One for the road?" the bartender called from the other end of the bar.

"No, all set," said David. He pulled a $100 bill out of his pocket, not waiting for the change.

Outside in the dark in the alleyway, he pulled out the phone and saw "missed call and voicemail." Foolish woman; she had no security code. He found the message and heard a man's voice.

"You've been pre-approved for a $50,000 loan, no credit check, no strings—"

David erased that message and saw another voicemail left several hours ago. He hit the arrow and heard another voice, this time rushed and straightforward.

"I'm running a little late, Annabelle. Had to work late, and now traffic is backed up on the approach to the bridge. Damned construction! Take the bus, and wait for me at the usual place."

A heartless bastard, making a pregnant woman wait in the dark after a day at work.

Any number of terrible things could have happened to her. Terrible things.

10

AFTER THE AMBULANCE had driven off with the pregnant woman, Gus bounded up the steps of the No. 7 bus and swung into the driver's seat. He shot a quick glance into the rear-view mirror, then into the empty street in front of him, closed the doors, and pulled out into the night. *Hiss!* The street was a blur, but he'd been driving this route for so long he didn't need eyes to show him the way. He drove by lights and colors. At the top of the hill, traffic lights marked a left turn in front of the new glass-and-steel high-rise building. Another left turn, and he was headed back towards the city and Market Square on his return run. It was easy once he hit Market Square, threaded through the narrow streets of the restaurant district, and made the turn back up Broadway.

He was the last of two generations of transit workers in his family.

"Not me, Dad," his son said when Gus told him he put in a good word for him at the transit office. "Won't catch me driving a bunch of losers around, smelling of diesel fuel and food truck hot dogs. I don't want to wear a groove in the street and my brain, following the same boring route, dealing with drunks, punks, and whiny kids who treat you like you're their personal chauffeur. Rather put a gun to my head."

Gus squinted against the glare of the tall streetlights as he passed over the river bridge. A faint odor of human body fluids hung in the stale bus air, emanating from the sticky pool left behind by the woman.

His cloudy eyes caught the off-rhythm flash of a blue and green neon sign for Frankie's Bar at the corner of 5th and Broadway. Gus turned right at the next corner, diverting to the bus garage for a quick cleanup. As he pulled into the service entrance, he saw a police car parked at the corner with two officers leaning up against the small phone-booth size office talking to the dispatcher. As Gus parked, the dispatcher came out of the little office and pointed at him in his bus. The officers turned and began walking toward him. *Stop. Hiss.*

Gus swung down the steps. "What's happening, officers?"

"We responded to your 911 call but had to divert. We caught up with the EMTs at the hospital, and they said there had been quite a situation on your bus. We have just a few questions to ask you for our report," said the taller of the two.

"Situation?" Gus played out the scene on the bus, hoping the guy in the baseball cap hadn't repeated what he had said about the "whale." "How can I help, officers?"

One officer started firing questions while the other scrawled notes in a small black notebook. Yes, a pregnant woman passed out and left something sticky all over the floor beneath her seat. No, he didn't know her name. Yes, there was a guy on the bus—well, no, he wasn't on the bus, but he was in the shadows across the street. Gus asked him to sit on the bus with the woman while he did his job—by the book—and called the EMTs to get that woman off the bus. Who was the guy? Don't know, didn't get his name. It was all so fast. What did the guy look like? Don't know, don't remember. It was dark. Gus had been in the street with the

EMTs. The guy had a baseball cap pulled low over his eyes, with some kind of bird on it. He went with the woman in the ambulance to the hospital. The EMTs should be able to give you a description, for God's sake.

Gus' impatience and thirst were growing. He'd need an extra shot in his beer at Frankie's if he ever got out of there.

The officer took a breath, and Gus let out a huff. "Why all the questions, officer?" Gus tried to sound concerned and not like he was ready to hit the guy in the face.

"The woman's cell phone and wallet are missing. Did you see them? Do you know what happened to them?" the officer said, staring Gus square in the eyes.

Gus strained to focus on the officer's face, which was a blur in the fluorescent glare of the garage lights.

"No, I didn't see them, and no, I didn't take them. Search me. Search the bus!"

"Now take it easy; no one is accusing you of anything, sir."

Sure—they blame the poor jerk driving the bus. Poor, stupid, underpaid, low-life slob who can't get a better job, and just waits for the opportunity to steal from pregnant, passed-out passengers.

"I just pulled in here to clean up the bus floor where she … well, leaked, and finish my shift," said Gus.

"This bus is out of service until we look it over," said the officer as he snapped the cover on the little notebook. "Your shift is over for the night. But we may have more questions, so stick around while we look things over, in case we have more questions."

The second officer shoved a card in Gus's direction. "Call us anytime if you happen to remember anything

"Sure will, officer," said Gus, swallowing the venom rising in his throat.

His eyes were getting worse with the diabetes, and Gus wouldn't remember anything because he couldn't see anything anymore. But that would remain Gus's secret. A bus driver who can't see faces? That would be the end of his not so stellar career and the end of an era.

The officers went aboard the bus and started their inspection, taking photos with a cell phone and asking questions that Gus couldn't answer, so he made them up. Satisfied, the two officers made their notes and drove away. In the garage, Gus fired up his pickup truck and headed for Frankie's Bar and his friends that he hoped would still be there. And the cold beer with a double shot he earned after this terrible shift.

11

ANNABELLE WAS SLEEPING soundly. All the horror and stress of going into labor on the bus, the preeclampsia, falling blood pressure causing intermittent loss of consciousness, and the pain and screaming had taken its toll. The delivery was dangerous, with the doctors working frantically to save both mother and child. Now she was sleeping and unaware of the drama that had unfolded during the past hours.

The dark-haired man in the chair next to her bed checked his phone again. *Sweet Anabelle.* He stared at her text from the bus.

"Jake not coming. On the bus. Something happened. Please, Shepherd Hospital. Why am I texting you? *You* don't fucking care."

She wanted him to care, but wouldn't let him, thought the dark-haired man, glancing over to her sleeping body, watching her chest rise and fall in sync with the beeping of the heart monitor. *You ended our affair, and that should make me want to tell you off and disappear forever. I may be a fool for running to you tonight.*

His gaze stopped at her long, blond hair, loose and somewhat matted, the result of sweat and being transferred from bus to gurney to ER, to delivery, to current destination on the birthing floor. He felt a rise within him, even as she lay there asleep in the standard hospital gown, a black mascara scar-like streak across her left cheek. He closed his eyes and could feel that hair, loose and warm, spilling over onto his bare chest. Holding those long tresses in his trembling hands, moving up and down in sync while she pleasured him. *Sweet, giving, needy, Annabelle.*

He had been the first to arrive at the hospital. No one questioned his explanation that he was a co-worker that she called in a panic because her husband couldn't be reached. No one bothered to ask for identification in the chaos. Devoted co-worker here for support. Once established, the relationship gave him access to her room and the nursery. A phone call took him out of her room and into the hallway, a welcome respite from his role as devoted, concerned co-worker to get back to business matters.

"Roger." He heard her soft voice, no more than a whisper, calling his name. She was waking again

"I'm here, baby. Your Roger is here."

She smiled, eyes closed, still half asleep, turned her head to the side, her body relaxing into the pillow and bed covers pulled up around her.

"My Roger."

12

ROGER, THE DARK-HAIRED man, was not her co-worker. Friend with benefits, maybe. He and Annabelle had met at a charity auction a year before. She was working at the silent auction tables as a volunteer at an evening museum fundraiser. He was a top-level donor who paid the $500 ticket fee for the privilege of bidding on high-priced trips and artwork and to eat three-star cuisine in the cold, cavernous atrium of the modern art museum. His wife, begging off with yet another headache, afforded him a solo appearance. Without her, he was in his element—smooth, elegant in a GQ sort of way, witty, and on the prowl.

Annabelle had decided after too many nights alone that she needed to get out of her empty house. She became a docent at the museum, helping out with an occasional evening lecture or weekend fundraiser. Her motives were not entirely pure and noble. The wealthiest and most distinguished of the city's men, eligible or not, were patrons and supporters of the museum, and she was not averse to meeting a handsome man to engage in stimulating conversation, if only for a brief moment while she checked his coat or looked up his table on the seating chart.

That's more than she got from her husband, Jake. When he wasn't buried in his computer or out five nights a week at his meetings, which were just excuses to go drinking with his buddies from various community organizations, he was complaining about why his shirts weren't back from the cleaners or that dinner wasn't what he expected. Yes, sitting at a table in a downtown museum and flirting with powerful, wealthy, handsome men was way better than that.

A coy conversation between Roger and Annabelle led to a drink after the museum auction. Annabelle had time on her hands, and Roger was a free agent for the night. The chemistry between them ignited, burned hot. That first night developed into a three-month, clandestine affair, with Roger's yacht their preferred hookup spot, docked at the quiet, private access side of the marina.

Roger was a gentle, insatiable, attentive lover, but Annabelle grew tired of the game. Her IT project development job was demanding, and Roger's pursuit of her had made for an exciting respite from her loneliness. But working all day and satisfying her lover at night chipped away at the excitement. And Roger became a little too possessive, wanting more of her life. She felt trapped in a game she feared would have a bad ending.

And there was Jake, who after a night of drinking with the guys would expect—no, demand—to have hot sex with his adoring wife when he finally made it home. She felt that her life had become a bad soap opera, as she wearily left her lover to go home to service her husband.

One night she arrived late and exhausted at the marina for a rendezvous with Roger, knowing that Jake was on his way home early and would be driving up their driveway in less than an hour. She stood in the doorway of the boat's lower cabin, sighed through exhausted tears, "I'm here, but this is the end." Roger was surprisingly unruffled. Apparently, he had wearied, too, of Annabelle's demand for secrecy and constant fear of discovery. Seeing a merciful out, Roger quickly put on his shirt, gave Annabelle a kiss on the forehead and was gone, leaving Annabelle standing in the boat's bedroom alone.

Stunned and relieved, Annabelle made it home a mere ten minutes after Jake. He was predictably drunk and feeling amorous.

Annabelle's explanation didn't need to be convincing or even believable. She knew the one thing that Jake couldn't resist, that made him powerless and stupid and gullible. A former dancer, Annabelle need only slip her long, sculpted, supple legs into a pair of thigh-high black stockings to render Jake totally helpless and thinking of nothing else. The sky could fall, volcanos erupt. Those silken legs wrapped tightly around his torso would right a hundred wrongs.

13

THAT SHOULD HAVE been the end of their affair, until Roger had spotted Annabelle at the bus stop on Market Square, about three months after their last meeting. She looked different. Still the beautiful blond with those long legs, but a little rounder. He knew every inch of that lithe, taut body, and there was something in her slow, steady gait that made him stop and stare. The sun was sinking, and as she turned, the long, low rays outlined a perfect little belly bump.

"Hey, watch it, asshole" a tattooed girl yelled as Roger walked into her. She barely glanced from her lighted screen, thumbs flying over the keyboard.

"Sorry, miss, I didn't see you," said Roger.

He shifted his attention from the collision to the spot where Annabelle had been standing, but she was gone.

The next afternoon, he returned to the square at five o'clock. A few minutes later he saw her again, this time with some women he guessed were from her office, chatting and laughing as they made their way to the bus stop. Undeterred, Roger stalked her daily until, a week later, he finally caught her alone on her way to the bus and steered her to a back booth in a small café off of Market Square.

Roger didn't have to ask.

"Yes, I am. No, it's not—at least I don't think it is. I don't know," said Annabelle, looking at the wall just to the side of Roger, avoiding his wide-eyed stare.

Roger was not about to sabotage his reputation with a scandalous divorce, but he did have one unfulfilled item on his wish list. A kid. This unexpected turn could, in some twisted way, fill the void in his family and the ache in his wife's heart for a child of their own. It would be his child, and with some convincing, hers as well. Could his part-time, shared son or daughter cure his wife's depression and their loveless marriage?

"Could it be?" Roger uttered slowly, torn between delight and despair.

"Of course, you asshole," said Annabelle. His eyes got even bigger at her remark, at once proud and terrified of the possibility.

"Jake thinks it's his, of course, though this could be the second Immaculate Conception, except in reverse," said Annabelle. "Seems his swimmers have had trouble finding the finish line. Not that they can't, but up till now, they are swimming with blinders on. Yours may have hit the target, but I'm not talking, and he's not suspicious. He's also not around much."

A pause, and Annabelle's demeanor softened, her eyes finally meeting his.

"Roger . . . oh, Roger," she murmured in a voice he'd heard before. He felt a sack of concrete in his gut at those words. Something was coming, and he wished he was somewhere else, far away from this inconvenient meeting that he had made happen.

"Roger, I don't know if Jake is going to be there for me. He's been away a lot more; I feel so alone," she said, staring directly into his eyes.

Annabelle looked desperate, which could play in his favor. Roger considered the options. Annabelle could be cooking *his* baby. His kid. The unchecked box on his life to-do list. He could claim paternity quietly, armed with an irrefutable DNA analysis while providing little Roger with a second family complete with a loving, doting new "mother" and a generous, anonymous trust fund. Or Annabelle could go rogue, call him out, and destroy his marriage, career, and his brilliant future.

"Yes, of course. Things have changed," Roger murmured. "If you need me, I'll be there, Annabelle," he said, staring into her eyes across the small wooden table, hoping his concern sounded genuine, and congratulated himself

———

Her text from the bus had sounded so desperate and alone. So here he was. He'd only been with her for a few minutes, but he'd better not linger too long. He was already feeling uneasy. Jake could show up any minute.

He had unexpectedly met Jake when he and Annabelle were at an art opening at a small gallery in the Market District. Jake had a habit of appearing unannounced. Roger always wondered if Jake didn't trust her, or if he was just the paranoid, controlling type.

Annabelle coolly introduced Roger as a co-worker, which startled Roger, surprised at her creative lie. She explained that they were colleagues, working on critical projects, working late to meet deadlines, analyzing results from research data and beta testing results.

So, it wouldn't be too much of a stretch for Roger to now be at the hospital for Annabelle, especially in an emergency situation. But plausible or not, he would rather not meet Jake in this setting at this time.

Roger took Annabelle's hand, lifted it to his mouth, and kissed it gently. "Sleep well, baby."

He turned away, picked up his backpack and noticed Annabelle's open computer bag on the floor by the door, visible from the hallway. As he moved it to the opposite side of the room, he noticed the necklace draped over her laptop in the bag and was puzzled. She always wore it. It was a gift from Jake. He knew she didn't take it off—not in the shower or to sleep or anything.

Jake will surely notice if she's not wearing it.

Roger pulled the necklace out of the bag, gently lifted Annabelle's sleeping head off the pillow, slipped the necklace around her neck, and secured the clasp.

A quick glance down the hallway showed a clear escape. He made his way around the corner past the nurses' station and stopped only for a minute in front of the nursery window. There he was, a little dark-haired bundle sleeping, wrapped tightly in a blue-striped receiving blanket. "Annabelle and Jake" was printed in big letters on the blue-bordered card slipped into the slot in the bassinet facing the nursery-room window.

Yeah. Maybe.

14

RACING TO MEET the bus, Jake pushed the pedal down in his BMW. Late again. *Oh, well, there's a bench at the bus stop in front of the flagpole.* He loved the roar of the engine, the smooth uptake and speed. *Better than drugs,* he thought.

Annabelle had pushed for the Lexus SUV with a built-in booster seat. Price wasn't a consideration. Business was good. But Jake wasn't the type to drive around in a lame, fucking SUV, no matter what make. The SUV was for Annabelle and the baby.

When Jake met Annabelle, they had been college students. Jake was from Orange County; a handsome, confident extrovert on a full academic scholarship, headed for a brilliant future in law or finance or something exciting and risky—whatever would make him very wealthy. He had enough of quiet suburbia, spending time between classes hanging out at the beach and chasing girls.

A master of the side hustle, Jake had a knack for listening to determine not only what other people needed but how to fulfill those needs—and make a little cash at the same time. He was a natural at pairing up lonely, awkward college students so they could walk into the Friday-night football game or the Fall Festival dance with a presentable date on their arms. The campus was his office, the 2,000 students his potential client base. Even the jocks and prom princesses sought out his services. For a quick twenty bucks, Jake could set up a personal introduction to the future Mr. or Ms. Perfect—or at least a warm, willing body for the next party, hookup, or campus event.

Before long, Jake's client list included half of the school's best and worst dating material. "Sick of Solo" was born, and Jake was raking in the cash. The profile and introduction were both services rendered. He made no guarantees of lasting love or even a hook-up—the results were up to the happy couple. No refunds. No complaint desk. The college had plenty of shy, awkward, or just despicable students who couldn't get their own dates, and each September brought in a fresh crop of potential clients.

By his junior year, Jake was the community college's wealthiest independent businessman with no problem getting his own dates, guaranteed to connect at a moment's notice. Sick of Solo rewarded its CEO with a used, 2000 black BMW convertible—his babe mobile—though he didn't need help attracting willing women to take his ride. Until he met Annabelle.

He spied her walking on campus, long blonde hair pulled straight back into a low ponytail, the long, soft curls tossed by the wind and bouncing off her ballet-straight back as she smoothly dodged students walking on the crowded walkways, their eyes glued to their digital phone screens. She walked as if she had an important appointment or was meeting a new lover. Purposeful and confident. He remembers her softness. Faded jeans that hugged her toned, tanned body. A cotton t-shirt under a soft plaid shirt, buttoned only halfway up. She wore little makeup, but it would only have hidden her flawless skin, perfect eyebrows, and green eyes.

He had just pulled up in front of the campus center, attracting a crowd of friends and potential clients.

He watched her wind her way through the crowd until she glided up the steps of the humanities building across from the campus center and disappeared behind the carved wooden doors.

The Freshman Intake weekend drew hundreds of new students looking for help with housing, activities, and social connections. Sick of Solo had a reputation as the best way to meet the best people on campus, and Jake was busy setting up a booth in the Campus Center and almost didn't notice her, standing at the table, fingering one of the flyers.

"Ah . . . can you tell me something about this Sick of Solo thing?" she asked in a soft but steady voice.

"You don't strike me as one who is solo very often or for very long," said Jake, extending his hand more out of a desire to actually touch this exquisite creature than to exchange pleasantries.

Looking down at the photo on the flyer, she looked up at Jake, down again, and said, "You're him. Jake."

"That's what they tell me." Jake flashed a winning smile. And your name is . . . ?"

"Annabelle."

"You are stunning. I hope you don't mind if I say so," he said.

She brushed his comment aside, glancing away as if she had heard it or some variation, before and too often.

"I have a full schedule this semester, I'm on several committees *and* have a job, so I don't have time to hang out at parties or bars trying to meet someone. Someone who is tolerable and won't make me want to poke my eyes out— or his—by the end of an evening," she explained. "A profile and two introductions for $30? Sounds reasonable. Where do I sign up?"

She had him at the poking-eyes-out thing. Beautiful, self-assured, and a sense of humor—at least he hoped she was kidding about the eye thing.

A few keystrokes and he had her; or at least her profile, including her name, address, phone number, dating preferences, dreams, desires. She would be an easy one to connect, but sadly she wouldn't have much luck through Sick of Solo. Jake didn't care what she was looking for; he already decided Annabelle was his cure for solo sickness.

After a week, Annabelle left a message and her number on the SOS's website. "One week and still SOS. Do you have a refund policy? Anna-Ring-Your-Bell."

Jake responded. "So sorry you're unhappy with our service. Would like more feedback. Meet for coffee today at two o'clock at Caffeine Blitz on the West Side?"

She replied. "Ok, sure. Just a quick one. I've got a class at 3:30."

Annabelle watched as Jake slid his BMW into a tight parking spot in front of the coffee shop. She felt a tug watching the car door open, his tall, lanky body revealing itself slowly—leather loafers, no socks, then the washed jeans hugging toned, muscular legs. His broad chest formed the top of an inverted pyramid. She wondered if she detected evidence of a six pack underneath his soft blue polo shirt. Stooping down at the car's side mirror, he swiped at his thick, wavy blond hair, walked across the street, and into the Blitz.

15

GUS PULLED HIS old Honda Civic into the bus terminal parking lot and parked it. The engine wheezed to a stop. The car had 190,000 miles on its odometer and was still giving it up for Gus.

His head still throbbed slightly from one too many shots last night. After the near-delivery on his bus, along with the ambulances and the cops grilling him, he had needed to tie one on. Gus didn't need an excuse to overindulge, but it felt better somehow, even if he was only talking to himself.

He grabbed his bag off the back seat. It held a half-eaten sub from the night before and a bottle filled with a mixture of water and vodka, just to get him through the afternoon lull before the commuter crush at five. He trudged to Bus 7, parked in its usual spot, when he noticed the same officers from last night standing in the dispatch office. Gus turned his shoulder to the window and quickened his step, hoping to climb onboard before anyone saw him. Just as he was mounting the first step, he heard a voice call out.

"Gus, over here. These guys want to talk to you."

Shit! Gus froze, then stepped down and shuffled to the dispatch office.

"Good morning, officers. What can I do for you this morning?" He spoke as cheerfully as he could, head pounding in cadence with every word.

"Just a few more questions. You said that there was only one other person at the bus stop when the lady went into labor on the bus? The one who is missing her phone and wallet

"That's right," said Gus. "I didn't see his face since his cap was pulled low."

"Anything else about him that you remember?" asked the detective, talking into his notepad.

Gus retreated into his throbbing head, as if he was trying to remember something. "No, officers, it was so crazy with the lady screaming and fainting and then the ambulances arriving. It all happened so fast."

"OK, was there anything else about that night that seemed out of the ordinary? Any other disturbances, strange people. Anything like that?" the officer asked.

Strange? In Market Square on my bus route? Take your pick. Images fought their way through his memory, fogged twice by poor recollection and the blurry haze his eyesight made of everything.

"Wait, there was something else, but I don't know if means anything," Gus said. "In the square earlier. I was picking up and there was a crush of evening commuters. They pushed to the door when I stopped, and I heard yelling when a girl with pink hair tried to jump the line. Someone stuck a hand against the door to block her, and she bounced off back into the crowd. And the pregnant lady got on. I heard some nasty comments and a few cheers from the crowd. The pink-haired girl was one of the last people on the bus. I've seen her waiting there before. Rides once in a while and always gets on at Market Square. Like I said, may not mean anything. That's all I remember. Can I go now? Got a schedule to keep. Got to get people to work."

The cops shook their heads, nodded, and waved him off.

Gus boarded his bus, tucking his bag snugly under his seat. He cranked her up, closed the door, and set off into the morning traffic. One block ahead he could see the early risers queuing up.

Stop. Hiss.

Morning, miserables. Good morning, indeed.

16

"MY BABY! WHERE'S my baby?" Annabelle cried out.

She groped for the call button, still groggy from the anesthesia, pain pills, and exhaustion.

"Ms. Martin," said a nurse in blue flowered scrubs, bounding through her door. "I'm here. So glad you're finally awake. What can I get for you?"

"My baby," cried Annabelle. "What have you done with him?"

"Now, relax. You've had a difficult time of it. Your baby is sleeping in the nursery. We'll bring him to you just as soon as the doctors have completed an evaluation and give the go ahead."

Another figure appeared at the door and hesitated, seeing the nurse beside Annabelle's bed.

"Jake—oh Jake! Finally," said Annabelle. "It's OK. Come in."

The nurse turned and nodded in agreement. Jake walked in slowly, putting his briefcase beside Annabelle's computer bag, and went to the other side of the bed. He bent down and gave Annabelle a kiss on the forehead.

"So sorry, babe," he whispered, as if embarrassed by his late arrival. "I had a late meeting—and this wasn't supposed to happen for a couple of weeks. As I was pulling in to meet your bus, I got a call from the hospital ER that you were brought in by ambulance."

Jake tried to sound concerned and apologetic, more for the nurse's benefit than Annabelle's. The former could be fooled, but Annabelle knew Jake only too well.

She grabbed Jake's hand, drew him close, and kissed him full on the mouth, perhaps lingering just a little too long for a woman who just delivered a baby. Jake looked up just long enough to see the nurse's eyebrow arch inquisitively.

Jake caught the nurse's glance. He pulled up and stepped back a little.

"Have you seen him yet?" she asked.

"No, not yet."

"Me neither. I've been sort of out of it. You missed a lot of excitement," Annabelle said with a touch of sarcasm, the "as usual" unspoken but intended.

"I'll bring the baby in right away," said the nurse as she slid the blood pressure cuff off Annabelle's arm. "He will be so happy to see his mommy and daddy for the first time."

Jake looked at Annabelle, who watched the nurse leave the room. She turned quickly and shot a sharp glance at Jake.

"How could you? I am *sure* I sent you a text from the bus to come to the hospital. I was going into goddamn labor on the bus! But it took you hours to show up!" Annabelle hated the needy, pleading sound in her voice. Jake did, too, and she knew it.

"I never got a text from you," Jake protested, sitting on the edge of her bed. "Are you sure you sent me one? They said at the desk that you were pretty out of it when you came in. You always like to make a dramatic entrance!"

"Check my phone, you bastard," Annabelle fumed. "You'll see the text I sent to you."

"Nice mouth, mommy," said Jake, stooping to pick up Annabelle's bag. He put it on the foot of her bed and started rummaging inside, searching for the phone.

"It's not here. Is it in your coat?"

"It has to be there. I had it on the bus," said Annabelle, frustrated. "You just don't want to admit you ignored my cry for help. Give me the bag."

As she reached into her bag, the motion recalled the scene from the bus, the pain and fear as she frantically reached into the bag and pulled out her phone. The desperate text—that she had sent to *Roger*! Panic gave way to relief, then the panic returned like a tidal wave. The phone, with the damning text message, wasn't here. For now, her cry for help was still her secret. But where was the phone?

"No phone—and my wallet is missing, too! I had just taken out $1000 in nice new bills for a deposit on the baby's photo shoot."

Jake gave Annabelle a look and closed his eyes, but said nothing. Annabelle had a thing about cash. She loved to see it, feel it, and felt powerful handing it over to a cashier for a purchase.

"Credit cards are so common," she often said. "The feel of a new $100 bill is so sexy, so powerful. People notice when you pay with cash."

"Yeah, and they are home free when they can steal $1000 in bills without leaving a trace," he replied.

"I was out of it for a while. No telling what happened to my stuff," Annabelle said, letting out a sigh. "Jake, you'll have to talk to the hospital staff. We've got to find them."

Annabelle's voice betrayed her uneasiness. *My phone and wallet.* Her mind raced, recalling the secrets those two objects kept. The phone calls and texts from Roger. Photos of her with both Roger and Jake, tucked deep inside her wallet.

"Annabelle, are you alright? Jake moved closer. "You look worried. Try to relax. I'll take care of it. Someone probably put them somewhere for safe keeping."

He took her bag and set it back on the floor. As he did, the nurse arrived, pushing a bassinet with a screaming baby.

"Here he is, your perfect little bundle of joy," said the nurse, scooping up their little boy and placing him into Annabelle's outstretched arms.

"My baby, what are you so upset about?" cooed Annabelle, forgetting about the wallet and phone, immediately engaged with her pink-faced chubby baby boy.

Jake felt out of place, outside the maternal scene playing out before him. He put his arm around Annabelle and bent to kiss his son, pushing back the shock of dark hair from his forehead.

"He's beautiful, isn't he?" whispered Jake.

"Yes, beautiful, and little, and ours."

Jake kissed Annabelle on her cheek, still damp from her ordeal, and headed for the door. "It's late, and we both—I mean we three—need some rest. I'll see what I can find out about the missing wallet and phone," he said. "Too much time has gone by. I'll be right back."

Out in the hallway, Jake looked back at them. They looked like a Madonna and child, framed in the glow of the monitors and the soft hospital room lighting. He was a beautiful little boy.

17

JAKE ASKED AROUND, but no one had seen Annabelle's phone or wallet. There was no safe for valuables. He must have talked to everyone in admitting, at the nurse's station on Annabelle's floor, and in the ER. Nothing. Jake was headed to the elevator when he saw the ER receptionist pointing to a man leaning up against the desk.

"Sir," she shouted, waving to Jake. "This police officer may be able to help you."

Jake walked over and started spilling out his story. "Officer, my wife lost her phone and—"

"Sir, I'm Detective Holt. I'm waiting for word on two gunshot victims—my next stop may be the morgue. It's the Wild West out there. I'd be happy to get a police officer to help you with your missing property. A theft would normally be handled by a uniformed officer. Can you give me some information that I can pass along?" *Information that would most likely be passed back to me,* Holt thought with resignation.

Detective James Holt's reputation for cracking cases was nearly eclipsed by his habit of going rogue, riding the edges, and preferring to keep others at a distance. When he worked a case, he preferred keeping leads, information, and activities to himself until he solved the case or it blew up. His wins had kept him safe until two weeks ago, when he had withheld a prime piece of damaging evidence, intending to reveal it at the end of a high-profile murder trial. The chief kept Holt's blunder out of the press. But Holt's punishment was to now be assigned to low-level street crimes, traffic violations, and an occasional robbery.

Missing property. How far you have fallen, Detective.

Holt scribbled in his notebook as Jake ran through the scenario on the bus, describing the missing phone and wallet.

"I'll get the ball rolling," Holt said, happy to be doing something to break the monotony.

As Jake walked back to Annabelle's room, his phone buzzed yet again. He had ignored three other calls while he was hunting down Annabelle's things, but he pulled out his phone to check his messages. Damn! The three missed calls were all from the same familiar number—his number one customer. And the most recent one that he didn't recognize. *Life goes on, and business is good.*

He hurried down the hallway just in time to see the nurse wheel the bassinet out of the room.

"Your wife is tired, and she's had an ordeal," said the nurse. You can stay if you like or go home and come back fresh in the morning," said the nurse. "You must be tired yourself."

"Yeah, I could use a break. If she wakes up and asks for me, tell her I—I love her and will be back in the morning."

"I certainly will," said the nurse with a smile and a wink. "Take it easy, Dad."

Dad. That was going to take some getting used to. Jake walked out into the parking lot, slid into his BMW, cranked the engine, turned up the radio, and rolled into the light evening traffic.

He was a father now. Jake had only thought vaguely about being a parent and never about the responsibilities that went along with it—until now. The baby was mostly

Annabelle's thing. From the moment two lines showed up on the pregnancy test, she was consumed by the thought of finally being pregnant and having the baby that she wanted so much.

Jake wanted Annabelle with the same intensity, he thought, from the moment he saw her. He had been happy with just the two of them, living a life without distractions or outside obligations and responsibilities. He was a man who liked full and undying devotion, but he wasn't one to hover.

"You seem so distant, unavailable," she used to say, leafing through yet another baby magazine.

Yes, distant, and busy. Annabelle's new distraction gave Jake time on his hands, and that never led to anything good. Jake pulled over onto a side street away from the hospital and pulled out his phone. He tapped the first number of three from his customer.

"Yeah, this is Solo-man. What's so damned important?" growled Jake. "Yeah, I got it. It'll have to wait until tomorrow. Got a little issue of my own here." Jake pulled the phone away from the high-volume cursing on the other end.

"Look," said Jake into the torrent of expletives. "You'll get your order tomorrow morning, or not. And without the drama. Got it?"

The other side was silent, then a soft, "I got it, Solo. Tomorrow morning."

"Yeah," said Jake. "Solo-man has you covered."

Jake looked at the next number on his phone. A voice-mail. New numbers could be new business—or trouble. He hit play, and listened to the unfamiliar voice. "A mutual friend gave me this number. I'd like to do some business. Call back."

Friendly sort, thought Jake. After the beep, he replied, "I just did. You've got my number, call back or not."

Solo-man had lots of clients and limited time, and his clients knew that it was first come, first served. *This newbie would learn the drill or be out.*

Jake pulled out and saw a neon sign a few blocks away that flashed "Bar, Eats."

Suddenly hungry, he pulled into a parking spot in front of the door.

Just like in the movies, there's always a parking spot for the star right in front. He hit the lock button on the key fob and listened for the beep. *Can't be too careful. All kinds of shady characters lurking about.*

Jake crossed the sidewalk, grabbed the handle to the bar's heavy wooden door. and swung it open, nearly colliding with someone coming out at the same time.

"Watch it, man," the guy growled at Jake, head down and bumping into Jake's shoulder, pushing him back towards the sidewalk. Jake spun around and tried to grab the lapel of the guy's crested blazer, but he stumbled on the uneven pavement. Jake steadied himself and took a couple of steps towards him, but the guy had already crossed the street.

Annoyed, he gave the car's key fob another hit and disappeared into the dark, musty bar. After a beer and a burger, he'd do a little business, and head home to get some sleep. He would need it to return to the drama at the hospital tomorrow and the reality of fatherhood.

He slid onto a barstool facing the mirrored wall with its shelves of liquor bottles at attention waiting to be called to duty. He never failed to catch his reflection in a mirror or window, admiring the smooth skin stretched against his chiseled jaw, framed by a shock of wavy, slightly long, slightly unkempt sun-kissed hair.

He sat up slightly, and stared intently into the mirror, unaware that the bartender had wandered toward his end of the bar.

"Someone you know?" joked the bartender with a grin.

But Jake didn't respond. Something didn't seem right. His mind flashed back to the hospital room, and the wiggling little bundle that was his son.

They say that fathers gaze into their newborn's eyes and see themselves, forming an instant bond. Jake stared wide-eyed at his face staring back from the bar mirror. The tiny boy that had stared back at him had dark hair—lots of dark hair, dark as the night. Annabelle was a blonde. And he was a blond, too. Jake wasn't hungry anymore.

"Make that a boilermaker, double shot," Jake yelled to the bartender, keeping his eyes fixed on his reflection. "And the check."

16

JAKE THREW A couple of bills on the bar, drained the last of the bourbon from his glass, and headed for the door. Now running to his car, he felt uneasy, thinking something hadn't been right from the moment he first saw the baby.

He had vaguely thought about having a son; or he liked the *idea* of having a son. He had only hazy notions about the reality of the work and commitment it would take to raise a child. A child in the mix would change the whole commitment level to Annabelle. *Well, what's done is done.* Now he felt that perceived smile from his son seemed more like a sneer. A crooked smile hiding a secret that only the baby and his mother knew.

He accelerated, taking a few turns too fast, not thinking about the traffic or the road ahead of him, but fixed on his new son sleeping in the nursery. That dark-haired boy didn't look like him or Annabelle.

Jake's business had taken more of his time and attention over the past few months, and business had been good. He was branching out and picking up new clients. He tried to think back over the past year or so. There had been lots of late nights, and he'd been gone on weekends. Could she have found another source of attention? Someone to feed her deep craving for affection? Had those long, black-stocking legs been wrapped around some dark-haired man from the gym or the office?

His racing mind matched his pressure on the gas pedal, taking him closer to home. He suddenly slammed on the brakes, skidding sideways into the oncoming lane before screeching to a halt, millimeters away from a Trek bike and its horrified rider. Jake threw open the car door, but before he could plant one foot on the wet street, the bike rider was gone, disappearing around a corner.

Jake slid back across the BMW's supple leather seat, grabbing the steering wheel with both hands, and let out a deep breath. Looking up over the steering wheel, he could still imagine the terror-stricken face of the biker. He squeezed his eyes tight and opened them, seeing nothing but the dark street and a few cars curling around his silver BMW splayed across the opposite traffic lane in the street.

Jake took another breath and felt his phone's vibration in his pocket. The name was a familiar distraction, but not for tonight; that would have to wait. He had more important things to attend to.

19

DETECTIVE HOLT SLOUCHED in his chair in the ER, blocking out the chaos around him. The hospital was like the Wild West, he had told the worried guy looking for his wife's wallet and phone. It was worse than that. At least the gunslingers in the old westerns were pros. These guys in the ER were amateurs, waving stolen weapons at each other, settling scores, defending their territory or just out for a night's recreation. The two he had brought in were repeat offenders, had only minor injuries, and turned out to be felons on probation.

He pulled out his notepad and reviewed the information the worried husband had given him. His two bandits would be a while. *Had the precinct started an investigation?* Holt thought he would get the ball rolling at the hospital, as he served out his sentence of fallen detective/officer in charge. Probably just another dutiful husband trying to appease his worried wife. On the other hand, what looks like just a missing phone and wallet case could escalate if the secrets the objects held got into the wrong hands. Could this be a jealous husband looking for blackmail evidence? Was that a small twinge in Holt's instinctive gut alarm?

Holt got in the elevator, punched the button marked "Birthing Center," and leaned against the wall. Ding! He walked out into the reception area, catching the eye of a familiar-looking red-headed beauty behind the nurse's station.

"How can I help you, officer?" she said with a wink, taking in all six-feet-one of Detective Holt in one long glance. "Our little patients haven't been up to any mischief, at least not yet."

Detective James Holt was used to attention from women and wasn't one to miss an opportunity. Or forget one taken.

That voice. The smile. Veronica?

"You never know," he returned with a smile, bending down slightly over her upturned face framed with red waterfall curls held in check with a silky blue scarf. He recalled this redhead in a turquoise blue bikini stretched out on a pool lounge chair, sipping a mojito against the backdrop of a blazing Caribbean sunset. *Does she remember me?*

"It's Detective Holt. Anybody is liable to get into mischief these days and may have to be put in their place."

James Holt was handsome and charming, and he knew it. He liked the attention, slipping into flirting mode at the flutter of a mascaraed eyelash. He wasn't as good at boundaries, though, and had the personnel file to prove it.

A stern voice behind him quelled his rising anticipation.

"And what can we help you with, officer—Holt is it?" Holt stood up, turned, and came face to face with the head nurse, and she wasn't smiling.

"Ah yes, ma'am. It's Detective Holt," he said politely. "I met the husband of one of your patients in the ER. Her name is Annabelle Martin, and she seems to have lost her cell phone and wallet. I'm preparing a report to assist in their recovery and need some more information. Can you help me?"

"Is she suggesting one of my staff is a thief?" the head nurse said indignantly. "I can vouch for every one of them. You have to practically be Mother Teresa herself to get clearance to work on this floor."

"Oh, no ma'am," Holt replied hurriedly. "No one is accusing anyone of anything. Just gathering information and offering some help. I was in the ER on another case, and her husband reported some missing items, but I've got time. I offered to give some assistance."

"Hmmm," said the chief nurse, one eyebrow arched high over a squinty glance. "What do you need to know?"

Holt went down his checklist for lost or stolen goods, scribbling fast to keep up with the nurse's curt replies, aware that Veronica kept glancing his way. He flipped the cover on his notepad. *How could she not remember me. That week in the islands.*

"Just one more thing, ma'am," he said. "The husband said his wife went into labor on a city bus and had a difficult delivery. She's really stressed out. With lost valuables, time is everything. Is there someone who could help look around— retrace her steps, check stairwells, that sort of thing? I'd like to be able to let them know we're trying."

The head nurse softened a bit, impressed with Detective Holt's show of empathy, and stopped.

"Let me see if an orderly is available," she said. "There's sometimes an extra hand at shift change."

She walked around to the other side of the desk and after a brief phone call smiled at Detective Holt.

"We're in luck, there is someone who can help. They're sending him up now. You can wait for him by the elevator. His name is Dewain—you'll see it on his hospital badge. The orderlies know their way around the hospital. I'm sure he'll be very helpful."

Just then, Holt heard the ding of the elevator bell, and a young man dressed in hospital scrubs with an ID badge around his neck walked off with a swagger that reminded Holt of his two cowboys down in the ER

"That's him," said the nurse, pointing at Dewain.

Damned if he didn't look familiar.

"Are you Dewain?" Holt approached and held out his hand. As Dewain did the same, Holt noticed the two missing fingers.

"Yes, officer. Dewain at your service," he said with a little bow. "My supervisor told me you need help tracking down some valuable items one of our new mothers lost. I'll give it my full attention."

I'll bet you will.

Holt did a mental search of perps with two missing fingers. He was pretty sure this gig wasn't Dewain's primary occupation.

20

THE OFFICER IN front of him wanted help finding some lost items. It was Dewain's lucky day. He knew all about finding valuables, especially if they didn't belong to him. And he knew every hiding place in the hospital where someone might try to stash them. "At your service, officer."

"It's Detective Holt, Dewain. Here's all I know," said Holt, feeling like he was unlocking the canary cage for a hungry cat.

"The lady's name is Annabelle Martin, Room 547 on the 5th floor birthing center. Came in through the emergency room off a city bus, about to give birth. She says her new iPhone and wallet are missing from her computer bag, which is in her room. We'll talk to her tomorrow. I'll meet you back here at nine tomorrow morning. She can give you more information, but she's had an ordeal, so we don't want to upset her. You'll need to do a thorough search inside the hospital and the immediate surroundings. Here's my card. Text or call if you find anything before we meet."

Dewain gestured a quick salute in agreement with his three-fingered hand. Just before they got to the door, Holt stopped and turned to Dewain.

"This is a nice lady, and she's had enough trouble today. Lose the smirk and the swagger before tomorrow morning," he cautioned, with just enough authority to let Dewain know he was in charge.

"Detective, what do you mean?" said Dewain, with his best offended face. "I'm here to help. Trust me."

———

Dewain was at the reception desk at nine. Holt emerged from the elevator five minutes later and motioned for Dewain to follow him. The door to Room 547 was ajar. Holt knocked on the door.

"Come in, but be quiet," said a low voice from the other side.

Holt gently pushed the door open and walked in with Dewain close behind him. Annabelle was resting, the baby sleeping quietly in his bassinet next to her bed.

"Excuse me, ma'am, I'm Detective James Holt."

"Detective, is anything wrong?" said Annabelle, feeling that tug in her stomach again. "My husband Jake didn't come back last night. Did something happen to him?"

"No, ma'am," Detective Holt said reassuringly. "Your husband approached me in the ER and told me about your missing wallet and phone. I would like to get a statement from you. I've asked the hospital to help search to see if we can find them. Dewain here is a hospital orderly, and he's going to do some searching in the hospital. We'll need a description of the items and as much information about your arrival as possible. With any luck, someone's turned them in and you'll be all set."

Annabelle looked wide-eyed at Officer Holt and then at Dewain, who stood silent, smiling his best friendly and compassionate smile at Annabelle.

"So sorry for your loss, ma'am," said Dewain, immediately regretting his choice of words. It sounded like a condolence for someone who had died.

Annabelle's eyes got even wider, and she shifted a bit and pulled up the covers.

"Well, I appreciate your concern and help, Dewain," she said uncertainly.

"Wrap it up, Dewain," barked Holt. "I have some business to return to in the ER and have to run."

Detective Holt left, and Dewain moved closer to Annabelle's bedside, hands in his pockets.

"Detective Holt said you lost a wallet and a cell phone," said Dewain, slowly scanning Annabelle from head to toe and back again. "Can you give me a description of both?"

"Well, the wallet is a black slim fold-over style, smooth leather, Coach brand," said Annabelle.

"Nice," said Dewain, holding her gaze.

Annabelle, feeling uneasy, lowered her eyes.

"Nice wallet, I mean, ma'am. Can you remember what was in it? I mean, was there anything that was unusual?"

Dewain couldn't help himself. He wanted to know whether what he might find would be of value to him. Cash could be his, and cards could be sold so they couldn't be traced back to him. He'd be a winner either way.

"There were two concert tickets for this weekend," Annabelle continued. "Good seats, too. Cost me $250 each. Guess I won't be going now."

Dewain faked a compassionate smile.

"Oh, hell," said Annabelle, flopping back on the pillows. "And the cash!"

Dewain edged a little closer. "Cash money, you say? How much exactly?"

"A thousand dollars. Ten brand-new hundred-dollar bills. Just got it from the bank on my lunch break. I guess I can kiss that goodbye," she said, nervously pulling at the covers.

"SH . . . . . . Sure *is* a lot of money!" he said, visualizing the bills in his pocket. "Anything else?"

"Yes, about ten credit cards," said Annabelle. "But my husband may have already cancelled them."

Dewain could feel his good fortune shrinking. *Better get on this quick.*

"Like the detective said, ma'am, the faster I get on this the better the chances. What can you tell me about the phone?"

Annabelle looked at her sleeping baby for a moment, then back at Dewain.

"It's the newest version of iPhone. Just came out a week ago. It's black with a turquoise turtle case with blue chevrons. I guess the number would help so you can call it—I'll write it down for you. The ringtone is "Stop! In the Name of Love" by the Supremes. Can't miss it."

"What about the security code?" Dewain asked.

"Why do you ask?" Annabelle said, feeling the gut tug again. She sat up a bit and looked closer at Dewain, who stood a little too close and smiled a little too much, looking cocky with his hands in his pockets.

"Just trying to be thorough, ma'am, that's all."

"Well, it's a new phone, and I hadn't set it yet," said Annabelle. The reality of all this was beginning to sink in. "And I didn't activate the tracking GPS."

Suddenly, Annabelle felt dizzy, and a little faint. "Can you hand me the water glass on the table over there?" she said.

Dewain reached for the glass, and she saw his hand. He had seen that look before—shock, revulsion, suspicion. He handed her the glass with the other hand, quickly putting the other in his pocket, responding to Annabelle's unspoken question.

"A little run in with a table saw, ma'am. And the table saw won. A long time ago."

"I'm feeling a little tired, Dewain. Thank you for your help," Annabelle said, turning her face away, wanting this visit to end.

"I think I've got everything I need," said Dewain as he turned to leave the room. *Or I will, if I get lucky.* "I'll get right on this."

The baby started stirring in the bassinet, and Dewain stopped to look at him. "What's your little boy's name?"

"Doesn't have one yet," said Annabelle.

"If he's the first, in my family he would be a junior," said Dewain. "Named after his father."

That, thought Annabelle, *might be a little complicated.*

21

THE HOSPITAL LOBBY was quiet at ten in the morning, unlike the way it had been at Jake's arrival at the emergency entrance last night. A few visitors were scattered in the waiting area. It was hard to tell the new ones from last night's leftovers. Some were slumped over in plastic chairs. Others were transfixed on their cell phones or leafing through old, tattered magazines. A few children, obviously wound up by too much soda or too little sleep, were taking turns jumping off one of the hard couches, largely ignored by the adults nearby, huddled in low conversation.

Jake passed through the lobby without making eye contact and headed toward the elevators. Alone in the elevator, he pushed the button for the fifth floor, leaning back against the back wall and closing his eyes. The elevator stopped on the second floor, and an orderly and a couple of nurses walked in, turning to face the closing elevator doors.

Jake closed his eyes again but listened to their conversation.

"Yeah, this chick is wacked out," a male voice said. "Almost had a baby on a bus. Lost a lot of stuff, and I'm on a mission to find it and be her hero. Of course, they had to give the mission to Dewain."

Jake slowly straightened and opened one eye just a crack. They were obviously talking about Annabelle. How many other women in this town almost had a baby on a bus?

"Dewain, stop your trash talk," a young woman snapped back with a giggle. "You may be able to charm some of the people, but not Cherise. I've been around too long and met a lot of guys just like you—full of yourself, busy looking for opportunities and unlocked doors. That stuff she lost most likely will end up in your locker rather than in her hands ever again."

Jake stared at the back of Dewain's head as it bounced back and forth as if keeping time to some inner music.

"Have you finished your detective work yet, Dewain?" the young woman asked sarcastically, giving his shoulder a soft mock punch.

Dewain reacted instinctively, holding up his left hand like a fighter fending off the blow in the ring. Jake saw what wasn't there—two missing fingers. He flinched at the sight, imagining how the two fingers went missing in one terrifying slide show, one awful image after another. He felt his stomach churn, remembering his own brother's tragic accident with a chain saw, nearly cutting through his leg after losing his grip while clearing brush on his grandfather's farm.

Had this jerk been in Annabelle's room, interrogated her, asked a lot of questions? Did he fluff up her pillow, bring her water, or give her a reassuring pat on the arm? Jake wanted to grab Dewain by the shoulder and spin him around. Smack that bobbing head and shut him up.

The elevator stopped at the fourth floor.

"Got to get back to being Sherlock Holmes," Dewain chuckled, glancing at Cherise with a wink and a too-big smile.

"Whatever, Snoopy Dog," whispered Cherise, leaning in close. "You do just that. And keep your sticky little fingers out of that lady's wallet."

Dewain tossed his head and swaggered off the elevator, waving a three-fingered goodbye.

22

***

ON THE FIFTH floor, Jake edged around the nurse's station and hurried down the hall to Annabelle's room. *She'll say I'm late again.*

He stopped for a moment in front of the nursery windows. The little bassinettes were lined up in rows with each swaddled bundle wearing a blue or pink stocking cap. A few wailing babies cut through the quiet hallway. One tired, grinning dad leaned up against the nursery window, tapping lightly as if his baby would look up and recognize its father.

As he rounded the corner, he heard voices in Annabelle's room. Then laughter. He knocked on the door and then pushed the door open. Annabelle was sitting up in bed, holding the baby, engaged in an animated conversation with the morning shift nurse.

"Come in, Dad," said the nurse, walking around from the side of Annabelle's bed. "We were just talking about you!"

"Oh, really," said Jake with a weak grin. "And what was so interesting about me?"

"Oh, whether your little baby gets his personality from you or his mommy," said the nurse, touching the baby's hair. "And look at all that dark hair. If I was a curious gossip, I'd be wondering where this baby got that dark hair with two blond parents."

Annabelle looked down at the baby in her arms and touched his chin. The baby opened his eyes and yawned. Annabelle sighed and smiled.

"Yes, my dark-haired little man," she said, pushing the hair from his forehead.

"You know, now that you mention it, I was thinking the same thing," Jake said to the nurse, shooting a look at Annabelle.

"Well, as I explained to your wife," said the nurse as she walked to the door, "Parents can be blond as a couple of Swedes, and the baby comes out with hair dark as night. Makes you wonder if there had been a visit from the mailman or pool boy nine months ago. A little side-step in the marital conga-line. But, like I tell all my new parents, don't call the divorce lawyers yet. That baby could turn to platinum blond in the next few weeks. Now, if he doesn't, I can give you my brother-in-law's number. He is the best divorce lawyer in town."

Annabelle laughed, while Jake stared at her and the baby. She smiled the contented smile of someone who had just gotten a free pass from detention. She didn't have to use the story she concocted to explain the mysterious dark hair, and Jake couldn't dispute the explanation of an expert.

"You two have a nice visit," said the nurse as she left the room, closing the door behind her. "I'll be back to get the baby in about half an hour."

"I thought you were coming back last night. And you took your time getting here this morning," said Annabelle, trying not to sound annoyed.

"Well, glad to see you, too," said Jake, walking around the bed. "Can I hold him?"

Jake scooped the baby into his arms. He studied this little creature that was his son, not in awe or with tenderness but searching for evidence. Did he have Jake's square jaw, or

Annabelle's heart-shaped face? He studied the baby's nose, lips, and the set of his eyes. For a newborn, he seemed to have big hands, like Jake's. Were his eyes brown or dark blue? Was he looking at his son, flesh of his flesh, or had someone else's DNA produced this dark-haired creature?

"I haven't been able to take my eyes off him either," said Annabelle.

Jake looked up at Annabelle, dewy-eyed and staring calmly at the baby. Even in her blue cotton hospital gown, she looked beautiful. Her long blond hair was a little matted, but without any makeup, she was still the girl he saw across the square years ago that day on campus.

"I was puzzled about the hair thing, too," Annabelle said nervously, trying to sound concerned. "I mean, how would it look, two blond parents and a child with hair as dark as night? I can just hear the jokes. Kids can be very cruel, you know," she said, squeezing a tiny tear out of the corner of her eye.

Jake knew Annabelle well. She always tried to get ahead of every argument, every accusation. The nurse may have been the perfect player in the game of "Let's tell Jake a convincing story." Had Annabelle conveniently prompted the nurse to give the explanation about newborns and hair color when Jake arrived? He couldn't be certain. What he was sure of, however, was that Annabelle knew how to use a lucky break to swing a story in her favor. He was no match for her manipulation, and he knew it.

"Yeah," said Jake. "You know, I was sitting in a bar having a drink and caught my reflection in a mirror, and it hit me. About the baby's dark hair, and you and I both being blond."

Jake put the sleeping baby back in the bassinette and moved closer to Annabelle.

"So, almost as if it was rehearsed, the nurse conveniently gave an explanation just as I walked into the room."

He sat down next to Annabelle. He took her hand in his, fingering her wedding band and then looked up at her. Annabelle felt his grip tighten, crushing the sharp edges of the diamond's setting between her fingers. He looked straight at her.

"That's one explanation. Do you have any others? Annabelle, dear?"

Annabelle glared at Jake, who was leaning in close to her face.

"You're hurting me," she said indignantly, wrenching her hand away and rubbing her fingers. "What are you suggesting?"

"I'm just curious, considering there could be a number of other explanations. What do you say, Annabelle?"

"I think you should give your curious, dirty little mind a rest," said Annabelle. "Enjoy the moment. You always wanted a son to do all those manly things that fathers and sons do. Everything you missed out on while your father was at one foreign military outpost or another."

"Look at him, sleeping there," her voice almost a whisper. "He's beautiful. He's got your perfect nose," said Annabelle, playing the vanity card.

Jake walked over to the bassinette and studied the baby's face.

Annabelle knew how to distract him. If she couldn't use her long legs, a little talk about Jake's good looks would hit him in the right place—his ego. He could never resist flattery.

The nurse had said to give it time. Jake surrendered to Annabelle's explanation and his desire to believe that he was wrong in his assumptions.

The door swung open, and the nurse swooped in to wheel out the bassinette.

"Time for Mom to get some rest and Dad to go elsewhere." The nurse gave Jake a stern, 'I mean you' look. "And it's time for this little guy to join the rest of the gang down the hall.

Don't worry, he'll be back in a couple of hours, ready for his morning snack."

Jake bent down and gave Annabelle a quick kiss on the cheek and headed out the door, barely keeping up with the nurse's half jog down the hallway.

Yes—time would be the ultimate judge.

23

SUCH A NICE lady to go through so much shit just trying to have a baby, mused Dewain. He checked all his favorite hiding places in the hospital. If someone from this hospital had jacked Mrs. Annabelle's wallet and phone and wanted to dump it and come back for it later, there was no hiding place that Dewain didn't know about. He was the master of secrecy. First stop was the sixth-floor supply room. With piles of outsized and torn bedding piled on metal shelves, it was the go-to place for a quick stash.

Dewain ran his hands between the stacks of sheets and pillowcases, top to bottom, front to back. With two fingers gone, the other three were somehow more sensitive to heat, cold, and changes in pressure. Perfect for hiding and finding.

Damn! He felt a hard lump in a stack on the bottom shelf. He kept his hand in the stack to mark the spot. With his other hand, he pulled back the sheets one by one. He peeled the last sheet off his hand, and there they were. Two bottles of Vicodin for a Jacquetta Pierce from the hospital pharmacy.

Ms. Pierce, you bad girl. Leaving your meds in this nasty storeroom.

Dewain chuckled, looking at the bottles with their neatly printed labels and child-protective caps. He had personally gone to the pharmacy to get replacements after he had explained that Ms. Pierce had misplaced her medications after her back surgery. It had been easy to slip the two bottles from her discharge bag as he wheeled her out to the main entrance. He left the small bottle of Oxycodone and the extra-strength ibuprofen alone—no need to be greedy. Plenty of opportunity.

I helped myself, and you helped me, Jaquetta. That's what makes the world a beautiful place.

Dewain liked discharging patients from the sixth floor. He always wheeled them to the back of the elevator, out of view of the other passengers. Six floors in the hospital's creaky elevators with stops on descending floors gave him more than enough time to rifle through a patient's bags and to pocket their meds. These unwitting suppliers stocked Dewain's personal and lucrative pharmacy.

Dewain shoved the bottles he'd hidden under the sheets into the pocket of his scrubs, pleased at the find but concerned. He and Ms. Pierce were both getting forgetful, and he worried that someone else might reap the reward of his work. He wasn't the only entrepreneur on the hospital's payroll. Some dealt in toilet paper, paper towels, and tissues. Others had a profitable linen-supply business. Dewain went after the big money, and a couple of slips like this could put him out of business. *Better step it up, Dewain.*

He stopped at all the likely hiding places, with no luck. Ms. Pierce's missing meds had been a bonus, but he'd found no wallet or phone.

There were other places to ditch stolen valuables that he wouldn't search no matter what the reward. The hospital laundry chutes were easy disposal points, with giant collection bins in the basement. The same with the kitchen trash barrels or the dumpsters off the loading dock. Nasty, dirty, and slimy. A $1 million Rolex watch could be tangled up in a stinking wad of those sheets or in the garbage, and Dewain would gladly let someone else take the prize. Maybe a rookie just starting out, hungry, or strung out—but not Dewain.

Hell, that wallet and phone could be anywhere from the bus route to the ambulance to the streets. Some lucky junkie could have found them and traded them for quick cash to get high. They were probably lost forever.

Dewain ended his search on the first-floor visitors' lobby as the last option. The grand piano was now a digital self-play, the hinged piano bench tucked deep under the keyboard. He knelt down next to the bench as if searching for something on the floor, and reached under the bench. His fingers quickly scraped the small shelf on the inside corner—nothing. He headed for the elevator.

If it's in this hospital, ain't nobody going to find it.

Dewain hit the fifth-floor button for the birthing center, rehearsing his speech to Annabelle, complete with concerned facial expressions and soothing tones of voice. He reached in his pocket and felt for Ms. Pierce's pill bottles, deciding which lucky junkie would be the beneficiary of his good fortune.

Then it hit him. *Some lucky junkie.* Dewain quickly hit the button for the fourth floor and bolted out of the elevator. He slipped into a stall in the empty men's room and locked the door. Some lucky junkie. He knew a lucky junkie, but it wasn't one of his usual customers.

Out on the loading dock, David had been blubbering something about a bus and a woman having a baby and the screaming, just before Dewain's fist had shut him up. David had been on that bus with Annabelle. He rode in with her in the ambulance. He had motive and opportunity. He even had her diamond necklace, showing it off in the dim alley light. What else did David have? A nice new cell phone? A wallet?

Dewain was no longer interested in Annabelle. He knew that David had been living in his parent's old house for years. Tonight was the perfect time for an impromptu interview. He had a lot of questions. It was time to pay his little "lucky junkie" friend a visit.

24

DAVID HAD SLEPT most of the day, his body tired from the long walk last night from the bar to his house on the West Side. The demons were silenced by the pills from Dewain. The sun had long set by the time he walked in the dark to the end of the driveway to retrieve that morning's newspaper. David's house stood dark against the dim glow of the streetlights. He stopped just short of the curved walkway that led to the front door. The security lights over the garage doors failed to respond to his approach up the driveway, which added to the dark cloak of the night, and made him uneasy. He had walked up to this house a thousand times. Now alone, he should feel safe there. And still, so many years later, he felt the old dread slowly creep up a well-worn path from deep inside. He was an unwilling hiker taking steps he'd taken before in a dark place of terror. He never knew what awaited him on the other side of that windowless front door.

David closed his eyes tight, breathing slowly, unable to move.

"This exercise will shake off shadowy demons," said a gentle voice deep inside his memory. *"In and out. Inhale slowly, counting to eight. Hold for four. Then slowly exhale to the count of eight. This is your safe place, David. You can go there whenever you want."*

The therapist hadn't been as successful in helping him cope with the flesh-and blood demon on the other side of that front door. His father had tolerated his young son's trips to the therapist, but he had refused to participate in the recommended family sessions. David stood in the dark cloak of night, quietly breathing in and out until he felt his feet move again.

A vibration from deep inside his blazer summoned an automatic response. His phone displayed a missed call and voicemail from a new number. He clicked play and heard an irritated voice blast, "No, you called me. Call back or not. You know the number."

He pulled out the slip of paper from his pocket and compared the numbers—it was Darcy's dealer. The nine hundred-dollar bills in his wallet gave David new confidence. The Oxy fix from Two Knuckles kept him steady, and he still had one to spare.

I'll definitely call back.

David slipped his phone back into his pocket. The darkness seemed a little brighter as he twisted the doorknob and walked into the dark entryway. He dropped his keys in the green carnival glass bowl on the carved mahogany hall table. His gaze drifted from the dark living room to the dining room and the tall staircase leading up to the second-floor bedrooms. A narrow hallway to the right of the stairs led to a door closing off the kitchen. A slim shaft of dim light spilled from under the doorway. Had he left a light on this morning?

He pushed open the kitchen door. It was just as he left it, except for the open door to the microwave. David walked to the counter and closed the microwave door. The room darkened with the suddenness of an extinguished candle flame.

David grabbed a beer from the fridge, walked into the dining room, and flipped on the light switch for the chandelier. The wrought iron fixture hung low over the table. Lights from twelve faux candles revealed the dark drop-leaf table with eight carved chairs tucked snugly under the oval tabletop.

Only three of the chair cushions bore witness to use. No one had ever been allowed into the house. It had been a waste of five good chairs.

"Prying eyes and wagging tongues. Who needs them?" his father would say.

Even so, every holiday his mother would make guest lists and pore over holiday recipes. And yet every year only the three of them would silently sit around this table, their invitations hopefully addressed and stamped but unsent.

David took off his jacket and emptied the pockets, heavy with the day's spoils. He opened Annabelle's wallet and spread the contents on the table. Photos. Nine hundred-dollar bills. A bus pass for the next month.

He took a closer look at the two worn photos. The woman was a younger Annabelle with different men at her side in each one. He picked up one and looked closely. In it, the couple's heads were tilted, touching, with their hands clasped. Annabelle's blond hair contrasted with her companion's dark wavy hair.

In the other photo, Annabelle's companion was blond. He was tall, and looked straight into the camera with a sly half-smile. There was no question they knew each other well. They were on a rumpled blanket by a lake, Annabelle in a gauzy shirt with the top three buttons undone, the hem of her gathered skirt lying across her tanned upper thighs and the man's large hand resting on her thigh. She was leaning against him, her arm crossing his chest, her hand tucked deeply inside his unbuttoned denim shirt. *Hungry or satisfied?* Either could describe her expression, as she gazed at him.

Clearly two different men were part of her life—both perhaps still in her life—tucked safely inside her wallet. The names "Annabelle and Jake" had been on the placard in the hospital, so one of the two could be Jake. Her husband? Lover? Father of her child? And who was the other one? Husband, lover? Father of her child? This new mama had some secrets. And secrets could be valuable—and profitable.

What are you hiding, Annabelle?

He scanned the receipts, saw the names of a few high-end boutiques, and turned his attention to the two concert tickets. Annabelle did like the best in clothing and concerts. Front row seats to the hottest rock festival of the year on opening night. Tomorrow night, in fact. Seven o'clock at the new amphitheater on Silver Dunes Lake. One for David and one for some desperate fan willing to pay a scalper's price to be front-row center. *Yes, that's a date.*

Just as he put the tickets back in his jacket pocket, Annabelle's phone started to buzz. David reached out instinctively, then pulled his hand back. No, he'd let it ring. He thought about his phone and the annoying number of robocalls he got. Of course, any number on her phone would be strange to him and could help unravel any secrets that might be profitable.

David stared at the number displayed and wrote it down. The phone stopped ringing. Could it be one of the mystery men in the photos?

David picked up his own phone and did a search on the number. He stared at the screen, and he felt a knot tighten in his stomach. It was the Shepherdsville Police Department.

Shit! Had he been carrying around a tracking device?

He sat down on one of the worn chair cushions and stared from his phone's screen to Annabelle's now-silent phone and back to his again. He could almost hear the phone mocking him in his father's familiar voice.

Stupid to think you're so smart. You think you can fool your father? Hiding like a scared little girl. I'll show you what to be scared of.

David closed his eyes, waiting for the sting of the belt against him. But instead, he heard Annabelle's phone ringing again, vibrating its way across the table. He could only look at it and the now-familiar number. He couldn't breathe. Finally, the phone stopped ringing.

He picked up Annabelle's phone and checked the settings for tracking and locations. He slumped in relief. Annabelle's new phone wasn't set to find itself or track her locations.

I'm not the only stupid one, Dad.

David put the silent black rectangle back on the table—small, but with the potential to reveal and destroy him. He wouldn't answer it or make calls from it, but it still could tell tales and reveal secrets without betraying him or its whereabouts.

David slipped the bills and tickets into his wallet and tucked the photos and receipts back into Annabelle's. He opened a drawer of the buffet and put her phone and wallet deep inside for safe keeping. He caught a glimpse of himself in the mirror above the buffet. There was no need to hide any longer so he took off the cap with the Ravens logo and tossed it onto the table.

Yesterday had been an interesting day. He'd struck it rich and had been a hero, saving the little mother in distress. And he may have stumbled onto some interesting opportunities and a few mysteries.

He turned off the chandelier and waited for his eyes to adjust to the darkness. The house was quiet except for the soft whirr of the refrigerator in the kitchen. David went back into the entry hall and flipped the front door deadbolt into place. He looked out the tall windows flanking the front door at the street, illuminated by the streetlights like spotlights on a stage. He leaned closer to the glass and stared at the darkness, catching a glimpse of a shadowy figure walking in and out of the glow of the street lights, coming down the street towards the house.

The figure came up quickly, almost running. David backed away from the windows but still had a clear view of the street. As the figure came out of the shadows and onto the front porch, David gasped; the figure put his face up to the same side window, peering in from the porch, banging on the front door.

Two Knuckles!

25

"**ANSWER THE FUCKING** door, David!" yelled Two Knuckles. "It's Dewain. You and I have some business to discuss. Open the door and talk to me or I'll be forced to find some other interested parties to share my thoughts with. About a missing wallet and phone."

David saw a porch light go on across the street. He flung open the door just as Dewain's fist was landing another blow.

"Shut up, Two K. What the hell are you doing here?"

Dewain retracted his fist and pushed through the front door. "Well, that's better. Didn't your mother teach you any manners?"

"What are you doing here? How did you find me?"

"Google is a beautiful thing, David," said Dewain, pacing the entryway, peering into the dark living room.

"I remembered your house from those days in middle school, and it didn't take much to find the old homestead. And look. Here you are in the flesh."

He walked over and stood square in front of David, locking eyes in the dark hallway. "I find that we have some unfinished business. I think, and I believe you'll agree, that you weren't completely honest with me on that loading dock last night. You were holding back on me, and I thought I'd pay you a visit just to satisfy my curiosity."

"What are you talking about?" said David, leaning towards him. "You got your money and had the pleasure of working me over. I offered you the necklace, but you didn't want it. Is that what you came back for?"

"The necklace was and still is, too hot to be of any use," said Dewain. "That shiny diamond necklace must have distracted me from what you were saying. I've come into a whole lot of new information about the situation that makes me think you have something much more valuable than a necklace on you."

"I don't know what you're talking about, Two K."

"Oh, I think you do, my junkie friend," said Dewain with a menacing whisper. "You see, a pregnant lady was brought into the hospital by ambulance yesterday. She almost had a baby on a bus. They brought her up to the fifth-floor birthing center."

"If you hadn't been so busy beating the shit out of me on the loading dock, you would have heard me tell you the same thing," said David. "That's where the necklace came from. You came here to tell me that you knew I lifted the necklace off that woman? You think you can blackmail me with that information, you freaking bastard? Well, sorry, but that information is of no use to you. I gave it back. I put it back in her computer bag in her room. Because you were right. Too hot, and too recognizable to pawn. Sorry, Two K. but you got nothing on me. Get out, and go shake down someone else."

David walked over to the front door and turned the doorknob. He turned around, only to see Dewain walking slowly into the dining room to sit down in one of the five never-used chairs, settling in.

"Happy to hear Mrs. Annabelle—that's her name, isn't it—has her diamond necklace back. But I've got a little story of my own to tell. Why don't you have a seat, David?" Dewain tapped the tabletop.

"I'll stand," said David, squinting in the faint light.

"You may think I'm just an orderly delivering trays and pushing gurneys around the hallways, but I'm a trusted, valuable member of the medical staff. In fact, when there's a special mission—a mission needing smarts and knowledge of the hospital and its workings—they call on me to take charge. In fact, that happened last night. And that, my junkie friend, is why I'm here sitting in your dining room. Would you like to hear more?"

David thought back to Bus 7 and its last stop. The bus driver had pulled him into the unfolding drama, but the driver had been on the street uninvolved the entire time David was on the bus. David's hat had been pulled low over his eyes, and it was dark. He never gave his name to anyone except Annabelle, but she was out of it and never really saw his face. He rode with her in the ambulance alone while the EMTs were in front and slipped away in the chaos at the emergency room. What more could there be?

Dewain leaned back in his chair.

"Miss—or should I say, Mrs.—Annabelle had her baby, and a cute little thing he is. Once she calmed down, she started to ask about her belongings. She was frantic and told her husband, who then told a nice police officer—a detective, really. The detective told the husband that he'd see if the hospital could track down the missing belongings, and of course, they called upon their most reliable and trusted orderly—yours truly.

"This morning, I was escorted to Mrs. Annabelle's room by the detective to get more information, and what a surprise to learn that her cellphone and wallet were missing. They weren't in her computer bag where they should have been. A brand-new cellphone, mind you, latest version Apple has to offer, and her leather wallet. Seems our little mama likes cash and had just been to the bank that day and took out a cool thousand dollars. Along with some other stuff, several credit cards rounded out the contents. Of course, my heart went out to the poor lady," said Dewain, shifting in his seat, running his hands up and down the smooth wooden arms of the dining room chair. "Didn't anyone ever use these chairs, David? Not a chip or dent or rough spot on it."

David was silent and shuffled his feet uneasily.

"Ok, back to my story. My heart was pounding hard thinking about my good fortune. If that phone and wallet were in the hospital or its grounds, I was sure to find them. Shit, I know every hiding place, access door, and hospital employees with secrets, and all that played to my advantage. Of course, if I found those belongings, that information would be mine and mine alone, along with the cash and a very marketable digital device. And who would be the wiser if I were to just bring back an empty wallet? A hero, regardless.

"So, I went on my search. Along the way, I found some meds that I'd stashed a while ago and started reminiscing about all the sorry junkies I've helped along the way. I thought about our little skirmish on the loading dock and remembered your pitiful story about a woman on a bus, about to have a baby. The necklace that you'd lifted from her. And the puzzle started to fit together. Rubik's cube tiles spinning into place. Rolled the lucky seven. I knew my man David had had the necklace, and he was my prime suspect for the wallet and phone."

"Now the credit cards aren't worth anything," Dewain sighed. "Probably cancelled by now. But you can imagine how disappointed I was that you were holding out on me, who was willing to deliver you from the evils of withdrawal to the tune of one thousand dollars."

Dewain rose slowly from the chair and picked up David's Ravens cap from the table. "You were wearing this last night on the dock," said Dewain, running his three fingers over the cap's bill. "Were you wearing it on the bus? Who could forget a purple raven on a hat? I wouldn't be surprised if there wasn't a reward for finding the missing items, and even a bonus for information leading to the suspected thief."

David breathed slowly, silently, keeping a cool demeanor. He'd had lots of practice hiding his emotions. Pleading or crying or sniffling only made things worse. He had learned from a pro how to suppress fear and anger, a skill that fit this moment.

"You're wrong, Two K," said David calmly. "Well, you're right about the bus. I *was* there. And you're right, she *did* lose the wallet and the phone. I saw them on the floor of the bus while she was screaming her head off. But there wasn't any way I was going to pick them up.

"Her water broke on the bus, like the Hoover Dam, releasing a sticky flow on the floor around the phone and wallet on the floor. Now, I'm not one to pass up an opportunity, but there could have been diamond-studded thousand-dollar bills in that mess, and I would have walked away. Don't know what happened to them once they loaded me with her into the ambulance. Probably in a bio-hazard bag in a dumpster at the bus terminal. You might be able to sneak around to the terminal and dumpster dive for a red biohazard bag. You're welcome to it."

Dewain listened to David's story, all the while remembering his early days in the hospital laundry, unloading carts of sticky, stinking sheets coated with human waste, and mopping up vomit and urine from hospital room floors. He felt his stomach churning while he recalled wiping goo and blood from patients' personal belongings. It was always up to Dewain to clean up those messes.

"Ok, stop, before I puke right here on the carpet," said Dewain. "You're lying as sure as you're breathing. A strung-out junkie with opportunity like that? They could have been covered in vomit from an Ebola virus victim and you would have scooped them up with your bare hands and licked them clean. No junkie is going to pass up a stroke of luck like that, no matter what."

Dewain rose from his chair, standing so close that David felt his hot, moist breath on his face as he spit out his words. Dewain grabbed David's arm with one hand, and grabbed his face with the three jagged fingers of his other hand.

"They're here somewhere," Dewain snarled, "and we're going to have a little search party to find them."

"You can tear this house apart if you want, but you won't find anything. You're such a great detective, huh? Searching the hospital for Mrs. Annabelle's property and coming across some of your own stash? Or I should say, meds that you lifted from some poor terminal patient going home to die in agony? So, you know all the hiding places? Access door codes? Center stage for every security camera? You've got yourself a nice little gig going there, don't you, Dewain," sneered David. "A free pharmaceutical shopping mall, with a personal customer list willing to pay premium prices. Yeah, go ahead and search. And then you and I will go back to the hospital and inform the officer and the head nurse and Mrs. Annabelle how you're so fucking qualified to be detective in that hospital."

They were eye to eye, breath to breath, glaring at each other in the semi-darkness. Dewain slowly released his grip and stepped back.

"I thought you were a reasonable man, Two K," said David. "Too much to lose and too little to gain. I didn't have her phone and wallet on the dock so I couldn't have lied to you." David was impressed with the sincerity in his voice and the quality of his story. He was sure that Dewain bought it.

"Now take your sorry self out of here, Two K, and report back to the police and Mrs. Annabelle that her things are lost forever. Or they are at the bus terminal dumpster. Tell them whatever you like, just get the hell out of my house."

"This ain't over, junkie," threatened Dewain. "You may be lying, and that wallet and phone are stashed somewhere, even in this room."

Dewain picked up David's cap and jerked it down on David's head.

"One false move from you and I can drop a few details to my detective friend about a dude I saw at the hospital wearing a cap just like this—the cops would be all over this place. Besides, you may need me again when your stash gets low, and you don't want to get turned away. Remember whose hand it is that fed you."

David took a slow, silent breath as Dewain walked to the front door and turned the doorknob. Suddenly, David noticed a shaft of light from under the kitchen door. The muffled sound of shuffling across the floor and a switch clicking on and off made Dewain stop in his tracks and turn. David froze and stopped breathing, hoping he couldn't see the terror in his eyes.

Dewain took a step toward the kitchen door, thinking he hadn't played his last chip after all.

"So, you're not alone tonight, David," Dewain whispered with a grin. "You a player now? You have a lot of nasty little secrets, don't you? Have you got a fine lady stashed away, making a little cozy dinner? A little voulez-vous for avec moi tonight? Is that why you wanted me out so fast?"

David's mind was racing to concoct another lie.

"Well, you got me there," said David, frantic for some details to satisfy Dewain's lascivious mind. "You know women—they do get impatient." He walked toward Dewain, blocking his route to the kitchen.

David could see Dewain's expression change into a sly smile.

"It's cool, David. A man has to have his space. But be careful. Too many secrets can boomerang on you when you least expect it."

David said nothing as Dewain disappeared out the front door and into the night.

David heard a shuffling behind the heavy wooden kitchen door. He pushed the door open as light flooded the hallway.

"Hannah?"

26

DEWAIN WALKED UP the street, in and out of the glow of the streetlights.

He's lying to me. Dewain punched his fist into his three-fingered hand. That stupid junkie thought he could outsmart him. Dewain could have squeezed it out of him, but didn't need any witnesses. He had to be smart about this. Just play it cool. The tune hadn't hit the last note. This bird will sing. Tomorrow he would report back to Mrs. Annabelle. He may not have recovered the lost wallet and phone, but he has some information that may be of interest to Mrs. Annabelle, her husband, and the detective.

It's not nice to lie to Dewain.

27

WHAT A MISERABLE two days! Jake needed the routine of his job and clients after sparring with Annabelle over the baby's surprising arrival and questionable paternal origin. He needed space, even if it was dealing with junkies and business partners. He stretched it as long as he could. He pulled into the driveway, clicked the garage door opener, and slid the BMW next to Annabelle's SUV. He cut the engine and sat for a moment, just until the overhead light clicked off.

The house he had left yesterday morning was the same, but everything else was different. Life with Annabelle had been very manageable. Even the pregnancy didn't get in the way of Jake's pursuits. But the arrival of the baby changed things. That little baby up in the hospital nursery made things a little more complicated. Annabelle seemed to know how to make things complicated. He should have been at the stop when Bus 7 rolled in. It would have been a routine pickup with a side trip to the hospital. Or if not routine, it would have kept the drama private. Flying under the radar was Jake's specialty, a necessity in his line of business.

Jake sat in the darkness, hands still gripping the steering wheel. He slipped out, locked the doors, and navigated in the dark to open the door to the kitchen. In the dark kitchen, the only sound was the clink of his keys as he tossed them onto the granite countertop. He flipped on the recessed under-counter lights Annabelle insisted on for the kitchen remodel, saying they gave a soft, calming glow.

He opened the cabinet and pulled out a bottle of bourbon and a glass, pouring two fingers neat. He lifted the glass to eye level, examining the amber liquid glowing in the low lights. She had been right; the lighting was calming.

Drink it all in. Tomorrow will be a different story.

26

ANNABELLE SHIFTED, TRYING to find a comfortable spot in the hospital bed. She pulled the thin blanket over her lap and turned to pull her pillow up when she felt the sharp pain in her back that traveled to her abdomen. She winced and bit her lip, falling back on the pillows and grabbed for the call button.

The doctors had told her she might have some pain from the ordeal on the bus and the difficult delivery. She breathed in and out slowly, gauging her pain level. With each breath the pain lessened. She released her grip on the button. *I don't want to give the doctors a reason to keep me here any longer. I can't take another day of this place.*

"Here you go, Mama, someone is hungry tonight. This one is going to be a good feeder."

"Let me have my little man," Annabelle said, reaching out as the nurse picked up the baby from the portable bassinet to hand to her. She sat up and felt the tug again, sending her gasping back against the pillows.

"Everything all right, Annabelle?" said the nurse worriedly.

"Oh, just a little sore. The doctor said to expect it."

"You've been through a lot. If you're having pain, we should call the doctor to take a look," said the nurse, putting the baby into the bassinette. "I'll get the on-call physician."

"Please—I'm fine. I'm just a little tired and need some help with these pillows," said Annabelle with a slight catch in her throat. "I want to hold my baby before I go to sleep. Really, I'm OK."

The nurse turned back, smiled her I'm-a-mama-too smile, and rearranged Annabelle's pillows before putting the baby in Annabelle's arms.

"There you go. Nothing like a sweet baby to ease the pain," said the nurse. "I've had four of them myself. Angels, all of them. I'll be back in about thirty minutes."

Annabelle nodded weakly and stretched a smile across her face.

She settled back as the baby rooted and then latched on, hungrily sucking and making soft noises. Annabelle leaned back against the pillows, trying to ignore the persistent pain in her back—or was it her abdomen? The baby had a quiet rhythm going. He was such a little thing, Annabelle thought. She studied his eyes, the curve of his nose, the chubby pink cheeks. She gently traced his eyebrows with her fingers, pushing back the shelf of soft hair that swept down his forehead. And those long eyelashes; his father's eyelashes. She sat up and leaned over and placed a soft kiss on his upturned cheek.

"How's it going, Mama?" said the nurse, peeking her head in the door.

"I think he's finished," said Annabelle. "Seems to have fallen asleep."

Annabelle sat upright and lifted the baby. As she stretched to place him into the nurse's arms, she winced and let out a gasp from a sharp pain, falling back against the pillows.

The nurse snatched the baby before he could fall. She hurriedly put him into the bassinet and pressed the call button on the side of the bed.

"Annabelle, can you hear me? I'm calling the doctor right away."

Annabelle tried to breathe slowly through the pain. She felt a strange warm wetness and pulled back the covers. The bed sheets were covered in blood. The room started to fade away. She barely heard the nurse shouting as the doctors and nurses burst into her room. From somewhere in the fog, she heard the nurse repeat, "Hemorrhaging. Pain."

And then it was dark.

29

"HANNAH?"

David walked into the kitchen and let the door swing closed behind him. The light over the sink was on.

"Hannah, are you here? Where are you?"

David scanned the room from one end to the other. He noticed one of the slippers from an old pair he had left at the door was missing.

David walked slowly over to the table, his feet barely making a sound in the silence. He grabbed a chair to pull it back and felt resistance. He firmed his grip and pulled again, and as he did, he saw the other slipper slide across the kitchen floor, ricocheting against the sink cabinet.

"Hannah, you know you can't hide from me," David whispered softly as he slowly knelt down, reaching under the table. "Come out from there, now!"

He reached further, but jerked his hand back, wincing from the pain. Along the top of his hand were three long bloody scratches. David dove under the table and pulled Hannah out and sat her down on the chair.

"Bad kitty!"

The cat stared at David unapologetically, licking her claws fresh with David's blood.

"Up to your tricks again, are you? Flipping on light switches and dragging my slipper around the room?"

Hannah jumped off the chair, strolled over to the slipper, put her paw on the inside, and began to drag it across the floor, reuniting it with its mate next to the door. The task completed, she turned, looked up at David, and lay down on the floor.

"You are a bad cat, but you may have saved my life today." David reached down, picked up Hannah, and gave her a hug.

"Yes, you are my lady tonight." David looked the cat in her eyes as if expecting an answer. "Now, how did you manage to turn the lights on and off?"

Hannah stared back but wasn't giving up her secrets. David smiled, put her back down, opened the refrigerator, and pulled out a beer. He straightened the slippers by the door, flipped off the kitchen light, and followed Hannah, who was one step in front of David, into the dark hallway and up the twenty stairs to David's bedroom at the end of the hall.

30

JAKE TOSSED BACK the bourbon in the dim kitchen, feeling the potent liquid warm his throat and calm his mind. He refilled the glass, downed it in one motion, and poured a third. It had been a long day and night.

He took off his jacket, tossed it over one of the matching overstuffed club chairs in the den, and sunk down into the other. The damned chairs cost a fortune—Annabelle insisted on the French embroidered silk upholstery. But then, that was one thing he found exciting about her. She insisted on nothing but the best. She had insisted on him, hadn't she?

He stretched his legs onto the matching ottoman, sliding forward on the seat, resting his head on the back cushion. The bourbon's calming effect was much more pleasurable than recessed lighting, he thought with a smile as he sipped slowly this time, savoring the warm liquid.

The silence and the alcohol made the frustrations of the last two days slowly slip away. There had been too much drama, too many questions, and too few, if any, answers. There would be time enough tomorrow for answers. He breathed deeply, beginning to drift into sleep.

On the edge of sleep, Jake heard the ringing. He sat up, wrestled his phone from his pocket, and stared at the screen through a bourbon haze. The hospital—what now?

Annabelle? The baby? The call went to voicemail; he waited and listened to the message.

"Mr. Martin, this is Shepherdsville Hospital. Your wife is experiencing some complications from the delivery. She's hemorrhaging, and we have taken her to the OR. The doctor doesn't think it's critical and certainly not life-threatening, but he wanted you to know in case you wanted to come in to be with your wife when she is back in recovery."

Oh, great, Jake muttered to himself with a slur. Perfect timing.

He grabbed his jacket and stumbled through half sleep and too much bourbon into the kitchen. He grabbed at his keys in the dim lighting and sent them onto the floor. Damn! He bent down, grabbed the keys, and flung open the door leading to the garage. With only the light from the kitchen through the doorway he didn't see his golf clubs leaning into his path as took a wide turn to the driver's side of his car. Catching the nine-iron hanging out from the bag, he spun around and bounced off the left front fender and fell backwards onto the floor.

For a moment, Jake lay on his back while his eyes refocused, staring at the empty socket of the garage ceiling light. Hadn't he been meaning to replace that? He felt a pain in his shoulder and leg. After years of playing high school football and pick-up rugby at college, Jake was a pro at assessing his body for injuries that could impact his looks or performance. *Face seems OK,* he thought, rubbing his chin and forehead.

He rose slowly, propping himself up, and swung upright, leaning on the car door for balance. He felt woozy now from the sudden meeting of his head to the cement floor. He opened the car door and slid onto the seat. Keys. Where are my fucking keys? He scanned the garage, piled with boxes, yard tools, and sports equipment. They could be anywhere. *Shit.* He slumped down in the seat.

Annabelle's situation was not life-threatening. They only suggested that I come in. No code red. No sense in risking my life when it's probably nothing and she'll be asleep or on meds, and not even know I'm there anyway. She's in good hands. It is probably best to sober up, get some sleep, and make it over there in the morning. That's the sensible thing.

Jake got out of the car, stepped over the golf clubs now strewn on the floor, climbed the steps leading to the kitchen, and stumbled in. Instinctively, he closed his eyes against the kitchen lights, which at this point were not soothing at all. What was soothing was the glint from the open bottle of bourbon left on the kitchen counter. The fourth pour went down almost without notice.

Jake hit the redial on the last call and got the nurse's station. "Jake Martin here. I had a call from the hospital about my wife, Annabelle. Something about a complication?"

"Yes, we did call," said the nurse. "When will you be here? She just went into surgery."

"How long will the surgery take?" said Jake, sipping the bourbon. "I'm out of town and can't get there until tomorrow. I feel terrible about my wife going through yet another trauma without my being there for her."

"Well, you never know about these things, but the doctor said it wasn't life-threatening. We can keep you informed as you make your way back into town. Do you have cell phone service where you are?"

"Yes, but it's spotty, and I may be out of reach at times," said Jake with a concerned and sober voice that impressed even him. "I should make it back early in the morning. If she wakes up before I arrive, tell her I love her and am doing everything I can to get back to her and the baby."

"She will be happy to hear that. Take care and have a safe trip."

"Yes, I will," said Jake, ending the call with a long sigh of relief.

He congratulated himself on a stellar performance. Safe trip, indeed. He staggered down the hallway to the bedroom, kicked off his shoes and stretched out on the bed.

He started to drift off when his phone, still in his hand, buzzed with an incoming call. What could the damned hospital want now? He didn't think he had the strength for an encore.

The number wasn't the hospital but was vaguely familiar. He let it go to voicemail, and listened to the message.

"Left a message for you earlier. Don't you answer your phone? I want to do some business with you. Call me back."

Tossing the phone across the room, Jake grabbed for the pillow, closed his eyes, and whispered to himself. Annabelle could wait. Business could wait.

The whole fucking world could wait a few more hours.

31

"**OPEN YOUR EYES,** Annabelle. Everything is OK."

Annabelle could hear the words but her head was spinning, and she couldn't determine where they were coming from. The voice wasn't Jake's. It wasn't Roger. She opened her eyes and a face took shape, with grey-green eyes staring at her. Slowly the picture got clearer, blue scrubs, glasses. It was the night nurse.

"Good, Annabelle. Wake up. You're OK. We called your husband, but he's out of town and can't make it here until tomorrow morning. Can you hear me?" the voice said.

"My baby," whispered Annabelle to the face in front of her.

"He's asleep in the nursery. He's fine, and you're going to be fine, too."

"Fine. Yes, fine," mumbled Annabelle, as she drifted back to sleep, exhausted.

From somewhere close by there was another voice. A man, but not Jake or Roger. The nurse was talking to someone else.

"No, you can't talk to her now. She's just back from surgery. You can talk to her tomorrow. Now get out of her room."

"But I've been assigned to investigate the loss of her phone and wallet and may have some information that she can verify. I know she'll want to know if it will get her valuables back," said the voice. Then, suddenly, there was another face, staring down at her from the side of her bed.

"Mrs. Annabelle, it's Dewain, the orderly. I'm trying to find your wallet and phone and need to talk to you. You're a little out of it now, so I'll be back tomorrow morning."

"Orderly, I told you to get out of this room. Get away from the patient!" the nurse said sternly.

Annabelle heard the orderly's feet shuffling and a door closing. Then the face of the night nurse loomed above her again.

"Don't worry, Annabelle. We won't let anyone else bother you tonight. Don't worry about a thing."

32

DAVID COULD HEAR *the voices; he was arguing with her again. Even from the back of his closet with the door closed, David could hear his father's voice like a sharp knife stabbing at his mother, helpless and unable to escape her husband's tirade. David felt like a coward, but he'd promised his mother that when he heard that voice he would run into his bedroom and hide, and stay there until she came for him. So he crouched in the corner of the dark closet, pressing Mr. Bunny tight against one ear, his trembling hand over the other, trying to block out his father's voice and his mother's pleading.*

"I told you to get rid of these things. But, no, you don't listen, you don't obey me," his father said in a slow, harsh, steady voice. "And you tried to hide them behind the bed. You think you can defy me and then lie and sneak behind my back?"

David pressed Mr. Bunny tighter against his ears. His mother didn't make a sound.

"Woman, I asked you a question. Why did you defy me? Get rid of these things. No use for them now."

"I just wanted something to remember my baby, Joseph," said his mother, her voice soft and pleading. "It's just a little blanket. He was wrapped up in it when they let me see him before . . . " Her voice trailed off.

"Memories. Who needs them? You still have a little boy to coddle and make into a sissy with all your fussing and baby talk. Dammed

disgrace. You would have ruined that other one, too. Baby is better off where he is. If you won't get rid of this blanket, I will."

Footsteps, a scraping sound against the kitchen floor, and then the smell of smoke. Faint at first, then stronger, rising up the stairs from the hallway and into David's hiding place.

Terrified at what his father may have done, David crept out of the closet and slowly descended the stairs, far enough to see over the banister and into the kitchen. His father had one arm around his mother's neck, the other held her hands behind her back, forcing her to watch her dead baby's blanket, burning in the kitchen trash can.

"See, it's not so precious anymore," said his father with a laugh. "Just a stinking, blackened piece of trash."

Something terrible came over David, standing on the stairs, watching smoke and flames rising up, consuming the blanket. He felt anger replacing his fear of this monster as he watched the scene before him. The smile on his father's face. His mother straining against his grip, trying to escape the horror of the loss all over again and the heat and smoke of the flames.

He slipped down the stairs, gaining momentum, and ran into the kitchen.

"Stop it, you monster!" He yelled out to his father, startled at his own words. "If you don't stop, I'll stop you."

David ran to the knife set on the kitchen counter, drew out a serrated carving knife, and yelled out again.

"Stop or I'll kill you, Joey!"

An evil grin spread over his father's face. Shoving David's mother aside, he moved slowly toward David.

"So, it's Joey, now, is it David? Well, maybe you are a man after all. Come on, let's see what you've got."

David stood there, holding the knife in trembling, little-boy hands, and raised the knife over his head, ready to strike. Just then, his father—moving like a hungry tiger—sprang at David with a roar.

33

DAVID WOKE WITH a start, lying in cold, sweat-soaked sheets. His arms were over his head, hands clasped together in a tight grip. His head pounded. Waves of nausea came and went. He slowly lowered his aching arms and rose up on one elbow, looking at the clock on the bedside table. The LED numbers glowed "1:15."

That familiar damned dream was almost as relentless as his damned addiction. Too much time had passed since his buy from Dewain on the hospital loading dock. He could feel the longing, the terrifying ache in his bones and brain, begging for a hit.

Where was the second Oxy from Two K?

He pulled himself up and stumbled to the bedroom door. His eyes slowly adjusted in the dim light from the street through the downstairs windows. He went down the stairs and into the dining room.

Blazer? Pockets? He felt the soft wool of the blazer hanging over the dining room chair. He felt around the outside pockets. Nothing. He found an inside pocket and thrust in his hand so hard the lining began to give way. Terror—then calm and excitement as he felt the round, hard shape of the Oxy tablet jammed into a corner. He pulled it from its hiding place. *There you are.*

He threw back his head and dropped the Oxy into his mouth, bringing up just enough saliva to make it slide down his throat. David sank into the chair and waited patiently for the pain to ease and was just about to climb the stairs when he heard a muffled ring tone. His head started to clear as it continued.

The musical refrain "Stop, in the name of love!" repeated in a tinny digital version.

Annabelle's phone. Now awake, David pulled the phone from its hiding place in the breakfront and stared at the bright screen. A number flashed on the screen marked "Unknown caller." Instinctively, his finger hovered over the green circle on the screen, but he waited until the music stopped. Safer to listen to a voicemail.

There were two messages. One was the message from the police department that had come in earlier. He tapped to listen to it.

"This is the Shepherdsville police department, Detective James Holt, badge #SPD364762. There is a reward for anyone who turns in this phone. If you get this message, call this number and ask for Detective Holt. The reward will be paid when the phone is turned in to the police department in person."

A reward? Maybe fortune was smiling on him. In person? A good Samaritan who happened to be on the bus with the frantic lady who was having a baby right there. Maybe, if he got desperate enough.

He punched the latest voicemail number and put the phone on speaker. A crackle, then a voice wrapped around David's throat like a python positioning for a squeeze.

"Whoever you are answering this phone, I'm on your trail. You can't hide for long. The police and I are breathing down your neck. Call this number while you still can."

The voice stopped; David dropped the phone on the table. The voice; the same one from the hospital loading dock and from just a few hours ago in this very room. *Two Knuckles.*

David sat down and looked at the phone again. First the police and now Two K. That thieving, drug-dealing, low-life hoodlum had fooled both a police detective and the hospital staff.

The police department and Dewain? A trusted advisor? *Bullshit!*

David didn't know who he feared the most. The police, who could only get him for stealing the wallet and its missing contents. Or Two Knuckles, who was not beyond any evil in the pursuit of money or revenge.

He reminded himself to play it cool, to relax. It was just Two K, enjoying the cover of the police, playing detective and looking for reward money. Or, he didn't buy David's story and thinks he knows he's got the phone and wallet.

David picked up the phone and stared at the number. *No, Two K—nice appeal, but I'll keep things to myself for now.* But thanks to his call, David now had his number. *Don't be too pleased with yourself, my two-knuckled friend.* David slipped Annabelle's phone back into its hiding place in the breakfront and went back to bed.

34

JAMES HOLT SAT up on the edge of the bed, opened his eyes and waited for them to adjust to the pre-dawn darkness. Shadows slowly turned into shapes and then became objects. Pants. Shirt. Belt. Badge. Service weapon. Everything was on the floor where he left them the night before.

He pulled on his pants and let the belt, still in the pant loops, rest open on his waist. He walked over to the window and lit a cigarette, blowing the smoke through the opening above the sill. The clock displayed five-thirty. The squad room would be quiet for another hour before the shift change. The best time for thinking and piecing together bits of evidence, interviews, and file notes.

The room came into view with the first rays of sunrise. He saw the sheets move, revealing the tantalizing shape of the red-haired nurse. There were some things that James couldn't resist. A good bourbon, tarpon fishing off the Florida Keys, and a sexy, available, and willing woman. Veronica was all three, and had an apartment conveniently located close to the precinct station.

He had recognized her immediately at the nurse's station in the hospital. An all-exclusive vacation in the Caribbean six months ago. They had met on a deep-sea fishing excursion for resort guests. She was quite the catch. After three days of hot sun, cool nights, and mutual exploration, they said their goodbyes at the airport, promising to meet again. An unfulfilled promise until that evening at the nurse's desk. Timing, opportunity, and a texted invitation was all it took. Who thought a traveling nurse position and a simple missing property case could bring them back together?

He stood for a moment, watching as her red hair fell across her naked breasts and onto the pillow as she turned, her left hand, feeling his empty pillow, searching. He could still taste her sweet-and-salty skin, dewy from her sweat mixed with his.

"James, get your fine ass back in bed," she whispered, still half asleep. "It's too early to leave me alone."

Thoughts of going MIA and spending the day with her crowded his mind. "I'll call you later," he said as she turned away, asleep again.

Holt kept his distance before his resistance could weaken. He pulled on the rest of his clothes, gathered his belongings, and made for the door. He grabbed his keys and closed the door softly behind him.

The windshield was wet with a heavy morning dew. He grabbed the crumpled Krispy Kreme bag from the back seat and downed the remains of a stale glazed donut in one bite. A man of many appetites, his desire for Krispy Kreme donuts ran a close second to his desire for the lovely woman he left sleeping in her apartment.

He stretched his tall frame in the seat of his black Mustang, turned the key, and listened to the purr of the engine. He glanced out the window to see Veronica's curves topped with flowing auburn hair pressed against the upstairs apartment window, waving goodbye.

His urge to join her warmed and terrified him. "Don't tempt me," he whispered, as he pressed hard on the accelerator and sped out onto the empty streets.

Playtime was over. Time to get to work.

35

INSTEAD OF GOING to the precinct, Holt headed across town to his apartment for a shower, shave, and a change of clothes. The red-headed vision gave way to the image of a three-fingered orderly with a smart mouth and a suspicious demeanor.

Ten years on the police force, hundreds of arrests, and months of study for the detective's exam gave him the skills and experience to earn the respect of his peers and a dozen awards for meritorious service. But one tool of the trade that never failed him couldn't be learned or bought. His gut kept nagging at him every time he encountered orderly Dewain in the hospital. He had handled triple-murder cases, kidnappings, sex abuse, human trafficking cases—the worst kind of criminals and situations this fucked-up city had to offer. But this small, seemingly insignificant lost property case dogged him. His gut knew what his mind and reasoning couldn't comprehend.

That cocky little shit robbed Holt of sleep as he tried to put together the few incidents and conversations that Holt had with him. Just Dewain's presence seemed to make the woman, Annabelle uncomfortable when Holt introduced him as the hospital's contact for the search for her missing valuables.

There had been no word from Dewain after his introduction and first meeting with Annabelle. Dressed in street clothes, Holt made his way through the early-morning traffic to the precinct offices. As he pulled into his parking space, his phone lit up with a text message. He picked it up off the front seat and saw a message from Veronica with a photo attached.

He clicked on the photo and enlarged it. He let his memory replay the highlights of last night. This naked anatomy could get in the wrong hands; he took a last long look, hit "delete," readjusted, and headed for the precinct.

––––––––

Holt sat down at his desk, pulled out his notebook, and reviewed the week's cases. The two shooters were still in the hospital. He would have to make a trip back to the hospital and follow up to drag their sorry asses to lockup as soon as they could be moved. Too bad they didn't have better aim; that would have saved him a trip to the hospital. A trip to the morgue made things easy. Done and done.

He flipped past the shooters and read the next set of notes scrawled hurriedly across the page.

"Husband of wife who went into labor on city bus. She is missing phone and wallet. Get hospital to help search. Nurse at desk, Veronica, volunteered to help out. Orderly Dewain directed by head nurse to search for the phone and wallet. Missing two fingers. Cocky. Prior arrest? Looks familiar. Check this."

He turned on his laptop and pulled up the National Crime Information Center database. He knew it was a long-shot but entered the name "Dewain" along with the few details he had—the name of the hospital, city and state, and the missing fingers. The system started searching the millions of pieces of data. It could take hours—he'd check back later. He grabbed his jacket, phone, and notebook and headed for the hospital.

36

DEWAIN SMILED AS he cleared a spot on the kitchen table littered with prescription bottles from the past week's take from the hospital. There had been lots of discharges last week; it was just so unfortunate that some of the medicines didn't make it home with the patients. Everyone knew that old, sick people who were in a hurry to get the hell out of the hospital can be forgetful. They leave their meds in the room or drop them in the parking lot or lose them in the car.

It happened all the time, which was fortunate for Dewain. Lots of logical explanations for missing meds. Who has time to track down a couple of scripts when patients are stacked up in the hallways and doubled up in rooms? Move them out of here, deal with the meds later. The hospital pharmacy was happy to refill those meds. More than happy. As a result, his needy, strung-out customers were delighted. Yes, he'd made lots of people happy this week.

He grabbed the carafe from the old Mr. Coffee on the counter, poured a steaming mug, and grabbed his phone to check the call log. No response to his call to Annabelle's phone.

Dewain told himself to be patient. He wouldn't make any more surprise visits to David in the night; he'd wait it out. Either way, he'd win. Creds with the police department, employee of the year from the hospital, and, if his hunch was right, a shitload of cash.

Today he would see Mrs. Annabelle again. No one would question a visit to give her an update on the hospital-requested investigation into her missing things. With a little prompting, she may even remember what David was doing at the bus stop and perhaps even identify him.

Dewain took a sip of coffee, scooped up a bottle labeled M. McDougal filled with Oxycodone 150/mg tablets off the table, and shoved it into the pocket of his blue scrubs. Mrs. McDougal was headed for hospice, and they would get her anything she needed. Probably wouldn't need half of these, or the three refills. There was enough here for at least three of his needy customers.

Dewain glanced at the clock on the microwave. Just enough time to catch the seven-thirty bus to the hospital. It was going to be a busy day.

37

THE ER WAS quiet; a far cry from the chaos of the other day. The receptionist, busy swiping the screen of her cell phone, didn't notice as Detective Holt strolled in the emergency-room entrance and walked up to the admitting desk.

"Can you really read that fast?" he asked.

"Yeah, I can. Can I help you?"

Holt smiled and decided this one was too young or clueless for his usual small talk. He pulled out his badge.

"Detective Holt, fifth precinct. I brought two shooters in here two nights ago." He pulled out his notebook, flipped a few pages, and continued. "Rodriguez and Davenport. They were in surgery and should still be here. I need to question them and, if they're able, take them to lockup. Can you point me in the right direction?"

The receptionist gave the badge and Holt a blank stare and clicked away at the computer keyboard.

"Yeah. They made it through," she said, staring at the screen. "Davenport and Rodriguez are tucked away in Room 427. They may be here for a while, though. You can go on up, Detective—ah, Holt did you say?"

Holt felt the receptionist's mood change. No longer transfixed on her phone or the computer, she leaned forward, locked her gaze on his blue eyes and smiled, waiting for a reply.

He warned himself that it was too early in the day to return that warm smile. He already had a nurse on the fifth floor who, he hoped, would be looking for an encore.

"Thanks, miss," Holt said in his best professional you-don't-want-to-go-there detective voice. "Have a good day." He turned quickly on his heels and headed straight for the elevator.

36

"**WELL, YOU'RE IN** early," the receptionist at the birthing center desk said with surprise.

"Never too early to start helping out," Dewain leaned over the desk, scanning the open files on the desk, straining to read the computer screen.

"Hey, this is confidential information. Keep your roving eyes on the other side. I've got my eyes on you."

He leaned back and put on a smile.

"Thought I'd check on Mrs. Annabelle this morning. I'm helping the police with their investigation. How is she this morning?"

"Better now. They are going to keep her one more day. Had a scare last night, and they had to take her into the OR. They're keeping the baby in the nursery this morning. Don't upset her."

"I'll be the model of diplomacy and tact," he said, turning on his heel and heading down the hallway.

He didn't have any real information for Annabelle. He didn't have her wallet or phone or know where it was or who had it. She must know something she hasn't been able to remember. He thought he might help refresh her memory.

The door to her room was slightly open. Dewain knocked lightly. "Mrs. Annabelle, it's Dewain, the hospital orderly from yesterday."

No reply. Dewain pushed the door open and slipped in quietly. Annabelle was sitting up in bed, eyes closed. Sensing someone in the room, Annabelle looked up, startled.

"Who are you, and what do you want?" she demanded. "Three nurses and a doctor have already been in here, and the other orderly hasn't brought me the coffee I requested from the lobby coffee bar. The hospital coffee tastes like dishwater. I don't see you carrying a grande macchiato with skim milk and a shot of espresso, either."

Spunky little lady. Selectively forgetful, too.

"No ma'am," said Dewain, pulling a chair close to the bed. "The hospital asked me to help the police find your phone and wallet. We talked yesterday morning. Do you mind if I sit down?"

"Well, I don't see that you have my phone and wallet, so I can guess what you have to say. Sounds like a standing conversation to me."

"Yes. I mean, no ma'am, I don't have your phone and wallet. Not yet. The police are on it too. I just wanted to see if you remember anything more about the night you came in, anything from the bus or the ambulance. Do you remember anyone else on the bus that hung around you, talked to you, sat next to you? Anything at all?"

Annabelle leaned back against the pillows, took a side glance at Dewain. "Since you're not standing, I'll try to think of something. It's all been so disjointed. I haven't been well since I arrived here, what with the birth and the scare last night."

She closed her eyes against the harsh glow of her beside lamp. She could feel Dewain's eyes fix on her, waiting expectantly.

"If I can suggest," Dewain said with a tone of command. "The bus ride. Can you remember anyone on the bus? Someone that stands out? That you talked to or who talked to you?"

Annabelle closed her eyes tighter, then relaxed. "There were so many people on the plaza that day. People pushing at the bus stop. When the number seven pulled in, there was such a crush of people trying to get on the bus. There was this woman."

A woman? Dewain didn't care about a woman. He wanted to hear about a man, with a hat on. He pressed on. "A woman? What about her?"

"She was pushing her way on. Almost knocked me over. She had funny-looking hair. Pink, I think. I was so tired, and my feet were killing me. And my bladder was about to explode."

"Ah, yes. The crowd." Dewain pushed, ignoring her statement about an exploding bladder. "And what about on the bus? Do you remember anything or anyone in particular?"

"Well, I take this bus at times, so pretty much the regulars. The bus driver—I think his name is Gus—drove like he has for years. Lately, though, he seems to drive a little faster and swings way into the bus stop, practically running up on the curb. The old guy is going to run over someone. So many people at five o'clock on the plaza."

"The bus." Dewain steered her back. "What about the passengers? Anyone out of the ordinary?"

"Why are you so interested in the people on the bus? Do you think someone stole my phone and wallet from my bag on the bus? That would be hard to do since it was tucked almost underneath me on the seat. Someone would have had to reach over my enormous belly to do that. I was sitting next to the window. I remember looking out once I got my seat to watch the rest of the crowd try to push onto the bus. I was tired and closed my eyes once the bus took off from the stop. A pink-haired lady got on, but she was standing in the aisle, earbuds in, texting on her phone."

"So, you don't remember anyone else?" asked Dewain, frustrated.

Annabelle opened her eyes and jerked away from Dewain's face, now just inches away from hers. His eyes were fixed on her in a motionless stare.

"Sorry, ma'am, but I got caught up in your story. What an ordeal for a woman in your condition." Dewain sat back in his chair, putting on his best imitation of concern.

Those eyes; that stare. Annabelle remembered that day on the bus. The person who sat next to her. He was staring, and she felt uncomfortable for a moment.

"There *was* this guy," Annabelle began slowly. "I remember he was staring at me. Kind of creeped me out. He sat down next to me. I don't remember much; I wasn't paying attention and hate when strangers try to chat me up. Women go on and on about harrowing pregnancies, or how they hate their kids, or about being sleep deprived."

"Annoying," said Dewain in agreement, hoping to steer her back to that day. "But that guy?"

"Yes, a young guy. He was staring at me—at my belly. Of course, most people do—or did. Used to be people would stare at my smile, or my hair, or my small waist."

Annabelle ran her fingers through her hair, pressing one hand gently on her still-round abdomen. "I'm afraid they won't be looking at those features anymore."

Dewain struggled for the right words to get her back on track. *What a self absorbed, whiny bitch.*

In the silence, Annabelle continued. "He was nice, in a creepy sort of way. Said his mother was having a baby soon. That's all I remember. Like I said, he was staring. I looked out the window, avoiding his eyes. I must have fallen asleep, because when I woke up, he was gone. Rode for a while until the bus was empty except for me. I get off at the last stop, and the shopping area there is closed at that time of day. My husband picks me up there and was supposed to be there, but he texted that he would be late. I was thinking about having to get off the bus in the dark all alone.

"I do remember the pain. I may have passed out. Later the nurses told me my water broke on the bus. Pretty messy. Like I said, there was the pain, and then everything went dark. In my mind, that is. I don't remember anything else until I woke up in this room."

"What about the ambulance ride? Can you remember that? Did anyone ride with you?

Annabelle shifted a little, moving away from Dewain. Something about the tone of his questioning made her uneasy.

"Look, I've told you all I can remember," she raised her voice in frustration. "Why are you pressing so hard? It's just a phone and a wallet. Is there something I should know? Do you have some information that you're not telling me?"

Suddenly there was a knock on the door, and Detective Holt walked into the room. "Dewain, you're making the lady uncomfortable. I could hear you from the hallway. Do you know something you're not telling her—or us?"

"How long have you been standing in the hall, detective?" Dewain asked as calmly as he could. It was just like the police to be sneaky, hiding behind doors and laying a trap. Dewain was familiar with that game.

"Long enough," Holt said, hiding his irritation. His cold stare told Dewain his interview was over.

Holt walked up to Annabelle's bedside and motioned for Dewain to step back. He took out his notebook and flipped to a new page.

"Sorry, ma'am. Sometimes the amateurs get a little too curious."

Annabelle settled back and smiled at Holt. He turned to Dewain, now standing at the door.

"You can go now, Dewain," he said dismissively. "I'm sure you've got other patients who would be happy to see you."

Dewain choked out a low "Yes, sir," and walked out the door and down the hallway.

But it wasn't going to be so easy to get rid of him. His conversation with Annabelle was far from over. After all, this was his turf.

39

DAVID ROLLED OVER onto his back, shielding his eyes from the bright sunlight streaming into the bedroom windows. He spied Hannah curled at the foot of the bed.

"Come here, Hannah girl," he said. But Hannah gave him a disinterested glance, stood up, circled in place, and sat down again with her back towards David.

He checked the clock on the bedside table: seven-fifteen. He rolled over again onto his stomach and grabbed his pillow, tucking it under his head. He felt a slow movement in the bed, then a soft warmth against his back.

"So, you do love me, Hannah," David said without turning. "I know, you're hungry."

David felt a jab against his back, then another, confirming his suspicions. Hannah jumped off the bed and walked to the open bedroom door, turned, and gave David a look that said "Well, are you coming?" David pulled on his robe and headed downstairs to the kitchen.

Hannah picked at the salmon and tuna supreme he put in her dish. David went into the dining room, retrieved his phone from his jacket, and checked his messages. No response yet from Darcy's connection. It had been six hours since his last Oxy. He punched the number again and let it ring. This time a voice answered.

"Yeah? Who is this?"

"Um, I'm a friend of Darcy's. She gave me your number. Looking to do some business."

"And how do you know Darcy?"

"Let's just say we had a business relationship. I interned in her office. She said you were in business, too."

"Well, Darcy's got a lot of business acquaintances. If you know *my* Darcy, you can tell me what kind of icing she likes on her cake?"

Yes, I do, thought David, cringing.

————

Fondant. Just saying the word to himself brought back the taste, smell, and texture. She used to eat that stuff like fruit leather. Bought it in sheets from a bakery downtown, and she would tear off pieces of the leathery icing and wrap it around her index finger, then suck it like a popsicle on a stick. She sent me out to get it like a damned delivery boy. Chocolate was her favorite. Always kept it in the refrigerator in her office. The call would come after four o'clock.

"Come here, David, I've got a craving for chocolate," Darcy would say seductively. "Get the fondant out of the fridge."

Darcy's staff knew that she was not to be disturbed for any reason after four. Even if the building was on fire and terrorists had invaded the offices. No one dared to open her office door, or even knock, after that time. David would dutifully retrieve a circle of chocolate fondant out of the refrigerator and lay it on her desk.

That day, Darcy poured two double shots of tequila from the Patron bottle on the credenza behind her desk. Then she pulled two tablets from her bottom drawer. She slowly placed the tablet on her tongue and downed one shot, offering the other tablet and a shot to David. He tossed them back quickly, hoping the drugs and liquor would dull his senses just enough to get him through her games.

She put the empty glasses on her desk, sauntered slowly over to David, laid her hands on his chest, and unbuttoned his shirt, sliding her outstretched hands on his bare chest and took his shirt off in a slow, fluid motion. She pulled him to her on the red Italian leather sofa and gave a playful push on his chest. He knew the drill. He lay back against the pillows as she climbed on top.

The booze, pills and Darcy's educated hands conspired against him. His brain was revolted by her clumsy attempts at seduction, but his body started shifting through the gears, accelerating as smooth and sleek as a Maserati Spyder. She tore small pieces off the circle of fondant. It was cold against his nipples, then warm and liquid as she sucked the rich icing off his chest. Next, a square for his belly button. David lay there, Darcy's face in his chest, her tongue drawing circles in the melting chocolate.

Darcy's hands clawed at his belt buckle. In the haze of the Patron and ecstasy, David surrendered to Darcy's power over him, feeling the cool fondant as she expertly wrapped it around—

———

"Hello! Are you still there? Tell me, what is her favorite kind of icing?" The voice brought David back.

"Yeah, I know. Fondant."

"Yeah, that's right. So, what do you need, Darcy's friend?"

"Oxys—80s. And I need them fast. What's the price?"

"Well, that's premium stuff and will cost you $150 each. Cash. Don't show up with merchandise to trade or a sob story. How many?"

David thought of the nine one-hundred-dollar bills in his wallet. "Six 80s will do it. How, and where?"

"I'll call you back with instructions."

"Today? I need them today," David said urgently.

"Take it easy. I take care of Darcy's friends. Chill. I'll be in touch."

David heard the click and watched the number disappear from his phone screen. It was no use trying to track the phone number. Probably a burner phone that can't be traced. Another two hours and he'd be crawling up the walls, tearing the place apart. He walked into the kitchen, poured a shot of bourbon, and tossed it back to fortify himself.

Breakfast of champions.

40

THAT SHOULD TAKE care of him for a while, Jake thought as he ended the call. It's better to make them wait a little. Shows who's in control. Damned junkies. Yes, he'd get back to this new friend in time. But first, he had a wife and baby to drop in on. He slipped his phone into his jacket, grabbed his keys, and headed for the hospital.

41

"**MIND IF I** sit down, ma'am?" Detective Holt motioned at the chair next to Annabelle's bed after Dewain had left.

"Not at all, please sit down," said Annabelle. "I don't mind answering a few questions, but I was beginning to feel like I was under the bare bulb being interrogated by that orderly. It's my wallet and phone that are missing, not the crown jewels! Do you know anything yet?"

"I'm sorry, ma'am, if he made you uncomfortable. We haven't turned anything up. I was hoping you remembered something from the night you came in. People who stand out. Any details about the bus or the ambulance transport."

Annabelle sighed deeply. "I told the orderly all I remembered. Can't you get his notes?

"I will, ma'am," said Holt, "but I need to get an official statement for the record. Just a few questions. Where had you put your wallet and phone? What's the last place you remember?"

"They were in the bag with my laptop. Usually in the inside pockets, but I was late getting out of the office, and I almost forgot them. One of the guys in the office was getting married, and I had my wallet out when they came around to collect contributions. I left it on top of my desk with my phone. I got as far as the elevator and stopped to check my phone to see if my husband had sent a text—that's when I noticed they weren't in my bag. I was going to stop in the ladies' room before catching the bus but instead had to drag myself back to my desk. Just grabbed them and threw them in the bag. Thought I was going to burst."

"OK, thanks for clearing that up, ma'am," he said with a half-smile.

Holt scribbled in his notebook and continued.

"And what about the bus stop? And the bus ride?" he asked. "Any details that stand out? Anything at all? In missing or stolen item cases people tend to think big events, where the small details can be most helpful. Try to recall that evening like a movie, frame by frame, and tell me if anything stands out."

Annabelle closed her eyes and walked her way through the scenes.

"I told Dewain that there were a couple of people on the bus that I remembered. There was a young woman with pink hair who tried to get in front of me when I was getting on the bus. People usually give me a wide berth." She chuckled. "Wide berth; that's funny, right?"

Holt cracked a smile, resisting an eye roll, and nodded. "Glad you kept your sense of humor through this," he said. "Anyone else?"

"I told Dewain about the young man next to me on the bus. He kept staring at me—at my belly actually." She let out a sigh and ran her hand over her rounded abdomen.

Detective Holt cleared his throat just enough to get Annabelle's attention. An effective tactic for getting people out of their heads and talking again.

"He made me uncomfortable with that stare, so I looked out the window away from his eyes, watching the crowd at the bus stop trying to push onto the bus. I remember I could see his reflection in the window—you know, like a mirror. He kept staring at me. I could almost feel it. He wasn't creepier than some of the clowns on the bus, but somehow this felt different. Anyway, he told me his name. Davon? Or maybe Derrick? I can't remember. But it started with 'D'."

Holt scratched at his notepad and looked up again.

"Anything else about this young man? Physical characteristics? Clothing?"

Annabelle leaned back again, closed her eyes, and resumed the video in her memory. Holt waited for what he thought was an eternity, when she sat up and opened her eyes wide.

"His jacket! He was wearing a blazer with a crest on it. I've seen guys with those jackets before. Yes, there was definitely some kind of crest on his breast pocket jacket."

Holt nodded. "Good. Anything else that you can remember?"

Annabelle closed her eyes again, but the screen had gone blank. "I fell asleep on the bus. I woke up somewhere along the way, and he was gone. The rest is just a jumble. I remember the pain, and they told me my water broke on the bus. We were at the last stop. The nurses told me Gus called the EMTs, and they took me to the hospital. The next thing I remember, I was waking up in this room, and—"

"Excuse me, ma'am," Holt interrupted. "You said Gus called the EMTs? Who is Gus? You didn't mention him before."

"Oh, yes, Gus. He's the bus driver. He has had that bus route for years, as long as I've been riding the bus. I don't take it every day, but he's always at the wheel when I get on at Market Square. Gus doesn't talk much, and he's one of the few who didn't make comments about my belly. He was driving the bus that night, and the nurses said that he called the EMTs. I don't remember anything about that part of the trip."

He nodded. "Anything else? At the hospital?"

"No, sorry," she replied, obviously distressed. "I can't relive that horrible night one more time. Please, I've told you everything I remember."

He nodded. "You've been very helpful. Very helpful." Holt pulled out a card from his inside jacket pocket and placed it on the bedside table. He was almost at the door when he stopped and turned to Annabelle again.

"One more thing, if you don't mind. Your wallet. Besides the hundred-dollar bills, was there anything else of value?"

"I had a few photos and receipts, but they wouldn't be valuable to anyone else but me, Annabelle said.

She suddenly went silent. A wave of terror swept over her as an image flashed in her mind. The photo of her and Roger together, pressed inside the bill compartment of her wallet, dog-eared from retrieving it so many times during their brief affair. It had traces of lipstick where she had pressed a soft kiss over his face. A photo she kept hidden from Jake.

Holt finally broke the silence.

"We're almost finished, Annabelle. You mentioned concert tickets?"

Annabelle closed her eyes, shutting off Roger's image and turned back to Holt.

"Yes, there were two front-row tickets to tomorrow night's rock concert at the amphitheater at Silver Dunes Lake. No big headliners, but it's the hottest ticket at the music festival. I get the same seats every year, seats 15 and 16 in the front row. That's the only thing that would be worth anything. I hate the thought of someone sitting in those seats that cost me $500."

Some thief or junkie could turn those into cash in no time, Holt thought. Or be stupid enough to catch the concert. This could be the best piece of information yet.

"One more thing, detective," said Annabelle. "When—if—you do recover the phone and wallet. Will they be returned to me? I mean directly? I'm lost without my phone. I saved a message from my mother before she passed. It's all I have of her. The money is gone, but there are irreplaceable family photos in my wallet." Annabelle closed her eyes and looked away, hoping her performance was convincingly urgent.

"I just want to hear my mother's voice again and know I haven't lost my memories, too."

"Well, we do have some internal procedures for recovered property," said Holt. "But it is returned to the owner after processing. I'll make a note about your request. You've been very helpful. If there is anything else you remember, please call me. Anything at all."

Annabelle lifted her hand in Holt's direction as if to wave goodbye.

Holt paused outside her room and looked at his notes. Not much new, except the creepy guy wearing a blazer with a crest on it. He made another entry into his notebook—Gus the bus driver. First, he'd talk to the two perps who had turned into canaries in the ER. Then he'd see what Gus remembered.

Maybe it was his gut instinct after too many years working in the criminal world or his own inclination to capitalize on the mistakes of others, but this missing-property case wasn't quite as simple as it appeared to be.

He thought about what he'd overheard of Dewain's forceful interrogation. Why the intensity? Holt had questioned hundreds of perps, and he was especially proud of his ability to smoke out the liars and those with secrets. He flipped open his notebook and made one more entry: "Squeeze Dewain."

He had walked past the nurse's station and punched the button for the first floor when one of the nurses called out his name.

42

"DETECTIVE HOLT?" HE recognized that voice; as he walked up to Veronica he fought unsuccessfully to block images from last night's reunion.

"Yes?"

She suppressed her own reply and said evenly, "I have a message for you. The two men you brought in yesterday want to talk. Seems like they have a lot to say."

She handed him a slip of paper with their room numbers written on them, slowly brushing the palm of his hand with hers. He glanced at her and then at the note—Room 357—followed by two hearts and three Xs.

"Thank you, nurse," he said, turning quickly. She knew how to push his replay button. He headed for the elevator, pushed little a too hard on button number three, and was relieved to see the elevator was empty.

Easy, Holt. You have three floors to regain your composure.

43

DAVID SAW THE number fade from his cell phone. *He said he'll get back to me.* The last Oxy was beginning to wear off, and anxiety was beginning to turn into panic in his mind and body. Darcy had made his skin crawl, but she was always willing to supply what he needed and even a little more, depending on how she rated their "work sessions." Two K was the worst kind of dealer, willing to make David suffer and to inflict pain for his own sick pleasure. Besides, Two K was already suspicious, and he knew too much. So, Mr. "I'll get back to you" would have to do for now.

David poured himself another cup of coffee and opened the front door to retrieve the newspaper. He sat down at the kitchen table and spread it out on the table, as he did every morning. Hannah jumped up on a chair then onto the table, curling up at the top right-hand corner of the business section and stared at David, as if to ask, *What are you waiting for? Don't you have something to do?*

David took a long swallow of the now-tepid coffee, put down the paper, and got up to get Hannah's breakfast. Some wet food and some dry mixed together. "Here you are, my girl," he said. Hannah gave him a dismissive look, strolled over to the bowl on the floor, sniffed as if to signal disdain, and settled down to eat.

David refreshed his coffee and flipped the paper to the top of the Arts Section with the bold headline: "Sold Out Concert—Biggest Ticket of the Year. Can't Boogie on Down if You Didn't Bookie in Advance."

The article listed the cover bands performing at the concert in the park the next evening, with rave reviews of past performances.

"Nostalgia for the carefree innocence of the past has made this the hottest ticket of the year. You can't buy one, but if you want to go, you can always go the "beg, borrow, or steal" method to make your score," the article advised.

Beg, borrow, or steal? David retrieved Annabelle's wallet from the dining room sideboard. Snug inside the bill compartment next to the remaining $900 were the two tickets to the concert. He splayed them on the table.

He looked at the tickets again. Front row, $250 each. He shifted them around on the table with his finger while mentally calculating his newfound wealth. The original sales price had been $250, but now—? Now the price of the hottest ticket in town just went up. A ticket like this would impress the hell out of someone. Worth maybe twice the price? There would be thousands of people there tonight, and it would be easy enough to slip into the crowd and make a quick sale.

Double my fortune.

44

DAVID PICKED UP the tickets and climbed the stairs to his bedroom. His muscles were beginning to ache. It had been six hours. He picked up his blazer from the floor and slipped the tickets into the breast pocket.

Suddenly, David felt a squeeze in his stomach and bolted for the bathroom. His hands shook as he grabbed some toilet paper to wipe the vomit from his mouth. His head started spinning. He pushed himself up to his feet, grabbed his phone, and searched the messages. Nothing yet. He wasn't going to last much longer.

Panic and anger exploded like a geyser within him. He flung the phone onto the bed. Almost on cue, it started to buzz. A wave of relief pushed out the nausea. That number again.

"Yes, I'm here," David mumbled, pulling himself together.

The voice on the other line was familiar—direct and even. "One hour. There's an old, covered bus stop on the north-west side of the river, down the road from West Essex Street. Bring the cash and come alone. We'll be watching. Leave it under the bench inside, get back in your car and drive out to Essex and park for twenty minutes—no more and no less. Come back to the bus stop and look under the seat. Get it and get out."

"Wait a minute! How do I know—" David heard a click and the screen went blank. His hand left moist fingerprints on the phone, and he felt another wave of nausea fueled by fear and anxiety. This dirty business didn't deal in trust and fair play. It could be a scam, a trap, or a death sentence.

West Essex Street had once been a playground for the rich and prominent people in town, with its private midnight river bank parties fueled by secret liaisons, booze, and drugs. Now it was mostly deserted, overgrown, and neglected by a conglomerate that bought hundreds of acres of property with the promise of building a new, exclusive riverfront community. Left abandoned, it was overrun with all sort of predators—a dangerous place for the unsuspecting.

He was familiar with terror. He could hear his father's voice. "Don't be such a baby. What are you afraid of? Just go down into the basement and get the jar of beans for your mother. And hurry up. Your sniveling and crying are delaying my dinner."

———

The wooden stairs moaned with each step. The light from the single bulb cast long shadows against the shelves of canned foods and laundry hanging stiff in the musty air. And down the short hallway at the far left was his father's locked hideaway where his father, a numismatist, kept his coin collections. There was no light from under the door to the locked room.

David walked carefully to the shelves that lined one wall. The glass jars of peaches, pears, stewed tomatoes, and green beans were dusty from the basement air. He had to stretch up on his toes to reach a jar of green beans on a high shelf, grabbing the large Mason jar with his two small hands. Mission accomplished. Letting out a sigh of relief, he had turned to climb back up the stairs.

Suddenly, David felt he was not alone. He hurried over to the stairs, eyes down, avoiding the basement shadows that seemed to reach out for him. Finally—the stairs and escape. He mounted the first step, looked up and froze. In the dim light, he could make out a large, grey rat perched on the stairs between him and the safety of the kitchen door above. He felt the jar slip from his hands, and heard the sound of glass shattering against the concrete floor. Alerted, the rat turned and fixed David with eyes that seemed to glow in the dark.

David heard his father's heavy footsteps and saw the kitchen door swing open. The light from the kitchen framed his father and the now distinct form of the rat on the steps.

"Clumsy! Scared of a little mouse? Clean up your mess, and get another jar. Knock on the door when you're at the top of the stairs."

The light, and his father, vanished. Alone in the dark, he heard his father turn the key in the closed door and his footsteps fading away.

———

Fear and dread from those old memories were amplified by withdrawal, and a different kind of terror swept over him. One hour. David made his way back to the bathroom and stared in the mirror. The face of a young shy schoolboy was quickly changing to a hard, chiseled, slightly aging addict who would gladly risk his life for one more fix.

What if it was a trap? He'd been fooled before. He turned his face to search out the faded hairline scar under his chin from a rendezvous gone bad.

An hour.

"We'll be watching you."

A not-so-subtle message that I'm outnumbered?

David grasped the edge of the sink as the nausea passed. The ache in his bones was crouching, ready to strike, advancing with each passing minute. In an hour he'd be willing to walk through a gauntlet of thieves and murderers, barefoot over broken glass for the hope of scoring something, anything. He knew it. And the voice on the phone knew it.

David threw on some shorts and a T-shirt, walked into a pair of docksiders, and grabbed his cap off the floor. In the dining room, he pulled the $900 from Annabelle's wallet and tucked it inside a large manila envelope, folded it in half, and tucked it in the back waistband of his shorts under his shirt. He grabbed his keys from the kitchen counter and headed to the garage.

He walked around the baby blue restored classic Jaguar and ran his hand across its sleek, smooth rear end, sending a wave of pleasure through his aching body. There was no sense attracting attention he thought, blowing a kiss. The truck was a better choice for this trip.

The old grey Chevy truck groaned and sputtered to a start. Looking like a poor, neglected relation next to the Jag, it was unremarkable in a crowd or on a deserted road. Just enough dirt for a respectable truck, with mud on the wheels and license plate.

Light flooded the garage as the door responded to the click of the opener. David backed out into the street and headed for the river.

45

DAVID ROLLED DOWN the truck's window and rested his arm out the window as he headed to his rendezvous. The breeze helped subdue his gnawing pain and growing panic. The roads on this side of town were in better shape because they led to some of the most prestigious addresses in town.

As he approached West Essex Street, the landscape started to change. Manicured lawns gave way to barren front yards guarding slightly sagging structures. The smell of the river changed, too. Remains of abandoned houses from a now defunct construction site littered with faded lot markers casting eerie shadows in the late morning sun, hidden now and again by gray clouds thickening in the sky.

The manilla envelope scratched his back as David repositioned himself against the cracked vinyl of the driver's seat. He had come this way to the river many times but not as a driver. And not in the front seat. And not as a junkie on a drug run.

This part of the river was reserved for the "better" families of Shepherdsville, and the Westwoods were among the best.

Joe Westwood, David's grandfather, made the family fortune in real estate. He loved to tell the story of how a knee-jerk decision to move out West and seek his fortune at the age of twenty-one had turned his life upside down.

He had always been a gambler and a good one but not the most honest. He played the bluff with the best stone face, and always seemed to come out on top. After an exceptionally big win, his regular high-states group grew suspicious, forcing him to pack what belongings would fit in the trunk of his white Thunderbird and leave town in the wee hours, heading West and making no stops. With not much more than a change of clothes, his T-bird, and over a hundred thousand in poker winnings stashed in a brown paper grocery bag, he made it to Nevada just outside of Las Vegas.

Flush with cash and a gift for winning, he pulled over to the side of Highway 604. He stood there as the sun was setting, a hot breeze adding heat to the already-scorching temperatures of the desert around him, looking at the bright lights of the strip in the distance.

"California can wait a little bit longer," he said to himself, as he slid back into the driver's seat and headed for the bright lights and poker tables of Sin City. It seemed like the right thing to do. Who would have thought that a couple of weeks later he'd be taking that same road out of town heading West with all his cash plus the deed to thousands of acres of hot, windswept Nevada desert land in the very spot where he'd providentially changed directions?

The money got him to California, a new life, and a new business selling and servicing air-conditioning systems, a skill he had learned during four years in the US Navy. Selling air conditioning in the San Fernando Valley was easy, and there were plenty of veterans who needed jobs. Soon, Joe met and married Dorothy, who would be his wife for fifty-two years and mother to their brood of three daughters and two sons. Over the next ten years of hard work and some of that old "luck," he quickly built a reputation as the first choice for AC sales and service in the Valley.

Life was good, but it was about to change dramatically. One day he got a frantic call from Dorothy.

"Joe, there's a man here at the house, and he says he needs to talk to you now," Dorothy whispered into the phone. "He said it has to do with a business proposition and that you need to come home right away. He's pacing up and down the living room, and frankly, he looks like he's about ready to explode. I've offered him coffee and even a drink, but he only says that he must talk to you right away! Can you come home now?"

Joe looked at his Rolex. He barely had time to make it downtown to a Chamber of Commerce meeting. More important, he'd miss the game with his regulars in a quiet room at the Dresden.

"Sure, honey," he said. Joe loved a winning hand, the art of the deal, and a reserved front table seat at the Ash Grove. But everything came second to his love for Dorothy.

She was waiting at the door when he pulled up in the driveway. He could see the visitor through the living room window as he stood at the fireplace glancing at his watch and looking anxiously towards the door.

The nervous visitor turned out to be a real-estate developer from Las Vegas who had been searching for the owner of five thousand acres of desert land in Las Vegas. Over the years, that vacant land had grown closer and closer to the Las Vegas strip as more hotels, casinos, and restaurants were built to feed the demands of one of the fastest-growing pleasure destinations in the country. That sandy, barren stretch of land was about to explode in value, and developers were on the hunt for the owner. Harry Baxter was the first to get a name and address, and he wanted to be the first to make a pitch. He came with letters of reference from a bank, a trunk full of cash, and was ready to buy. Joe and Harry did business together over the next few weeks.

After many rounds with the bankers, attorneys, and tax advisors, Joe was now one of the few billionaires in Southern California. He kept a parcel of land just off the Vegas Strip and built a modest but upscale hotel/casino named The Silk Slipper in honor of the French silk evening slippers that were Dorothy's passion and Joe's delight.

Joe's fame, wealth, and good luck continued to soar until one late night on the road from Los Angeles to Las Vegas. Joe and Dorothy headed for Las Vegas after a late-night fundraiser despite Dorothy's pleas to get some sleep and leave early the next morning. About thirty miles from their destination, Joe fell asleep at the wheel and ran off the road. The Cadillac flipped several times and ended up in the dark desert. It was hours before the Highway Patrol came upon the car far off the main road, its dimming headlights pointing toward the strip away from the road. Dorothy, who had fallen asleep soon after they left the hotel, had been found a hundred yards from the car, ejected after the first impact. Joe was still in the driver's seat after succumbing to multiple head injuries.

The newspapers covered the accident and the funeral. But the question around town was who would get the fortune and the casino. The Westwoods were public figures with a steel-door private life.

The press had a field day with speculation and digging up dirt on the five Westwood children. In the end, Joe had been generous to many foundations and nonprofits and to the Crystal Cathedral where he and Dorothy became friends and supporters of Robert Schuler, then a pastor and a personal mentor.

With so much money to spread around, Joe had set up his five children with trust funds, with a stipulation. Money would be set aside for his children's children so they would always have a place to live. Joe Sr. loved his children but was a realist. He knew that no matter how he lived his own life, his children would make their own choices, and he wanted to protect his grandchildren from the consequences of their bad choices. If or how that would happen, he wasn't concerned. He left enough money for his lawyers to take care of any sticky situations that might come up.

Driving down the road, David felt a pull. It wasn't conscious, but something from a memory long ago. He yielded to his subconscious and made a sharp right turn, went down two streets, and pulled up in front of 3 Penny Stock Lane. He let the engine idle. He wasn't staying. No need. The house was still the same, except for a few minor adjustments. The sweeping porches on three sides now had overhead fans compensating for the lack of breeze from the river on a quiet day. The dock stretched to the dock house and the boat lift, far out to the deep water. There was no boat now, just an empty slip staring blankly at the river and beyond. He could almost hear Grandpa Joe calling. "Come on, David. We're going to give those fish a run for their money!" Grandpa Joe was the master of clichés, but David loved him for it. Grandpa Westwood's house had been part of the estate. It was sold and made part of the overall monetary settlement.

The sputtering and jerking movement brought him back to the present. The old truck wasn't used to idling, so David put it back in gear and pulled out onto the main road. One hour. He checked his watch. *Can't be late.* He pushed his aching back against the edge of the manilla envelope and the cracked vinyl seats and winced.

46

AFTER A FEW turns in the deserted streets, David spied the bus-stop shack ahead. Years ago, the bus was an acceptable and efficient way of getting to the river for the privileged and working class alike. The bus system linked the downtown business district and the low-income sections, and then continued to the river, which was kind of a demarcation line, leading to neighborhoods being revitalized after years of neglect.

Joe Jr., David's father, a child of the 60s, took his time finding himself with the aid of pot and LSD and the promise of a never-ending cash support system. While his friends were studying for the SATs and filling out college applications, Joe Jr was driving his MG convertible around town, throwing parties on the bluff at the curve of the river, and drinking himself into the next morning. As a rich young Westwood, he had his pick of the girls from any prominent family in town, but Joe wasn't interested in anyone who could appear to be superior to him in any way.

With disdain for those returning triumphantly from Yale, Stanford, or UGA with diplomas in hand and prestigious careers, Joe Jr. courted and married Hannah Walker, a shy, quiet, woman a few years his senior who could only be described as "pleasant looking." It was a lavish Irish wedding, with kilts and bagpipes filling the church with

Celtic hymns and the reception with raucous Irish reels and dancing.

The new couple returned from a month's honeymoon in Ireland and Scotland to take up residence and a place in society, but thanks to Joe's smug attitude and his wife's lack of pedigree, they were never warmly received. Realtors with the luxury listings wouldn't return Joe Jr.'s calls.

They settled for an old, rambling home and spent a good portion of their inheritance restoring it to its former glory. It could have come straight out of "It's a Wonderful Life," with a wide front hallway flanked by a living room and dining room. A door at the bottom of a winding staircase led to the kitchen. Double French doors opened off the living room to a glassed and screened sunporch that ran the full side of the house. Upstairs were four bedrooms—the master, David's room, a playroom, and what would become the nursery.

David's mother managed the house and took care of their son. Married to a controlling, defeated, but wealthy man, she didn't have the opportunity to develop the skills to compete for a job, let alone a career.

David's father realized too late that the good fortune of unearned wealth was really a thief that robbed him of realizing his own abilities, confidence, and dreams. He took out his bitterness over the town's rejection and his lack of purpose on his wife and son. He was an angry and defeated man who lacked the education or skills to make it on his own. He was a kept man; the trust fund would take care of his family without any effort on his part. He was essentially useless.

47

DAVID SLAMMED ON the brakes and backed up. Lost in memories, he almost missed the bus-stop shelter, now partly hidden by overgrown bushes and weeds. The bright colors had faded, exposing the worn gray wood. Broken boards poked out of the sides like shattered bones, unattended and neglected.

The truck's engine sputtered to a stop. David looked through the dusty truck windows and checked behind through the cracked rear-view mirror. The swirling road dust settled around him. He was alone.

David slid out of the truck. He felt a wave of nausea, and the smell of the shack, the river, and whatever was overflowing from a nearby trash barrel brought him to his knees. He wiped vomit and road dust from his mouth with his sleeve, steadied himself, and stood up.

Walking through the undergrowth and bushes, David realized he was not alone. With each step he heard rustling from somewhere in the brush—the feet of creatures making their escape from an approaching intruder. Coming closer, he heard a thump from inside the shelter and then froze in mid step. A racoon scuttled out of the bus shack, scrambled over the trash from the garbage barrel, and disappeared into the bushes.

But a three-headed dragon with fire flaring from all six nostrils or ten rabid racoons couldn't stop David from completing this mission. Not even the stench of human waste and piles of rotting food inside the putrid shack were enough. Shards of light seeped through the broken sideboards, creating ugly shadows. David held his breath and reached his right hand beneath the wooden bench built into the back wall. In the dim light, he inched his hand along the underside of the bench, feeling for a shelf. As his hand moved down the bench, he could feel small vibrations of unseen creatures as they scurried out of reach. One more swipe, and there it was. A small shelf, just far back enough to be out of sight. This wood was smooth and new, built for this specific purpose.

His lungs ached. He let go of the envelope and pushed it to the back of the shelf. David heard the bushes' rustling noise outside. Was someone coming? He pulled his hand out quickly, slicing it deeply against the rough underside of the bench. A shock of pain shot up from his palm into this arm and seemed to explode from his head. He held up his hand in the dim light and felt a raised line and the broken edge of a splinter lodged deep in his palm. He gulped the fetid air, and, bent over with nausea, stopped short of kneeling in the muck around him. He grabbed the manilla envelope with his other hand, shoved it into the shelf, and ran out, leaning over the back of the truck and gasping for air. In the bright sunlight he could see the shaft of the splinter through the raised skin of his palm, an angry red pool of blood forming at the entry point. A jagged red line with flecks of what could be rust made its own gash parallel to the splinter.

David took off his shirt and wrapped the sleeve around his throbbing hand. Twenty minutes. He's supposed to leave and come back in twenty minutes. What was a short wait now seemed like an eternity. He got back into the truck and crossed his left hand over to the gear shift. He cradled his right hand in his lap, shifted into first gear, pressed on the gas, and headed for West Essex Street to wait.

"We'll be watching," the voice had warned him. David studied the tree lines as he drove away from the bus shelter but didn't see anyone. Not another vehicle was on the streets or parked in the dirt roads angling off the main road. After a few turns, he pulled over on the shoulder of West Essex. Not far from where he turned off River Road he killed the engine and waited, his injured hand throbbing. The clock on the dashboard showed 11:20. *Not very reliable on this old truck.* His phone said 11:23. The voice had warned him, "Twenty minutes—no more, no less ..." *OK, 11:43 then.*

Traffic was picking up on West Essex. His gut, head, and hand were throbbing now with two sources of pain. Watching the rearview mirror, David saw cars turning off West Essex to the River Road behind him. Could one of those cars be the drop? A black SUV with what looked like a mom with a bunch of kids slowed down and made the turn. Not very likely, unless she's got a little side business going. The kids would make a great cover. A couple of city maintenance trucks turned off. David wondered if they would make a stop to pick up the trash and debris at the old bus stop.

He looked at his phone again: 11:40. Maneuvering with his left hand again, he shifted into first and sat idling. "No more, no less." Just then, something strange caught his eye in the rearview mirror. A car pulled up to West Essex from River Road—the first car he'd seen coming up from River.

David watched the car turn right onto West Essex Street. As it got closer, he saw a BMW emblem on the hood. He couldn't see the driver as he accelerated past David. He did catch the license plate, "SOS J + A."

The truck's clock registered 11:39. David made a quick U-turn onto West Essex, a left on River Road, and sped back to the bus stop.

The truck made a third set of tire tracks on the sandy shoulder in front of the bus stop. He wondered if someone was still watching as he picked his way through the brush at the shack's entrance. The sun had shifted away from the trees and poured in from a hole in the roof. He reached his left hand under the beach at the shelf, careful to avoid any splinters. He pulled a small white envelope from the shelf and walked quickly back to the truck, grabbing a bottle of water from a pack in the truck's bed. Ignoring the throbbing in his right hand, he grasped the bottle and unscrewed the cap in one motion.

Back inside the truck, he tore open the envelope. Six tablets lined the bottom crease of the envelope like a new stone walkway. *I'll take a pathway to heaven right now,* he thought. He carefully lifted out one of the tablets and dropped it in a ceramic coffee mug he had stashed under the driver's seat. "I need you now," David sang sweetly as he took the butt end of a hammer and smashed down on the tablet, breaking it into pieces. He tossed the crushed tablet into his mouth and washed it down with a long drink of water.

Racked with the pain of withdrawal and the throbbing from his splintered hand, David closed his eyes and leaned back on the seat, letting every fiber in his body go limp while he waited. Then he felt the rush, like an incoming tide. The throbbing disappeared, and he felt warmth and peace cover him. The Oxys were premium, as promised. He sat motionless, yielding to the tablet's power over him, taking him far away from his pain, the smell of the garbage, and the rotting shack.

The tapping was faint at first, then louder. David woke and turned his head to see a woman tapping on the window next to his head. Then he noticed her uniform, her body cam perched on her shoulder, and her badge shining in the high-noon sunlight.

David let the envelope slide off his lap between his legs to the floor and pushed it under the seat with his heel. He sat up, rolled down the window, and flashed a smile.

"Hello officer. Can I help you?" he asked.

"I saw that you were parked on the shoulder and wondered if you saw the signs posted along the road," said the young female officer. "About the racoons? We've had some confirmed attacks of rabid racoons, and they just love hiding places like this old bus shack. What brings you out here?"

The officer was studying David's eyes but glancing into the truck for anything that might be more interesting than a young man stopped on the side of the road—like the rumpled blue shirt with red blotches on the sleeve, rolled up on the passenger seat.

Fuck! thought David, following her glance at his shirt. He read her nameplate and smiled again.

"Officer Grant, ma'am," he said, feigning confusion and embarrassment. "Actually, I think I'm a little lost. I was supposed to pick up some firewood from a guy clearing land somewhere off this road, and I may have taken a wrong turn. Nothing but tree line for miles. I stopped up the road and walked into the woods and tripped on some brush. I got a splinter in my hand that bled a little," he gestured at his shirt. "I'm trying to get my bearings. Have you seen a guy along here or heard chainsaws anywhere?"

The Oxy was pumping pleasure with every passing moment. David didn't need this audience to share in the finale of euphoria that was coming. He had to get rid of her fast and get out of here.

We're watching you.

"I have a first-aid kit in the cruiser. Want me to take a look at it? You should probably get some medication on that before it gets infected."

David clenched his right hand into a fist, hiding the splinter, feeling no pain. *Medication? You have no idea how well medicated I am, Officer Grant.*

"I'm fine, officer, ma'am," said David, a little too loudly. "No need to bother."

The officer gave a second visual sweep of the truck, from the shirt to David's hand, the mug with a hammer in it, and the half-empty water bottle. Even a new officer with just a few weeks' experience could see something might be suspicious. But the blazing sun drenching her dark uniform, the stench of the rotting garbage hanging in the still air, and a low stomach rumble thanks to an overdue lunch break made Officer Grant decide against a search.

"Well, just wanted you to know about the racoons, especially if you'll be in these woods loading wood. And get that hand looked after." She gave the door a hard thump with her notebook and walked back to her cruiser.

"Yes, ma'am," David called after her, feeling his face break into an almost clown-size smile. He watched her drive off. Then, about a hundred yards up the road, he saw the flash of the cruiser's brake light. She made a quick U-turn, pulled up beside him and rolled down the window. David did the same.

"I'd get that taillight fixed. Looks like the glass is cracked, about to fall off. And watch for critters."

David watched her go again, sighing with relief. He grabbed the window crank just as the tide rushed over his body, sinking him helplessly against the seat. Through glazed eyes, he watched the cruiser's retreating dust cloud rise in the rearview mirror.

46

JAKE PULLED INTO the hospital parking lot. Discharged patients with orderly escorts and family members were lined up at the front entrance curb line waiting for pickup. The hospital lobby was crowded with doctors, nurses, and orderlies. People were lined up at the admissions desk. Visitors trailing colorful mylar balloons with "Get Well Soon," printed on them spilled out of the gift-shop door and headed for the elevators.

Jake threaded his way through the crowd, stopped at the small café for a grande macchiato with a shot of expresso, and went over his story again. He'd been out of town, no access. Lots of traffic, phone out of juice. It would all go more smoothly if he had a gift for Annabelle, but the hospital gift shop wasn't exactly her taste. No, he'd just go in cold and apologize. Take it like a hapless, penitent husband, and it would be fine.

Jake nodded a hello to the nurse at the birthing-center reception desk and headed to Annabelle's room where the door was ajar. He could hear Annabelle talking in a tone he hadn't heard her use before.

"Aren't you just the most beautiful creature I've ever seen," she cooed with a giggle. "Oh, you like that, do you? Smile for me again, my handsome little boy. Almost as handsome as your father, and just as captivating. You've stolen your mama's heart. You're a happy boy. We will make sure of that, your daddy and me."

Babies hadn't been in the plan. Jake always said she was just enough for him. Annabelle thought that maybe Jake didn't want to share her with anyone, not even a child. In some ways, he was like a child himself, needing lots of attention. Could Jake and Annabelle make room in their lives for this little intruder?

The baby grasped Annabelle's finger and hung on. Jake watched silently as Annabelle gazed lovingly at the baby and whispered sweetly to him.

Jake pushed the door open as Annabelle started humming a tune he didn't recognize. *Annabelle was singing to the baby? His Annabelle?*

"Hey. Nice tune," he said. Annabelle remained transfixed on the little bundle in the blue and white receiving blanket. She continued humming and smiling.

Jake took in the image. Was this the same Annabelle from a few days ago? Even after her harrowing ordeal and two days in the hospital, she was so beautiful. Here, without even a light swipe of lipstick, she glowed. She looked at ease with the baby cradled in her lap. His tiny hand held tight to her little finger. Jake almost felt like an intruder in this intimate moment.

"Come over here, Jake. Look, he's smiling."

As he moved closer Annabelle shifted, making space on the bed.

"Come, sit beside me. Isn't he beautiful?"

"Yes," Jake said. "In a *manly* sort of way." Annabelle looked up to see him smiling that smile. Then the wink.

Annabelle smiled at Jake. Despite her exhaustion and the baby in her arms, she suddenly felt calm and safe, intrigued by Jake's playful comment.

Annabelle welcomed his warmth as he leaned to stroke the baby's cheek. The baby grasped Jake's finger with his other tiny hand, completing their little family circle. Annabelle rested her head against Jake's shoulder, and she could feel him relax, yielding to her touch.

"You know, Jake," she said softly, "this little man of ours needs a name. A hospital admin came in this morning to get the paperwork ready for our discharge and reminded me that the baby needs a name before he leaves the hospital. For the birth certificate."

"Well, that's easy," he said, as if addressing the bundle between them. "Henry, after my grandfather and Rourke for his middle name, after your father. Henry Rourke Martin. A strong name for our manly little man."

"I was thinking more like Jake, Jr. with a couple of middle names," said Annabelle. The baby studied his parents as if he was also considering their choices.

'I appreciate the thought, but I was Jake, Jr, and always felt like people were always looking past me to my father. I had his name, and somehow I was supposed to have his manner, character, habits, ambitions—a little reincarnation of the original Jake. Follow in his footsteps."

The Jake Martin that the public knew was nothing like the father he experienced, Jake thought. A quiet, private, almost stoic man, emotionally unavailable to his wife and children. They had all the outward signs of success and played the role of a happy, successful, loving family, necessary for a man of his position and public image. Jake would have given up their country-club life, the flashy red Mustang for his birthday, and even his gold AMEX card in exchange for hanging around with his father—laughing and talking like he had seen his friends doing with their dads.

"No 'little Jake' for this guy." Jake said, definitively. "He's an original, and his name will reflect that."

Annabelle studied her husband's face. She had seen that look before. Determined, in a settled kind of way.

"Well, then 'Henry Rourke' is out, too," said Annabelle. "An original he is, and his name should be too

Their banter and easy conversation took Annabelle back to a time when things were simple and easy. Just the two of them, relaxing on the couch in her tiny apartment on campus, playfully disagreeing on what pizza to order or whether she had to have anchovies on her side of the pie. Disgusting, hairy little fish. Just the sight of them made Annabelle want to gag. They used to sit close, even though her apartment had cozy chairs from the consignment shop and Jake's favorite— a retro papasan chair from Annabelle's grandmother's attic.

Annabelle breathed him in—the earthy scent of his cologne mixed with pure Jake—a blend of forest and ocean breeze. Here was the man she fell in love with, making baby noises and smiling delightedly at their son. In that moment, nothing else mattered. Not the missed pickup at the bus or the unanswered calls, the late nights wondering where he was or who was keeping him from her. What was once a couple of selfish egotistical individuals was becoming a family. Could a baby change everything?

"Hey, babe, look." Jake held their baby and pushed the dark hair off his perfect forehead. "I think his hair is getting lighter. Won't be long until he looks just like his dad!"

Annabelle's perfect family vision shattered as he said it. "Just like his dad." Roger looked a lot like Jake—strong chin, wavy hair. They were both tall and muscular. Just one tiny difference made her uneasy, and it could take away what she wanted more than anything. That dark hair. She thought about her several nights of indiscretion. One martini too many. Jake's too-frequent absences when Annabelle needed him. It had been foolish of her to think that a convenient substitution would take away her loneliness.

His hair is *getting lighter. It has to.* She pushed away the dark thoughts ruining her vision of their happy family.

"Annabelle, what do you think?" asked Jake.

She looked at the baby. "Yes, I can see it, too," she lied, willing his remark to be true.

Jake put his arm around Annabelle's shoulder and pulled her close. Her body melted into his embrace, and she turned to kiss his cheek. Immediately he turned and kissed her with a new passion that surprised them both.

"Thank you, Annabelle," said Jake, ignoring the pang of guilt for not being there for her. "This has been an ordeal for you, and I am so sorry that you had to go through it alone. You've given me a beautiful son."

He wanted to say more. *Forgive me for lying to you about yesterday; for drinking too much and sleeping while you went through surgery. For being a selfish, uncaring, unfeeling jerk. For being late at the bus stop and not being there for you. For all the hundreds of times I failed you. For the secrets and deceptions over so many years.* But maybe he was like his father. Those words would do for private remorse, but the stoic gene inherited from his father kept him from saying them out loud.

"I'm sorry, Annabelle. I want to be the kind of father I wished I had. You pick out the name, whatever you like. He's my son. I'll probably call him something like Buddy or Sport, anyway."

"We will make him happy," Annabelle whispered, gazing at their son, now asleep in Jake's arms.

"Yes, we will," echoed Jake. He stood up slowly and placed the baby in his bassinet next to the bed.

Jake turned his attention back to Annabelle. "They are releasing you today, right? What time should I be here to take you both home?"

"Actually, not until tomorrow. The doctors want to keep us one more night. There are some final tests for me—precautionary, they said. The baby is ready to go, but there's the matter of the baby's name and the release paperwork. I can't get out of here too soon. I'll ask the nurse to call you. There's still no word on my cell phone, so I'll have to get a new one once I get home."

Annabelle pushed aside the thin hospital blanket and stood beside the bed. She grabbed the edge of the bed and steadied herself. Jake rushed over and put his arm around her shoulders.

"Are you sure you're ready for this? Here you have lots of people taking care of you and the baby. Once we're home, we'll be on our own."

"That sounds perfect to me. It's about time we got on with our lives."

Jake kissed Annabelle on the cheek and turned to go. "Call me whenever you're ready, babe, and I'll be here."

"Don't forget to bring the infant carrier. The hospital won't let the baby out of here without it."

Jake winced when he thought of a baby seat in his BMW. *That will take some getting used to.*

49

"HAVE YOU DECIDED on a name for this little guy yet?" The floor nurse had a hint of aggravation in her voice. "We need help around here, but he's a bit too young to push a meal cart."

"Yes," said Annabelle. "I have. Charles William. I'll call him Charlie, but his father will probably call him Sport."

The nurse rolled her eyes. "Men. Who can figure?"

She put down a stack of discharge papers for Annabelle to sign. "Your doctor will be here around four o'clock for a final check, and your pediatrician will be making his final exam and releasing documents around five o'clock. I'll pick up the paperwork in about an hour. You can get things ready to leave around five-thirty."

Annabelle picked up the pen with the hospital logo on it and filled in the blanks—baby's first and middle name. Charles William. She heard her door open again.

"Was there something else, nurse?" said Annabelle without looking up.

"I believe there is," said a deep, familiar voice.

Annabelle's hand gripped the pen tight. Her heart jumped at the sound of that voice. Roger slipped into her room and closed the door behind him.

"Roger, what are you doing here?" whispered Annabelle, shocked and angry at his surprise visit.

"I came to see you, my dear, and the baby. I think I have a right to be here, don't you think?"

He walked over to the bassinette, reached down, and stroked the baby's hair.

"What a handsome little guy, Annabelle. I believe he has your eyes. Yes, looks like his mother. And the shape of his mouth is all yours. But look at that strong chin and that shock of dark, almost black, hair. *That* must be from his father."

Roger turned his gaze from the baby to Annabelle, his eyes gone steely gray. She felt the anger in his expression—a smoldering fire about to explode.

"Roger, you have to leave now. Jake could come in here any moment. There is nothing here for you. I thought that was clear. It was over long ago."

Annabelle studied Roger's face. His expression didn't change.

"Oh, Jake won't be back for a while," Roger said. "In fact, he just left, didn't he? He's already had a busy morning, out to West Essex Street and back. And he stayed home last night, like a good husband. No, he won't be interrupting us for a while."

"How do you know that?" Annabelle voice was panicked. "Have you been watching him? Us?" *Jake was home last night? How can that be?*

"Yes, your husband has been a busy boy," said Roger, shaking his head and ignoring her question. "Not hard to track with that license plate of his."

"He had some business with his grandfather's old property, Roger," Annabelle lied. "He told me all about it."

She forced her mind back to Roger, standing too close to her baby. He walked over to Annabelle. He reached down and picked up the stack of discharge papers and glanced at her entry under "baby's name."

"So, our little guy has a name, has he? Charles William. Strong enough. Good name. Where in these papers does it ask for the father's name? I'm curious to see what you put for that."

"You're despicable, Roger. Jake is his father. You know that. Is that what you've come for? To stake some kind of claim?"

Annabelle took the papers from Roger's grip. "Leave now, for my sake and the baby's. For your sake. Don't be a fool—that dark hair will lighten up, just like his father's. You aren't his father; you couldn't be."

"Oh, now it's 'get out of here, Roger.' You texted *me* when you were about to give birth on the bus, not that sorry so-called husband of yours. It was *me* you wanted. Face it, Annabelle."

"I did text you. I was out of my mind with pain—I didn't call Jake, but that was a mistake. Please, Roger, you are not part of my life anymore. It was over months ago, and it's still over."

Roger moved closer to Annabelle, put his arm around her shoulder and pulled her to him. "You know I *could* be this boy's father, Annabelle. From the looks of things, I could be a big part of your *and* little Charlie's lives."

Annabelle felt repulsed by his touch and pushed him away.

"No, you couldn't be the father. You see, all that time there was something between us. I was lonely, but I wasn't stupid. Tucked away, guarding the castle gate—I had an IUD." Annabelle had pulled that little lie out of nowhere and settled into it.

"All it took was that little piece of plastic to deflect that possibility. So, you were armed with a pop-gun, not a rifle. No one will be calling you 'Daddy.'"

She could see him start to wither under her explanation. Big Roger wasn't so tough after all.

"No matter what you say, Annabelle, time is on my side. What you say may be true or may be a convenient lie to get me out of here. But time will tell. By the way, I think Charles

William is a perfect name. I won't change it. The child will be confused enough when the time comes. It's goodbye for now, anyway." Roger walked over to the bassinette, leaned down, and kissed the sleeping baby on the forehead.

Annabelle eased out of the bed and picked up Charlie, holding him close. "Get out. Don't come back. Leave us alone." She turned her back to Roger and clutched Charlie tight, waiting to hear the sound of her door closing behind him.

On the way out of the room, Roger snatched a rumpled receiving blanket from Charlie's bassinette. He tucked it inside his jacket and walked out into the hallway, past the nursery and the nurse's station and took the elevator to the underground parking garage.

I'll leave, Annabelle. But not empty-handed.

Once inside his car, Roger pulled out the blanket, held it to his face, and breathed in the new-baby scent. But there was something else. Roger turned on the overhead light and unrolled the blanket, revealing a circle of now-yellowed matter—spit-up from the baby. His stolen, stinking memento lost some sentiment for a moment until Roger realized his uncanny luck. He was holding the key to the mystery of the baby's dark hair. A messy little burp had given Roger what he needed to prove that Charlie was his.

50

THE THROBBING PAIN was back again. It had been four hours since David had taken the crushed tablet beside the dilapidated bus shack. His palm looked worse and hurt like hell, maybe from his botched attempt to remove the splinter himself. He would attempt almost anything when he was high. Sterilize a needle with the flame from a kitchen match and pick at the skin around the splinter until he could grab it with a tweezer and pull it out clean. He had done it many times as a kid. Better to do it himself than run to his mother, or worse, his father.

Clumsy boy! He recollected his father saying. *Stop your crying. It's just a little splinter. The needle will only hurt a bit, just need to get at it to pull it out. You know your yelling makes Dad nervous, and I'm not as gentle when I'm nervous.*

The splinter was still there, now surrounded by shredded skin where David had attempted to free it. The rusted needle, spent matches, and a bloody washcloth lay on the kitchen table, evidence of his high-induced botched extraction. Hannah was curled up on the kitchen table, witness to the scene. She gazed blankly at David, laughing a low guttural purr at his inept first aid.

David winced as he curled his fingers around his car keys. The relief of the first Oxy was fading. He grabbed the envelope with the remaining five tablets and shook one out. He popped it in his mouth, grabbed his coffee mug, and finished off the cold morning coffee. One more would make the pain go away.

He put the envelope back on the table. An hour in the ER and the splinter would be gone. He grabbed his cap, pulled it low over his eyes, and headed for the hospital.

The ER was quiet. In it were a few kids with sniffles, a crying baby, and a guy in running shorts holding a baggie of ice against a swollen ankle, a wad of paper towels on his bloody knee.

David walked up to the registration desk.

"Excuse me, ma'am," he said to the clerk who was scrolling through Facebook on her phone in her lap.

"Excuse me," he repeated a little louder, coughing this time.

"Take a number," the receptionist said, still staring at her phone. She waved her hand in the direction of a number-ticket dispenser at the end of the counter.

David pulled off a ticket, took a seat, and scanned the room. The crying baby was now gone, leaving only a sniffling child with his parents and the injured runner.

David leaned back and started to doze off, cradling his throbbing hand in his lap. He woke up to see the sniffling little boy standing in front of him. The boy wiped the sleeve of his Batman pajamas across his flowing nose and coughed, sending out a spray of droplets onto David's outstretched hand.

"What's wrong with you, mister?" he said between sniffles.

"Oh, I got a bad splinter in my hand, and I need the doctor to get it out."

"Does it hurt?" said the little boy, eyes wide open at the sight of the bloodied, swollen palm with the dark line embedded deep beneath the skin.

"Yes, it does, but the doctor will take care of it, Ben," said David with a calm, reassuring voice.

"Who is Ben?" asked the little boy, his runny nose blowing bubbles with each word. "My name is Wally."

David felt his face flush as he realized his mistake. "Oh, sorry, I was thinking of some other little boy I once knew, Wally."

"Freak!" Wally turned and ran back to his father across the room. A woman with a chart called out "Number 95!," and Wally and his dad disappeared behind an exam-room door.

When the clerk finally called his number, David followed a nurse into one of the examination rooms.

"They said you've got a bad splinter. Let's see what we have here," he said.

David turned over his hand, exposing his splintered palm, and the nurse winced. David barely recalled his own attempts at extrication.

"The skin around the entry is pretty chewed up," the nurse said and shook his head. "I'll numb it up and you won't feel a thing. This is a pretty big splinter; it's deep at the entry point, and it looks like it's sitting pretty close to a vein. Sometimes the wood is rough, and when it's pulled out it can tear the skin around it, or in this case the vein. I've seen these pump out a lot of blood. What's your blood type?"

David stared at his hand. Numbed by the drugs, he had poked aggressively at the splinter at home, trying to remove it himself. *A few deep jabs with the needle in the wrong direction, and I could have drowned in a pool of my own blood.* He felt a wave of nausea but steadied himself.

"Um, I don't know," said David. "Is this serious?"

"Just a precaution. Let me take a blood sample just in case. You should know your blood type anyway. Comes in handy if you're in a car or hunting accident."

The nurse went on, describing the gruesome ways one could bleed to death from self-administered first aid. David felt uneasy. He scanned the probes, needles, and tweezers laid out on a tray covered with a sterile white cloth. The nurse went into a side room, returned with a lancet and some other supplies, and got to work.

"Now, this won't take a second," he said, jabbing David's finger with the lancet. He turned David's finger over so a drop of blood could splash onto a glass slide. He covered it with a second slide, slid both into a plastic container, and sealed it shut. He wrote David's name on the container and set it down.

A round drop of blood formed a red liquid drop on David's finger, swelling, ready to drop. "You're a bleeder, I can see," the nurse said with an approving smile. "We like those. Easy to get a drop or a tube of blood. Hate it when I have to stick over and over just to get a couple of drops."

The nurse then directed his attention to the splinter. David closed his eyes to calm himself. He couldn't feel the needles or tweezers probing to extricate the splinter, but he still had a sensation of something jabbing at his hand. There was a vague pressure as the needle dug deeper, opening the skin around the splinter, trying to loosen it from the muscle and bone in David's hand. He felt the pressure of the needle come and go, and the nurse wiping away more blood.

"Got it!" The nurse proclaimed, pleased. David looked over to see him holding the bloody splinter up in a pair of tweezers, a big grin on his face.

David's stomach turned.

The nurse washed the wound, put on antiseptic, and wrapped it in gauze.

"Now, a tetanus shot, and we're all through," said the nurse. Without breaking stride, he grabbed the syringe and jabbed David's arm in one continuous motion.

"Wait—one more thing. That was a nasty splinter, and I had to really dig to get it all out. The anesthetic is going to wear off and you're going to have some serious discomfort for a while. Would you like a prescription for some pain medication? You don't have to take it, but it would be good to have just in case."

David stared at the nurse, stunned by his good fortune. *I get a splinter trying to pick up drugs in a filthy shack and now you're asking if I want some drugs for free?*

"Yes, that would be great," said David, as calmly as he could. "Not that I'd take it unless I really needed it. You can get hooked on that stuff."

"That's true, but this is only a ten-day supply. Two a day as needed."

The nurse opened a laptop on the side counter. "I'll send a request to the hospital pharmacy. Take this copy with you. You can pick it up before you leave."

David scanned the pharmacy order form. Hydrocodone, 325 mg. 20 tablets. Detailed directions and warnings filled the page, complete with skull and crossbones.

"You'll get a letter from the hospital with the results of the blood type. They will send a wallet card for you."

"Thanks," said David. By the time he found the pharmacy the prescription was filled and waiting for him. He slipped the bottle into his pocket and retraced his steps down the short hallway flanked by exam rooms and followed the exit signs out into the ER waiting area.

51

"WAIT, SIR, STOP!" David heard the nurse calling. Panicking, he looked behind him as the nurse ran towards him, waving something in his hand. "Your hat. You left it in the examination room. Ravens fan? I used to follow them when I lived in DC."

"Thanks very much," said David, relieved. He pulled the cap low over his eyes and exited into the street. The sun disappeared behind a patch of gray-tinged clouds, then appeared again, bathing the hospital landscape with sunlight.

He stepped off the curb and jumped back, nearly colliding with an ambulance thundering into the parking area, its sirens winding down outside the ER doors. It screeched to a halt, and the back doors were flung open, disgorging two paramedics. On cue, the ER doors swung open for two nurses running towards the ambulance with a gurney. As if in a macabre ballet, they deftly lifted a seemingly lifeless form swathed in a thin white blanket onto the waiting gurney. As one, they spun the now loaded gurney around and, in the best form, leaped and exited the staging area as if a theatrical scene had ended, and disappeared behind the open ER doors.

The sirens, the ambulance, the gurney. David closed his eyes. and he was there again. It had been dark, and he had been the one who came out of the back of that ambulance with Annabelle, covered in a thin blanket. He had been a reluctant member of the cast that night. It was supposed to have been a simple little robbery. A little cash to buy some drugs. An easy mark. David didn't like complications. And things now seemed much too complicated.

The wallet and phone were supposed to compensate him for a lost opportunity. Two K was a problem, with his suspicions and threat to expose him to the cops. That detective looking for the phone and wallet was a problem. A new dealer who liked to play hide-and-seek in a disgusting shack infested with vermin and rabid raccoons. Well, that wouldn't be a problem for a while, at least. David felt the prescription bottle in his pocket.

"You, out of the way," yelled an EMT, rushing toward the ER doors.

As the EMT disappeared inside, another figure emerged from the building. David fixed his eyes on the dark-haired man walking through the crowd. He was clutching something. As the man came closer, David recalled that he had seen him before—but where? The man appeared to be walking straight to David, as if he knew him, too.

The man caught David's stare and walked up to him. David tried to turn away, but the man blocked his escape.

"Who are you staring at? Get lost on your way to the game?" asked the man sarcastically, pointing to David's hat.

"Sorry, sir." Said David. "Didn't mean to be rude"

"Creep."

David turned, watching him walking toward the parking lot, now on his cell phone. His mind flashed back a few days to another scene at this hospital. It was the dark-haired man who had been on his cell phone outside Annabelle's hospital room. He had been leaning up against her door in the hallway. He hoped the man hadn't seen David hiding in the hallway that night. Or had he? *My hat.* Would this way of hiding his face from prying eyes betray him? The memories of that night flooded back. The bus, the screaming, the ambulance, Two Knuckles. Slipping into Annabelle's room. He closed his eyes against the chaotic memories, forcing them out of his mind.

"I said, move on!" The EMT was now rushing out of the Emergency Room entrance, pushing an empty gurney toward a waiting ambulance.

David didn't know how long he had been standing there. He hated hospitals. And crowds. He felt all at once exposed, vulnerable. He pulled his cap lower over his eyes, turned, and hurried down the street to his truck.

52

THE SQUAD ROOM was quiet this afternoon. The sun fil-
tered through the faded, tattered awnings of the bail-bond
shop next to the precinct, casting a blurred light through the
film of street grime on the windows.

Someone had scrawled "Pigs" on the window weeks ago.
Offensive at first, it eventually took on the look of a retro
street art poster. One of the guys saw a maintenance worker
put a ladder up against the wall outside and climb up with
a squeegee and some spray cleaner. Before he could pump
the nozzle, two officers and a detective ran outside and
threatened him with a citation and $500 fine for destroying
police property.

The swivel chair wheezed as Holt settled in behind his metal
desk. Not one for spending money on renovations, the chief had
found a forgotten lot of 1980s office furniture in a warehouse
and got rid of the old worn wooden desks and bookshelves.

"Metal will last for years, even with the rough treatment
it gets in the squad rooms," the chief announced to the City
Council with a smug grin. "You can't destroy it. No stains
from coffee cups or spilled food cartons and pizza boxes.
Wipes clean with a little Windex and a paper towel. This furniture is a real find."

The council had cheered while presenting him with a
small plaque for his cost-cutting efforts.

The staff and officers hated it. Their consensus was that the furniture was cold, noisy, uncomfortable, and institutional. Not much different from the cold steel of the lockup.

Holt mashed the start button on his computer and went through levels of security to access his email and files. He scanned lists of memos on administrative topics, regulations, and updates on cases. Another safety meeting. A reminder of a community outreach event on Friday, "Coffee with a Cop." The subject line included, in bold caps: "**MANDATORY— YOU WILL BE THERE, HOLT!**"

Shit! Another one of those touchy-feely "get to know the neighborhood" events at the local park. He'd have to dress up as a cop and smile and shake hands with people. A command performance. *Yeah, I'll be there.* He made a note—three o'clock, Hull Park.

Scrolling through his emails, he stopped at the subject line, "Bus driver interview report —Bus No. 7 incident—Missing valuables." He clicked to read the message and leaned forward. The dateline was two days ago, right after the incident. The officers had done good work, providing a few more details. There had been a guy at the scene hiding in the shadows wearing a baseball cap with a bird on it. No physical details of the guy, but he rode with the EMTs to the hospital. It was going to be a busy day. First, he had to find this bus driver, Gus. Then, track down the EMTs who transported Annabelle that night. Someone must know a little more.

And then there was Dewain. Holt logged into the database. As he suspected, without a last name, the search pulled up a lot of Dewains in the area. He scanned the list, scrolling quickly until he saw a Dewain Johnson. The hit was an obituary. Dewain Johnson, age forty-three, from a nearby town, had died from pancreatic cancer. Mr. Johnson had been a marine. Volunteered at the Special Olympics. No photo. In lieu of flowers, send donations to the VA hospital.

Holt stared at the screen. A long shot, but he had seen flimsier connections pan out. It was worth finding out a bit more about Mr. Dewain Johnson. A veteran would have a service record with a social security number and finger-prints on file. Holt had a gift for sizing people up, and he placed Dewain the orderly to be in his early thirties. He scribbled the details about Dewain Johnson in his notebook and pushed back in his chair.

Annabelle had said it was just a phone and a wallet. Something in Holt's gut was telling him something else. A suspicious orderly a little too anxious to get information about the missing items. A creepy guy who sits down next to the woman, stares, asks lots of questions, and then disap-pears. And then, a guy lurking in the shadows at the bus stop. A dead Dewain Johnson resurrected?

Holt had seen a lot of coincidences and had lost a few cases he thought were solid because of them. But something about this situation made him suspect there was a bigger prize at stake here than just a phone and a wallet. He loved puzzles, and this one had a lot of missing pieces. Made it even more interesting.

Whose picture would this one reveal?

53

TRACY TUGGED AT the waistband of her uniform. It was her first day fulfilling the obligatory community-service requirement for high school graduation. She had avoided it until now. Just a few months from graduation, her advisor made it clear—no community service, no diploma. Even though her mother was her advisor's tennis buddy and a big contributor to the high school, even her polite requests, followed by a little arm bending as well as the promise of additional donations, hadn't been enough to make the requirement go away. To add to the inconvenience of spending two hours a day, three days a week for the next five weeks, Tracy had to wear this stupid uniform. The gathered skirt of the shirtwaist dress looked like something from the 1950s. It was humiliating.

Worse still was her assignment. Clearing out and cataloging linen-storage closets, starting with the third-floor closet. The admin assistant sent her to hospital maintenance where she was assigned to Joe, first shift maintenance supervisor, for the duration of her service hours.

Joe unlocked the door to the linen closet. The odor from musty linens and stale institutional detergent made Tracy's eyes water. "Yeah, the linens in these storage units have been piling up for years," said Joe. They came back from the laundry stained, torn, or no longer usable and got dumped on these shelves. Some of these are probably older than you are."

She stared at the racks overflowing with mismatched linens of varying shades of white, yellowed from years of storage in the airless, musty storage area. She shuddered to think of where they had been, who they had been under and on top of. What had they soaked up and then been relieved of in the hospital laundry? *What had happened on these sheets?*

"Fill out this inventory sheet," Joe explained, pointing to the page. "Write down as much information as you can. Sheets go in this rolling bin; the towels go in the other. Once the bins are filled, call down to maintenance and we'll pick them up and bring you empty ones. Sounds like fun, huh?"

Joe let out a laugh that sounded more like a snort. Tracy forced a smile, hiding her revulsion. She fixed him with a "get out of here" look. He dropped the clipboard on one of the shelves and left.

As soon as the door clicked shut, she pulled her phone and earbuds out of her uniform pocket, hit her favorite playlist, and got to work. At least some music would make the task bearable.

It wasn't so bad after all. Shut away in the storage room, no one could see her in the ridiculous uniform. She had a strong Wi-Fi connection, and she didn't have to deal with cranky patients, smelly food trays, or snarky orderlies.

The bins were filling up by the end of the first hour, even though she had emptied only a couple of shelves from the first rack. She pulled another large, folded sheet off the shelf and heard a clattering sound against the cement floor.

She peered around the corner of the metal rack. Nothing. She got down on her knees, lifted the corner of a yellowed sheet off the floor, and looked underneath. She reached under the rack and back to the wall. Her hand felt a hard round object. She pulled it out and sat back on her heels, eyes wide. A prescription bottle, full to the top with white tablets. The label had someone's name and instructions for use, but the type of prescription stood out. "Vicodin 7.5 mg. One every six hours for pain."

Tracy grasped the bottle in her hand, lined up the arrows on the cap and bottle, and snapped off the lid. She stared at the round white pills crowded in the amber bottle.

What were these doing here? Not likely that they just got stuck in the pile by accident. The date on the bottle was just a few days ago.

Joe told her that these sheets had been here for ages, shut up and forgotten about. *Not by everyone, Joe. And certainly not by Nicholas Karpinski.*

For a moment, Tracy imagined poor Mr. Karpinski, writhing in pain somewhere, tearing apart his hospital release bag for his bottle of Vicodin, swearing that he had brought it home from the hospital. Mr. Karpinski could search away, but he wouldn't find it. Somehow it had gotten tangled up in the sheets. She wasn't supposed to find it either, but she did. She probably should take it to Joe so Mr. Karpanski and his meds can be reunited.

Tracy stood up and leaned against the bin full of yellowed sheets. She snapped the lid shut and dropped the bottle inside her uniform pocket, the small cylinder disappearing under the folds of her gathered skirt.

She took out her earbuds and texted her boyfriend. *Tomas. Party tomorrow night will be mind-blowing. Bringing a new guest. Be there. Trace*

This assignment was turning out to be better than she had expected.

54

GUS ROUNDED THE curve of the hill in the No. 7 bus, heading toward Market Square. Another Friday, another shift, another week of driving this metal trash can on wheels. He heard the hiss of the brakes as he slowed down, stopping just short of the taillights of a black Nissan at the light. The sun was getting lower every evening, making it harder for his failing eyes, clouded with cataracts, to see the road and judge distances.

Stopped at the light, he squeezed his eyes tight, over and over, hoping to raise the filmy curtain with each blink. "Get out of my way, you idiots," he muttered under his breath, heavy with the scent of mouthwash to cover the double bourbon he'd tossed back during his lunch break, concealed in his lunchbox thermos. He thought the bourbon cleared both his head and his eyes. He needed it to steady his hands on the wheel. The light above turned a hazy green, and Gus hit the horn hard. *Move it!*

He knew this bus with all its creaks and noises. The hissing sound was a little shrill this evening, with a higher pitch followed by a little knocking at the end. He needed to get the maintenance crew to check that out. He had been driving Bus 7 for over twenty years. Longer than some marriages. Longer than all three of his put together.

Bus 7 had once been a beauty—as beautiful as a green-and-yellow municipal bus could be. Shiny and new, right off the transporter. They had a little ceremony at the terminal, dangling the keys in the air, a little applause, a few cheers, and finally dropping the keys into a much younger Gus's waiting hand.

That young Gus had a pile of top performance reviews and Employee of the Year awards; he deserved the new bus for his route. It was good PR for the city, too—a new, state-of-the-art bus winding its way through the business district for all the professionals and hard-working citizens, whisking them away and delivering them to their destinations in style. "Your tax dollars at work," the mayor had said on television that evening.

Tonight, the square was crowded as usual. He pulled up to the stop at the edge of the square.

Stop, hiss, clunk.

No, that didn't sound good at all. He pulled the lever to swing open the door; the narrow passageway into the bus quickly clogged with pushing and shoving humanity. Through his cloudy eyes, he could still make out the regulars slogging back and forth on number 7 to their nowhere jobs, eyes glazed like his, though their condition was brought on by apathy, despair, or boredom. Early morning or at the end of the day, they all looked the same.

From somewhere behind the crowd at the door, he picked out a pink haze coming closer, climbing the steps.

"Keep your freaking pervert hands off me, loser," the pink haze yelled to someone behind her. "This ass isn't part of the ride."

He'd seen her before, although he couldn't swear by it. A couple of days ago there had been a crush at the door. Yeah, the pregnant lady almost got knocked over by Miss Pink Hair. Some guy was there to save the little Mama-to-be from being trampled at the door. Nice young man from the community college—he had seen many of those crested blazers over the years. He didn't need 20/20 vision to recognize that emblem.

Who could have predicted the rest of that trip? Gus shuddered, remembering the screams from his last remaining fare at the end of the route, the rush of EMTs, and the mess left behind from a near-delivery. Luckily, there was that guy at the last stop who went with the EMTs to the hospital.

Gus looked in the rearview mirror. The bus was full, passengers standing shoulder to shoulder in the aisle, every seat full. He grabbed the lever to close the door when a young man wearing the school blazer climbed up the stairs and grabbed a hand strap, not able to move back any farther down the crowded aisle. Gus turned his head and stared at the crest on his blazer at eye level on the young man's pocket.

It was the same jacket. Little mama's protector, and the guy at the last stop had been wearing that crested blazer. He'd been the only person at the end of the line, and he came out of the shadows. He didn't protest when Gus practically forced him to ride with the EMTs. Had he been waiting for something? For her? Seemed like the plot of a trashy detective novel. He had a whole library of them, dog-eared and coffee stained, mostly left behind on the bus over the years.

He chuckled. *Yeah, and I'm the detective hero in this story.*

"Hey driver, get moving!" Someone yelled from the back of the bus.

Gus pulled the lever and the door creaked closed.

Creak, hiss, clunk.

Gus pulled out of Market Square and headed down the street. He hoped the bus could just get them to the end of the line and then the terminal before falling apart.

55

JAMES HOLT FINISHED his second donut and his third cup of dishwater coffee and said his farewells to the thinning crowd at the neighborhood "Coffee with A Cop" event in the park. It was a short drive to the bus terminal and his appointment with the driver of Bus 7.

"I told the other two officers everything I remembered about that night," said Gus. "Don't you guys write reports or something?"

"I read the report from the other officers," said Holt. "Just wanted to see if by now you remembered anything else about that night. Anything unusual. Anything new that you hadn't told the other officers."

Gus sighed. "Everything was going as it normally does on that route. The lady had been on the bus before. The bus turns and makes a circle back at that point. We were about to make the last stop when all hell broke loose. She was screaming and carrying on. Then she passed out. I saw a guy across the street just standing there, so I yelled over for him to come and help. And a lot of help he was. He just cowered in the back of the bus, trying to be invisible. Sent him in the ambulance to the hospital with the woman. She made such a mess, I had to come back to the terminal instead of completing my shift."

"The police report didn't have much of a description of the young man," said Holt. "Can you describe him?"

Gus shifted in his seat. With his eyesight and the dark streets, he wasn't much for details. Gus thought about making up a description when he remembered the blazer.

"Well, one thing I didn't tell the other officers was what he was wearing. I didn't think of it until I had a young man on the bus this afternoon with the same blazer. It had a crest on it from some fraternity at the community college. I told the officers about the baseball-type cap he was wearing. Had some kind of bird on it. Don't know what kind. Probably some kind of baseball team.

"And another thing I remembered. Not so much remembered as struck me as strange. Market Square was crowded that afternoon. Lots of people queued up to get on the bus. Lots of pushing and jockeying for position. When the bus pulled up and I opened the doors, the pregnant lady was first in line. When she started up the steps, a pink-haired girl tried to push her out of the way. The guy—the one with the blazer—came from nowhere and blocked the pink-haired girl. She almost knocked little mama to be on the ground. He sat next to little mama for a while, then exited through the back door.

"It's probably just a coincidence, detective, but the guy at the last stop also had a blazer with the same crest on it. Gave me a strange feeling. Was he waiting for someone? For her? I read too many murder mystery novels. But there was something strange about seeing the same blazer in two different places."

Gus sat in silence as Holt scribbled in his notebook. "Thanks, Gus. That's great information. I think we're done here."

Gus flashed Holt a crooked smile. He bumped into the chair as he stood up.

"Steady, there." Holt said, standing up and offering him a hand. He pressed his card into Gus's outstretched hand. "Call me if you remember anything else."

"Sure will, detective," Gus said as he left the conference room. He put his uniform jacket in his locker, took a swig of bourbon from his water bottle, and headed for the door.

Solving your little mystery isn't at the top of my priority list, detective. Don't count on me calling you any time soon.

56

ANNABELLE SHIFTED IN the passenger seat. It was a different kind of awkward.

The last time she sat in the SUV she had been sitting in the driver's seat, eight months pregnant, her baby bulge pressed against the steering wheel. Now it was Jake at the wheel. She felt a twinge of fear and discomfort—a sense of loss of control over her life.

Jake had picked her up at the hospital carrying the infant car seat. He looked the same as always, but there was something different. It's as if his arm had grown a new appendage—something she had seen on other young, handsome, sexy men who were now fathers. Jake's confident, sleek stride was gone, replaced by a different cadence caused by the weight of the baby seat dangling from his hand, tilting him just so slightly. He looked older, a little unsteady.

She glanced over at Jake, his hands now firmly gripped on the steering wheel, quietly muttering profanities as a stream of people crossed in front of them at the hospital entrance.

"Could you get a damned move on before I mow you down?" he spoke through the windshield as a woman dragging a young man by his casted arm darted in front of him. Jake stomped on the brakes and hit the button to roll down the window.

"Please, Jake. The baby!"

The baby. It was no longer just the two of them in this reality. Annabelle put her arm on Jake's shoulder and turned to see their son sleeping peacefully, eyes closed with a tousle of dark hair peeking out from under his blue stocking cap.

"Get ahold of yourself, Jake. It's not just you anymore." Jake mashed the window button again. The car was silent except for the soft whirr of the window gliding back up.

Jake looked at his clenched hands gripping the steering wheel, and shot a glance at Annabelle, now turned and looking into the back seat. Her silky skin, soft cheekbones, long eyelashes, and cascading blonde hair were the same as when they had met. But then her long, loving looks had always been for Jake. Now she looked past him to the baby, concerned with *his* safety and comfort.

Someone else was now the target of her loving gaze. Her hand on his shoulder, the rebuke. She was transforming before his eyes. He felt strangely suffocated by the confines of the SUV, a prisoner with a life sentence in a six-passenger leather and glass cell.

"Jake, are you alright?" Annabelle's worried voice broke the silence. "Let's get going before the baby wakes up. I want to get him settled into his new home. Our darling little man."

Jake took a deep breath, eased up on the brake, and pulled out onto the circular drive, watching the hospital entrance as it disappeared in the rear-view mirror.

Darling little man? Jake tried to see himself in the boy's eyes, the shape of his face, the slope of his nose. He couldn't look at him without the dread of uncertainty he felt about the dark hair. Instead of drawing Jake closer to Annabelle, the questions and uncertainties about their baby brought back his fear of exposure from his past infidelities and the secrets that had nearly driven them apart.

He made the last turn down their street and up the driveway as if on autopilot. The garage door opened, slowly

revealing his BMW, a symbol of his other life with its fur-
tive dealings and pleasures known only to Jake. There was
no reason to change anything, he thought. No need to make
any adjustments or choices just yet. He just needed a little more time to discover the mystery behind the baby in
the back seat.

57

DAVID WOKE UP just as the sun began its descent into late afternoon. He picked up the prescription bottle from the bathroom vanity. Only two of the four tablets remained from the bus-shack buy.

No worries. He planted a kiss on his gauze-wrapped right hand, still pleased by his good fortune in scoring the prescription. Sleep had kept the gnawing feeling of withdrawal at bay, but it clawed at his gut now that he was awake. He shook out an Oxy directly from the bottle into his mouth and then put it back into the medicine cabinet. Two gulps of water, and he was set. *Don't get greedy, David,* he cautioned himself. *Pace yourself.*

He slipped on his watch lying on the nightstand. It was two hours before the concert. The other scalpers would be out early to catch the first desperate character hoping to score for tonight's performance. He slipped into a navy pullover, a pair of jeans, and loafers. He grabbed his Ravens cap off the kitchen table and headed for the garage before doubling back to pick up Annabelle's phone. He couldn't trust Dewain. He'd been there once already.

The anesthetic from the splinter had worn off, but the drug was now taking over. He grabbed the truck's shift column, mashed the clutch, and shifted into reverse. As the garage door rose, David pulled his wallet out, felt for the hard corners of the concert tickets, and tossed Annabelle's phone into the glove compartment. He flashed a smile in the rearview mirror, saw the edge of the garage door disappear from view, and slowly backed out and into the street heading for Silver Dunes Lake.

56

DEWAIN PULLED HIS timecard from the rack just inside the employee-entrance door. Five more minutes, and the time-clock would advance to the next 15 minutes. There was an angle to everything, and Dewain knew them all.

He leaned back against the wall next to the clock and nodded to the line of employees who were clocking out and leaving for the day, listening to the steady click of the timeclock as one after the other cheated themselves out of fifteen minutes of free pay. *They weren't nearly as smart as he was.*

"Hey, Dewain. What are you standing there for?" Cherise took Dewain in slowly from head to toe, flashing a grin. She came out of the line and walked to him, turning to lean up against the wall and pressing her hip tightly against him.

"Well, I was going to clock out, but I'm having second thoughts about leaving this spot." He moved his hips slightly, rubbing up against Cherise. He let out a low groan and turned to her, his eyes closed, licking his lips.

"Mmm, girl. You're so close. I can almost taste you."

"Shut up, you pervert," Cherise said playfully. "You've been neglecting me lately. How about you and I leave this world for a while tonight? Hang out? Hook up? I've got a bottle of wine at my place and a very wicked mind. Could be fun."

Dewain was silent. He let her words hang out there for a moment. He wouldn't respond too quickly. It was best to let her hang for a moment. Build up the tension, the excitement. He could feel Cherise pressing closer. He looked in her direction, but not in her eyes.

"No can do tonight, baby. Dewain has some business to take care of. But after business could come a little pleasure. How about I swing by later tonight if you still have some of that wine? I'll text you when my business is wrapped up."

He slid his hand against the wall and rested it on her backside.

Cherise pressed hard against his hand, stood up from the wall, and walked to the timeclock. She slowly pulled her timecard out of the slot, turned towards Dewain, and bit the corner of the card. She flashed a smile and mouthed, "Later."

He smiled and got in the growing line to clock out. The timeclock read 5:09, perfect to capture the next time period.

It was still a little early to head to the concert venue. He drove to get a fast-food burger and a vanilla shake and ate in the parking lot.

Dewain was used to junkies. They would lie to their own grandmothers if they thought they could somehow get some money. Annabelle had told him the wallet had two tickets worth $500 for tonight's performance. Front row. If David had been lying about the wallet, those tickets could give a junkie enough cash to score again.

Scalping tickets outside the venue was risky. With the recent shootings around the country at events like this there was certain to be security and cops crawling all over the place. All David had to do is show up with the tickets, and Dewain would score twice. First, to let the stupid junkie know that he made a big mistake lying to him. and second, Dewain would have the $500 tickets to cash in on. *Either way, I win and he loses.*

David would suffer the consequences for lying. Dewain would have some serious cash to impress a certain lady waiting for a text that night. He had to bring her something special to celebrate his good fortune. *Or, if the guy doesn't have shit, she still gets a night of pleasure with Dewain.*

He popped the last bite of his burger into his mouth, emptied the shake cup in one long swallow, tossed the trash over his shoulder, and headed for the Silver Dunes Lake.

59

HOLT HAD BEEN a detective for over fifteen years, and not much escaped his powers of observation. People look you in the eyes when they don't have anything to hide. But they look away, blink, or look back and forth when they are lying. They might talk too loudly, talk in circles, or just clam up.

He had interviewed hundreds of witnesses, and Gus was hiding something. Not about the guy on his bus or anyone else he may have noticed. Holt observed that Gus had problems with his eyes. The way he closed his eyes tight in reaction to the glare of the headlights of buses returning to the terminal. His eyes didn't move when Holt got up, walked around the table, and then sat down, almost like he couldn't follow Holt's movements. Gus squinted and blinked a lot, pretending to study Holt's file that had images of baseball caps with birds on them. Holt knew someone couldn't identify what they can't see. Gus wore no glasses—a bus driver with bad vision? No wonder he couldn't provide details.

He mulled over the pink-haired girl and the crest that Gus had mentioned—a crested blazer and a hat with a bird on it.

The two missing tickets would be a long shot, but some amateur might think he'd scored two tickets to the best event of the year and might actually decide to catch the show, or come and try to scalp them for cash. Thieves are creatures of habit and think they won't get caught, thought Holt. If they're stealing it's probably either for drugs or for sport, someone who likes taking chances. Let's see if the bird man shows up tonight with the tickets. Holt hoped they'd make it easy for him whoever it was.

I've got a date with a redhead who doesn't like to be kept waiting.

60

BY THE TIME David arrived at the Silver Dunes Lake amphi-theater, the parking lot was full. He pulled in to overflow parking in the wooded area adjacent to the parking lot. Shepherdsville was proud of its initiative to restore Silver Dunes Lake, the adjacent lagoon, and the picnic area. The highlight was a 10,000-seat partially covered amphitheater that quickly became *the* spot for music, theater, community events, and the Saturday farmer's market.

David pulled out his wallet and transferred the tickets to his pocket. Easy access would cut the time he was exposed to any security employees looking for scalpers.

David had done this before. Robbery was only one of his methods to get cash to feed his habit. Darcy was on the A-list for high-ticket events in the business and social community. For her participation and generous support, free tickets to sports, music, and art events arrived weekly and were among David's rewards for services rendered. David faithfully saw that the unused tickets were put to his good use by scalping them and lining his pockets.

David surveyed the crowd. He enjoyed the bargain-ing, especially when he held the advantage, holding what someone else was anxious to pay for. He took off his cap and tucked the brim into the waistband of his pants. He knew customers would want to see his eyes. He walked slowly through the crowd, his left arm at his side, the index and middle fingers extended, indicating he had two tickets for sale.

The crowd was growing, impatiently waiting for the gates to open. David stepped into the crowd, weaving his way through it a second time. Then, there it was. A fifty-ish man looking straight into his eyes, arms crossed, two fingers extended. David quickly scanned the surrounding crowd. He spotted a security guard a few feet behind the man, looking in David's direction. David walked past his potential buyer, past the guard, and back into the crowd.

A few steps on, he spotted a couple that was arguing. He walked closer and got the signal from the young man. He broke off and followed David to the edge of the crowd. No security around.

"What have you got?" the young man asked, nervously looking back at the woman and pulling out his wallet.

"What you want, I'm sure," said David, enjoying the man's discomfort and desperation. "Two prime seats up front—front and center. They don't come cheap, but I don't suppose you want to disappoint that beautiful lady. Five hundred."

"I'll take them," said the man, peeling off five one-hundred-dollar bills from a fat roll pulled from his pocket.

David reached into his back pocket for the tickets when he spotted a familiar face across the crowd. For a moment, their eyes locked. Dewain laid his three-fingered hand on his chest. A sinister grin slowly spread across his face as he started jostling his way through the crowd in David's direction.

"The tickets, man," said his eager buyer, pushing the five bills at David as Dewain rushed towards them.

"Sorry, no sale." David, flustered, pushed his way past the guy and darted into the crowd that was now standing shoulder to shoulder, straining against the ropes blocking the park's entrance. He pushed into the middle, trying to head for his truck and escape when he felt something drilling hard into his left shoulder. He turned around and came face to face with Dewain. They were immobilized by the crush of the crowd.

"Well, David, what are *you* doing here? I didn't know you were such a classic rock fan. I, on the other hand, am quite a fan. Looking to buy a couple of tickets. Would you be able to help an old friend out?"

Dewain gripped David's arm to maneuver him out of the crowd. He knew David wouldn't make a scene. As they pressed through the crowd, David heard someone yelling in his direction.

"Hey—hey! Come back here!" David's disappointed buyer was waving for David. The commotion directed the surrounding crowd's attention to David.

"Sure, man!" called David, sensing a chance to escape. Exposure worked for him, but not for Dewain, who relaxed his grip. As David pushed hard into the crowd, Dewain was pulled in the opposite direction. Now freed of Dewain, he pressed on to the couple, now both waving him closer.

"You still got those tickets?" the man asked.

"Yeah," David said. "Keep quiet, would you? This place is crawling with security."

The man reached into his pocket, pulling out $400.

"I said $500." David glared at the man, who just stared back.

"Second chances aren't as good as the first, my friend," the young man said to David. "And there's a security guard just ahead of us."

David whipped his head around and saw that the ropes had been pulled back with the crowd now funneling through an hourglass opening in the gate.

Shit! He pulled out the tickets, grabbing the cash from the man, fumbling with his bandaged hand.

"Enjoy the show, you thieving bastard!" David said as the woman grabbed the tickets from his hand. The transaction was over. David started pushing his way out of the crowd and away from the gate.

61

TWO FRONT ROW tickets at a bargain price. Quite a score. The young woman smiled and stood up on her toes to plant a kiss on her boyfriend's mouth. "You're such a badass, Ricky."

The house lights flickered.

"I want to get a beer and some nachos before we find our seats," Linda said with a pout.

"The lines are ridiculous," Ricky pointed out. "Let's get something later."

Linda's pout turned into a glare. Ricky followed her to the shortest concession line as the house lights started to dim. Spotlights illuminated the stage for the opening act. Music blasted from the speakers sending ear-splitting vibrations washing over the cheering crowd. Balancing beers and two big plates of nachos, they found their section and began their descent to the front row.

"Hey—where are you going?"

Ricky turned and saw a young guy in a green t-shirt labeled EVENT approaching them. His name tag proclaimed "Hi, I'm Steve!"

"You have to wait until they finish this number. "

Ricky glared at the usher, shifting the nachos now dripping queso down his arm. "I have front-row seats and we're tired of standing and waiting in lines," he growled.

"Can't go down while they are playing," said Steve coolly. "There are a couple of empty seats in the back row. When this number is over you can make your way down."

Ricky resisted the urge to smash the guy's face with the nachos. Linda was swaying to the beat of the band, somehow not spilling a thing. Ricky nudged her to the empty seats.

They finished off their nachos just as the band finished its first number. Ricky stood up. "Let's go, Linda," he said and headed toward the stairs.

"I need to use the little girl's room, baby," Linda said sheepishly. "No lines now. Hold onto my beer."

Linda disappeared around the corner just as the usher motioned to the crush of people at the top of the stairs to move *now*. The band had started the next number as Linda made her way back. "Let's go find those badass $400 seats," she said, grabbing her beer.

Ricky saw that the usher was now holding up a crowd at the top of the stairs. He glared at Linda, and she shrugged. So, they both sat down again, beers in hand, silently waiting for the end of the next number. At the last note, they finally made their way down the stairs to Row 1, seats 15 and 16.

"Ricky, you are the man!" Linda's eyes were shining as she pulled him down into the seat next to her.

"Do you love your badass man, baby?" Ricky asked as Linda scanned the premium seating section.

"We're sitting with the *big money* tonight, baby!" she said, taking a long sip of beer. He took that as a yes.

62

THAT LYING SON-OF-A-BITCH no-good junkie! That damned couple had given David an escape from Dewain's plan to drag David into the woods behind the parking lot, extricate the tickets in the most painful way he could think of, and then—well, he hadn't worked out the details yet.

There were many choices. He felt the cold steel of the swordfish knife in his pocket. Quality craftsmanship for any dirty job. A souvenir of an unfortunate encounter with a wealthy but foolish businessman. One slash with the finely-honed steel blade and David wouldn't be lying to anyone again. Or maybe he should just mess him up a bit—slice off a couple of fingers like old Dewain. They'd be brothers, sort of. Or just torture him with threats but not execution, making him willing to do whatever he wanted.

Dewain squeezed the knife tighter in frustration. He needed to be careful; the knife would do its work without regard to whose flesh kissed the blade. Dewain took his hand out of his pocket as he neared the edge of the crowd. He turned to scan the crowd once more, but David and the couple had melted into the crowd as it pushed toward the open gates. Late concert goers passed by, rushing to get to their seats. He could hear a voice announcing the opening band as he turned to walk out of the crowd and straight into a tall man.

"Why Dewain, what are you doing here?" Holt put his hand on Dewain's shoulder, signaling him not to try and run.

Dewain's stomach dropped. *First, I lose David, and then I score a fucking detective.* He felt the weight of the knife in his pocket, suddenly a piece of damaging evidence. Dewain relaxed his body. He looked up at the detective and flashed a smile, his eyes wide with just a hint of surprise. "Well, Detective Holt," he said. "I guess I'm here for the same reason you are—to see the concert. Or at least try. I guess you caught me there, Detective Holt. My Auntie Faye begged me to try to get some tickets for tomorrow night. Poor Auntie Faye can hardly make it to her Bible Study in the evening, but she loves her rock and roll. How could I refuse her—she's been like a mother to me. I thought I might be able to purchase some—well, from someone who had extra tickets, but they are so expensive! Can't afford scalper prices on an orderly's salary. Auntie Faye will have to be satisfied with a CD or something more in my price range."

Dewain looked up at the detective, conjuring a sad, concerned expression to replace the smile, pleased at his performance.

Holt studied Dewain. The nervy little prick must not know that Holt knew Annabelle had told Dewain about the tickets. So what scalper was he looking for? He either planned to steal them or strongarm whoever has them. Or maybe Dewain had found them, sold them, and has a load of cash in his pocket.

"Oh, I think we're both here to find the tickets that were in Annabelle's lost wallet," Holt said matter-of-factly, staring Dewain square in the eyes. He paused to see Dewain's reaction.

"Is that why you're here, detective?" said Dewain, stalling. *Think fast. He's on to something, and it might be you.*

Holt remained silent, using the uncomfortable silence to force Dewain to respond to his comment about Annabelle's lost wallet.

"You're never off duty, are you detective?" Dewain asked amicably. "Very admirable. I'm just a hospital orderly on my night off, trying to do a nice thing for an old lady. You say Mrs. Annabelle had concert tickets in her missing wallet? They must be worth a lot of money. Such a shame. You know I'm here to help in any way I can."

This isn't my first rodeo either, detective. I can play this game, and I like it better when we play by my rules. Ignore, divert, and switch.

"Yeah, I could use your help, Dewain. You say you were getting tickets for your Auntie—uh, *Faye*, was it?"

Dewain nodded. "That's right. I need to get back to her this evening. She will be so disappointed. You don't have any connections or spare tickets in your pockets, do you detective? A little bonus for your hospital detective-assistant?"

Dewain looked past Holt to see a man charging up behind him, staring at his phone, muttering to himself. "Watch out!" he called, but before Holt could turn the man hit him in the back, knocking him forward and dislodging Holt's metal Yeti water cylinder from his hand onto the ground at Dewain's feet.

The man barely looked up and continued on his way, now yelling to someone on the other side of the gate.

"You alright, detective?" asked Dewain as he picked up the water bottle.

"Yeah. It takes more than that to throw me off," Holt replied. He let the words hang in the air like a warning.

Dewain handed the metal container back to Holt who pulled a napkin from his pants pocket and wrapped it around the bottle. "No telling what nasty things it picked up off the ground. I'm sorry your auntie will be disappointed," said Holt. "I've got some work to do here. And if you do get any more information on the tickets, let me know, partner."

Dewain watched as Holt walked through the crowd, heading for the entry gate and flashing his badge at the security guard.

The bastard doesn't need a ticket, thought Dewain as he walked away. *I've got more information, but not for you. A little matter to settle with a lying junkie. It's playtime.*

63

HOLT FELT DEWAIN'S eyes watching him as he walked to the entry gate. He turned in time to see him heading in the direction of the parking lot. Holt walked over to the concession stand, flashed his badge, and asked for a paper bag. He slipped his water bottle into the bag and walked over to a security booth next to the entry gate. He flashed his badge to the officer inside and put the bag on the table.

"Keep this for me, will you? Evidence. I'll be back for it."

The security officer looked up and gave him the thumbs-up. "We'll be here an hour after the concert ends, officer."

The evidence safely stowed, Holt walked over to an attendant who was scanning tickets for the latecomers. He showed his badge and said, "I'm Detective Holt, here on official business." The attendant gave him a look reserved for cops trying to get in free to sold-out headliner events.

"Is that right, Detective?" he conveyed his irritation. "Sure, step right in." The attendant's words floated on a wave of marijuana and bourbon. Holt shook his head at the mixture of opportunity and stupidity. Another time, and he would have taken the opportunity to put down this guy for showing up stoned and drunk. But Holt had other business and no time for punks.

He entered the arena, scanning the seating layout. The arena held about 10,000 people, and he estimated this was going to be a full house. There were four sections, two with seats directly facing the stage. He pulled out his notebook and flipped through the pages for his interview notes with Annabelle. Seats 15 and 16.

He made his way down the far-right aisle, maneuvering through clueless people fixated on their cellphones and others loaded down with backpacks and carry bags, balancing beer, wine, and food from the concessions on the periphery of the open-air arena. The sun had almost set, casting a low glow that washed across the seating and crested at the stage.

Holt stopped about ten rows back from the stage. He scanned the seating layout on the back of the program and compared with the two front rows. The jostling crowd was the perfect cover for this surveillance. And there they were—empty. First row, third and fourth seat from the center aisle.

As the house lights started to flash, signaling the crowd to find their seats for the opening act, Holt walked down the aisle to the side of the stage, climbing the steps backstage.

"Hey, where do you think you're going?" a burly guy yelled. He was wearing a t-shirt that barely covered his vivid arm and neck tattoos. "If you don't get off this stage, I'll have the cops throw you out!"

"I *am* the cops."

Holt held up his badge, the lights illuminating the metal emblem in the center. The stagehand put up his hand, gesturing there was no need to come closer. "OK, that's cool," he said.

This guy's seen one of these before, Holt thought.

Holt positioned himself backstage, out of the crowd's view but with a clear sightline to Annabelle's seats. The opening band took the stage, tuning up and finding their marks. The house lights went down, and the band launched into a raucous version of "Take It Easy."

The crowd roared its approval. Thirty seconds into the number, the bass player switched sides with the vocalist, blocking Holt's view of the empty seats.

He redirected his gaze from the empty seats and scanned the aisles for movement. In the dim light, he could see a crowd gathering at the top of the stairways, but no one was moving, With the last note of the first number, the crowd funneled down the aisle, scrambling for their seats. Holt shifted his position as the band moved in and out of his sightline, his eyes now fixed in the direction of seats 15 and 16 as the band launched into another number. Holt thought his eardrums would explode.

Through the band's shifting dance moves, Holt saw that the seats were still empty. After the second number, the lead singer introduced the band members. Holt's eyes darted from the seats to the top of the aisle. A few stragglers began to descend the stairs, taking seats along the way. Finally, only a man and a woman continued their descent to the front row. Introductions over, the band shuffled positions again, blocking Holt's view of the seats.

"Get the fuck out of the way," Holt silently screamed in frustration. He moved out of the shadows for a better position.

This could be it.

Just then, the band burst across the stage in a frenzied dance number, never missing a note, exposing and then blocking the empty seats. Holt fixed his eyes towards the seats, hoping for a glimpse. The drummer launched into an ear-splitting solo, sending the musicians to opposite sides of the stage; Finally, Holt had a clear view. A man and a woman were in seats 15 and 16. He counted the seats again and looked more closely.

One of them was wearing what looked like a baseball cap.

64

THE CROWD PRESSED from all sides, pushing to get into the arena before the warm-up band started. David shoved the four hundred dollars into his pocket and started to thread his way back to the parking area. He reached behind him, relieved that his hat was still wedged into his waistband.

The darkness enclosed him as he stepped into the parking lot from the ring of lights that circled the arena. He made his way to the grassy area where he saw his truck, now wedged between a pricy BMW and a late-model brown Ford Explorer, its grimy back window covered with various band stickers.

He walked to the driver's side and stopped short. He stepped back behind the BMW and stared at the license plate: SOS J+A. He'd seen that license plate before. It had come around the corner from the direction of the drop site, just after he had left the money yesterday at the pickup.

Alone in the parking lot, he walked around the Beamer and peered into the driver's side windows. The car was clean inside—no used coffee cups, papers, stray clothing. A neat freak. As he walked past the passenger side, he saw an envelope lying on the front seat. He bent to peer through the window, but couldn't make out the writing. He pulled out his cellphone to use the flashlight. The music from the arena swelled and subsided, followed by a roar from the crowd.

Quiet again, he heard the low crunch of gravel under footsteps, coming nearer. He turned and saw a man and a woman winding through the parking lot in his direction. The concert was just beginning. A couple unable to score some tickets? David pocketed his phone and silently slipped into his truck, sliding low into the driver's seat. He pulled out the cap digging into his lower back and tossed it onto the passenger seat. As the couple approached, David heard a beep and saw the flash of lights as the BMW's doors unlocked.

When he heard the car doors open, he lifted his head and froze as he saw a woman getting into the passenger side. The door slammed shut. He waited for the purr of an engine, but it was strangely quiet. He peered again and saw the outline of a man's hand against the passenger-side window, then reaching and pulling in the car's dark interior. He knew those soft thuds against leather— two bodies urgently taking advantage of a dark, deserted parking lot.

David pulled Annabelle's phone from the glove compartment. He set the camera to video, hit zoom, and lifted the phone up, facing into the BMW's side window. The wind parted the tree limbs just enough to allow some light to shine on the scene inside the car. David held the camera steady until he detected silence again.

Then he heard the low murmur of an engine as headlights cast a cone of light into the dark trees. David looked into the rearview mirror as the BMW backed out. He couldn't see the driver in the glare of the headlights. He watched as the light turned and then dimmed as the car backed out onto the road and sped away. David rose up from his hiding place and hit "Play." Two bodies becoming one, wedged into the Beamer's leather bucket seats and low-slung interior. The man's face was just a shadow moving in and out of the darkness. But the woman's face was captured in the intermittent light, eyes closed in the throes of passion. He felt his stomach lurch as a wave of heat and then chills washed over him. His mind raced, and images flashed in his brain like a music video, one after the other, disjointed but with the same face in each three-second frame. In the light and even in the dark, he could recognize that profile, that body.

It was his former boss, Darcy.

65

DAVID STOWED ANNABELLE'S phone back inside the glove compartment. He knew Darcy well enough; she was a woman without limits and with a voracious appetite for money, power, and control. Who was the driver of the car? What was she doing in the car he had seen at the drug meet? A lover? A new, pathetic young man, trapped by the secrets of his lucrative internship, now hooked on her game of drugs for sex?

Or was it a colleague—another professional drawn into her drug network?

David closed his eyes in a futile attempt to wash the images of Darcy out of his consciousness. He took a deep breath and looked into the empty space where the car had been. He didn't see the man walking fast up from the direction of the arena, making straight for his truck. He heard a loud bang on the door and came face to face with Dewain on the other side of the driver's side window.

David reached to lock the door of the old truck, but Dewain was quicker. He flung open the door and grabbed David by the shirt.

"Get out! And be quiet. You and I are going to take a little walk."

David's eyes searched the dark parking area, frantically looking for signs of life, some kind of movement—people who might hear or see what was happening and offer an escape. The lot was deserted. He and Dewain were the only characters in this act, alone on a dark stage, about to play out this scene. Dewain may have scripted it, but David hoped he could improvise to avoid a bad ending.

As Dewain pulled David out of the truck, he tightened his grip and led him into the woods through the thick brush behind a heavy cloak of pines and oaks. Without pausing, Dewain cocked his arm and landed a blow on David's jaw and sent him to the ground. He pulled the knife from his pocket, released the blade, and stood over David who stared, watching the blade flash menacingly with every turn of Dewain's wrist, catching the moonlight through the trees.

"Fuck, Two K!"

"You got it right, junkie. Exactly right. You thought you'd screw me out of your good fortune. How much did you get for them? A hundred? Five hundred?"

"What are you talking about?" David rubbed his jaw. He felt a trickle of blood make its way down his upper lip and to his chin.

"Get up, junkie. I've had enough of your lies. I saw you haggling with that couple. I saw it go down. I would have relieved you of the money then, but this setting suits me better. I figure those tickets were worth at least $300 to someone."

"Here, take the money," David rose slowly and pulled the four bills from his pocket. This was not a time to count out $300 for Dewain and keep something for himself. David held the four bills up, waving them in the dark.

Dewain stepped forward and grabbed David's bandaged hand, jerking him forward. David winced in pain. Dewain's eyes locked in on his victim, his breath fast and hot on David's face. Dewain slowly brought his other hand to David's face, laying the steel blade edge on his now throbbing cheek.

David had seen that type of look before, just before the beating would begin. He felt terror and then an almost calm yielding to whatever was coming. Resistance was futile.

"It would have been so much easier if you hadn't lied to me. See, we would come to the same result. Hand over the tickets and save yourself the trip to the concert and this nasty business we have to take care of."

David looked down and could see the tip of the blade resting on his cheekbone just under his eye. He stood motionless, silent, barely breathing.

"Yeah, you got away with your lies before, but this one is going to cost you, junkie. Now and later. You see, the cops are very interested to know who had those tickets. And whatever else you are still holding that belongs to that poor woman from the bus."

Dewain inched the tip of the blade upward against David's lower eyelid. The cold steel made him blink against the blade, barely slicing the edge. The terror returned.

"You won't be such a pretty boy with only one eye. I know what it's like; the come-on smiles, the invitation to party. Then the shock when they see my hand. We'll be like brothers, suffering similar afflictions. You lied to me twice now; I think that justice is an eye for an eye?"

"Please, I'll do anything, Dewain."

"Oh, yes you will, my little junkie friend."

David felt the blade press harder and stood rigidly, staring at Dewain.

"One move and I may slip and take out more than necessary. Unfortunate."

David closed his eyes, then heard a loud snap. He felt the blade slide down his cheek as Dewain released his grip on David's hand and stepped away. David heard the snapping of branches underfoot, then voices approaching. He didn't move, but opened his eyes. A couple was walking towards him.

"Come on, Shirley. You know I love you."

A man's voice got louder. David saw a young man and woman passing through the brush. The man was pulling her along as she offered slight resistance.

David saw them disappear into the woods and realized that Dewain and the money were gone.

From a distance he heard the roar of the crowd. There was a bright glow from the light show, and fireworks lit the sky, signaling the end of the concert. Soon the parking lot would be crawling with concertgoers in various stages of intoxication, searching for their cars and maneuvering towards the exits.

David took a deep breath and leaned against a tree, out of sight of the amorous couple. Numb from fear and terror, he reached up to feel his eye socket. Still there. He breathed again, wiping what felt like a drop of blood starting to congeal against his lower eyelid. The panic began to subside.

He picked his way toward the light and out of the woods. He found his truck, cranked the engine, and threw it into reverse, almost taking out an elderly couple in his blind spot. No time for apologies; he pushed the gas pedal and carefully picked his way out of the park and into the safety of the streets.

66

HOLT STOOD BACK in the shadows, waiting for the opening band to finish their set as he kept the seats and the couple in view. He pulled out his cellphone and zoomed in on the couple who were taking several shots. The woman was swiping on her cellphone; the man was looking away at the crowd. Were they a couple of thieves who had been taking advantage of a defenseless pregnant lady on a bus? Or innocent people who bought tickets from the guy with the hat and the blazer who had been on Bus 7?

The set over, the crew swarmed the stage to set up for the headliners. The lights went down again as the headliners took the stage to unearthly pyrotechnics choreographed to the band's opening number. The crowd roared.

Holt looked past the guitarist to the couple in the front row. She was still swiping her phone, stopping to take photos of the band and then, Holt imagined, posting them on Instagram or Facebook. *The more evidence, the better.*

Holt had no need to cause a scene during the concert, even if it would be easy to get a security guard and pull them from their seats while the crowd was distracted. He would wait until the concert was over. These concerts always hired off-duty cops for a little muscle if things got out of hand, given the combination of too many beers and hard stuff from the concession stands and whatever drugs made their way into the arena past the guards. The air was tinged with the scent of marijuana and cheap beer.

Holt took the back stairs from behind the stage and circled around to the front of the arena, scanning the area at the entry points, looking for an officer. He saw a few security guards, their neon orange and yellow vests standing out. Then he spotted a young female officer seated at one of the entry points, cellphone in hand, swiping and laughing.

"Care to share what's so amusing, Officer McGee?" Holt asked after spotting her name. He held out his badge.

"Oh, not much, detective, just catching up on some family posts until the crowds start coming out." She slipped her phone into her pocket and stood up.

"These 'rent a cop' gigs can be pretty boring," said Holt. "I've been there myself. Have you been inside to catch the show at all? The crowd is pretty fueled up on music, alcohol, and who-knows-what pharmaceuticals they brought with them. You might want to maintain a presence just to deter anyone from playing outside the lines."

"No, sir," she said. "I figured if anyone needed me, they would find me."

"Well, you were right on that—I'll need your assistance once the concert ends. There are two people I've been watching, Section B, front row, seats 15 and 16. Tickets for those seats went missing from a wallet belonging to a woman involved in a situation several days ago. I'm going to detain those two as they leave the concert and bring them in for questioning. They might be innocent fans looking to buy tickets from a scalper, or they could be the thieves who stole them from a wallet."

"Excuse me, detective. I'm new on the force, but it's just a couple of tickets and a wallet. Why the surveillance by a detective? Stuff like this happens all the time. Usually, a report is filed, and we notify the owners if the stuff turns up, which it never does."

Holt wasn't about to explain his fall from grace to this rookie.

McGee's pocket started buzzing. Holt gave her a look. *Don't even think about it.*

"Well, things aren't always what they seem to be. My fifteen years on the force taught me that. Officer McGee, I suggest you shut off your cellphone. Here's a surveillance assignment; watch and learn. I need you to get a visual on the people in those seats. Be ready to track them out of the arena when the concert ends. I'll wait at the top of the stairs and I'll follow them too. Once I've got them in sight, you move forward and out into the edge of the lighted area in front of the entrance gates. I'll follow behind them, and we'll close in. No theatrics. Just stop them, and I'll come up behind and take over. Got it?"

"Yes, sir." She turned and headed to Section B down front. Holt followed, stopping back from the top of the stairs. He watched as the officer slowly walked down the stairs, stopping periodically to glance left and right. All eyes were on the performance on the stage. At the bottom of the stairs, she turned and walked to the right, in the opposite direction of the target seats.

Good job, McGee. Don't be too obvious.

At the end of the bank of seats, she turned and passed the couple in Annabelle's seats. She paused to look up at the stage and then into the seats and continued walking at a steady pace. She was better than he had expected.

The band finally wound down to a close, finishing the set with an ear-splitting rendition of "Bohemian Rhapsody" that electrified the crowd. The set ended, and the crowd let out a roar of applause and whistles, chanting "encore!". The band left the stage, came out for a few bows, and then launched into a cover of Bruce Spingsteen's "Dancin' in the Dark." The applause subsided, and the crowd was on its feet, moving with the beat. The sky exploded with fireworks. Finally, the house lights went up, and the crowd began to filter out.

Holt spotted McGee in the crowd and gave her the nod. *Showtime.*

67

HOLT WATCHED AS the officer positioned herself to the left side of the stage, keeping a comfortable distance behind the couple as they slowly headed up the stairs with the crowd. For a moment, Holt lost the couple, then spotted McGee halfway up the stairs close enough to give a "Got them" nod to Holt.

"Hey, watch it, asshole. Keep your fucking hands off my wife!" Holt heard voices rising above the crowd on the stairs and hoped everyone would play nice a little longer—this was no time to have to break up a fight.

"Who's the asshole?" another voice yelled. All movement stopped as a guy with a blue mohawk faced off with a college kid in a button-down shirt. The crowd moved around the two, some pulling cellphones out. Holt saw a security guard threading his way towards the combatants, opening a wedge in the crowd.

"Take it outside," he heard the guard say to the two men who had begun to face off. They gave each other one more glare, then turned and moved on in opposite directions, and the crowd continued moving up the stairs and out into the night.

The young couple reached the top of the stairs. Holt nodded to McGee, now just a few steps behind them. As he reached the top of the stairs, McGee peeled off to the left and disappeared into the crowd, making her way to the rendezvous point. Holt fell in behind the couple as they went out through the turnstiles. McGee was right on schedule, coming towards them. As they reached the edge of the crowd waiting for rides or Ubers, Holt gave the nod, and McGee closed in.

"Sir, ma'am, could you step this way please?"

"What is this? What's going on?" Ricky pushed Linda behind him, positioning his body like a shield.

Holt approached from the rear. "Please follow the officer," he said firmly, holding out his badge.

The couple followed McGee to a small security booth just outside the turnstiles, out of view of the crowd. Ricky looked back and forth from McGee to Holt and then to Linda. Each one had fastened a tight grip on the other.

"What's this about?" Ricky asked, facing off with McGee. Linda stood gripping his arm, shooting belligerent looks at the officers.

"Did you enjoy the show?" Holt asked conversationally, sitting on the edge of the desk.

"What?" Ricky said, moving closer. "What kind of question is that? Are the cops running a bullshit feedback project? You've got nothing better to do than drag us in here to see if we liked the bands? Don't they let you work the cases with real bad guys?"

Oh, a smartass. This should be fun, Holt thought.

"Move back, sir," Holt said, eyes locked on the man. "You must have liked the bands enough to fork out $500 for two front-row seats. Maybe you're trying to impress the lady?"

"What are you talking about?" said Ricky, trying to piece together Holt's statement with the four hundred he had paid the scalper. "I liked the bands. What is it to you?"

Holt relaxed a bit, and looked over the man's shoulder at the woman still clutching the man's arm. She stared back and crossed her arms under her ample chest. She smirked as Holt's eyes darted from her face to her chest and back again.

"Those seats belonged to someone else," Holt continued. "A nice woman in the hospital whose wallet and phone went missing a few days ago. The tickets to those seats were in that missing wallet. You were ushered into those seats tonight. I'm interested in how you became the owner of those tickets."

Holt crossed his arms and waited. He considered himself an accomplished interrogator. What, if anything, would the couple confess to if they've been up to anything in the past few days? The silence stretched on as Holt and the couple considered their next move.

Ricky softened his tone and looked down at his hands. He pulled Linda close, his arm around her waist.

"Look detective," he said. "I don't know what you're talking about; I don't know anything about a missing wallet. This is the hottest concert in town, and I did want to impress my lady." He gave her a little squeeze and a smile. "We didn't have tickets, and I bought some from a scalper. We lucked out; the guy wanted five hundred for them, but I got them for four. That was it—a quick transaction. And that's all."

"Really. A guy has two tickets with a face value of five hundred and sells them for four? He could have gotten much more for those seats," Holt shook his head skeptically.

"Maybe he just wanted to get rid of them fast. Don't know and don't care. We lucked out. That's all I know."

It wasn't a crime to buy tickets from a stupid scalper. Holt knew he couldn't hold them much longer. He pulled out his notebook.

"This guy who sold you the tickets. What did he look like?"

"Just a guy. Youngish, maybe 30. Brown hair, brown eyes."

"Creepy brown eyes," offered the woman. "And nervous. He twitched like he had ants up his butt."

"How tall?" Holt continued.

"About 5-11."

"What was he wearing?"

"A button-down shirt. Light blue. And jeans."

"And a hat," said Linda. "But he wasn't wearing it. Had it stuffed in the back waistband of his jeans. Saw it there when he walked away though the crowd—had some kind of bird on it. He looked too old to carry around a baseball cap like that, stuffed in his pants like a little kid. Creepy SOB."

"Did you see where he went?" pressed Holt.

"The place was a crush before the concert," said the man. "We could barely move. He grabbed the money and disappeared, heading toward the parking lot, I suppose. Look, that's all we know. Anything else, detective?"

"Yeah, I need your names and phone numbers." Holt wrote them down and pulled a card out of his pocket. "You're free to go. If you remember anything else, give me a call."

Ricky snatched the card up and ushered Linda out of the security office. Holt watched as they hurried out and disappeared into the parking lot.

Holt saw McGee nod to the couple as they exited in front of her through the turnstile. She walked over to Holt, an expectant look on her face.

"Did we get the bad guys, detective?"

"Not today, McGee. Just a couple more pieces to an interesting puzzle. That's what this work is—collect the pieces and they start to fall into place."

"Yes, sir, Detective Holt. Is there anything else you need from me?

"No, that's all. Thanks for your help."

Holt leaned against the wall and went over the notes he had scratched down. Nothing much to go on, except the hat with the bird. That preppy fellow with the bird cap had the tickets—did he have the wallet and the phone, too? Was he a local who knew he could score some serious cash for those tickets? The creepy guy from Annabelle's last bus ride? The guy with the bird cap pulled over his eyes who Gus told to ride with the EMTs the night Annabelle was rushed to the hospital? He picked up his metal water bottle wrapped in the paper bag and walked out of the security office.

68

ROGER FOLDED THE baby blanket over the sticky yellow circle of spit-up. He knew Annabelle was lying. He could always tell; their relationship had started with and was built on lies and deception, making it exciting. Dangerous. Addictive.

They had both enjoyed the cat-and-mouse game with Jake, the open trap waiting to snap. How close could they get? How far could they push? How close could they play without Jake catching on? The lies were part of the game. They fed off the intrigue and deception. It was better than foreplay.

Annabelle had eventually ended their affair. Roger knew that he had served a purpose, but she was done. She had texted him to come to the hospital when she was in labor because she was desperate.

Now the stakes were higher. He lifted the blanket again and breathed in the smell of baby oil with a faint odor of spit-up. Her baby could be his son. Finally, after the heartache and dashed hopes that had nearly destroyed his marriage—a child. With time, his wife would forgive him and accept his son as her own. She had to.

He and Sharon had met during their college days at University of Georgia and had married just after graduation.

They both had exciting careers—he in investment banking; she managing a thriving nonprofit. Roger felt complete, but Sharon wanted a child. While he was making a slow climb to the top, she grew increasingly distant and depressed.

The stress of Roger's job and Sharon's disappointment drove a wedge between them. He became good at making excuses for attending social, civic, and business events alone. Successful, handsome, and charming, he had no lack of offers for companionship, which he found increasingly difficult to decline.

He took Sharon's choice to isolate herself as consent, and she didn't protest. Roger, now a "married single," became part of the downtown after work crowd at Bailey's Pub near Market Square. Back on the black-tie circuit, Roger was a favorite dinner partner at some of the high-ticket events in town. The Museum Charity Art Gala was a last-minute fill-in for a colleague with a case of the flu. One drink, a few rounds of bidding, and he would be out of there.

That was the plan.

He didn't intend to be captivated by the beautiful woman at the check-in table that night. He'd seen so many beautiful women, but there was something different about Annabelle. Beautiful, yes. But she had confidence and an easy way of handling the crowd that night, fielding questions, finding table numbers, and joking—flirting—her way through the chaos to keep the line moving. He was mesmerized. She had to ask twice for his name before he could respond.

There was something in her voice that night and in the way she followed him with her eyes as he walked towards the ballroom. He paused at the doorway and took a glass of champagne from a waiter. Turning back, he saw she was still looking at him. He lifted his glass, tipped it towards her, and smiled. She responded with a wicked smile and a slight nod. He was hooked.

It wasn't difficult to hide the blanket from Sharon. She had moved into the guest room months ago. He had gently folded the blanket, put it in a plastic bag, and slipped it under their king-size bed. In the morning, he pulled it from its hiding place. Roger rubbed the soft cotton blanket in his thumb and fingers, imagining it wrapped gently around the baby that might be his son. Annabelle's son. And in time, his and Sharon's son. He closed his eyes and saw the three of them posing for family photos. In front of the Christmas tree. Dressed in khaki shorts and white shirts on the beach at sunset. At Charlie's soccer game. His son would bring life back to his marriage and his wife.

My son.

Despite a day of meetings and deal making, his mind focused on the little blanket in the plastic bag in his bottom desk drawer. The sun splashed pink and orange as it began to sink towards the horizon. He begged off cocktails with his last client and showed him the door. Alone at last, he grabbed his phone from his pocket and scrolled through his contacts, stopping at Jonas Dirkfield. He tapped the number and heard Jonas' voice.

"Roger. What's up, man? Haven't heard from you in a while," Jonas responded with surprise. "What can I do for you?"

"Well, Jonas, I have a situation that I think you might be able to help me with."

"I will if I can, Roger. What do you need?"

"It's a personal matter and highly confidential. I'm coming to you, Jonas because you are a man of integrity and discretion."

"Of course, Roger. And a friend. Tell me what you need."

Roger put the baby blanket on the passenger seat, taking care to roll the precious evidence to the inside.

"I have something that I need tested. A DNA test. It's a baby blanket. The baby left some evidence on the blanket that could answer some questions for me. I will supply whatever needs to be analyzed for comparison. Of course, this is a highly personal matter, so I'm counting on your complete confidentiality and discretion. The results should come to me only. Can you handle this for me, Jonas?"

"Well Roger, once you give me the blanket we will determine if we have a viable samples for the test," said Jonas. "If there is a problem, I have some connections at the hospital who owe me some favors; they could get samples instead. I should have results for you in a couple of days." There was a silence, then Jonas coughed nervously. "Ah, Roger, are you hoping for a positive outcome or an escape route?"

"Jonas, you can be assured my intentions are honorable. And please, no questions. The less you know the better."

"Right. I'm in my office now, Roger. I was just about to pour myself a couple of fingers of bourbon to get through the night. Join me?"

"Be there in in thirty, Jonas—with the blanket. Thanks."

Roger ended the call, slid the phone into his pocket, put the car into drive, and headed for Market Square.

69

DAVID COULDN'T MOVE his head. This had happened before; an oversupply of Oxys and a bottle of bourbon were too seductive for restraint. One drug fueled the other, taking over his body and mind. He was a willing captive, surrendering completely. So much good fortune. So many round white pills. One tablet tames the demons and relieves the pain. Two, sliding down the throat on a ribbon of Class A bourbon, and you're dancing with the demons, every sensation heightened, until the demons turn on the master, scraping the bones and tearing the muscles apart, splitting the skull, dropping the eyes from their sockets in terror and pain.

David couldn't tell if he was alive or dead. He could see the room through the sheer curtain of a clouded eye. The room had landed on its side somehow. He could see a bottle of Makers Mark on the coffee table, the screw top lying beside a double shot glass filled with the amber liquid. He could see the bottle of Oxys from the hospital lying on its side next to the bourbon bottle, co-conspirators in his fall into hell. That beautiful splinter. David tried to rub his bandaged palm with his thumb, but nothing moved.

Like steppingstones, bright white pills formed a path from the rim of the open bottle to the shot glass. *My stairway to heaven*, thought David.

"I'm coming, my darlings." David tried to push off the couch but sank deeper into the cushions. He sensed the movement before the cat entered his line of vision.

David tried to call the cat, but could form no words. Hannah sauntered over to David, pausing at the foot of the couch, and stared at David with what looked like disgust. She crouched, took a long stretch, turned, and walked over to the coffee table.

One fluid leap and she was on the table.

Careful, Hannah, David spoke in his head.

Hannah looked over at David, blinked, and then set her eyes on the shot glass. Hannah stepped carefully over the pill bottle, brushing it lightly, dislodging more of the pills onto the table. She glanced at David again, immobilized on the couch. He stared back at her, still restrained by the drugs, as if watching the devil caressing tools of torture laid out on a tray. The cat moved deliberately, like a dancer on a stage scattered with dangerous obstacles.

Hannah picked her way over the shot glass, around the bottle of bourbon, and back to the pill bottle.

David willed the cat to get off the table.

As if responding to him, Hannah headed to the table's edge. She paused across from the shot glass and lifted her front paw, resting it on the edge of the glass, then slowly lowered it to the table. She fixed her eyes on David, turned to jump off, and with a swish of her tail, knocked it over, sending the bourbon washing over the Oxy pathway. David watched in horror as the bourbon soaked the tablets that dissolved like an abandoned sandcastle at the ocean's edge.

David's head exploded.

Hannah walked to the couch, jumped up, and curled up against his chest. He thought he saw a smile come over her little cat lips. The miserable, worthless cat.

He tried to swipe at her, but his arms were useless. He could only lie there and watch one pill after the other collapse into the puddle of bourbon. His mind exploded with rage and went dark again.

70

IT WAS LATE, but lights were still on in the crime lab when Holt pulled into the precinct parking lot. The squad room was quiet, except for a couple of uniforms going over the arrests of the day with the detective on shift. Holt threw his notebook on his desk and walked downstairs to the crime lab, holding the Yeti coffee mug still sheathed in its paper-bag cocoon.

"Randy, what are you doing here so late? The boys and girls out there not playing nice tonight?" Holt quipped.

Randy Schiff was a young, ambitious forensic scientist, new to the precinct but not the force. So far, he had fended off suitors from larger metropolitan areas. Shepherdsville had enough crime to keep him busy, and the "boys and girls" were getting more creative every day, making things interesting enough to keep him in Shepherdsville.

Holt sat the metal cylinder on Randy's table. "Got a little rush job for you, Randy, my friend," said Holt.

"Your bits of evidence are always rush," said Randy, shaking his head.

Holt ignored the head shake. "I need to get some fingerprints off the metal and match them to a smart-mouthed punk, if I'm right. It's my water bottle, so some of the prints may be mine. Actually, it was a bit of luck that I got the prints at all."

"Let's see if this is your lucky day, detective." Randy pulled on a pair of clean gloves and picked up the cylinder at its rim and began dusting. Oval, grooved images appeared on the surface like ants. "Not a lot of single prints, here," he said, staring at the container.

"The guy picked it up, so I hope there is something you can use. I'm counting on you, Randy."

Randy rolled the container over and kept dusting. "Ah, here are some good ones." He shot images of the prints, then grabbed some lifting tape and transfer cards. "Come to papa," he muttered, proceeding to lift three full and two partial prints from the metal surface. He slowly pulled the tape from the mug and pressed it to transfer cards, revealing the grooves and shapes that could shine a light on a criminal hiding in the dark.

"Got to log this as evidence, Holt, so you'll have to get yourself another Yeti."

"And that's a rush, Randy. You know, got to get the bad guys off the streets. Especially this one, if my hunch is right."

Holt turned, walked up the stairs and out of the precinct into the parking lot. He pulled out his phone and checked the time—almost midnight. Why not? He found the number and waited for an answer.

"Is that you, Jimmy?" An angry voice cut through the night air. "Where the hell were you? I sat in that sleazy bar fending off a circus of drunken men and one classy looking woman waiting for you. No call. No text. No nothing, you bastard. So, what do you want, now, Jimmy? The light is no longer on at this Motel 6."

"Baby, you know how it is," cooed Holt apologetically, with an emphasis on the "baby." "Duty called. It took longer than planned. All the time I was thinking about you, waiting so patiently for me in the bar. I could hardly concentrate thinking about you sitting perched on a barstool, those luscious legs in black stockings welcoming me from the cold, mean streets."

Holt waited, listening to the slow, steady breathing on the other end.

"I should lock the door and keep you out in those mean streets where you belong, you SOB. But since I'm still dressed as you requested, I may as well get something out of it. Get your sorry, sweet-talking ass over here, Holt."

"Aw, Veronica. I'm already there. Parked in front of your building. Buzz me up, will you please?"

Holt pulled the outer door open and hit the buzzer above Veronica's mailbox. At the same time, he felt a vibration in his jacket pocket. He pulled out his phone and saw the text message from dispatch. *Underage house party on south side. Alcohol and drugs on property. Proceed immediately. Possible multiple drug overdose.*

Holt sighed. He'd have to miss his party tonight. Stupid kids. They'd get no sympathy.

The inner door clicked once, then twice, and a voice called out from the small speaker on the wall.

"Holt, are you there? Get on up here before I change my mind again."

"I'm really sorry, Veronica. Just got a text from dispatch. Bunch of kids with an empty house; daddy's booze, and mama's pills went way too far. Got to go. I'll make it up to you. You know I will."

Silence. Then a final click.

He bolted out of the building, got back into his car, cranked the engine, and sped out into the night, headed for the pricey end of town.

71

HOLT FOUND THE house easily, lit up like daylight in the otherwise dark street.

Police cars and ambulances were scattered in the street in front of the house and up the circular driveway. The partygoers too drunk to run or hide were scattered on the lawn, on the sweeping porch, or on the curb. EMTs crisscrossed the lawn, looking for the worst drug overdoses. A few were lying on the lawn with a team of first responders working over them. Parents, alerted by their frightened kids who were not too drunk, arrived with a squeal of tires, bolted out of their cars before the wheels had stopped turning, and raced from child to scattered child, frantically searching for theirs.

Police cruisers were parked at either end of the street to form a periphery and prevent anyone from leaving the scene. Beer cans, liquor bottles, plastic beer cups, and shot glasses were strewn over the lawn and the porch. The night air carried the scent of bourbon, beer, and vomit, freshly delivered by a few kids relieving themselves in the azaleas and rhododendrons in the once pristine front yard.

Holt pulled a handkerchief out of his back pocket, stowed there for just this type of occasion, and covered his nose against the stench. A tough guy with a weak stomach, Holt got a lot of grief at crime scenes. Blood and sticky bodily fluids made his stomach turn. He fought the urge to join a green and purple-haired boy leaning over the manicured boxwood shrubbery.

Holt flashed his badge to the officer in charge, who was standing by one of the ambulances, taking notes and giving orders

"What have we got here?" he asked, shaking his head.

"Ah, these kids—looks like mostly high school age—managed to create the perfect storm. Parents away for the weekend. A full liquor cabinet and a fresh keg on tap. One of the kids said someone dropped a handful of pills into the punch. Anyone who drank the home brew is going to be sick and high. We're taking some punch that was in the living room for testing. Most of these kids are just pretty well tanked, and nature is taking things into its own hands. Lots of spontaneous vomiting and urinating in the bushes. We've got two overdoses that we're trying to stabilize and get to the hospital. A young boy and a girl. They're alive but not responsive."

"Got any names?" asked Holt.

"Just the girl over there. This is her house." The officer checked his notepad. "A Tracy McMillan. She's 17 years old. Her parents are somewhere in the Australian outback. An older sister is skiing out west for the weekend. They really trashed the house. Every piece of pool furniture and potted plants are in the pool. Sickening."

The officer pointed to two teams of EMTs huddled on the front lawn over a young girl and a guy. Holt was shocked to see what looked like two children lying on the ground. The EMTs loaded the girl onto a stretcher, holding up an IV drip and a blood pressure monitor while they whisked her into the back of an ambulance. As Holt stepped back to let them pass, he saw something clutched in the girl's left hand.

"Stop a minute," he said, taking her hand and pulling her fingers off what was an amber plastic prescription bottle.

"Her pressure's dropping," yelled one the of EMTs. "Let's go!"

Holt looked at the bottle as the ambulance doors slammed shut and they sped out of the driveway, sirens blaring and lights flashing. He turned the bottle in his hand and held it in front of the headlight of a police cruiser. The prescription for 30 Vicodin tablets had been filled at the local hospital, issued to a Nicholas Karpinski three days ago. The girl's last name was McMillan.

How did Mr. Karpinski's drugs get invited to the party?

Holt walked up to the officer in charge and handed him the prescription bottle.

"Found this in the girl's hand just as she was being loaded into the ambulance. It needs to be bagged and catalogued as evidence. Notify the EMTs in the ambulance who just left so they can alert ER and the hospital."

"Thanks, detective. Probably lifted it from a sick uncle or something. Stupid kids." The officer radioed the information.

"Seems like you've got everything under control here, officer," Holt said. "I'm going to head on over to the hospital and get the conditions of the girl and guy, see if they failed to kill themselves so I can get a statement."

"Yeah," said the uniform, shaking his head. "Controlled chaos."

Holt turned and got back into his car, pulled out his notebook, and scribbled down the name on the prescription bottle and the girl's name. He felt his phone buzzing on the passenger seat. The screen lit up with a text that had a photo attached. He tapped on the photo, taking in every inch of the nearly naked form in an alarmingly provocative pose. He tossed the phone back on the seat, leaned back, closed his eyes, and grabbed the steering wheel. This was how she was going to punish him? He took another long look.

The glare of headlights spilled through Holt's windshield as the second ambulance curved down the driveway and made its way into the street. Holt moved up behind the ambulance just as it went full sirens and lights. As it picked up speed, Holt followed close to the end of the street.

He heard his phone buzz again and glanced at yet another photo. At the end of the street, the ambulance made a left turn toward the hospital. Instead of following it, Holt turned right and floored it, fueled by excitement, lust, and an urge that would not be denied.

Get ready, Veronica, Holt thought. *I see you're still up. And now, so am I.*

72

VERONICA WAS PROBABLY still wearing her black silk teddy, waiting for him at her apartment with a glass of wine and sin on her mind. She had a creative mind, too. Like a missile fixed on its target, he sped into the dark night, headed for her place. He pulled into her parking lot, killed the engine. and felt his phone start to buzz.

"Hey, Jimmy, it's me," said Veronica. "Tonight is off. My kid brother just showed up. World War Three broke out at home between him and my mother, and he's a mess. And I had planned to be such a bad girl tonight."

Holt leaned back against the headrest and closed his eyes.

"OK. I can fill in the blanks," he said. "Later."

"Oh—Jimmy! Something you might want to know. Word is all over the hospital about some kids who overdosed at a party. Vicodin that turned out to be from a patient discharged a couple of days ago."

"Yeah," he replied. "I got a message from the hospital. The guy who overdosed is going to be alright. The girl's in ICU. What do you know about this?"

"Nothing for sure, but there have been a lot of meds missing lately. Mostly from discharged patients. Rumor is it's an inside job. Must be a fricking amateur. Who would give someone stolen meds that are still in the prescription bottle?"

"Yeah. Thanks for the tip. Take care of your little brother. I'll take care of the bad guys."

73

DAVID WOKE UP, still on the sofa, face down on a pillow. His body ached. The Oxy tablets that had dissolved in a puddle of bourbon were now dried and hardening on the glass coffee table. He didn't know how long he had been lying there, but he knew that when he could get up he was going to kill that cat.

He sat on the edge of the couch, clutching his pounding head. Then he saw it—one white tablet, only half dissolved. He picked at the pill fragment, scraping it off the table with a fingernail, and sucked it off his finger. He grabbed the bourbon bottle and took a swig, forcing the pill down his throat. He winced and leaned back against the cushions, waiting for the drug to take effect. The half-dissolved pill quickly released its magic, and he felt his body respond and the pain subsiding. After a few minutes he opened his eyes, and there she was, curled up on the coffee table, her tail wound loosely around the bourbon bottle.

"Fucking cat!"

Hannah swished her tail and sauntered slowly off the table and onto the couch.

"I'll deal with you later," David said to Hannah, as she curled up in his lap.

He stroked her back and scratched the top of her head. With his stockpile gone, David was again forced to be on the hunt. The cash was gone. The tickets—the last thing of value from the wallet—were gone. Maybe there was something he had missed in there?

David pulled himself to his feet and walked slowly into the dining room. He pulled out the phone and wallet and laid them on the table. There was still the reward for the missing phone and wallet. As if part of the plan, Hannah followed behind, moving silently from floor to chair, and sat like a sentry guarding some precious booty.

David went through every pocket of the wallet again. He pulled out the faded photos. *Worthless.*

He tossed them on the table. Then he picked up the phone and saw a string of missed calls and a voicemail. Probably the police department hoping someone would answer. He listened to the voicemail and heard a familiar voice.

"I know you've got that phone, you lousy junkie. You've held out on me for the last time. I know you've got more that you're hiding." Click.

Dewain's greed was making him careless. He'd now left two messages on Annabelle's phone.

David had first seen Annabelle that chaotic night when he sat in the seat next to her. Then he was sitting across from her as the ambulance careened through the streets to the hospital. She had been such a perfect mark. But when she went into labor and his plan failed, he almost felt protective of her, protecting her from himself and what he was planning. He felt somehow connected to her and her baby; hadn't he saved the baby's life, too? Somehow this made up for the little brother he couldn't save.

David shuddered as he recalled the images of a lifeless infant, dressed in white, lying in a tiny box. He had used the baby brother story several times to gain the sympathy and trust of his other marks, but Annabelle's obvious impending delivery gave it a different reality. Now, seeing her things on his table made it seem right that he had them. He had saved them from getting into the wrong hands.

Hannah stood up, arched her back, and leapt off the table on the track of some unseen prey beyond the dining room doorway. As she did, her paw hit the phone's screen, bringing up a photo stored in Annabelle's phone. David picked up the phone and studied Annabelle's image—a beautiful blonde with a slightly tilted smile, green eyes alive with a sexy, sassy look for whomever was snapping the photo. He swiped across, revealing more photos. Selfies with friends. A couple of sunsets. And a blond-haired man, leaning up against a sporty BMW. The kind of photos from glossy magazine ads.

He swiped a few more times when something made him stop. The man again, crouched down un the rear of the car, smiling, his hair tousled by the wind. He was pointing to the vanity license plate as if it was the best thing about the car. David had seen that license plate before. By the river and at the concert on the car parked next to him—the one Darcy had climbed into. It was as if the smiling guy was sending David a secret message. The license plate read "SOS J+A."

David dropped the phone on the table and sat down. He stared at the image. J + A? Wasn't that J + Annabelle? He stared at the man's eyes in the photo. He heard a voice inside his head "…yes, it's me. Your connection." The phone started to vibrate, blurring the photo. Was the joke on David? Or on Annabelle's husband? Was Annabelle's baby's father a drug dealer? The screen flashed "voicemail," and David clicked to retrieve the message.

"This is the Shepherdsville police department. If you are hearing this message and have this phone, you can turn it in at the precinct station for a $10,000 reward. No questions asked. Bring it in person to the officer on charge at the desk." Click.

David pondered his options. Someone really wanted this phone. And he needed money. But no questions asked? *Probably have a pair of cuffs with a note attached reading "amateur thief who believes in fairy tales" waiting behind the desk.* He would be in an orange jumpsuit quicker than a hooker sheds her G-string.

What's a $10,000 reward to the phone's owner with a steady stream of cash and a reason to keep things confidential?

Hannah jumped back up on the table, looked at the screen, turned her head, and lay down, her paw pointing to the phone.

Hannah's little acrobatics had opened a new money door.

For a fucking despicable cat, you are worth your weight in gold.

74

JAKE EASED ONTO a bar stool and ordered a double scotch, neat. This place was starting to become familiar since he had found it the night Annabelle had been rushed to the hospital. He stared into the mirror behind the bar and recalled his confrontation with Annabelle about the dark-haired little bundle that was his son. Had the wallet and phone been stolen, or was it just more of Annabelle's carelessness? He was distracted by emergencies, pulled away from work and his business. Who could deny him that little rendezvous at the Lake earlier that night to catch a concert with a special business partner and steal a little pleasure to relieve the stress of the day's drama?

"One more, Hal," said Jake, tapping the edge of the glass. He could feel the tightness in his neck loosening with each gulp—liquid fingers gently pressing the pain down and away. The second glass went down easily, moving magic hands across his shoulders and down his back.

"Steaks are good tonight," said Hal, wiping a bar rag in a slow circle on the worn oak bar top. "The cook won a couple thousand on Keno yesterday, puts him in a better than average mood. Medium rare, right?"

"Sure. I could eat. And a glass of your best cab."

The bar was emptying out. Couples lingered in a couple of booths along the wall. At the end of the bar, a middle-aged man wearing khakis, a turtleneck, and a tweed jacket was trying to hit on a couple of twenty-year-olds. He was buying, and they were happy to accept.

Two stools down, a woman in an off-the-shoulder red spandex minidress toyed with her martini, spearing an olive with a toothpick and then dropping it back. As it plopped into the glass, she turned toward Jake with a smile and a giggle, her breasts nearly dislodging from the thin edge of the plunging neckline. Jake managed a weak smile and then turned his back to her and pulled out his phone. There were some missed calls, numbers he didn't recognize. Except for one voicemail—he did a double-take, nearly dropping his phone. It was from Annabelle's old phone. He looked at it again. He had gotten Annabelle a new phone after hers went missing. The police suggested that her new phone should have a new number so the old phone would still be in service in case anyone used it to make a call.

He listened to the voicemail.

"Yeah, I'm using Annabelle's missing phone. But you don't want to call the cops. And you don't want me to call your wife, either. We have some business to take care of, and then you can get this phone back. By the way, I like your license plate 'SOS J+A.' More later."

Jake didn't recognize the voice. His mind raced over the past days. Who would put him and the license plate together? Who did he meet—talk to—over the past few days? And how did this guy get Annabelle's phone?

Jake's mind raced over the time since the phone went missing. With Annabelle in the hospital and all the drama there, he hardly had time to do anything. Nothing more than dealing with the usual clients who knew better than to try some shit like this. He had a sixth sense for stalkers—no alarms there. There was the concert with Darcy, of course, but no one was the wiser about that little arrangement.

Someone was out there putting the pieces of a Jake puzzle together, but who? What other pieces does he have? Jake felt exposed. Vulnerable. That was usually the situation he created for others, not the other way around.

He examined the few remaining customers in the bar reflected in the mirror. Suddenly they all looked suspicious with their cell phones in hand or lying on the table. One couple in a booth across from the bar was snapping selfies, their backs to him.

Jake slowly went over the facts again. Annabelle's phone and wallet went missing the night she was taken to the hospital. No one had seen either of them since. The hospital search turned up nothing. And the police hadn't heard a word about them. Who was that officer I talked to in the ER? He was supposed to look into it.

Jake searched his jacket pockets. He pulled out his wallet and fanned through the thick wad of bills and credit cards. There it was. 'Detective James Holt, Shepherdsville Police Department.' So much for follow-up. It was time for the concerned husband to check in. Holt might have some leads on this case—enough to tip off Jake so he can find this mysterious caller before the police did.

75

AFTER ROGER LEFT the baby blanket wrapped in a package marked "Confidential" in the hands of Jonas' executive assistant, he headed home. In for the night, he turned the lock on the carved wooden front door and threw his keys and phone in the oyster dish on the entry-hall table. The living room was empty. Down the long hallway he could see a sliver of light from under the closed guest bedroom door. Sharon probably had another one of her convenient headaches, Roger mused.

He stopped and imagined a future scenario—walking in the door on a Friday evening to the sound of laughter. His wife Sharon and son Charlie sitting on the floor together in the living room, building blocks and stuffed animals strewn on the carpet, the two lost in play and each other. His weekend with Charlie. *Our* weekend with Charlie. Jonas would deliver the DNA results soon, and Roger could begin to convince Sharon to help him make this fantasy a reality.

He grabbed the remote on the way into the kitchen and poured his usual two fingers of scotch to help him unwind and tolerate the evening news. He flipped through the channels, finally turned off the television, and threw the remote on the Italian leather loveseat. He refreshed his glass and grabbed his phone on the way up the stairs when he saw a message light up the screen—a text from Jonas Dirkfield. *Call me.*

He tapped on Jonas's number and waited through several rings.

"Just saw your text, man. What's up?" said Roger.

"Roger, this isn't a rush job, is it?"

Roger let out a laugh. "Easy, Jonas. Not that kind of rush. And the fewer questions the better, remember? Thanks, man."

"One thing," said Jonas. "The material on the blanket wasn't sufficient to test, but we found a few strands of hair clinging to the blanket fibers. Lucky find."

"Thanks, Jonas."

Roger took a long swallow and let the scotch burn slowly down his throat. Was luck turning his way? There was no rush. He needed time to plan the big reveal to Annabelle, figure out how to convince Sharon she's going to be a mother after all, and maybe start setting up the nursery.

76

HOLT PULLED INTO the emergency-room lane and squeezed his car between two ambulances idling near the entrance. He got out and held up his badge, bypassing security, and threaded his way through the tangle of humanity, heading for the admissions desk.

The admissions nurse looked up at the badge he held out.

"Detective Holt. I'm looking for two teenage drug overdose victims—a male and female brought in tonight. Overdoses from a party."

"The paramedics said you were following them here from the scene," said the nurse, punching keys while blankly studying Holt. "That was an hour ago."

"Oh—I got sidetracked by an emergency call." A delicious image flashed across his mind and then quickly faded.

What's the status, and do you have room numbers?"

"The young man is pretty out of it—responsive but not talking," the nurse read from the screen. "The girl, I'm afraid, is unresponsive. They worked pretty hard on her when she came in, and just put her in ICU on the sixth floor. Talk to Dr. Ramos in room eleven, triage; he was the attending physician when they came in."

"Thanks, you've been very helpful," said Holt putting on a concerned look. He found the triage room empty except for a tall young man in a lab coat writing on a clipboard amid a crush of equipment strewn about, circling an empty bed.

"Dr. Ramos?" asked Holt.

"Yeah, that's what my coat says." Dr. Ramos sighed and finished his entry as he slowly sank down onto the edge of the ICU bed. He scanned the badge in Holt's outstretched hand. "Sorry, detective. Busy night. What can I help you with?"

"I was told at the desk that you worked on the teenage girl and guy that came in about an hour ago? Overdoses? I was called to the scene and hope you can give me some information. They were the worst of the casualties from that party. Any idea what they took?"

Ramos picked up the clipboard and looked through his notes.

"Toxicology isn't back yet, but from the looks of them, some pretty heavy stuff. The young guy threw up most of what he took in the ambulance and triage. The EMTs said the girl was found holding an empty prescription bottle for thirty Vicodin. She was unresponsive—the EMTs administered CPR and injected naloxone enroute. We continued CPR until she stabilized and put her on a ventilator. She's in ICU. Her parents are somewhere in Australia. Her older sister is en route."

"And the guy?"

"Tomas Johnson. He's pretty trashed but will be OK; he's under observation. He's awake, but not talking. Parents came in about half an hour ago. They are in the cafeteria, so he's solo at the moment. That's all I know until the toxicology report comes back. Third overdose incident this week. Stupid kids. Both of them were transferred to ICU on six."

"Thanks, doc" said Holt, as he headed for the elevator and the ICU.

On the ICU floor the charge nurse positioned herself between him and the corridor to the girl's room. "I'm not letting you back there, Holt. You have no compassion. Always asking questions with that disgusting fake-worried face. You won't get anywhere near her tonight."

"So, you think she'll make it through the night?"

"Nice try." The nurse pantomimed locking her lips. "Tighter than an old maid's corset. Now crawl back in that elevator and find someone else to harass."

77

ON HIS WAY out of the ICU, Holt recognized one of the EMTs who had been at the party scene and called out to him. "Hey, got a minute? Weren't you at the scene where the kids overdosed tonight?"

"Yeah, some pretty scary shit. They got you working teenage mayhem these days, detective? It's been a busy week. Drug overdoses, accidents, woman going into labor on a bus. Better than cable."

"Yeah, I hear you," Holt shook his head ruefully. "Wait—a woman going into labor on a bus?"

"That's right. My partner and I got a call from a bus driver at the end of the Market Square line a couple of nights ago. Never heard so much screaming. She passed out in the ambulance. Blessed peace!"

"The woman. Was she alone?"

"No, the bus driver had this young guy ride with her to the hospital. Don't know who he was. Didn't say a thing. Just sat in the back of the ambulance."

"A young guy, you said? Wearing a blazer with a crest on it?"

"Yeah, and a Ravens hat. You know, the Baltimore Ravens. Pulled over his eyes. When we got to emergency we lost track of him. Sort of disappeared. Do you know who he was?"

"No, but I'd like to," said Holt. "But no one seems to know anything about him. No one got a good look at him. I hear the hospital installed a first-class surveillance system recently."

"Got them everywhere. Inside and out. Gets us coming and going—'Smile, you're on Candid Camera'—my grandmother watched reruns of that. Practically swallowed her dentures from laughing so hard."

"The videos. Know where can I get them?"

"Security office, second floor. Pretty boring stuff." The EMT's shoulder walkie talkie went off, cutting their conversation short. "Got to go, detective. Three-car collision on West Elm Street. Going to be a busy night."

Holt headed home. He would be spending some time watching movies tomorrow.

76

HOLT MADE IT back to the hospital early the next day, groggy after too few hours of sleep. He boarded the elevator and got out on the sixth floor ICU. It was quiet at this hour, with the beep of monitors playing a soft symphony against muted voices. He stopped a few feet from the elevator doors and saw the charge nurse looking over some files.

As he looked down the long line of ICU pods, a door at the far end opened. A tall, slim woman emerged and slowly closed the door. She walked up the hallway to the nurses' station, a hand raised up to wipe what Holt supposed was a tear from her eye.

She spoke softly to the charge nurse, who patted her arm. The nurse then walked down the same hallway the woman had come from. The tall woman walked toward the elevator, her long black hair flowing loosely over her shoulders.

Holt remembered Dr. Ramos' comments about the female victim having a sister. *He didn't say anything about a beautiful sister,* thought Holt.

She stopped in front of the elevator and reached out a manicured finger, silver bangles jingling, and punched the down arrow. Holt walked up behind her just as the elevator came to a stop.

"Excuse, me, ma'am," Holt said, pulling his badge out from his pocket. "I'm Detective Holt, and I was called last night to the scene of a party out on the west side. I've come to the hospital to check on two of the young people who were transported with possible drug overdoses. Last night the ER doctor told me that the young girl was in ICU, and I just saw you coming out of her room. Do you know her? The faster we move on these cases the more likely we are to get valuable information that can get dealers off the streets. This may sound insensitive, and I don't mean to upset you, but could I ask you a few questions?"

"Detective Holt, is it? That young girl is my sister. Is she in trouble?" said the woman.

"No one is in trouble, ma'am. We're just trying to piece together what happened."

"I'm Bianca, Bianca Hawkins, detective. I'm her sister. Our parents don't know anything about this. They are somewhere in the Australian outback. I just can't take the sound of those machines and seeing my sister lying there so still. I had to get out of there, for just a moment."

The elevator doors slid open.

"I'm so sorry, Ms. Hawkins. I know this is a terrible time. Can I get you something at the coffee shop on the first floor? We can talk there. Just a few moments of your time."

Bianca nodded as Holt nudged her gently into the elevator just as the charge nurse came from behind the desk, glaring. Holt flashed her a smile as the doors closed.

In the coffee shop, Holt set down two cups of steaming coffee on the well-worn table and pulled out a chair. "First, let me say I know this must be very difficult for you and your family," said Holt. "I don't want to add to your troubles. We don't have a lot of information about what happened, and anything you can share might be helpful. I'd like to ask just some preliminaries, first. Can you tell me your sister's name?"

"Tracy—Tracy McMillen. She's just seventeen. Headstrong and wild. We're very close, despite her age. We talk or text almost every day. She's had a time with that boyfriend of hers. I don't trust him."

"The doctor said his name was Tomas Johnson."

"Yes, that's him," said Bianca, taking a sip of coffee. "I don't know him well, except what I hear from Tracy. My parents don't like him either; they banned him from the house. Tracy likes to come to my condo and hang out there. Tomas would show up, and the two of them would disappear together. God knows where they went or what they were doing. There is always alcohol in the house, and we all like to party. But drugs? I'd like to know how she got them."

"Well, Ms. Hawkins, so would we."

"Please, it's Bianca, Detective Holt. I left for a ski trip in Utah two days ago. We were catching the last of the snow at the high elevations when my boyfriend wrapped himself around a tree and had to be airlifted back home. I caught the red-eye last night and pulled up to my parents' house just as the last police car was leaving. They told me what happened, and I came straight here. I couldn't even see her until this morning when she was in a room in the ICU."

Bianca gripped the coffee container so hard it splashed onto the table.

"Have you ever heard the name Nicolas Karpinski?" asked Holt, wiping away the coffee spill. "Is he a relative or family friend?"

"Nicolas Karpinski? No—never heard that name. Why do you ask? Was he at the party? Is that where the drugs came from?"

"An empty prescription bottle was found at the scene. It was issued to a Nicholas Karpinski two days ago at this hospital. Thirty Vicodin, prescribed for pain. Are you sure you haven't heard of him?"

Bianca stared at Holt, eyes wide in pain and disbelief, and shook her head. "No! I can't get my head around all this.

Tracy is smart and determined. She's graduating with honors this year. She's doing her community service requirement at this very hospital, putting in her hours every week. She complained about sorting sheets in a laundry storage room, but she can be responsible."

Anger washed across Bianca's face. "Did this Karpinski guy give those kids drugs? I'd like to ask him a few questions, detective. I'd like to rip his heart out with my bare hands. My sister is fighting for her life." Bianca put her head in her hands and began to sob. "I have to go. I have to get back to Tracy."

Holt patted her arm. "We're going to find out what happened, Bianca. You've been very helpful." He pulled out a card and slid it across the table. "Please call me if you remember anything that might help in our investigation. Anything at all."

Bianca picked up the card.

"Thanks, detective," she said, a tear making its way over a perfect cheekbone to the curve of her mouth.

Bianca stood and walked toward the elevators. Holt took a deep breath.

This is business, Jimmy. Let this one go.

79

HOLT WATCHED AS Bianca disappeared behind the elevator doors, then took the stairs up to the sixth floor. As he rounded the corner at the third-floor landing, he nearly collided with Dewain barreling through the third-floor stairway door.

"Whoa!" Dewain hooted, nearly knocking Holt off his feet. "Where are you going in such a rush, detective? Someone chasing you? Bad guys after you for a change?"

Dewain laughed and peered over Holt's shoulder, down the disappearing staircase.

Holt steadied himself and took a deep breath. "Well, if it isn't junior Deputy Dewain. I could ask you the same question. Lurking around the back stairs?"

"Taking the stairs is good for the heart and the calves. What brings you to the back of the house today? Still looking for that nice lady's phone and wallet? Cracked that case yet, detec-tive?" Dewain said with a grin, emphasizing each syllable.

Holt studied Dewain who stood with his arms folded, rocking on his heels, head tilted in a half-mocking, half-defiant stance. His mouth curved in a smirk while his eyes stared straight at Holt. Holt felt a chill standing close to Dewain on the narrow landing between two flights of stairs with the only exit around Dewain and through the heavy steel door to the third floor hallway.

Holt moved forward, forcing Dewain to drop his smirk and move back and away from the door.

No matter how good the bad guys are, they always make a mistake.

"No one is chasing me, Dewain," said Holt, leaning forward. "I'm on the hunt for drugs. Vicodin, to be specific. Seems some teens threw a party and mixed booze with Vicodin—thirty tablets to be exact—from this hospital. Sweet young girl is fighting for her life at this moment. Somehow those pills got from a patient discharged from this hospital and were dumped into a dangerous cocktail ingested by about forty teenagers. Two ended up here last night."

Holt paused, but Dewain didn't blink. If he knew anything, he wasn't letting on. He either didn't know anything or was just that good.

Holt went on. "Nice girl from a nice family. She was doing her senior-year community service here, sorting laundry in a storage room. We're going to find out how this happened."

And there it was. Holt detected just a slight narrowing of the eyes. A couple of rapid blinks. Something registered that made Dewain flinch just a bit, and Holt saw it. He needed to keep Dewain close so he could figure this out.

"Drugs are terrible, detective. I tell my little brother all the time—be clean, stay straight. Drugs will kill you. The girl—is she going to make it?"

"Don't know, Dewain. She's in ICU and fighting."

Holt sensed Dewain's focus was drifting. To the girl alone in the ICU?

"So, do you have an assignment for me, detective?"

Holt pulled a card out of his pocket and pressed it into Dewain's hand. "If you hear anything about drugs going missing around here, let me know. These things happen sometimes in hospitals. Usually there's a pattern; it's not just a one-time thing. You're the eyes and ears around here, Dewain. Give me a call if something comes up."

"Yeah, sure, Detective," replied Dewain. "Now watch your speed on these stairs, or Deputy Dewain will have to give you a ticket."

He started down the stairs, turned at the stair landing, and pointed at Holt, his hand a three-finger pistol, and took a shot.

Later, detective. Dewain is on it.

60

HOLT PUSHED OPEN the door on the sixth floor. The last two flights of stairs left him a little winded. He needed to lay off the booze and hit the gym again.

The door to Tomas's room was open slightly. Holt could see that he was alone.

Holt knocked on the door and heard a faint, childlike voice say, "Come in."

Tomas Johnson's voice didn't match the tall, muscular guy lying in the bed. Holt could see that under his scraggly beard, Tomas's face was still a little green and puffy.

"Oh, I thought you were my parents. Who the hell are you?" Now the voice matched the body—deeper and stronger with a tinge of defiance.

"Detective Holt, Fifth Precinct," said Holt, waving his badge. "I'm investigating a party last night held at Tracy McMillan's house. I saw the EMTs working on you at the scene. From what I saw, you're lucky to be here talking to me. I just talked to Tracy's sister, and Tracy's not so lucky."

"Tracy!" Tomas tried to sit up, then fell back again. "My head is about to explode. Where's that nurse?" He jammed the call button in his left hand. "What about Tracy? Is she going to be alright?"

"She's on a ventilator in ICU. What can you tell me about the party? Where did the drugs come from?"

Tomas groaned.

"Is Tracy your girlfriend?"

"No, man. We hang out, do stuff. Her parents don't like me. You know, not her 'kind.' Tracy's cool. She's fun, not like the girls in her crowd—those rich, stuck-up princesses. She likes crossing over the line."

"So, she's a good girl who likes to be bad? Where did the pills come from? They found a prescription bottle for thirty Vicodin at the scene. What do you know about that?"

"Why should I tell you anything?" The defiant tone was back. "Am I in trouble? I was just there. Do I need a lawyer? My parents are coming back from the cafeteria any minute. They think I got food poisoning."

"Look," said Holt. "I don't care about your love life or Tracy's need for thrills. And you're not in trouble unless you're withholding information. If you know where the Vicodin came from and who brought them, I suggest you tell me before we're having a bigger discussion with your parents."

"Shit." Tomas considered his next move. "OK. Tracy brought them."

"She bought them?" asked Holt. "From whom?"

"No. Listen. She *brought* them. She found them at the hospital—this hospital. She was doing her community service—sorting sheets or something in one of the storage rooms, and this bottle fell out —Vicodin. She called me and said she was bringing a guest to the party. I didn't know she meant that shit. I warned her—that's some heavy stuff."

"How did the drugs get into so many of the guests?"

Tomas continued. "There was a lot of booze in the house. The more we drank, the more she kept going on about the pills. So we mixed up some beer and booze, and she tossed most of the pills in. Word got out, and everyone was doing shots of the stuff.

"We were in the kitchen. Tracy poured some of the mix into a cocktail shaker and went out to the pool. She still had the prescription bottle in her hand and popped the last pill and washed it down with a shot. I was feeling sick, and I guess I passed out then.

"Someone must have called the cops about the noise or something. I remember being in an ambulance and the smell of puke. The EMTs said I brought up most of what I took. Made a mess of the ambulance. Next thing I remember is waking up here with my parents standing next to me. That's all I know. God! Tracy! Her parents are in Australia or something. They're going to fucking kill me when they find out I was there, if my parents don't do it first."

Holt looked up from scribbling in his notebook.

"Well, you did good here, Tomas. Thanks, I'll follow up on this. And don't worry, you're not in trouble. Between the drugs in your body and your parents, I think you'll have enough trouble for a while."

61

DEWAIN WATCHED AS Holt disappeared up into the dimly lit stairwell. He had no sympathy for stupid kids who couldn't handle drugs. Besides, he had his standards. Didn't deal with high school kids. Kids have parents or uncles or family friends who are lawyers and law enforcement, and they get a thirst for blood when something happens to their innocent little darlings.

Somehow the teen druggie had been in the hospital laundry storage room. The third-floor storage room held the soiled, ripped, and otherwise unusable linens. It was also the perfect layover spot for Dewain's drugs—from a discharged patient and later to an eager customer. As far as he knew, no one else went in there. He had a sweet little business going and didn't need an outsider disturbing his little empire now. *Yeah, Dewain is on it, detective.*

Dewain walked back through the exit door and headed for the elevator and the ICU. As he walked, he heard a nurse call out his name.

"Dewain, I need you to go to Room 385 in a few minutes and take Mr. Williams downstairs. He's being discharged." She pulled up the discharge list and found his name.

"Mr. Antwon Williams, seventy-nine, came in three days ago for gall bladder surgery. You have to make a stop at the pharmacy for his meds. There will be a taxi waiting for him outside the main entrance. No family, poor guy."

"My pleasure, ma'am. I'm here to serve." The nurse rolled her eyes and wrote Dewain's name next to Mr. Williams' name on the sheet.

"Be gentle," she added. "He's had a rough time."

Gall-bladder surgery. Lots of referred pain. And Mr. Williams was all alone. No one to get in the way of relieving Mr. Williams of some of those meds. He probably wouldn't remember to take them anyway. Or might take too many. *It's for the best.*

It was easy. The poor guy was lost in a fog and didn't even notice as Dewain slipped the bottle of Percocet into the pocket of his scrubs. He wheeled Mr. Williams out the door and helped him into the cab.

"Here you go, Mr. Williams," said Dewain as he put a bag with the rest of the meds in his lap. "You're all set."

Now, how to get close to a sick little girl in ICU?

62

THE INTENSIVE CARE Unit was a tough place to go unde-
tected. Dewain traversed every floor of the hospital during
his shift, planning his route and cover story for a trip to the
sixth floor that night. He checked the work sheet to see who
was assigned to the ICU that night and who might need a
break from trucking supplies to the sixth floor. He ran down
the roster until he saw "Wesley Anderson." Ah, Wesley, a lazy
SOB. He was always looking for a way to sneak out back for
a smoke and a nip. Dewain could come to his rescue.

Wesley was holding court in the staff lounge on the fourth
floor with a couple of nurses and a new orderly. Dewain
strolled in and bent down next to the newcomer's ear and
spoke loud enough for all to hear.

"Watch out who you take advice from, Dude," he said with
a smile, staring at Wesley. "This one's liable to get you in a
shitload of trouble."

The orderly looked up at Dewain, "It's Burt," he said as he
stood, unfolding his six-foot-one-inch frame.

Dewain looked up at Burt and held up the palm of his
three-fingered hand.

"Whoa, Burt. My mistake. Easy big guy. Don't mean to
interrupt your little party here."

"What you doin' here, Dewain?" said Wesley with a faked
concern look. "Thought you were on day shift."

"Now, *this* is the one you really need to look out for, Burt," Wesley said, pointing to Dewain. "Don't tell me you were a bad boy, Dewain, and got knocked up—as we say—to second shift?"

"No, my man. I'm solid. Just getting a few extra hours in. Anything I need to know about our guests in ICU?"

Wesley straightened up in his chair, lost his smile, and looked straight ahead. He was a preacher's son and had mastered the art of clearing the throat, leaning forward like he was leaning on a pulpit, and taking a deliberate pause. When he had everyone's attention, he cleared his throat again.

"It's quiet all right. They brought in a young girl from a house party on the west side. Overdose—Vicodin, alcohol, and who knows what else. Cops brought her in. May still be up there.

"That little girl took some heavy shit. It was so bad she stopped breathing. The respirator bells and whistles went off a couple of times, so they shot her full of lorazepam, and now she's in a coma. No family here except an older sister. Word is going around that the drugs came from this hospital, a patient discharged a couple of days ago—Karpinski."

The room was quiet. All eyes were on Wesley.

Dewain broke the silence.

"Heavy shit, Wes. Was Karpinski her uncle or something? Kids will do anything to get their hands on drugs—even stealing them from some sick old relative."

"Don't know about that," said Wesley. "I do know she was working in the third-floor laundry-storage room. High school community service; Joe from maintenance got her set up yesterday. Only that girl knows how she got them, and she's not talking— yet."

Dewain knew that Karpinski was the old guy with colon cancer he had wheeled out a week ago. The third-floor storage room was his safe waystation for pilfered drugs. And now it had been breached by an adventurous teenage girl who happened to pick door number three for the big jackpot. What does she know? What does Joe know? He closed his eyes, let the pinball drop through the levers, and took a deep, silent breath.

"That's some heavy shit, Wesley," said Dewain in his best shocked-yet-concerned voice. "Poor kid. Let's hope for the best. What a day to volunteer for ICU. I was looking forward to a few slow, quiet hours and some extra cash."

"Well, if that's the case, I'll put you to work," Wesley offered. "I'm supposed to take the supply cart from the third floor up to ICU. But I'm kinda busy here right now orienting this young man and informing and consoling the ladies. That's me—master multi-tasker."

The nurses rolled their eyes and stood to leave. "Master bullshitter is more like it," one said, and they all laughed. "Later, Wes."

"No problem, man. I got you covered, Wes," said Dewain as he followed the nurses. "No problem at all."

He took the stairs down to the third floor. The hallway was deserted. He unlocked the laundry-room door and closed the door behind him.

Dewain ran his hand through the stack of yellowed sheets piled on the rack in the back corner of the room. He wrapped his hand around a small vial of insulin and put it in his pocket, satisfied. Lights out, he cracked the door and scanned the hallway. All clear. He heard the door lock shut behind him as he turned and disappeared through the exit door, headed for the ICU.

63

DEWAIN FOUND A supply cart and headed up to the ICU. The elevator stopped at each floor, loading and unloading passengers at each stop. He moved farther back in the elevator at each stop, studying the faces of oncoming passengers and avoiding eye contact with hospital personnel. No need for someone to recognize him.

The nurse's station was deserted when he got off the elevator. The waiting room was quiet, with just a few family members huddled together on uncomfortable chairs at the far end of the lounge area. Perfect.

The ICU was a series of glass-enclosed pods that formed a circle around the nurses' station. The lights in the pods were low, peppered by the red and blue steady flashes of monitors that cast an eerie glow through the white curtains between the beds in the pods. Most of the curtains were drawn back, giving the nurses in the station a clear view of the patients and the monitors. Lines were attached to the patients like vines, their tendrils holding fast to the motionless bodies. Doctors, PCAs, and nurses moved quietly between the pods, whispering softly, taking vitals, and making notes.

Dewain wheeled the cart around the circle, keeping his head down to avoid the cameras and straining to read the names on the pods from the corner of his eye. He was halfway around when a glass door opened at the end of the semicircle directly behind the nurses' station. The curtains in this pod were drawn, revealing only shadows inside. Then a uniformed police officer and a woman with long black hair came out of the room and walked past him. He waited until they had disappeared into the elevator and moved the cart in position beside the pod's door. *Tracy McMillan.*

The glass door was slightly ajar. He could hear the cadence of the respirator and the slow and measured beeps from other monitors as they dutifully kept the young patient alive.

As he reached to push the door open, he heard the wailing of an alarm. Flashing lights above a door near the front of the nurse's station kept time to the repeated blare of the alarm. In an instant, nurses and doctors swarmed into the pod, working on the patient in a well-orchestrated routine that looked more like a back-alley assault as they forcefully attempted to stabilize the patient.

Dewain loved it when a plan came together. A code blue provided the perfect cover for the next thirty minutes or so. He slipped on a pair of latex gloves, the two empty fingers on his hand flopping like puppets in a macabre play. He pulled a syringe from the supply cart, cupped his palm around it, and slipped quietly into the pod.

She looked small in the bed as wires and tubes fed her and drained her bodily fluids at the same time. The respirator pumped air into her resistant lungs, forcing life into the body she had almost destroyed. Dewain could see the flashing lights still going strong a few pods down. He filled the syringe with insulin and studied the still form.

"You thought you were lucky, finding all those Vics in the storage room," he whispered to the lifeless form. "Bad girl, taking Mr. Karpinski's drugs from the storage room. Look what you've done to yourself. Actions have consequences, little girl."

He found the line to the saline drip, pierced it with the thin syringe needle, and pushed the plunger. Then he opened the line, sending the insulin into her vein, on the way to her heart.

Dewain put the vial and syringe into his pocket and slipped out the door. It wouldn't take long, and he didn't want to be pulled into the code trying to keep her alive.

The alarms suddenly went silent. He could see the shadows of personnel still huddled around the patient, absorbed in the experience of pulling yet another patient from the jaws of death.

He grabbed the cart and parked it next to the still-deserted nurses' station, continued walking the circle to the stairs, and slipped out. From the other side of the door, he heard sirens sound again and feet pounding their way to Tracy's ICU pod.

Yes, little girl, actions have consequences. You put Dewain in danger, and that's never a good move.

He slipped off the gloves, shoved them in his pocket, and headed down the stairs, making his way to the back entrance to the loading dock. On the way, he pulled a red biohazard bag from a first-aid station and shoved the syringe, vial, and gloves inside. He threw the bag into one of the red barrels with the black biohazard icon next to the refuse piled up for removal, slipped out the door, and disappeared into the alley.

64

SOPHIA READ THE note attached to an envelope marked confidential. "*Sophia, here's the drill. Rush. Top secret. Total confidentiality. Results go to me only, hand delivered. Thanks, Jonas.*"

Another rush from Jonas? OK, which of his wayward friends was in trouble?

Sophia had come to Dirkfield Labs after working for independent labs, mostly testing employees for drug use and forensic samples. Jonas, her boss, had been CEO of a startup company on the cutting edge of home DNA testing kits. After that startup had been acquired by a pharmaceutical manufacturer, he formed a new corporation focused on the next wave of genetic testing.

Sophia had met Jonas while he was working at his first startup before the acquisition had been finalized. She demanded the highest standards of quality and accuracy; as his business grew, he persuaded her to run his labs.

Sophia walked the envelope down to the lab. It was closing in on five-thirty, and the lab was empty. In her element, she opened the envelope and prepared the dried substance and hair samples for testing. Rush? Jonas knows it can take three days for results, even if the sample is perfect and the procedure is flawless.

Sophia knew not to ask questions. She prepared the paperwork, marked it "Confidential," and directed that the results be sent to her alone. She slipped the samples and paperwork into a lab-processing envelope and she stamped the outside of the envelope "Priority/Rush."

It was now close to six-thirty. The rest of the lab was lit by the glow of the monitors on desktops and the lab equipment that were silently analyzing data and DNA samples and churning out reports that would revealed tomorrow's secrets for good or ill.

She turned out the office lights and put the lab envelope on her assistant's desk along with a note telling her to process it first thing. She headed out for a late drink with an attractive professional she had selected on Bumble. If he were her guy, he would be waiting for her at a small, corner table away from the bar. And if he had read her profile description of her perfect date, a Grey Goose dirty martini with four skewered olives would be waiting for her.

65

DESPITE THREE CUPS of coffee, David's brain was still fuzzy. He could feel the ache of withdrawal in his arms and legs, radiating out from his joints, setting him on fire.

He went over the plan in his mind. First, a call from Annabelle's phone to her dealer husband demanding $25,000 and thirty Oxys. If he refused to cooperate, David threatened to send a note to the cops and Annabelle about her husband's little drug business.

Surely the husband wouldn't be stupid enough to call the cops. If he resisted, there was the evidence David had about the little evening out with Darcy in the front seat of the BMW; he was sure Annabelle would love to hear about that. Her husband would pay whatever he asked to protect his lovely wife and new baby.

David knew that dealers like him would have lots of customers; maybe he wouldn't suspect the guy who took the wallet and phone off the bus. Just a lucky junkie customer who hit the jackpot and found this phone. Could be anyone.

He found the slip of paper with the number that Darcy had given him days ago and punched in the numbers on Annabelle's phone. The screen lit up with the number and "Jake." Ah, now he had a name. Jake. J+A. The phone rang and rang, and then a snarling voice answered.

"Who is this? How did you get this phone?"

David's hands shook, and he could feel drops of sweat pooling above his eyebrow and trickling down his face. He took a deep breath, closed his eyes, and spoke in a slow, measured voice.

"Listen good. If you don't want your wife to know about your dirty little side business dealing drugs or your other women, put $25,000 and thirty Oxys in a manilla envelope and leave them in the back of the trash can behind the old maintenance building at Henry Street and Lewis Drive at ten tonight. No cops. Just leave the envelope and then drive to the boat launch under the bridge. Wait thirty minutes and not a minute less. You'll be watched. Then go back to the trash can. You'll find the phone in a plastic trash bag in the same place. This is the only message you'll get. Don't be late, and don't get creative, Jake."

"Who the fuck is this?" The man's voice escalated in anger. "You think you can squeeze me for money? You don't know who you're dealing with."

"I know more than you think. About your drug-dealing. And your late-night hook-ups with a well-known financial CEO. You wouldn't want your pretty wife to know what her cheating, low-life husband has been up to, do you? Don't fuck this up, Jake. Bring $25,000 and 39 Oxys—that's a small price to pay. Ten o'clock—be there."

A jolt of pain shot through David's fingers as he pushed the red dot on the screen. He walked back into the living room, used the blade from his pocket knife to scrape the sticky lumps of dissolved Oxys off the glass coffee table, and then licked the blade. One hour, and his torment would be over. He scraped again, licking the blade clean, ignoring strands of Hannah's fur embedded in the gooey mess.

One more thing. David deleted his calls from the stolen phone. He slipped on a pair of rubber kitchen gloves, sprayed a paper towel with window cleaner, and wiped the phone over and over, cleaning any prints he may have left. He pulled a manilla envelope from the kitchen drawer, dropped the phone inside, and then put the envelope into a plastic trash bag and taped it shut. Only 40 more minutes. He had just enough time to get to his observation spot across from the crumbling building.

66

JAKE THREW HIS phone onto the counter, went into the garage, pulled down the retractable staircase to the attic, and climbed up into the darkness. The attic was piled with boxes full of Annabelle's grandmother's Wedgewood china, Christmas decorations, and photo albums. Jake threaded his way through the matrix to the back corner and a worn, faded cedar chest filled with old metal toy soldiers.

His father had been a Marine who collected vintage battle memorabilia, including a full complement of miniature Confederate and Union soldiers, complete with weapons, horses, and tents, to recreate Civil War battles. Jake could remember the elaborate staging of the battle of Gettysburg on the ping-pong table in the basement and his father rearranging each piece with battle-ready precision. The basement smelled of the potting soil spread on the table, mounded up for hills, scooped out for valleys. The scent of pine and oak hovered over the miniature landscape from freshly cut twigs and pine branches that formed wood lines, forests, and brush.

Jake had inherited the collection after his father's funeral. Jake had been estranged from his father ever since he had turned down a commission to West Point and a military career. His father's cedar chest arrived one day with a note from his father's lawyer that said this was the only thing he was going to get from his father's estate.

Jake had never been interested in playing soldier, not as a boy or as a man, and he didn't intend to keep his father's final attempt to shame him for what his father considered disgracing the family and his country. As soon as it had arrived, Jake had hauled the trunk out into the street at the end of the driveway, hoping someone would take it in the middle of the night. Annabelle had been shocked to find the fine steamer trunk in the gutter and begged him to bring it back. The vintage metal toy soldiers were collectors' items, she argued, maybe worth a fortune. At least have them appraised.

So the trunk with its military cargo made it back to the garage that night, and it had followed them from place to place ever since. When they decided to make the move to Shepherdsville, the movers wanted an extra fee to haul the heavy trunk into the attic. He hated the sight of it as it mocked him in his father's voice. It was an intermittent reminder, as he moved from place to place and job to job, of his father's prediction that he would always be searching for what he had thrown away—a chance for an honorable life of service to God and country and a nice military pension.

The night before the movers arrived for the move to Shepherdsville, Jake found the yellowed envelope from the attorney so many years ago. He pulled out the folded letter and held the envelope upside down. A tarnished brass key with a faded blue ribbon attached had fallen out onto the table. The ribbon had certainly been his mother's touch, an attempt to soften the hard, razor-sharp corners of her sober and stoic husband. If he had to keep this cursed trunk, at least now he could get rid of the damned, heavy soldiers inside.

Jake pulled a trash bag from a roll in the kitchen and headed into the attic. The bare bulb cast shadows to the far corners of the space that took on grotesque shapes. The trunk beckoned him from the back corner. He slipped the key from his pocket and forced it into the lock. After years of damp, dusty storage, the lock resisted the intrusion until it finally gave up. Jake snapped the lock open and lifted the lid.

In the low light, the soldiers looked like they were engaged in a self-destructive battle; tiny rifles and bayonets pressed against metal flesh and uniformed limbs in a chaotic, frantic charge. They had settled in a mound, jostled from years of moving.

"Glad to see you're still on duty," Jake said to the tangled mass.

He started pulling handfuls of soldiers out of the trunk and into the plastic bag. The appraiser said they were impressive but hardly valuable, cast at a time when every little boy his father's age had large sets of toy soldiers.

"Oh, we can keep them for our little boy, someday," whispered Annabelle, as she examined one fierce-looking blue-coated soldier, rifle held high, bayonet pointed down to the ground as if poised above a gray-coated enemy.

Our little boy ... Jake couldn't think of that now.

When most of the soldiers had been transferred, he saw it. A small fold of tape protruding from what looked like the bottom seam of the chest lining. He cleared out the remaining soldiers and fitted his index finger through the loop. He felt his heart jump, just as it had the first time he found it and discovered the real value of his father's legacy.

The appraiser he contacted had said he was interested in the chest but agreed to look at the toy soldiers. Jake had found the key to the trunk, grabbed a bag, and transferred the soldiers to the bag, much as he did this night. As he cleared out the chest, one of the soldiers' arms caught the ribbon loop at the bottom and held fast. Jake had given it a hard pull and lifted what appeared to be the bottom of the chest. The final sentry guarding the secret succumbed to pressure, revealing row upon row of $20, $50, and $100 dollar bills bound neatly with discolored rubber bands, stock certificates bearing Jake's name, and several bank-deposit books, wrapped in his father's marine parade sash. A note in his father's hand atop the treasure read:

Jake—So you finally found it. I always thought you were a lazy, frivolous boy, and would squander whatever was handed to you. You never cared about what was important to me, and probably looked at the soldiers and shut this trunk cursing your cheap meaningless inheritance and your cruel and heartless father. I wanted you to work at this. Be curious and figure it out. Stop thinking you're a powerless victim. Well, here it is. Finally, do something with your life that is honorable and true and right.

And, if this isn't my son Jake reading this note, you are one lucky bastard. You probably bought this trunk at a yard sale for $50, or found it discarded at the dump. Enjoy your good fortune.

Jake pulled the false bottom up and placed it on the floor. The contents had dwindled since he had first discovered it. Dad's secret gift, once revealed, paid for the luxury houses and funded Jake's fledgling financial business, the cars, the trips. Annabelle didn't care how things happened. She was happy to be driving a new Mercedes to the country club for lunch with her friends, discussing their next trip or what celebrities they had met at the charity fundraiser or the trip to Las Vegas.

Over the years, Jake had cashed in some of the stock certificates. He had immediately transferred the bank accounts to a private account in his name only. Most of the cash was still there. He never counted it—the thick packs of bills lying three deep across the bottom of the chest, silently keeping their secrets. Where did the money come from? Jake didn't really care. The note hadn't been signed "Love, Dad."

Jake lifted a banded bundle of bills and started counting. When he had a stack equalling $25,000, he pulled the rubber band back over the rest of the stack and placed it into the chest. He carefully lowered the false bottom into the chest with the ribbon flap. He grabbed the bag of soldiers and dumped them back into the chest, locked it tight, and shoved it back into the corner under the eaves replacing the boxes that had been stacked on top. He headed down the stairs, clutching the $25,000.

Jake went out to the garage and opened the trunk of the BMW. He lifted the cover to the spare tire well, removed two plastic bags, and took them into the house. Silence wasn't cheap. His blackmailer wanted $25k and thirty Oxys. The guy was a junkie, but not stupid.

He went back into the kitchen and split the bills into two stacks. He opened one of the bags, put the Oxy tablets into a plastic baggie, and pulled two manilla envelopes from a pile in his office. He counted out ten $20 bills from the stack from the attic chest and put them aside. He then made two stacks of the remaining bills and placed them side by side into the first envelope along with the plastic baggie of pills and folded the flap down without sealing it. Jake flattened the envelope to measure the height of the bills and the shape of the envelope around the pills.

He then grabbed a stack of newspapers from the entry hall, opened them flat. and stacked them up to the same height as the bills in the envelope. Using one of the bills as a guide, he cut the newspapers into two stacks the size of the bills and put the reserved twenty-dollar bills at the top and bottom of each stack, securing them with rubber bands.

Then Jake loosened the knot of the other plastic bag. It held blue pills, and he spilled them onto the table and counted out thirty. These little beauties weren't for sale but would be perfect for this occasion. He had gotten them from a supplier who had a sourced them from his contact in Mexico. The counterfeit pills had the same shape and color as Oxys stamped "M30."

A few days later he saw a news report about a drug bust in New York with a photo of his supplier flashed on the TV. The fakes looked like the real thing with the "M30" stamp but were laced with lethal doses of fentanyl and heroin. The Feds were all over it. His good fortune had turned. He stashed them in the wheel well for safekeeping. They were perfect for a blackmailing junkie who thought he could squeeze Jake for ransom.

He put the deadly pills into a plastic baggie and placed that into the second manilla envelope that held the fake stacks of bills. He closed the flap and placed the envelopes side by side. When they were sealed, the envelopes would look and feel exactly the same.

Jake sealed the fake ransom envelope, went out to the garage, and put the other envelope and the two bags of counterfeit pills back into the BMW's spare-tire well. He slid into the driver's seat and pushed the garage door opener. The door rose slowly, revealing murky shadows in the empty street.

He thought about his dear old dad as he shoved the deadly ransom package into the glove compartment.

It gives me a lot of pleasure to know you are paying to keep your resourceful yet disappointment of a son out of a very messy situation. Thanks, Dad. You owe me this.

67

DAVID TOOK HIS position across from the maintenance building, far enough into the woods to get a clear view while he remained out of sight. The moon was a crescent sliver hanging high in the sky. It barely cast a shadow in the thick brush that concealed him from anyone on the path, but it provided enough light to reveal the side of the rusted trash can. The congealed fragments of bourbon-soaked drugs that David had scraped up had reduced the pain level in his joints caused by his crouched position.

He checked his phone again: 9:58. Two more agonizing minutes. David breathed in slowly, held his breath, counted to eight, and breathed out again, making a soft whistling sound between his barely parted lips.

It's all over, now, David. Mother is here. He's gone. He can't hurt you anymore. Breathe. Breathe! Slowly in, and now hold your breath. Count with me while I squeeze your hand. One, two, three, four, five, six, seven, eight. That's right. Now, breathe out slowly. Part your lips, and blow it out with a whistle. That's right, feel the love in the clasp of my hand and breathe out the bad feelings. In and out. He'll never hurt you again.

At precisely 10:00, David heard the crunch of footfalls on the grave. Even in the dim light he recognized Jake from the concert parking lot as he walked down from Henry Street past the building. David watched him turn and follow the path to the trash can. Jake crouched while looking around cautiously and pulled a package from under his jacket, putting it behind the can out of David's sight line.

A sudden sharp crack split the silence like a rifle shot. David stopped breathing and closed his eyes. He felt the brush around him move as something ran past him in the dark. He opened his eyes to see a deer disappearing into the woods.

Jake heard the sudden noise too. He stood up, looked back and forth in alarm, and reached under his jacket again. He slowly walked up the path away from the trash can and stopped where the path made a sharp right turn by David's hiding place back to the street. A break in the cloud cover exposed the moon, shedding enough light for David to make out a gun as Jake made his way toward the source of the sound. David crouched deeper into the shadows. Another cracking sound, and Jake turned quickly, running down the street to his car.

David fell back into the brush, overcome with tension and the delirium of withdrawal. He waited a few minutes before leaving his cover.

The stench of rotted garbage and small, yellow eyes staring at him from the dark wasn't enough to stop him from sweeping his hand on the ground, following the curve of the rusted, leaking trash can until he found the manilla envelope and pulled it from behind the can. He ran his shaking, sweaty hands, crusted with dirt, over the package. He could feel the outline of two bundles the size of bills and a package filled with something round and hard.

David ripped open the envelope, groping inside for the bag of pills. The pain intensified with every contact of flesh on the flat, unyielding surface of the envelope. He grasped the plastic bag and yanked it out with a frantic motion. The unsealed plastic bag quickly disgorged its contents, and David heard the soft patter of pills falling at his feet.

Instinctively, he dropped the envelope and clutched the bag with both hands, folding it over and over in a futile attempt to stop the stream of escaping pills. He saw the tiny yellow eyes of a creature darting back and forth in the dark, scrambling in pursuit of what might be an unscheduled snack.

David fell back and sat in the trash and leaves around the can, his free hand sweeping the ground for the disappearing pills. He unfolded the bag in his trembling hands, fingers searching the corners. In one motion, he pulled a round pill from the corner of the plastic bag and shoved it into his mouth. He swished his tongue around to create a pool of saliva, sufficient to swallow the pill. His mind and body raging, he felt for the envelope. Stupid, stupid Jake! He had tried to get creative, leaving the bag open like that. This mistake was going to cost him.

David felt under his jacket for the phone, wrapped in a plastic bag. His aching body was responding quickly to the pill he swallowed, clearing his mind and deadening his conscience.

He had asked for thirty pills, and he didn't have them. David would take the money and whatever was left of the pills. But Jake wasn't getting his wife's phone.

David ran his hand over the phone in the plastic bag. The pain was subsiding fast. He found the envelope with the money and tucked it under his arm. He pulled himself up, shoved the plastic bag into the envelope, and peered down the path. He checked his watch. Five more minutes.

The small, yellow eyes had disappeared. It was strangely quiet, no rustling of leaves or trash. David raced down the path, slid into the seat of his truck, and pulled the plastic bag and two bundles of bills out of the envelope. In the dim light he saw the familiar face of Andrew Jackson staring at him. He put Annabelle's phone into the glove compartment, found a pen, and scratched a note across Jake's now empty envelope. *"Seal the bag carefully the next time. Only two pills in the bag. If you don't give me 30 more, you won't get the phone."*

David kept low as he found his way in the dark to the drop-off point. He felt curiously strong and steady. He felt his anger—no, rage—building. He reached in the dark around the can to find something to fill the empty envelope. The leaves and dirt felt uncommonly soft and pliable in his hand. He raised his fist close to his face and saw a dead rodent staring blankly at him. He shoved the macabre object into the envelope, folded it closed, and dropped it behind the trash can. From the distance, he heard a rustling of leaves and a crunch of gravel that was sure to be Jake coming back for the phone.

Surprise, Jake.

David rose to a crouch and headed into the woods away from the can. This area next to the abandoned building was a dumping site for unused furniture and construction trash. David hid behind a rusted refrigerator, its door gaping open against a pine tree. He heard the rustling stop, then a sweeping sound. The crunching started up again at a faster pace, then faded into silence.

As he waited in the dark, he saw yellow eyes appear in the distance, then closer until they seemed to be marching toward him, a rodent army circling an enemy. David felt a surge of strength, mixed with a sudden rage at these would-be captors. All his senses were exploding. He could see the creatures clearly now, some on their haunches, posed for attack. He lowered his arm and with a wide swoop, swept across the ground, fingers extended and then clasped around a writhing soft body, its teeth bared, eyes glaring.

Hello, ma'am, is this David Westwood's mother? I'm principal Kramer at the Lakeview Middle School. I'm afraid we've had another unpleasant situation here at school. We are still sorting out the details, but your son David got into a fight with a boy who accused David of taking his lunch. What started out as a stare-down turned into a brawl, and the other boy is hurt pretty badly. His parents are on their way to the hospital right now. The lunch in question was found in David's backpack. David insists that the boy lied and needed to be punished. Can you come immediately?

David pulled his hand toward his face in the dark, locked eyes with his squirming attacker, and slowly squeezed his fist until its head flopped forward over its limp body. The full force of this phantom drug coursing through his body sent a surge through his arm as he flung the lifeless creature into the woods. He wiped his hand on his pants and rose from his hiding place, crept cautiously to his truck, and drove off down the deserted road.

66

JAKE CHECKED HIS watch and counted down the final minute before he drove back to the abandoned building to retrieve Annabelle's phone. Jake wasn't worried about the fake stack of bills. Junkies would trade their grandmothers for drugs. The plastic bag with the pills was the only thing this junkie was interested in. With just two of those little pills in his system, he wouldn't live long enough to complain. Jake stretched out in the driver's seat, took a last look at his watch, and headed down the path toward the trash can.

The sliver of moon was high in the evening sky, lighting the way. Jake felt around the back of the trash can for the envelope with Annabelle's phone. His hand bushed over what felt like small pebbles. He felt around again and found a bulging envelope. He grabbed it by a corner, tucked it under his arm, and headed back to his car.

Back in his car, Jake saw two beams of light round the corner behind him, reflecting off the rearview mirror. Jake ducked and sat motionless until the vehicle had passed. Alone again, he unfolded the envelope, turned it upside down—and out fell dirt and a bloated dead rat, its front paws twisted into a grotesque death pose. He stared in horror at the filth on the leather seat.

That fucking little junkie.

He threw the envelope on the seat to cover the rat's carcass and saw the note scrawled across the envelope. What he had thought were pebbles on the ground around the trash can had been the Oxys, spilled from the plastic bag. He leaned over, opened the passenger side door. And, using the side of the envelope, flung the rat out into the street. He heard a soft thunk of the rat's carcass as it hit the ground.

Jake didn't like getting double-crossed. He had to find a way to get the phone before this junkie was strung out enough to turn it into the police for the reward or worse, to Annabelle. The phone now had Jake's voice recorded, setting up a buy.

His mind raced over possible methods of retaliation. He knew he should probably let it play out. The guy was no doubt celebrating his good fortune, popping several of the salvaged Oxy look-alikes laced with fentanyl, likely enough to ensure death. And if not, he'd be back for more.

Jake put the Beamer in gear, pulled out into the deserted street, pushed the pedal to the floor, and sped off into the night.

69

DAVID FELT SO cold, and his head was pounding. He could barely see the faded white lines on the road ahead as he sped through the dark, his foot heavy on the pedal. He took his hands off the steering wheel and grasped his head, trying to squeeze out the pain. He closed his eyes against a sudden searing brightness that exploded inside his head. He didn't see the car arriving around the bend until its headlights were coming straight for him. He jerked the steering wheel to the right; the truck headed for the trees as the approaching car flew past on his left, close enough for him to see the terror in the young driver's eyes.

David pulled off the road. Panting in pain and terror, he watched the car disappear into the night, its image getting smaller in the rear-view mirror and the headlights getting lost again in the trees and brush. His heart pounded, and the trees seemed to be spinning. A pill that should have brought him pleasure and a release from pain had turned into searing agony and terror.

What had Jake given him? David's body shook with rage. Whatever was inside his body was trying to kill him.

David searched the passenger seat for the opened bag and pulled out the last tablet. He held it up in the orange dashboard light. One more could stop the pain and cold, could stop the world from spinning. Had Jake had counted on a quick overdose to solve his problems? *Well, you don't know this junkie.* David rolled the tablet slowly between his fingers, caressing the soft curves and rounded edges for a moment before shoving the pill back into the bag.

New terror gripped David. No drugs, no connection. The money! He grabbed a stack of bills and turned it over, catching Andrew Jackson's stern face on the top of the stack. Pain ran down his fingers and up his arms as he removed the rubber band. The neat stack burst open in his shaking hands, spilling over the seat and floor of the truck. The bills were perfectly cut pieces of newspaper. David grabbed a handful from the seat, crumbled the paper in his fist, and let out a scream. His tortured mind and body couldn't contain his rage.

No drugs. No connection. And no money. His mind raced, and the rage he felt was like an antidote to the drugs. The demons were laughing at him, as Jake was probably doing right now, thinking he was a stupid junkie. He tried to block the taunting laughter, but it got louder. David knew that when it subsided, he'd have another kind of pain. He needed money for good drugs, and he knew how to get it.

David looked up and down the road. He was alone on the side of the road with no approaching headlights. He pulled back onto the road and sped toward his destination. The demons cheered him on, making him giddy with the thought of his next act. He pushed harder on the gas pedal, a smile forming through the grimace of pain that still coursed through muscle and bone.

90

IT WAS JUST before closing time when David pulled into the parking lot at the Anchor Inn. He brushed off his clothes and wiped his runny nose several times with some paper napkins that were strewn on the truck's floor. There was another car parked outside, a good indication someone was drinking to get up the courage to go home or dulling the senses enough to forget something or someone. He pulled a pair of latex gloves from the box under the passenger seat and tucked them into his pocket.

Inside, he took a seat at the end of the bar closest to the door, looked up from under the bill of his Ravens cap, and nodded to the woman behind the bar. Grateful for an excuse to get away from the drunk trying to get her phone number, the bartender slowly walked over to David.

"Name your pleasure, and make it quick," she said. "We close in twenty."

David liked her immediately. On the wrong side of fifty, she had the slow walk of someone with a bad knee. She squinted when she stood in front of him as if she needed glasses. A perfect victim for another time.

"A shot of Makers Mark and a Bud on draft, Beatrice," said David, reading her nametag. She gave him a squinty wink, turned, and walked back, pulling a beer out of the cooler in mid stride.

David turned his attention to the drunk at the bar, fumbling for his wallet and keys. Not many middle-aged men wore a suit and tie at the Anchor Inn. But David didn't care if he was wearing a clown suit—he just needed him to have cash and be drunk enough to need a ride. The guy made one last plea for mercy from Beatrice. His voice changed from pleading to anger, and he reached over the bar and grabbed Beatrice's arm.

"Get your hands off me, you lousy drunk," she said shrilly. "I'll call the cops, and you'll get comfort alright—locked up with some pervert in a jail cell."

For David, the scene appeared to be playing right into his hands. The demons in his head chanted with delight at the trap he was about to lay as he finished his drink. He could hardly hold back his ache in anticipation as he watched the drunk.

David got up and walked to the end of the bar. "Hey, buddy, take it easy." He grabbed the drunk by the arm, his eagerness adding extra pressure. He pulled him away from the bar, looked at Beatrice, sighed, and said, "No need for the cops, ma'am. I've just gotten off my shift at the hospital, and I'll give him a lift home. I've seen too many of these guys wheeled into the emergency room missing body parts after trying to drive."

He turned back to the drunk. "You got a name, buddy?"

"Eddie."

In one fluid motion, Eddie looked at David, turned away, and vomited on the floor. Beatrice gasped. David bent over to hold him up, then sat him down on his barstool.

David pulled the gloves from his pocket and slid them onto his shaking hands. "My shift was over, Eddie. Now it seems I'm on overtime."

"Well, Eddie," said Beatrice. "Now look what you've done! You've been drinking all night, and you don't drink for free."

Eddie moaned and put his hand over his back pocket. "Here, take it," he whispered into the bar top.

Beatrice came around the bar, slid Eddie's wallet out of his pocket like a professional, and gasped. She found a line of shiny credit cards alongside a thick wad of bills bulging from the cash compartment.

Beatrice grinned as if she had won the lottery, while David's brain danced in circles. "Eddie, you're a good customer and a great tipper," said Beatrice as she peeled off five $50 bills.

She retreated behind the bar, stepping around the pool of vomit underneath Eddie's feet. "Now this little incident is between you and me—right, mister?" Beatrice asked David.

"Of course," he said. "Discretion and confidentiality are part of my professional code. Between you and me, this never happened."

"Now will you get him out of here, please? It will take me another hour to clean up this mess. What's your name, son?"

"Dewain, ma'am. I'll take care of him."

91

DAVID GRABBED EDDIE around the waist, pulling one limp arm over his shoulder, and led him through the door and into the parking lot. He leaned him up against the side of his truck and with one quick motion swung the door open just as Eddie's knees began to give way. Eddie opened his eyes wide, grabbed the door handle, leaned over his shoes, and threw up again.

David jerked Eddie upright and loaded him into the passenger seat, removing his bulging wallet from his jacket pocket before slamming the door. He flipped it open to pull out the remaining cash.

Four rows of credit cards were tucked tightly into the leather slots that covered both sides of the open wallet. David pulled out the Centurion American Express Card and the JP Morgan Palladium Card. He fought the urge to put them in his pocket—but credit cards were no good to him. He reluctantly slid them back into the wallet and shoved the cash into his pocket.

He got into the cab and tossed the wallet on the dashboard. Now to dispose of the evidence, David thought, planning the route. Eddie slumped back in the seat, his head wedged between the headrest and the passenger door.

David started driving to the river, taking the deserted back roads and driving at the speed limit.

"Where are we going?" Eddie mumbled without moving. "Hey—who are you?" He opened his eyes, his voice quickening, and through a slur repeated his questions.

"Take it easy, buddy," David said, staring straight ahead. "I'm a friend. It's all under control."

"My head is pounding!" Eddie lifted a hand to his forehead and moaned.

"Yea, you tried to drink the bar dry single-handed tonight, buddy" David said in a low measured tone. "I've got something that will make the pain go away. Works for me when I can't take the pain."

David checked his rearview, then the side mirrors, and pulled off the road under some low-hanging trees. He leaned over, opened the glove compartment, and pulled out the plastic bag that held the last pill from Jake jammed into its corner.

"This will fix you right up, buddy." David pushed the pill into Eddie's palm. "Don't drop this. It's the last one."

Eddie reached out his hand in the dark cab of the truck, fingers trembling and lifted his hand to his mouth to put the pill on his tongue with all the reverence of a communicant.

"Here," said David, offering Eddie a half-empty water bottle. "This will help it go down."

Eddie drank hungrily, held the bottle tight, cradled it against his chest, and fell back into the seat, eyes closed, and head wedged against the door.

"Seat belt," Eddie mumbled, hands instinctively groping for the strap.

"No, you won't need that, buddy." David reached across Eddie and pulled the door handle up, pushing the door partly open. He leaned him against the door.

David started the truck and quickly turned to pull out onto the road again. He had played this role before: the young hero, looking after the less fortunate. He knew the script by heart, all the stage directions and marks to hit.

Young hero rescues hopeless, sick, worthless drunk from a bar.

Young hero takes drunk for a ride, relieving him of his pain and his wallet.

Truck speeds up. Passenger door opens unexpectedly around a curve; drunk can't save himself from falling and disappears into the ditch on the side of the road.

Truck taillights fade into the distance, blink for a mournful left turn, and disappear.

Blackout. Curtain.

92

DEWAIN HAD CREATED a nice setup for himself at this hospital with a new identity that no one ever questioned. He had a profitable business supplying drugs to his junkie customers and a willing, available co-worker for the mutual satisfaction of their appetites. He operated with ease, going where he wanted with a set of keys to unlock the perfect hiding places for his inventory or an empty room with a clean bed and just enough privacy to make his lady's day. But now he felt exposed and hunted.

He didn't like being in the hospital this early, either.

But this current situation left him no choice. He needed to act fast before he began his shift. No one would question his presence if he was a little early. With his all-access employee badge, he moved easily though the hallways, taking the stairs to avoid being trapped in the elevator with someone who might become suspicious.

The hospital rumor mill was always hot, but the death of a young girl from a prominent family as a result of stolen hospital drugs threatened an inferno of suspicion. Some staff knew more than others, but some were not surprised that drugs from the hospital had ended up in a high school kid's party punch. Those with inside knowledge of employee side gigs might be putting the pieces together. Young girl doing community service. Working in *that* storage closet. A certain orderly who used it as his personal hideaway. Dewain needed to get any of those drugs out of there and fast.

Dewain headed down the corridor to the third-floor storage room when someone grabbed his arm from behind. He turned to see Cherise with an index finger over the wicked smile on her face. He glanced up and down the empty hallway and unlocked the storage room door. Cherise pushed him into the dark room. As soon as the door closed behind them, Dewain grabbed her shoulders and pulled her close.

"What in the hell are you doing, Cherise?" His grip tightened. "There are eyes everywhere in this hospital."

"Oh, baby, you're hurting Cherise, and she likes it," she cooed in the dark. "I saw that cute little ass of yours making its way down the hallway and I knew where you were going. Word is you have business in this storeroom."

"So you think you know something, Cherise?" He loosened his grip and pushed her away. "Just can't keep your hands off me, huh, Cherise? Didn't you get enough of this the other night?" He leaned in, his face just inches from hers. "I've got some work to do here, and I only have a few minutes."

"Oh, I get it," she said, pulling back. "Business can't wait, but I can?" Cherise knew where to push.

"Baby, I'm always ready for you," he said, pulling her closer in the dark.

"Locked and loaded? You're a dangerous man, Dewain." Cherise straddled his leg and pressed harder.

Dewain's hand found its way up her skirt and along her inner thigh. As Cherise began to moan, Dewain heard a noise from out in the hallway. He froze and pulled away.

"Oh, baby, don't stop now!"

"Shut up, Cherise."

The door handle turned hard against the lock. They could hear muffled voices talking outside the door, then fading as they moved away.

"You've got to get out of here, Cherise. I've got something I need to do before those people get back."

"Yeah, there is something you have to do. Finish what you started," she pushed up against him.

"Listen, Cherise, get out of here, and we can take this up later."

Cherise put her hand on Dewain's chest and pushed him back. "You mean later, after you get that stuff out of here? It's all over the hospital. Dewain's little waystation for drugs from discharged patients. Dewain's little side hustle. That preppie volunteer exposed your little racket. There's all kinds of speculation about how she ended up dead."

"Yeah, well people end up dead in hospitals all the time," said Dewain. He grabbed Cherise by the arm and squeezed tight.

"You're hurting me, Dewain, and not how I like it. We've got a thing, you, and me. Besides, I admire a man with a head for business. Let me help you." His fingers tightened around her arm, and she felt the heat of his breath as he drew her close.

"Ok, baby. Once you're in, you can't get out. You already know that bad things can happen when people get in the way."

Dewain clicked the flashlight app on his phone and aimed it at the tall shelves stacked with yellowed sheets.

"Slide your hands between each of the sheets. Take the lower shelves. Pull any bottles out and put them in this bag."

He pulled a cloth laundry bag from another shelf and put it on the floor.

"Do it fast. Stuff a few towels in the laundry bag so the bottles won't rattle." He clicked the app and the room went dark. "Don't need to alert anyone with a light under the door."

It took a few minutes before each stack had been skimmed and the bottles were in the bag. Dewain cracked open the door to an empty hallway. Cherise slipped out with the bag and was down the hall when Joe from maintenance stepped out of the elevator with a security officer. Cherise shouted something to them about a suspicious person on the floor, pointing them down the corridor away from the storage room.

She was smooth as silk, Dewain observed with relief. As he silently pulled the door closed, he felt a hand grip his shoulder from behind.

He turned around, coming face to face with Detective James Holt.

"Well, Dewain, I thought I'd find you here," Holt said with a smile.

93

DEWAIN CAUGHT HIS breath, then exhaled slowly and returned Holt's smile. He reminded himself to stay cool. Easy does it. He knew how to do this.

"Well, officer—how unexpected. Is there a break in the phone-and-wallet caper, or do you need my assistance on another case?"

Dewain studied Holt's face. His smile was as hard as the stone carvings on Mt. Rushmore.

"Right on both counts, Dewain. I got an interesting tip on the case, and you are just the person who might be able to help. The tip was about a hospital storeroom, a dead high school volunteer, and a side hustle selling stolen drugs from the hospital. And here you are, Dewain, exiting that very storeroom. My intuition was right. This must be my lucky day."

Dewain didn't like Holt's smile. Someone must have been talking, breaking the code of silence. It was a mystery he needed to take care of, but first, he had to get rid of this nosy cop.

"Whoa, detective. What are you talking about? I took an oath, remember? I'm part of the team."

Dewain kept his smile, relaxed his shoulders, and leaned against the door frame.

"What are you doing here?" asked Holt. "I checked the schedule, and you're not on it."

Dewain closed his eyes and shook his head. "No one goes by the schedule. We get so many new admins it's never right. And besides, we've got a relaxed policy—we're more like a family than employees. As long as shifts are covered and you have the right creds, no one really cares."

He studied Holt's face, which was expressionless. Even Dewain didn't believe this lie, but he hoped Holt would buy it until he could think of a better one. "I stopped in to talk to a buddy in the laundry, but he wasn't there, so I took it upon myself to bring up some retired linens. This is where they end up."

"A kind of laundry graveyard?" said Holt. "The perfect place to stash some drugs, which by the way, was another bit of information we got. Since you seem to have access, you won't mind if we take a look between the sheets? One detective helping another out, Dewain?"

Dewain recalled Cherise carrying the bag down the hallway. There were stacks of sheets in the storage closet, and they had had so little time to be sure that everything had been removed. He reminded himself to stay calm. Any hesitation or pushback might make Holt more suspicious.

"Official police business, eh? Sure, detective."

Dewain unlocked the door and turned on the lights, revealing rows of shelving piled high with linens. The hurried search rescue mission just minutes before had pulled sheets out from the stacks, some hanging over the shelves, a few on the floor.

"A little messy, isn't it?" said Holt. "Almost looks like someone was searching for something." He turned towards Dewain, waiting for a response.

"You got that right, Detective. If I was investigating a burglary, I would say this place was ransacked. Your informants may be on to something."

"Maybe they missed something," Holt said. "They always do. Leave behind a piece of evidence that cracks the case."

Holt pulled a pair of latex gloves from his jacket pocket and started pulling out sheets from the shelves and dropping them on the floor. With each thud of cotton on cement Dewain held his breath. He watched as Holt moved over to a shelf toward the back of the room where sheets were stacked like soldiers in perfect formation. He and Cherise must have missed that stack when they were searching earlier.

"I'll take that stack in the back," said Dewain. "They look pretty dirty. You got a pair of gloves for me, detective? You know, to protect the integrity of the evidence? I saw that on CSI once."

"No, Dewain, you've just come from this room. Your prints are probably all over this place."

Dewain began pulling sheets from the neat stacks, listening for the rattle of tablets or a bottle hitting the floor. He was down to the last two sets of sheets in the bottom stack and recognized the familiar hump of a bottle under the sheet. Dewain glanced over his shoulder to find Holt standing behind him.

"Find something, Dewain?"

Dewain felt his knees weaken. His prints *were* all over this room and were likely on this prescription bottle from days or weeks ago when he had hidden it. "No, detective. Just taking a breath. These sheets are nasty!"

"Step aside, Dewain." Holt had seen the small rise in the top sheet. "Like I said, they always leave something behind."

Dewain's shuffled aside on leaden feet, eyes fixed on the rise in the sheet. He took a deep breath as Holt pulled back the edge of the sheet, revealing a small plastic prescription bottle, safety cap in place.

"Bingo! See, Dewain—something is always left behind!" Holt pulled out his cellphone and took photos from different angles.

Dewain felt sick. How had he and Cherise missed this one? He looked at Holt, eyes wide. "What is that?"

"Maybe you can tell me, Dewain. This is your territory."

"Looks to me like someone's medications got caught up in the dirty sheets in the laundry, detective," Dewain shook his head sadly.

"Or my source is correct." Holt said, shaking the bottle. "Someone stashes drugs in this storeroom that they've stolen from the pharmacy or patients until they have a buyer. Running a profitable little business with a ready supply of product. Hiding it in a place where they wouldn't be discovered. Sweet."

Holt studied Dewain for a reaction. Dewain's eyes were fixed on the amber bottle. If he knew something, he was not giving it away.

Holt read the label aloud. "Mrs. Barbara Thompson. Thirty tablets of Oxycodone, take as needed for pain." Holt twisted off the cap and turned the bottle upside down. The tablets spilled out on the musty sheets. "I'd guess Mrs. Thompson never got a chance to take even one."

Holt scooped the tablets into the bottle, put the cap on, and put it back on the sheets. "This is my lucky day," he said. "We're done here."

"You're a witness to this, Dewain. The bottle was full, just like we found it. I need to get this room sealed off and call forensics to look for more evidence. This could break open a couple of cases—the missing phone and wallet and a dead high school volunteer."

Holt called the precinct, gave them his whereabouts, and asked for forensics to conduct a search for evidence.

Holt turned to Dewain, who was slumped up against the storage rack.

"Go to security and have someone come up here to secure this room. I'll wait here—don't want anyone coming in here to compromise a possible crime scene."

Dewain's mind raced, searching for a way to sidetrack that bottle from landing in a crime lab. "I can come back to assist forensics, detective," said Dewain.

Holt detected a little waver in Dewain's voice. There must be something he's afraid they'd find.

"No need to return, Dewain," Holt said with a smile. "Forensics, hospital security, and I will take it from here."

They stepped out of the storeroom. Dewain turned, locked the door, and went to the security office. He had better play this one out.

Security sent up an officer to join Holt outside the door, and forensics showed up about a half hour later. Holt recognized Alvin Truitt, one of the newest lab techs, rounding the corner. In just six months, Alvin had distinguished himself as being among the best in the lab.

"Alvin, I see they've sent the lab star for this one," said Holt.

With the security officer as an observer, Holt and Alvin searched the room and took photos and prints. They bagged and labeled Mrs. Thompson's prescription bottle as evidence.

"This is a rush," said Holt, handing Alvin the bagged bottle.

When they were done, security locked the door. Holt pulled a roll of crime-scene tape from Alvin's materials bag to tape the door.

"We don't want to alarm anyone, detective," said the security officer. "Let me use some tape we use for maintenance instead. Innocent until proven guilty, eh?"

"I'll give you that, officer, but it's on your head if this room is compromised in any way." Holt replied.

Holt took a last look at the locked and sealed storeroom door that was crisscrossed with orange maintenance tape. He was pleased with the day's work. The bad guys always seem to leave something behind. One stray prescription bottle might be all it took to shut down someone's dirty little side hustle—and maybe reveal a killer.

94

HOLT CHECKED HIS messages and phone, but there was no word from Veronica. For a moment he entertained an image of those long legs wrapped in those silky black stockings. He could feel the pink satin garters on his fingers as he disengaged the belt's metal hooks and eyes, soft skin against buttery silk, and imagined the soft clink of metal and silk as it fell to the floor.

He swallowed hard, told himself to snap out of it, and headed for the hospital;s security office. He pressed his badge against the door's reinforced glass window and tapped until the guard inside opened the door.

He wasn't expecting the wry smile and big brown eyes from under her uniform hat.

"What can I do for you, officer?" Maybe she could help break up a drug operation at the hospital and nail a suspicious orderly—but those were still only suspicions. He didn't know who the bad actors might be; it was better to keep that to himself.

"I've been investigating a missing property case that may have occurred at the hospital a couple of days ago, Officer Renfrew," said Holt, reading her name off the nametag pinned on the crest of her breast pocket.

"Three days ago, around six-thirty in the evening, a young woman was brought into the emergency room by ambulance.

She had gone into labor on a bus. I understand you have security cameras in the ER. I would like to look at any video for possible evidence in this case."

"Well, Detective Holt." She took a breath. "We installed a new security system in the hospital a couple of months ago, and not only do we have clear security footage for multiple entry points to the hospital, but an almost instant retrieval system. Just give me the date, approximate time and location, and I can call that up for you."

She looked up and smiled at him. "Oh, and I'll need for you to fill out a couple of forms and sign about ten times, detective. After that, I'm at your disposal."

Holt quickly filled out the forms and handed them back.

"My, you are quick, Detective Holt," she said with a wink.

Holt coughed and said in his best professional manner, "I'd like to see the tapes from three days ago at the emergency room entrance where ambulances pull in. Around six in the evening. Can you pull those up?"

Officer Renfrew dispensed with the banter. "Sit here, Detective Holt, to get a good view of the videos. Watch this screen." She tapped the top-middle monitor.

A few clicks later a scene began to play. It had been a busy night, with groups of people and gurneys moving back and forth, EMTs scrambling in and out, triage nurses and orderlies meeting them and assessing the arrivals while they were being pushed inside.

"Can you switch cameras to the inside? Same time frame?"

A few more clicks and the emergency-room bays were in view. Holt searched the images and saw a pregnant woman on a gurney with two EMTs and a nurse at her side as they rushed down the corridor. Holt made a note of the time stamp. He watched as the images moved down the hallway out of sight.

"Is that what you were looking for, detective? Should I replay it?"

"No, Renfrew. Let it run for a bit."

Holt stood up and moved closer to the monitor screen, studying the images—nurses, doctors, patients, and others wandering in and out of view. Nothing appeared to be out of the ordinary for a typical night of mayhem and misfortune.

"Wait! Stop the feed!"

Renfrew clicked loudly on the keyboard, and all the figures in the video were caught in a game of freeze.

Just inside the bottom left-hand corner was a young man wearing what appeared to be a suit jacket and a baseball cap. The man turned his head as if he was looking for something or someone, with his face to the camera. The hat was pulled low over his eyes, but Holt could see an image on the cap.

"Here. Zoom in if you can, officer. The bottom left-hand corner. The guy with the hat."

Officer Renfrew clicked, and the image grew, filling the screen. Across the front of the hat was a bird—the logo of the Ravens football team.

Holt stood silently, his eyes moving like a scanner taking in the image. The face was obscured by the hat's bill, which was creased and worn on the edge.

"Zoom out and continue," said Holt without turning away from the screen. "Witnesses say there was a man with a hat that night with a bird on it. Let's see where he is going."

The video began again. The man walked slowly down the hallway and almost out of view. Holt heard the keyboard clicking as the camera switched to fix on the man as he walked into the next camera's view and then the next-next one's. Holt watched as the man walked across the screen, his back to the camera, passing others in the hallway until he came up behind a figure dressed like an orderly. The bird-hat guy stopped and tapped the shoulder of the orderly, who turned around. They stood talking for a few moments in the hallway.

"They know each other," Holt said softly to the screen.

Holt was accomplished at reading body language. It was instinctive—sizing up a situation fast, saving himself from a bullet or a blow to the head many times in his career. He read this situation on the screen as two people who knew each other but weren't close enough to be old friends. A cautious encounter, but not their first.

"Freeze it!"

A click, and the video became a photo.

"Now zoom in, please." Holt's eyes were riveted on the screen as the faces grew from blurry dots to fill the screen.

Holt squeezed his eyes shut tightly and opened them again. There staring back at him was Dewain with his narrow eyes riveted on the bird-hat man, his mouth twisted into a smirk.

Officer Renfrew stood up next to Holt and stared at the images on the screen. Holt was transfixed by the image, barely breathing.

"Do you want me to start the video again, Detective Holt?" she asked, turning to face him.

"No, Renfrew. I've found what I was looking for."

95

MARJORIE PUT HER skim double-foam single-shot mac-chiato on her desk and hit the desktop's power button. Why hadn't Howie cleaned up his mess before he left last night, she thought as she picked up his trash, including a large soda cup half full of brown liquid, two Payday candy wrappers, and an open bag of Cheetos bleeding orange powder on the keyboard.

What a pig!

She grabbed two Lysol wipes out of the bottom desk drawer. She was not his freaking mother.

She liked getting to the lab early. It had only been six months since she had started in the lab as a records clerk—a "foot in the door" job. She hoped her degree in criminology and her work ethic would move her out and into a white lab coat.

Marjorie uploaded the file of completed DNA lab tests, highlighted the block, and pushed print. Copies rose out of the depths of the printer and stacked silently on the tray. She could get those into envelopes and ready for mailing before anyone knew they were late, she assured herself.

Most tests went to the courts or law enforcement, evidence in one crime or another. She sorted the copies into stacks for mailing when she came across something different. A paternity report, sourced by Sophia, the lab's executive director. It was already two days past the completion date and was marked "Rush."

Marjorie found the file and attached it to an email to Sophia. The report listed the two identified parties connected with the birth at Shepherdsville Hospital. Marjorie hit "new email" and attached the DNA report file, sending it marked "Rush" to the hospital, attention of Yolanda Springer in the records department.

That's going the extra mile.

———

Yolanda Springer was in charge of the hospital's records department. She had a reputation for demanding accuracy and following procedures, and she didn't like to be rushed. Back from a week's vacation in Hawaii, she sat down at her desk and draped a paper lei over her computer screen. She put down her coffee and focused on an email in her inbox marked RUSH! CONFIDENTIAL! "If I see one more 'Rush' from Marjorie at Dirkfield, I'm going to lose it," Yolanda fumed. It was barely eight-thirty and she already had a stack of paperwork to put into files for patients scheduled for discharge today.

Barry, Yolanda's assistant, looked up from the stack of papers on his desk, turned to Yolanda, and closed his eyes. "Yolanda, you're starting with the attitude early today."

"Barry, my attitude would get a whole lot better if you could run this up to the fifth floor for this patient, Annabelle Martin." Yolanda printed out the report and put it into a white envelope, writing "Confidential" in the lower left-hand corner.

"If it saves me from listening to you bitch the rest of the day, give it here." Barry stood up from behind the desk and swiped the envelope that was waving like a flag from Yolanda's fingers.

"I'll be an angel all day, Barry," she cooed, fluttering her long, fake eyelashes.

"Humph. I don't see any wings," he said, walking away. Barry turned around at the door and flashed a half smile at Yolanda who was already mumbling about something else. *Horns, maybe, but no wings.*

96

HOLT WAS LOST in thought driving to the precinct over roads that were nearly deserted at this time of the morning. He mulled over the image of Dewain and the man with the Ravens hat. Dewain, who had been asked to find out what had happened to Annabelle's property, had talked to the suspect from the bus who'd been identified by his Ravens hat. What else and who else did Dewain know?

Holt was used to juggling cases with lots of loose ends. They eventually stitched themselves together, weaving a net that often trapped the guilty.

The precinct was unusually quiet. The message light on his phone blinked a steady plea for attention. Holt shook his head. That blink used to signal a double homicide or something equally exciting. But since his "reassignment," it was someone reporting a missing cat or a drunken husband. He punched in his code and half listened to one message after another, making a few notes for the street cops on day shift. The last one made him sit up.

"Officer Holt, this is Jake Martin. I met you at the hospital. My wife, Annabelle, was brought into emergency—almost had our baby on a city bus. Her wallet and phone were missing from her bags. I hoped you had some leads on them. The wallet isn't so important any longer, but I would really like to get the phone. You know—messages and contacts are hard to replace. Call me when you get this message."

Holt snorted. The money and credit cards were worthless? And after three days, the phone would probably be trashed. He scribbled Jake's message and phone number on the notepad and tucked it into his pocket.

He pulled a stack of papers from the corner of his desk and pulled out an envelope marked "Lab, Confidential." He tore the envelope open and pulled out the results of the coffee-mug's fingerprint analysis. He scanned the form. Instead of Dewain Johnson, the name of the person who had clasped the steel cylinder was George Anderson, thirty-five years old. He had a string of past addresses that dotted the map from California to Louisiana and ended at the south end of the city. George Anderson had a long list of criminal activity: DUIs, assault, robbery, drug possession, and drug trafficking. No outstanding warrants. How had the real Dewain Johnson been resurrected by George Anderson to live a second life as a hospital orderly?

Holt closed his eyes and held his breath for a moment. He played a video in his mind of the man he knew as Dewain picking up the coffee mug and handing it to him that night at the concert. The mug was new, and Holt was the only other person who had touched it. He had taken it from Dewain by grasping it with a napkin so he wouldn't destroy Dewain's fingerprints. It was by the book.

Holt's mind flashed back to the night the hospital nurse offered Dewain's assistance when the woman's wallet and phone went missing. Holt might miss some clues along the way, but his gut never lied to him. He'd been at this for so long, familiar with the muck and mayhem created by criminals. He could often tell when someone was guilty of something.

He sorted the pieces like letters on a scrabble board. Dewain's encounter with the guy with the Ravens hat.

Dewain/George's eagerness to get close to Annabelle in the hospital. The missing drugs and rumors of a drug network at the hospital. The young volunteer's overdose. And her death? The natural result of an overdose or a murder cover-up?

These were questions that only George Anderson could answer, and Holt knew just where to find him.

97

BARRY GOT ONTO the elevator, pushed the button for the fifth floor, and rested his lanky body against the wall in the back corner. The elevator bells announced the arrival of new passengers like trumpets at a debutante's ball and tolled in mourning at their departure. The bell tolled for the fifth floor, and he threaded his way out the door and sauntered up to the nurses' station.

The nurse on duty looked at Barry's nametag. "You're from records, I see," she said, looking up and over her glasses.

Well, you must be fricking Sherlock Holmes, woman.

He straightened himself just a little more, forcing her to look up even higher. "You're a tall one, aren't you!" she said, taking off her glasses.

Freaking Sherlock Holmes, Magnum PI, and Columbo!

"Yes, Nurse Champion," said Barry, leaning in close to read her nametag. "That's what my mama said."

Barry put the envelope on the desk, pointed to it, and said, "This report needs to get into Annabelle Martin's discharge papers. Just came in today, marked confidential."

Nurse Champion leaned into the screen, fingers flying over the keyboard. She straightened up, shook her head, and turned to Barry.

"Well, it's going to remain confidential, even from Mrs. Martin. She was discharged hours ago. Her file has already gone back to records, so you'd better take it back to Yolanda. She's not going to be happy with whoever was supposed to be in charge when she was gone. Nurse Champion paused, looked up, and fixed her gaze on Barry. "No, not happy at all."

She grabbed the envelope and pulled out a pen; Barry swooped in and snatched the envelope from her desk.

"Wait. Yolanda isn't in a great mood this morning." Barry tucked the envelope under his arm. "She's going to launch a Defcon-three investigation about why this wasn't in Ms. Martin's file before she left the hospital. And I'm in her line of fire, since I was supposed to monitor her email while she was sipping Mai Tais in Hawaii. She will never trust me again. And she's scary enough on a good day."

"Well, I don't want to deal with her either. You owe me big for this. FedEx is our friend, Barry." She pulled out an Administration Request Form with the Birthing Center and Hospital logo across the top. She wrote a note using Annabelle's address with instructions to send the envelope by overnight service and marked it "Confidential Mrs. Annabelle Martin."

Barry grabbed the note and the envelope. "I'll take a copy and put it in her file, out of the range of prying eyes. No harm, no foul. Everything in its place. And no enduring the wrath of Yolanda."

Barry took the stairs to the administration office and put the envelope and the note in the FedEx basket. Back in the lab office, Yolanda was holding court with the staff, recounting her attempts at paddleboarding in Maui and giving Barry the distraction he needed to slip the DNA report copy into Annabelle's file.

96

IN HER DIRKFIELD office, Sophia tossed her bag and coat on the Italian leather chair in front of her mahogany desk, and turned on her computer. She checked her emails, looking for the DNA report Jonas had requested.

She knew it should be there; she had even attached a note saying it was a rush and to hand-deliver it to her.

I'll have someone's head if this one goes missing or worse. Or it will be my head.

Jonas was a friend, but his impossibly high standards in the lab didn't leave room for mistakes. The only mistake Sophia had made the night she had prepared the sample was to go on a late date with a disappointing "dream" connection who nowhere resembled the photos posted on his online profile.

She continued scrolling through her emails until she saw one from Marjorie with a report attached. Marjorie was a relatively new tech; she was ambitious and had a tendency to sidestep protocol and overstep her bounds.

The subject line read "Rush." Sophia's heart sank. She felt hot and nauseous. Emailed reports could have gone under the eyes of a number of lab techs and admins before they made it to her.

Sophia called the lab, and soon Marjorie was on the phone.

"Yes ma'am, I sent you that email with the report. No ma'am. It didn't have a confidential note on it. It did say rush, so I sent it to you."

"Marjorie, this report was a highly confidential report requested by Jonas himself. It had specific instructions attached to it. Did you follow the protocols for highly confidential DNA reports? It was for my eyes only. No one else, not even the named individuals or institutions."

Marjorie remembered the copy she had sent to the hospital. She started to panic. Her throat went dry as she recalled sending the copy to the hospital lab to put in the mother's file.

My attempt to go the extra mile will march me straight into the front of the unemployment line, she told herself. *Sophia can't know.*

"Marjorie, are you there?"

Marjorie took a silent deep breath. "Yes, ma'am. It was marked "Rush," and when I saw your name, I attached it to an email and sent it to you. I didn't see a note. Notes sometimes get lost. You know how things get mismarked and screwed up in the lab sometimes. But I handled it carefully."

Marjorie smiled and congratulated herself for responding without really lying at all.

"Alright, Marjorie. Thanks." Sophia sat for a moment, and then opened the attached lab report, printed it out. and put it in another manilla envelope. She picked up her cell phone and called Jonas' private number. After a few rings, she heard his voice.

"Sophia, you have something special for me?"

"Yes, Jonas. Just came in this morning. I can bring it over to you now if you like."

"No, bring it to the bar around the corner from my office around seven. I'm meeting the guy who is interested in the results of that report for a drink. An old friend of mine.

"A single old friend?"

"Nominally married. I'll have a drink waiting for you if you need an incentive. Dirty martini with olives, right?"

"Jonas, you know all my weaknesses," Sophia replied. She swiveled her chair, thinking about Jonas' intriguing friend.

She was curious to meet her boss's "sort-of" married friend, but it was made especially enticing by the promise of an ice-cold dirty martini with four olives waiting for her.

99

THE PRECINCT WAS coming alive as other officers and staff trickled in for the day shift. Holt gathered his notepad, bolted the rest of his now tepid double-shot espresso, and headed to the door. It would take about forty-five minutes to make it to the hospital for a surprise visit to George/Dewain. He swung open the front door and nearly collided with two officers coming off the night shift.

"Holt—hold up a minute," said the younger of the two.

Holt waved him away, kept his head down, and walked past them toward the parking lot. *Night shift*. They think they're all Dirty Harry, stalking the bad guys in the shadows.

"Hey," the officer called out, running after Holt as he opened his car door.

Holt looked up and saw the officer running across the parking lot.

"What is it, Ramon," he asked the rookie cop.

"We just came from the morgue, detective. Someone dumped a body over the side of the road near the river early this morning. Middle-aged man, professional looking, you know, suit and tie. Hadn't been dead very long. The guy reeked of vomit and bourbon. No ID, just a cocktail napkin in his pocket from the Anchor Inn bar near the hospital."

"So, write a report and give it to the chief." Holt grabbed the car door handle. "Why did you chase *me* down?"

"Chief is going to want to give this one to you," said Office Ramon. "Turns out the coroner knew the stiff. City councilman. Married to the daughter of one of the largest hospital donors. It hasn't hit the morning news yet, but the chief's phone is going to start ringing when it hits. He's going to want some answers so he has something to say to the press."

Ramon stood his ground and stared at Holt. Holt stared back, turned, and started walking back to the precinct.

"OK, Ramon, write your report, and I'll see what our city councilman was up to last night."

Ramon was right. The chief met Holt at the door and sent him to the morgue.

The coroner was waiting for Holt in his office. Holt hated the morgue. He could handle the most dangerous perp on the streets without breaking a sweat. But dead bodies in roll-out drawers made his stomach churn and his hands grow cold. The echo of the wheeled platforms as they slowly revealed the cold, stiff human forms in various stages of decomposition reverberated in his brain for days.

They walked down to the morgue together. The coroner droned on while Holt tried to quiet his churning stomach. The coroner pulled back the sheet and pointed out contusions and lacerations, presumably from the fall and roll until the body came up against a pine tree off the shoulder of the road. The palm of the man's right hand was facing out, arm broken and askew from the fall.

"No signs of foul play, as far as I can see. No blows to the head, gunshot wounds, or stabbing." The coroner listed the possible horrors as if he were reading a grocery list.

Holt made notes as the coroner talked, a welcome distraction from looking at the battered and bruised body.

"Shall I turn him over, detective?"

"No, sir. I've seen enough," said Holt weakly.

The coroner pulled the sheet back over the body and returned it to its steel-wheeled temporary coffin.

Back in his office, the coroner gave Holt a copy of his report.

"You know this needs to be handled quickly and with discretion, Detective Holt. I've known Councilman Eddie Ortese for many years. He was instrumental in my campaign and has been a great supporter of the hospital and the community. He spoke to youth groups about the dangers of underage drinking and how he beat alcoholism through Alcoholics Anonymous. But you can see from the report that his blood alcohol level was .08—he was legally drunk. We also found a high level of Oxycodone and fentanyl in his urine. Who would have guessed? Tragic. His family has been notified and are on their way to identify the body."

Tragic was right. Any dirty little secrets were exposed under the yellow fluorescent lights of an underground macabre theater of death. The dead had no hiding places; no way to spin their stories, to confuse the facts, or to silence any testimony.

"The officer on the scene said there was a cocktail napkin in his pocket," said Holt. "Do you have it?"

"It was taken in evidence, but there is a photograph in the file. It was damp, so we figured it could have been from his last stop. Strange, though, because the two officers who brought him in said there was no vehicle near or at the scene. No skid marks on the road. No sign he had been driving or was ejected from a vehicle as a result of an accident. And he was found on the right side of the road. I'm not a detective, Holt, but I've seen enough of these cases to draw some conclusions. He wasn't alone last night. Anyone driving would be found on the left side of the road. This guy was riding shotgun."

100

HOLT CHECKED THE time. He had occasionally warmed a bar stool at the Anchor Inn. Its proximity to the hospital made it an easy stop after transporting gunshot or domestic-violence victims to the hospital at all hours of the day or night. Not a trendy bar with craft beers or umbrella drinks, it had low lights and barstools with cracked vinyl seats. Just enough private booths lined the windowless walls to offer a hiding place for consenting adults out of view. This was not the place to order top-shelf cocktails. Here, beer and whiskey chasers were served up by bartenders whose demeanor matched the splintered four-tops tossed around in too many late-night disagreements. The bar and food, the lighting, and the "mind your own damn business" code were the same for lunch, dinner, or into the wee hours. If you had a reason to hide, disappear, or just be left alone, the Anchor Inn was your destination.

The scent of wood, whiskey, and burgers on a seasoned griddle greeted Holt as he walked through the door of the bar. He recognized a couple of regulars already slumped over their drinks. Shadowy figures were barely visible in the booths at the back. A few tables held business types looking for a break from the hospital cafeteria or strangers needing some liquid refreshment to ease the pain or boredom of life outside the bar doors.

Beatrice usually worked the night shift, but she was behind the bar talking to Gordon, the day bartender. Holt found an empty barstool at the end of the bar and waited, catching Beatrice's eye as she turned his way.

"Well, Jimmy. It's been a while," said Beatrice with a smile. "You going to haul out one of my paying customers this early in the day? They haven't even had enough time to get rowdy. But the couple in the back booth have already broken a number of laws against God and their respective spouses since they came in an hour ago."

"Beatrice, if I wasn't on duty, we could break a few laws ourselves right here, right now," Holt said, his blue eyes fixed on hers behind her horned-rimmed glasses. "You know I can't resist you when you wear your bar apron low across your hips like that!"

"Shut up!" said Beatrice with a laugh. "What can I get you? Your usual, or can I make up something special to get you through the day?"

"One of your classic Rob Roys could make me surrender my badge, but I'm on duty and actually here on business. Official business. Looking for some information."

"Jimmy, when it comes to police business and giving information, I have a very unreliable memory. But I'll help if I can. The code, Jimmy. You've been the beneficiary of it yourself. Can't break the code."

"This is important, Beatrice. A man in his late fifties, brown hair, brown eyes, about two hundred pounds, was found dead early this morning along the side of the road near the river. Dressed like a businessman—suit, dress shirt, and tie. Badly bruised, lacerations. Broken arm. There were no vehicles in the area, no skid marks. No identification on him, but we know who he is. The only thing that he had on him was a cocktail napkin from the Anchor Inn. Still damp, so we think he might have been here last night.

Smelled like bourbon and vomit. They say it was all over his shoes. Was there someone like that here last night?"

Beatrice immediately saw a picture of Eddie slumped over the bar after too many drinks, vomiting on the floor and his shoes. Beatrice had been here before. *Play it cool.*

"So, you found a dead body with a cocktail napkin in his pocket," said Beatrice, leaning her elbow on the bar. "So what?"

"So, this guy was a city councilman, a family man, a pillar of the community. This is going to be a big story, and the more we know the better chance we have of controlling the spin in the media. We think someone may have dumped him on the road. Happened late last night or early this morning. You close at one in the morning. Anyone here like that last night?"

Beatrice weighed her options. The Anchor Inn was situated between the hospital district with hotels and shops and the lower-income neighborhoods with small businesses providing services like barber shops, cleaners, and nail salons. Overserving was a matter of opinion, and the code offered protection for anyone who paid for their drinks. Cooperation with the police, especially with someone like Jimmy, always worked in her favor.

"Off the record?" Beatrice watched Holt's expression and body language.

"Depends," said Holt, pulling out his notepad. "This place was just a stopping-off point. Information that gives us a lead could make you a hero. What do you say, Beatrice?"

"OK, Jimmy, but keep my name out of it. The guy came in about ten last night. He said he came from some fundraiser that was boring as hell and started ordering two fingers of bourbon, one after the other.

"It was a slow night, and about twenty minutes to closing, he was the only one at the bar until this other guy showed up. Eddie, the dead guy you're talking about, was very drunk, out of it, sitting at the end of the bar. This other fellow came in, sat at the other end of the bar, and ordered a drink. I told him we were about to close so it was last call, and he said fine. Meantime, Eddie was passing out, and I wanted to close. I tried to get him up onto his feet when he started getting belligerent. This other guy got up and tried to stand him up. Eddie was so drunk he threw up all over.

"I had to close the bar to get and him out. I was going to call a cab, but the guy offered to drive him home. Good riddance as far as I was concerned. He stood Eddie up and walked him out the door, and that's the last I saw of them. I was here for another hour cleaning up the mess Eddie left behind. I came in early this morning to make sure the place didn't smell like vomit before the lunch crowd came in. Not surprised he's dead; he made a good try of suicide by bourbon."

Holt scribbled in his notebook.

"Did you happen to see what kind of car the other guy was driving?" asked Holt.

"No, I didn't see them after they walked out the door, but it was quiet in here, and I heard what sounded like an old pickup. Heard the doors slam and the engine gunned a couple of times, and then it was gone."

"What about this other guy? What did he look like?"

"I'd never be a star witness who remembers every detail about someone. I was so angry about having to clean up the floors covered with bourbon and vomit that I didn't pay attention. He was kind of young, maybe in his thirties or so. Not too tall. He had on a jacket, one of those zip up ones like you'd wear hiking. Said he worked at the hospital. He put on a pair of those hospital gloves after Eddie lost it. And he was wearing a kind of baseball cap. Purple with a bird on it."

Holt stopped writing and looked up. "He was wearing a cap? Did it have any writing on it?"

"Yeah, I think it said 'Ravens.'"

Holt's brain was spinning, his mind jumped back to the video at the hospital.

"You're sure about that?"

"Yes. Jimmy, you're freaking me out. Who was this guy?"

"Beatrice, he was taking one of your very drunk customers out of the bar with your permission. Did you get his name?"

"Oh yeah. His name was Dewain."

101

ROGER LEANED BACK against the leather banquette and slowly ran the stir stick against the rim of his second Manhattan.

Jonas was late as usual. It was getting crowded in the bar with barstools and tabletops filling up with weary office workers in no hurry to head home. He watched the door open and close, letting in a slice of light from the street with each customer.

Through the crowd, now standing around the filled high tops, Roger saw Jonas and a tall slender woman with long, dark hair picking their way to his table. Roger stood up from his seat, waving them over. "Jonas—always fashionably late."

Jonas spied the two Manhattan glasses and one dirty martini on the table. He smiled his approval and turned to Roger, then to Sophia.

"Roger, please meet Sophia, the director of the lab."

Sophia took a long look at Roger and then past him to the martini, which she decided was of more interest. She slid into the banquette, putting her attaché case beside her, and quickly made short work of half of the martini and three olives. Roger and Jonas took a seat on either side. Jonas waved the waiter over and ordered a double scotch on the rocks. He was a regular, and the drink appeared in less than a minute.

Jonas turned to Roger. "I wanted Sophia to deliver your lab report in person." Sophia smiled, staring into her martini glass, the one remaining olive only half submerged in the murky vodka and vermouth.

Roger gave Sophia a weak smile and shifted his gaze to the attaché case on the seat.

"Thanks, Jonas. Sophia, I don't mean to be rude, but I am very anxious to get those lab results. Can I see them?"

"Of course, Roger," said Sophia. "I have them right here." She pulled the envelope out of her attaché and handed it to him. He grabbed the envelope, folded it in half, and slipped it inside his jacket.

"What, no drum roll? No big reveal? Not even going to take a peek inside?" Jonas joked.

Roger downed the rest of his Manhattan, set the glass on the table, and stood. The envelope felt hot against his chest, about to ignite every nerve end in his body. He was filled with anxiety as feelings of hope and fear of disappointment did battle in his head. Was the baby boy sleeping in Annabelle's arms his son?

"Jonas, I can't thank you enough," he said. "And Sophia, it was nice meeting you."

Sophia stared into her now empty martini glass. She looked up and watched as Roger picked his way through the crowd to the door. A slice of light, and he was gone.

"Well, that was quick," said Sophia, as the waiter set a double dirty martini on the table.

"Yeah, Clyde is one of the best waiters in town," said Jonas laughing.

"No, not the martini, Roger," said Sophia. "I may need a couple of these to comfort my bruised ego. Even if he is married, I've never seen a man make such a fast retreat."

"Don't take it personally, Sophia. Right now, no woman on earth could distract Roger from the slip of paper in that envelope."

After another round, Jonas and Sophia made their way through the raucous crowd and headed out to the parking lot. After she left, Jonas spied Roger leaning up against his car, the DNA report clutched in his hand.

"Roger, are you OK?"

Roger grabbed Jonas, his arms locked around him in a suffocating hug.

"Whoa, easy there," said Jonas, stepping back.

"Congratulate me, Jonas," said Roger, wiping his eyes. "I'm a dad."

102

IT DIDN'T TAKE long for Charlie to take over the Martin household. Annabelle slept a lot, waking for feedings and cooing over her baby boy. Jake did his best to unpack the receiving blankets, infant diapers, and formula and to set up the nursery. At her insistence, Jake put the formula on the back shelf of the pantry. Annabelle had read that breast feeding was best for the baby, with the added benefit of helping her lose her baby fat and flatten her stomach. The three Martins found their rhythm and settled into a new routine.

Jake found Annabelle standing over the baby's crib, slowly twirling the mobile above his head—blue giraffes and orange elephants dancing in a circle. The sound of her voice blanketed the sleeping baby with a lullaby. The soft glow of the circus lamp on the dresser lit up her face, and whatever jealously Jake felt for his son melted away.

"Annabelle," Jake said quietly. She turned her head and smiled, a silent summons to join her. He put his arm around her waist and she rested her head on his shoulder. Neither said a word, lost in the silence of the moment, watching the rise and fall of the baby's chest as he lay sleeping, fists relaxed, lips parted.

"He's so beautiful, isn't he Jake?"

Jake tilted his head and pressed his hand gently against her back, pulling her closer.

He felt himself slipping away from the sweet moment. His life didn't really have room for a child. He needed space, privacy, the cover of late meetings and business trips to live his life. He had businesses to run that paid for his—their— life. Jake studied the baby's face, willing to see his own nose, chin, or eyes in that sleeping face.

"Our little man," said Jake, surprised at the sincerity of his own voice.

"Do you really mean that, Jake?" said Annabelle. She turned her head to look up at him. "Do you believe that? All those angry words and accusations in the hospital. It was horrible, and I was horrible to you. We were horrible to each other. I don't want that for us—for Charlie. I want us to be a family."

"We are a perfect match, Annabelle, in love and war it seems," said Jake. "We know how to hurt each other, but we also know how to end the conflict. My parents were at constant war with each other, and it damaged everyone. That can't happen to Charlie. If we ride into battle, it will be under the same flag in the same direction to protect our son from all enemies—including ourselves. I'm willing to try if you are."

Jake smiled at Charlie, pleased with his Oscar-winning declaration.

Annabelle pulled back to face Jake. She felt safety in his arms, but felt a twinge—the familiar feeling of past embraces that conveyed his regret. She returned his embrace, completing the final scene of their script of confession and forgiveness.

"I will try, too," said Annabelle, relieved. "This is Charlie's new home. We can make it ours new home as well."

She leaned on Jake's arm and reached out to hang onto the side of the crib. "I'm a little tired, Jake. I need to lie down a bit. The hospital sent a lot of instructions for me and Charlie that I should look over. And there should be an envelope with his footprints. I want to frame that for the nursery. Can you bring the bag from the hospital into the bedroom?"

In their bedroom, she changed into one of Jake's t-shirts. She climbed onto their king-size brass and iron bed,and crawled between the taut sheets. Jake put her bag on the floor and bent to kiss the top of her head.

"I'll get Charlie and change his diaper when he wakes up," said Jake. "You try to rest."

After he left, Annabelle pulled the hospital forms and booklets for new mothers from her bag. She had been the oldest of four siblings and had had plenty of practice taking care of babies while her mother ran a successful design company. She flipped through the booklets on diaper changing, baby safety, and breast-feeding. Her breasts were one of her best features, so she ignored the section on cracked nipples, pain, and leaking.

From the stack of papers she opened an envelope with the hospital's logo. Inside was a certificate with Charlie's footprints. Annabelle smiled and ran her fingertips over the tiny impressions of Charlie's ten little toes. Then she lifted the sheet of paper and kissed it. As she did, Annabelle heard their housekeeper coming up the stairs, calling "Miss Annabelle! Miss Annabelle!"

"Up here, Madeline, in the bedroom. What is it?"

"The FedEx truck brought this just now. It looks like it's from the hospital, hand addressed! Looks very official. Confidential." Madeline ran her finger under the "Confidential" in the bottom corner.

Madeline leaned in and went on in a low frightened tone. "When my Uncle Benny was in the hospital, they sent him a FedEx envelope after they sent him home. Not good news. It was hand-addressed, too. Uncle Benny almost had a second heart attack just looking at the envelope. This one is kind of skinny, so it can't hold much bad news—"

"Madeline, you do go on sometimes. Give it to me. It's probably just another bill they forgot to give us at the hospital. Nothing to get upset about." Annabelle took the envelope and watched as Madeline hurried down the stairs.

"Why is Madeline so upset?" asked Jake, coming up the hallway.

Annabelle held up the envelope. "Just this from the hospital. Madeline thought it could be bad news. It's probably just another bill."

Jake took the envelope from her hand. "You don't need to be bothered with this. I can take care of the bills."

"In that case, there are a lot more in the bag." Annabelle playfully snatched the envelope back. "I'll put them all together and give them to you later."

A cry came from the nursery, and Jake headed back down the hallway. Annabelle settled back onto the bed, sorting the papers. When the bag was empty, she tore open the FedEx envelope and pulled out a white envelope.

But it wasn't a bill from the hospital. Her eyes darted across the page, stopping at "DNA" and "paternity." Annabelle felt dizzy and realized she was holding her breath. She gripped the paper tightly and read the names at the top of the report. The baby's name was Charlie Martin. Her Charlie. And the father was Roger Littlefield.

Annabelle was dizzy. There were columns of numbers—DNA markers—filling the page and at the bottom of the page, the determination. "Results confirmed the father tested is the biological father of the child."

Annabelle gasped, then pressed her hand to her mouth. Who ordered the paternity test? Had Jake ordered the test behind her back? How did the lab get the baby's DNA? The room seemed to dim, and she recalled Roger's angry face and his threats when he had been in her hospital room.

From somewhere outside her fog, she heard Charlie crying and footsteps in the hallway. Jake!

Annabelle quickly folded the report and put it back into the envelope, sealing it shut. She slipped it between the pillows just as Jake came into the bedroom, holding Charlie. Jake had a big smile, and the baby was precariously perched on his open hands, a new, folded diaper balanced on Charlie's stomach, his blanket trailing on the floor.

"This seems more complicated every time" said Jake with a grin. Annabelle stared back at him, gripped by panic and fear.

"What's wrong, Annabelle? Is everything alright?" He sat down next to her on the bed, cradling Charlie in his arms. "I should have insisted you hand over the hospital bills. They can scare the shit out of anyone. You don't need any unpleasant surprises now."

"No, I don't," said Annabelle taking Charlie's little hand in hers. "Not now."

103

DAVID STOOD IN the square looking up at the Tower building, counting to the sixteenth floor—Darcy's office window.
"Hey, watch out, buddy," yelled a man pushing a baby stroller
past David where he stood, oblivious to people trying to
walk around him. Startled, he moved aside, still staring at
Darcy's window. The office lights were on, bright against the
approaching darkness.

David caressed the bills in his blazer pocket, his reward
for giving a disgusting drunk a ride and—maybe—an escape
from a miserable, meaningless life. The money meant he
could relieve his own torment. His muscles ached as he
squeezed the bills harder, recalling Jake's double-cross
with the tainted Oxys and fake bills. David would deal
with him later.

He knew that Dewain had an endless supply of quality drugs, but doing business with Dewain had proved too
risky. Besides, he had other plans for Dewain, too. Anger
intensified his aching from withdrawal, soothed only by his
sure-fire brilliant deception and perfect cover. When they
started looking for someone to finger for the death of that
old drunk, they would look for someone named Dewain.

So, Darcy was his only hope. David slipped into the building, dodging office workers spilling out of it, and crossed the
atrium to the elevators. He had time to finger-comb his hair

and practice a sexy, calm smile in the mirrored walls. "Hello Darcy," he spoke sweetly to his image in the mirror. No, too ragged. "Hey Darcy," he tried again. Better, said his reflection with a smile. He could be anything in order to part Darcy from the stash of drugs in the bottom drawer of her desk.

The elevator came to a halt on the sixteenth floor. As he made his exit, David pulled the cap over his eyes and ducked to avoid the camera. He heard a voice call, "Hold the door!" David held the doors open, a million needles piercing his palm.

"Thanks, bro," said the young man as he slipped on his suit jacket, his tie loose around his neck. As he brushed past him in the doorway, David caught the faint scent of Darcy's perfume. *Someone had been doing a little overtime this evening,* he thought as he walked to Darcy's office.

There was a small slit of light under her office door. The door opened easily—her new intern must have been in a rush to get away. David knew that feeling. He pushed the button to lock the door to the hallway as it closed behind him.

"Is that you, Colin? Decided to have that second drink after all?" He remembered that raspy low tone with a hint of sexual energy summoning him into her inner office.

He pushed her door open. Darcy sat at her desk clicking through emails, eyes fixed on the laptop, a slowly darkening cityscape behind her. A bottle of tequila and two shot glasses—one with a lipstick imprint—sat on the credenza behind her.

"Hello Darcy. I see you're working late tonight."

Startled, Darcy looked up at David leaning against the doorway.

"What the hell are you doing here, David?" said Darcy, her tone changing from honey to venom. Darcy closed her laptop and stood, eyes fixed on David. "Get out of here. I told you never to come back."

"That's the spitfire I remember," said David, taking a few steps toward Darcy. "Just like our last meeting when you uttered the same sweet words to me."

"So, what are you doing here? It's late, and I have a meeting to get to."

Darcy put her palms on her desk and leaned over, revealing her black lace bra pressing against her blouse. "You must want something. I'm not available, you know."

"Not interested. In fact, it's really very simple—I need your drugs. And you're going to give me as much as I want. See, isn't that simple?"

Darcy glared at David, then smiled, stood up and started putting a stack of papers into her briefcase. "And why would I want to do that, David?

"Well, because you've been a very bad girl, and I have something that can prove it."

"You're out of your mind if you think you can hustle me."

Darcy's voice betrayed her fear that he was a strung-out junkie with nowhere else to go.

"You'd say and do anything to get your hands on some of my drugs. Well, get out now, and I won't have you arrested for trespassing and harassment."

David walked closer and stood beside her, the two framed by the floor-to-ceiling windows. She was caught off guard by his proximity. She stood still, trying to gage his intentions.

David sat down on the edge of the desk, facing her. She repulsed him. He put his hand on a stack of papers and shoved them aside.

"You're going to give me whatever I want because you're a dirty little drug dealer caught in a web of lies with another woman's husband—who is also a drug dealer. I saw the two of you at the concert at Silver Dunes Lake few days ago. I was parked next to him when you got into his BMW.

"He tried to kill me with some nasty Oxys laced with something. I know that the two of you are business partners as well as lovers. I've come to you first, but don't think I won't go to him too. What a pity that his lovely wife, who was still in the hospital after giving birth, would find out that her husband was with another woman. That wouldn't play well in the news, would it? Prominent CEO and community leader turned drug dealer lures young college interns in her employ into her dirty web using drugs and alcohol—"

"You have nothing," snapped Darcy.

She moved quickly around the desk until it was between her and David. She grabbed the Danish hunters knife she used as a letter opener and brandished it at David. The blade flashed menacingly in the dim light, catching light from the streets below.

David felt a rush, like a hungry cat who has cornered a mouse. So this mouse was going to fight back. The letter opener was one of her favorite toys. He forced disturbing memories out of his mind—the pleasure and pain of that knife against his skin. His body ached for the drugs he knew were inside the bottom desk drawer. His hands trembled as he forced himself to stay calm.

David pulled Annabelle's phone from his pocket.

"Nothing, you say? Well, I have you and Jake—yes, I know his name—getting into his car for a few minutes of some fun in the front seat before you both drove away."

He waved the phone in front of her.

"I was able to brighten the dark shots like daylight; it's a nice little movie. No mistaking the two of you. Jake wants this phone; he even offered to pay me a lot of money for it. But then he tried to double-cross me."

The demons had him in their grip; he felt bitter about being an easy mark and for ending up at Darcy's mercy again. He glared at her, found the video on the phone, and pressed "Play."

Darcy watched the small screen, never changing her expression. David smiled. He had caught the master manipulator with her panties down, literally.

"Stop!" said Darcy, turning her head away. "I've seen enough."

David took a step closer.

"Don't come any closer, you bastard. So Jake wants that phone? I'll pay you double what he offered. You can have a nice supply from my stash, too. This is your lucky day, David."

The demons in his head screamed in his ears. "I want $50,000 for the phone and whatever drugs are in the drawer *and* in the safe. That's my price," said David.

Darcy swallowed the gasp rising in her throat. "That's a deal, then. Put the phone on the desk, and I'll get the money."

"First, put the knife on the desk, Darcy."

"Not until you're out of here," she snapped.

David slipped the phone into his jacket pocket. "Well then, I'll keep the phone as collateral."

Darcy's eyes were locked on David. She moved around the desk and opened a small wall safe, withdrew several stacks of bills, and tossed the money on the desk.

"You know where the drugs are, David. Help yourself."

With one eye on Darcy, David opened the bottom desk drawer. There, in neat plastic bags, was an addict's fantasy of assorted capsules, cocaine, marijuana, and hashish. He grabbed a Louis Vuitton shopping bag from under the desk and shoved the drugs and the money into the bag. He tore at one small bag of white tablets, desperate to free one to satisfy the demons in his head.

"Just can't wait, can you, poor pathetic junkie?" she jeered. But David didn't hear her, transfixed by the plastic bag, unyielding against his shaking fingers.

Darcy moved closer to him, her hand gripping the jeweled handle of the knife. She walked behind him, unnoticed in his frenzy to open the bag. She placed the blade tip against the back of his neck.

"The phone, David," she whispered, her lips almost brushing the top of his earlobe.

David felt the cold blade press into his flesh, triggering an adrenaline rush. In one motion, he swung around, grabbed Darcy's hand holding the knife and brought it down hard on the desk. It tore through the plastic bag, sending white pills across the desk and onto the floor.

Darcy was no match for David, fueled by the sight of the freed Oxycodone. He shoved two tablets into his mouth and turned back to face her. Still holding onto her hand clutching the knife, he pressed the blade against her neck.

"No, you don't get the phone, Darcy. You are just like Jake. You wanted to kill me with that knife and take the phone, didn't you? Fucking double-crossing bitch!"

David pressed harder, sending a small stream of blood down Darcy's neck. She tried to grab at David's arm, sending the blade even deeper.

"It will be so sad when they find you, a victim of your own hand, lying on the floor surrounded by illegal drugs. What a story that will make."

David pressed the blade deeper into her neck, slicing through the artery. The stream of blood burst like an open fire hydrant. Darcy scrabbled at David's jacket, her eyes fixed on his in a wild stare. He shoved her backwards, avoiding the spray and the growing river of blood. She staggered and dropped to the floor, still clutching the knife.

Panting with rage, David reached for the bag of pills and sprinkled some on the floor, white dots against the sea of red pooling on the polished floor. It was necessary to sacrifice the pills to set the scene for the police, but such a waste.

He grabbed the shopping bag full of money and drugs, folded it over, and slipped it under his arm. He wiped down the desk drawer handles. Darcy's lifeless body lay on the floor, the knife lying just inches from her outstretched hand.

David slipped out of the office, crossed through the reception area, and cracked open the outer door. He stepped into the empty hallway, carefully closing the door with his sleeve pulled over his hand. Down the hallway he heard the elevator bell. He stepped through the stairway door just as the elevator doors opened. Three floors down, he slipped back into the hallway, took the elevator down to the street, and disappeared into the night.

104

HOLT SHOOK OFF the image of the cold, dead councilman lying in the morgue. He returned to his car, pulled out into the road, and floored it. Evidence was stacking up like pieces in a Jenga game. Dewain Johnson wasn't really Dewain; he was a George Anderson with a rap sheet. The hospital security video showed clearly that Dewain knew the guy wearing the Ravens hat who arrived at the hospital with Annabelle in the ambulance. All this time, Dewain knew who might have the phone and the wallet—he'd been lying and playing Holt. And now Holt had a dead councilman who had taken his last ride with a hospital orderly named Dewain—who was wearing a Ravens hat. Stolen drugs had been stashed in a storeroom where a now-dead high school volunteer had spent only one day. And now Dewain—George—had shown fear.

Holt's phone lit up with the forensics lab number. He picked up the call and heard Truitt's voice.

"Detective Holt, I picked up some clean prints from the hospital storeroom and ran them against the database. There had been a lot of different people in that place—I've got a list that I'll send over to you. Mostly hospital personnel."

"What about the prescription bottle, Truitt? Did you get any prints there?"

"Not on the outside of the bottle. It was pretty clean. Whoever put the bottle in the sheets used gloves or wiped it clean."

Holt leaned back against the seat, shaking his head. "Shit."

"What's that, Detective?"

"Sorry, Truitt. Is that all?"

"As I was saying, the outside of the bottle didn't have any prints. But I opened it and dusted the inside of the cap. I ran it. Detective, I ran it several times. This is the weird part; the print matched a couple prints from the storeroom. But it didn't match anyone on the hospital staff. The print belongs to a George Anderson. And he has a three-page rap sheet."

Holt smiled with relief. "Thanks, Truitt. Good work. Really good work." He tossed his phone on the seat and pressed the accelerator.

Not only was Dewain a lying thief and impersonator. He was also a murderer.

105

"I'M MORE THAN happy to help the police get to the bottom of this terrible, terrible situation."

Holt knew that voice. He stopped in front of the television screen in the ER waiting area. There on the screen was Beatrice, standing outside the Anchor Inn, talking to a couple of news reporters and surrounded by a crush of onlookers holding up cell phones capturing every word.

So Beatrice would keep this confidential? Somehow the story had made the evening news and would soon go viral.

"Was the councilman a regular customer?"

The reporter stuck a microphone in Beatrice's face. She hesitated, then spoke slowly with a compassionate tone. She was clearly calculating her response.

"The councilman was a fine man and a good customer. It's a tragedy for him and his family. The Anchor Inn has always been a favorite place for locals as well as the movers and shakers of our community."

"Was the councilman drunk when he left the bar the night he went missing?"

"I can't say he was drunk," said Beatrice. "I'll leave that to the experts.

"Aren't you obliged to stop someone from getting behind the wheel and driving drunk?"

Holt stared in horror at the Beatrice on the screen, feeling his advantage in this case slipping away with her words.

"Well, I've told the detective in the case all this, so I guess I can tell you. He didn't leave by himself. And yes, we do have a policy to offer a ride to someone we think could be a danger to himself and others. But Councilman Ortese got a ride home—at least that's where he was headed. He wasn't driving."

The crowd went wild. Cell phones flashed like those of the paparazzi at the Oscars. The reporters leaned in even closer. Holt could see a smug smile on Beatrice's face. She was enjoying every minute of this!

"A nice young man in a Ravens hat offered to give the councilman a ride home."

"Did you know the nice young man?" A reporter leaned in with his microphone. The crowd around Beatrice fell silent. All eyes were on her. She paused once more and looked straight at the camera with a serious expression. "His name?," pressed the reporter. "Do you know his name?"

Holt held his breath. *No, Beatrice. For God's sake, don't do it!*

"He said he worked at the hospital," said Beatrice. "His name was Dewain."

Holt felt his knees buckle and grabbed for a chair. The waiting room was deserted except for a man staring into his phone and a woman trying unsuccessfully to calm down a child who was alternating screams with sobbing. No one was looking at the television screen.

He had to find Dewain and hoped he wasn't on a break watching the evening news. Holt started toward the reception desk when he saw a nurse run from behind the desk, coming towards him.

"Officer, we need you—and fast. A black SUV just dumped two shooting victims outside the main entrance. One of the victims has a gun in the waistband of his jeans. He's shot in the arm, but if he's left-handed there could be a lot more victims. He's conscious and threatening to start shooting. Please!"

Holt nodded and followed the nurse down the hall. Dewain would have to wait.

106

CHERISE PULLED TWO beers from the fridge, popped the caps off on the edge of the counter, and strolled back into the bedroom.

"Here, baby," she leaned over Dewain and gave him a kiss.

"Enough, woman," he teased, and kissed her back. "Turn on the TV, baby. My one day off, and you've held me captive in this room all day. I need to see what's happening in the world."

Cherise put on her best pouty face and turned to walk away. He sat up just enough to run his hand over her buttocks; she paused so he could complete a full circuit.

She tossed the remote to Dewain, and he turned on the evening news just as Beatrice was finishing her interview, marked as "Breaking News." The crawl gave details of the councilman's murder. Dewain punched up the volume as Cherise slipped back into bed.

Dewain put his arm around Cherise and pulled a long draft from the frosty bottle.

"Hey, I know that old woman," Dewain said to Beatrice's image on the screen. "Been in that dive a couple of times. What a dump."

"A nice young man in a Ravens cap gave the councilman a ride home," Beatrice was saying. Cherise shook her head.

Dewain sat up, pulling Cherise up with him. "Did she just say a Ravens cap?"

What had his junkie friend been up to?

Cherise shrugged her shoulders and settled back on the pillows. "Yeah, baby, it's a bird, from that football team. Hush, I'm listening to this."

The TV reporter asked Beatrice whether she knew the man who had taken the councilman from the bar.

The crowd around Beatrice fell silent. He tensed, waiting for her reply.

"His name," pressed the reporter. "Do you know his name?"

The camera zoomed in until Beatrice's face filled the screen. "He said he worked at the hospital" said Beatrice, "and his name was Dewain."

He picked up the remote and hurled it at the television. That lying, double-crossing, son-of-a-bitch!

Cherise jumped up, screaming at Dewain as she pointed to the screen. "Are you crazy? That thing cost me two paychecks!"

Dewain felt strangely calm as the station shifted to a commercial. Cherise's voice seemed far away. He slowly put on his clothes and shoes. He walked over to the dresser and put on his watch and pinkie ring and ran a comb through his hair. He pulled open a top drawer of the bureau, pulled out his Glock 42, and popped in a new magazine. He put the gun in his jacket and zipped the pocket halfway.

Cherise silently watched Dewain from across the room. It was like watching a perfectly choreographed dance from a movie. Dewain paused, and she finally spoke.

"Dewain, what did you do? That old woman said it was someone from the hospital named Dewain. Was that you? That councilman is dead."

Dewain slowly walked around the bed and leaned over Cherise, an unnerving calm about him as he stared straight at her.

"I haven't done anything, Cherise. And don't ask me what I'm going to do because I *am* going to do something. If the cops come knocking on the door—and they will—keep your mouth shut. Don't open the door for anyone."

107

BACK HOME, DAVID poured the contents of the shopping bag onto the dining room table. Stacks of money and bags of drugs made a pile of pleasure and relief. The two pills he had taken in Darcy's office had done their trick, and he was reveling in his cache and his brilliant disposal of his former boss and tormentor. Not a hitch. Not a witness.

Jubilant, he sat down and wrapped his arms around the pile. With a quick motion, he threw it in the air, like a child throwing confetti at a birthday party. Hannah leapt from her perch on the sofa and onto the edge of the table.

"Let me have my moment, Hannah." said David, putting on his best little-boy voice. Hannah curled and uncurled her tail, letting it fall gently on David's arm still stretched out on the table.

"Thank you, Hannah. You always understand me." He stroked her back and kissed her softly on the head.

David picked up a bag of white powder and brought a stack of Darcy's $50 bills into the living room. He could hear the television across the room—he must have left it on last night. Hannah followed and jumped up on the coffee table, paws resting on the remote.

"No, Hannah, leave it." As she walked over it, a paw pressed the volume control and David heard familiar music announcing a special news report.

David cleared a spot on the glass coffee table and shook out a small pile of white powder. He peeled off a fifty and divided the powder into three lines. Then he rolled the bill up and inhaled the first line.

Hannah stepped on the remote again, and the volume got louder. David read the top banner on the screen: *Councilman found dead in tragic accident.*

Startled, David sat up. The reporter described how the councilman had been discovered dead on the side of the road not far from the Anchor Inn with a bar napkin from that establishment in his pocket.

"The bartender talked to our reporter in an exclusive interview." The image cut to Beatrice standing outside the bar.

David stared at the screen. That lying bitch! They'd agreed keep it quiet. He should have taken her, too.

Hannah jumped up on the sofa and curled up next to David. Her soft touch was reassuring, and he reached out to stroke her tail. She could always calm him down.

Beatrice's name flashed on the screen below her image as she went on.

"Well, I've told the detective this, so I guess I can tell you. He didn't leave by himself. And yes, we do have a policy to offer a ride to someone we think could be a danger to himself and others. But Councilman Ortese got a ride home—at least that's where he was headed. He wasn't driving."

The reporter asked a question, but David only heard Beatrice's voice.

"A nice young man in a Ravens hat offered to give the councilman a ride home."

The reporter's lips moved again, David leaned over the last two lines on the tabletop, inhaling deeply.

"His name?" pressed the reporter. "Do you know his name?"

David watched Beatrice's face, now filling the screen.

The demons whispered, *"David. David did it."*

But then Beatrice spoke, silencing the voices in his head. "He said he worked at the hospital. And his name was Dewain."

The hospital connection was brilliant; David congratulated himself.

The voices chanted, "*Dewain is David. David is Dewain.*"

"But no one knows that," David said out loud, and Hannah seemed to purr in agreement.

He turned off the television. Beatrice's story would call off the cops, but Dewain was another matter. As if on cue, David's phone lit up with Dewain's number. He let it go to voicemail. It lit up again and again, and finally went dark. David tapped on voicemail and heard Dewain's voice—slow, measured, and eerily calm.

"I'm coming for you, David." Click.

106

HOLT RACED AHEAD of the nurse to the front entrance. "Call for backup, now!"

He broke through the crowd gathered inside the doors at the front entrance. One victim was on the ground with wounds to the leg and shoulder. He had a gun in his waistband, alternately screaming out threats and demanding help. The other victim was motionless, lying at the edge of the walkway. Holt drew his weapon and walked out the door, gun pointed squarely at the screamer.

"Reach for that gun and I take out your other shoulder," he shouted as the man grimaced in pain.

Holt moved forward; his gun fixed on the victim. *Couple of amateurs,* Holt thought as he watched the guy collapse in pain. He bent over and pulled out the gun as the screams turned into whimpers. Applause erupted from the audience behind the glass front door.

He nodded to the crowd just as a squad car with sirens blaring sped up to the entrance. Two uniformed men, guns drawn, ran out. Holt held up his hand. "Party's over. Got it covered, guys," he said to the officers. He lowered his voice and added. "Must be trash day. Someone dumped these two pieces of shit out of a moving car five minutes ago."

After Holt filled in the officers, he asked if they could clean the situation up. "I'm here on another case and got pulled into this."

"We can take it from here, detective. Go get the bad guys."

Holt went back into the hospital. The crowd had dispersed, but an elderly woman in a wheelchair was waiting for her ride home. "Nice work, Dirty Harry," she said. "You made my day!"

Holt smiled and headed for the main desk. He flashed his badge to the receptionist, who smiled and gave him the thumbs up.

"I'm looking for a Dewain Johnson. He's an orderly here at the hospital. Official business. Where can I find him?"

"What's he done now?" She said smiling, tapping furiously on the keyboard.

Holt leaned in as the receptionist shook her head. "Sorry, detective. He's not here. It's his day off."

109

DAVID GATHERED THE open bag of cocaine, a bag of heroin, and one amphetamine capsule and took them to the kitchen. He turned on the undercounter lights, illuminating the granite countertop. He pulled out a plastic syringe, a large metal spoon, a paper cup, and a disposable lighter out of the bottom drawer.

It took a while to dissolve the powder and granules, but David was an experienced mixologist. He watched the liquid begin to bubble in the spoon. He filled the syringe and replaced the cap, putting the syringe in his pocket. He turned off the lights, walked out of the kitchen, and sat down on the stairs facing the front door. He was ready for anything.

———

Across town, Detective Holt rounded the corner and pulled up in front of Dewain's apartment building. It was a four-story steel-and-glass structure with a lighted entryway flanked by potted plants. Tall pencil evergreen trees stood at each end of the building. He could see a railing on the rooftop, with lights strung on poles. Music spilled over the railing onto the street below. It seemed pretty pricey for an orderly's salary.

Holt went through the outer doors into the building to another set of inner locked glass doors. He scanned the mailboxes, searching for maintenance or a super's button. Just then a young woman inside the building walked toward the locked door and flung it open. Holt slipped in, heading for the elevator. He found Dewain's apartment at the end of the hallway on the third floor and knocked hard on the door.

"Police, open up. This is Detective Holt. You'd better talk to me, Dewain, before the Ravens fan finds you. "

110

THE POUNDING ON Dewain's apartment door made Cherise jump, sending her vodka on the rocks crashing to the floor.

She stood and stared at the door, expecting it to burst open any minute.

Dewain's command echoed in her ears, and he'd been right. That Holt guy was just outside. The pounding got harder and the shouting got louder. Cherise picked up her cocktail glass, walked into the kitchen, and poured another two fingers of vodka over fresh ice. Finally, silence. A small business card slid under the door across the floor.

Cherise heard the sound of footsteps moving away down the hall. She picked up Holt's card and read the note he had scrawled on the back.

"They always leave something behind."

111

CHERISE WOKE THE next morning and shielded her eyes from the sun filtering through the windows. Her head pounded, and her tongue stuck to the roof of her mouth. It had taken three shots of vodka before she finally got to sleep last night. She was alone in the apartment. Where was Dewain, and what has he done?

She looked at her phone. She had twenty-five minutes before she would be late for her shift at the hospital. She could make it from Dewain's apartment in twenty, easy. *He didn't say I couldn't leave.*

112

DAVID WOKE UP on the floor, next to the stairs. Hannah paced back and forth in front of the kitchen door.

"Yeah, Hannah, I see you," he whispered.

David got to his feet. He checked his pocket for the syringe, still secure, and pushed open the kitchen door. He emptied a can of food into Hannah's bowl and set it on the floor, but she walked past the bowl and paused in front of the door that lead to the basement. She sat down and scratched at it.

"Eat, Hannah," he said, motioning to her bowl.

He pulled out a coffee pod, inserted it into the machine, and hit brew. Hannah stood up on her hind legs, front paws on the basement door and looked over at David. Then she sprawled onto the floor, nose at the bottom of the door. He walked over and felt a rush of cold air coming from the basement.

David turned the lock and opened the door. The basement was dark. He flipped the light on but heard a pop.

"Bulb must have blown," he said to Hannah who followed behind.

He could feel a draft of cold air blowing in as he descended the stairs. He stopped halfway to reach for the flashlight he kept on an open stud next to the stairs. He pushed the button. Nothing—the batteries had gone dead.

As his eyes adjusted to the dark, he could make out furniture and storage boxes piled in rows. It's like a maze down here, he thought, picking his way around the tall stacks. He came around the corner and felt the full blast of air. One of the basement access windows, high up near the ceiling was open. These old houses had at least one window just above the ground level on the outside for light, tall and wide enough for access from outside for repairs or emergencies.

He hadn't remembered opening that window. David shivered, but not from the air blowing in. He felt exposed, vulnerable. Any number of creatures could come in through that open window. Hannah brushed past him and looked up at the window.

"Yeah, I'll get it."

He pulled an old chair over to the window and climbed up, pushing the window shut and securing the lock.

"There, that should do it, Hannah."

Hannah ran ahead towards the basement stairs. But at the bottom step she stopped, turned, crouched down low, raised her haunches, and hissed into the darkness.

"Yes, Hannah," he laughed. "You're my protector. My lioness. My fierce bobcat. Let's go!"

Hannah didn't move. David reached down and carried her upstairs.

Hidden behind stacks of boxes, another set of eyes stared, watching the two ascend the stairs and close the door behind them.

113

THE BACKUP WARNING alarm of a garbage truck woke Holt with a start. It took him a full minute to realize he was still in his car, parked down the street from Dewain's apartment building. He looked at his phone, buzzing on the passenger seat. The screen was covered with alerts from the precinct. *Emergency meeting at nine in the morning with Captain Stevenson, concerning Councilman Ortese.*

It was seven-thirty. He was going to be late. He took a swallow of yesterday's cold coffee, put the car in gear, and pulled into morning traffic. He checked his voicemails; no messages from Dewain. With his name connected with the councilman's death, he'd be laying low somewhere, away from the hospital.

After a quick shower, shave, and change of clothes, he was in the conference room by eight fifty-five. He found the last seat. The chief and the precinct captain sat at either ends of the table. Holt brought a list of evidence or circumstances that tied Dewain to a number of unsolved cases. When it was his turn to report, he recited the list.

The missing wallet and phone. A meeting with the guy with the Ravens hat in the hospital the night they went missing.

Purloined drugs missing from patients released from the hospital.

The hospital storeroom used as a waystation for an inside drug operation, and Dewain's thumbprint on the inside cap of a prescription bottle of Oxys hidden in the storeroom.

A young volunteer who died from an overdose of drugs that had been stored in that room.

A named suspect in the suspicious death of a city councilman.

Holt figured Dewain for a two-bit, low-life hustler, even a drug dealer. But murdering a councilman? It didn't figure. He had to find Dewain, and fast.

The chief and captain stood up, signaling the meeting's end. Holt looked up at the chief to see if he was aware of the work he had already done on the case. The chief stood silent, his expression a cross between needing a laxative and contemplating a homicide of his own.

"Now get out there and get this guy." The captain picked up the file from the table. headed for the door, and stopped short. He searched the crowd of officers, and spotted Holt.

"Holt, in my office."

114

HOLT PREPARED HIMSELF for a lecture. He replayed the last one—his fall from grace and reassignment to petty crime—in his head. Not being a team player. Hindering an investigation and losing a major conviction by keeping leads and evidence to himself. Fraternizing with the public. Showing up unshaven and smelling like beer and Listerine. He followed the captain to his office and sat down, ready for a speech. He could have given it himself.

"Holt, that was an impressive list of possible evidence linking the suspect "Dewain" in the councilman's death to several open cases. The problem, as I see it, is that you were the only officer in this precinct familiar with the first five bullet points. I thought a bump down to street crime would teach you to share information with others and play by the rules."

Holt looked down at his shoes, ready for the howling to start.

The captain sat behind his desk and folded his hands on top of the file.

"You're one of our best, and you know it, Holt, so I'm not going to give you the satisfaction of hearing and ignoring my warnings again. We've got a dead councilman, and we got a call from the precinct covering the Plaza downtown. It seems that a CEO was found in her Market Square office with a slit throat, surrounded by a sea of Oxycodone. A cleaning crew found her this morning. No witnesses, but her intern showed up an hour later. He had seen her alive when he left a little after seven the previous night.

"He said he crossed paths with a young guy who got out of the elevator on the sixteenth floor just as the intern was leaving. The guy said to him, "Late night, eh?" like he was familiar with the place. Said the guy was wearing a Ravens hat. Unless we have a shitload of Maryland transplants who can't leave the house without a ballcap featuring a bird on their heads, sounds like it could be your guy who drove off with our councilman. Seems this dead woman wasn't Lady Madonna, either. Had a reputation.

"So, listen good. We've got two dead bodies connected with a guy named Dewain wearing a Ravens baseball cap."

Holt took a deep breath. "His name isn't Dewain, captain. I left that out. The name belongs to a nice old dead guy who was resurrected by a Mr. George Anderson, a former frequent guest of the state and federal prison system who is now working at the hospital. The hospital had offered me his help with my missing-property case, but I was suspicious of him from the start. I haven't revealed to him that I know about his stolen identity yet; trying to keep him close. I had him yesterday, but he slipped away—now he's hiding somewhere."

The captain glared. "Good God almighty, Holt. Stop talking. I can't take any more of your Lone Ranger bullshit. Get everything you know to the other detectives and officers. We've got to find this guy. The mayor is very unhappy. Get him, dammit!"

115

THE BASEMENT WAS dark again. The last rays of sunshine moved up and over the basement window and climbed the side of the house. The only light in the basement came from under the kitchen door. The chair David had used to close the window made an almost-comfortable bed. Dewain stood up and stretched his legs. He'd slept in worse places. He checked his watch; it was six-thirty in the evening. He'd been there for nearly twenty-four hours ago after watching Beatrice's performance in his apartment.

Dewain saw the light disappear from under the door at the top of the stairs. He stood still, listening, then slowly climbed the stairs. The doorknob turned easily. He slipped inside the kitchen and silently closed the door. He could feel his Glock against his side as he walked into the hallway and into the living room.

David was sitting on the couch, bent over the coffee table. A rolled bill transported a line of powder into his nose. He sniffed hard, wiped his nose with his jacket sleeve, and fell back against the cushions.

Hannah saw him first. She crouched down low, all her muscles tensed, ready to spring at the intruder. David heard her hiss, followed her gaze, and saw Dewain walking towards him with a gun pointed at him.

"Dewain, what the fuck are you doing here? How did you get in? Put the fucking gun down!"

"You're getting sloppy, David. Leaving windows unlocked. Pissing off your connections. Picking up prominent drunks in bars. Leaving witnesses behind who can talk to the cops. And your biggest mistake was lying to that nice old bartender. Fingering me for your dirty deed. 'Dewain from the hospital?' That was your last lie, David."

Dewain moved closer, his eyes fixed on David. Hannah hissed and rose up on her haunches. Dewain turned his eyes on Hannah, lowered his gun, and fired.

"Shit!" David scrambled off the couch, tripping over the edge of the coffee table. A thin trail of smoke rose from the bullet hole in the cushion where Hannah had been sitting before she leaped.

David backed away from Dewain. He slid his hand across his pocket feeling for the syringe. Still there.

His eyes darted around the room, searching for Hannah. Then he saw her behind Dewain, peering from behind the draperies. She silently crossed the living room to the bottom of a tall bookcase next to Dewain. Hannah stopped and looked at David, then Dewain, and back to David. She crouched low and took a few steps.

"Dewain, take it easy with that thing." David backed up. "Do you want money? Drugs? The phone and wallet? Take them. I may have lied about that—but you know junkies, Dewain."

David kept Hannah in his peripheral vision, not daring to shift his eyes away from Dewain. She was on the club chair next to the bookcase flanking the flat-screen television. David had stacked some books on their sides, protruding past the end of the shelves like steps to form a perfect ladder for Hannah to climb to the top.

"The reward for the phone and wallet is nothing compared to what you can squeeze out of that woman's husband—he has his own side hustle in drugs," David continued. "The phone has a video of him banging his girlfriend—you could blackmail him! The guy is loaded. He'd pay millions for it. Take it, Dewain. And the wallet has photos of his wife and another man. Squeeze both ends at the same time!"

Hannah climbed the book steps to the top of the bookcase, curling up and out of sight except for the tip of her tail.

"You pathetic, stupid little junkie," spat Dewain. "I'm going to kill you and your cat, too. You think you can cross me? I could kill you now with one little squeeze of the trigger. I'll have it all, and you'll be dead."

David put up his hands and started walking slowly towards Dewain. "I've got them hidden, Dewain. I'll get them and make it easy for you. If you kill me now, you'd never find them."

As David moved closer, Dewain stepped back. "I'll show you where everything is," David motioned to the dining room.

Dewain stepped aside, his back to the bookcase, and gestured for David to walk in front of him. As he did, Hannah crept to the edge of the top of the bookcase just above Dewain's head.

Dewain jammed the gun barrel into David's back. "Stop right there, junkie. Maybe I'll just shoot you here and find them myself."

Dewain leveled the barrel of the Glock to strike between David's shoulder blades. David turned his head and looked around into Dewain's cold eyes for a fraction of a second, then up to Hannah, coiled like a spring. As their eyes met, Hannah let out a howl and leapt onto Dewain's head, hissing and clawing at his face and neck.

"Get off me!" screamed Dewain. The gun was tangled uselessly in the three fingers of his hand. Arms flailing, he tried to pull the cat off, but Hannah held on, slashing at his neck and planting her hind claws into his back.

David dropped to the floor and crawled behind the club chair, crouching out of the line of fire.

"I'll kill you, you fucking cat," screamed Dewain as he grabbed at her. Hannah let out a howl and clawed at him. Dewain swung his arm, using the barrel of the Glock like a hammer to stop Hannah's assault. Just as she swiped at him, the gun went off, peeling off the side of Dewain's face, splattering flesh and blood over the wall and books.

Dewain dropped to the floor in a heap. As he fell, Hannah jumped free and landed beside him.

David crawled out from behind the club chair.

"Come here, Hannah," he whispered. Hannah leaped over Dewain's lifeless body and curled up beside David. He stroked her back with shaking hands. "You are my cat, my lioness, my protector."

David surveyed the scene. The smell of fresh gun residue, torn flesh, and blood hung in the air. He looked out the window at the street. No crowd was gathering, no porch lights were on. No sirens wailing in the night. No police cars bearing down on his house.

He got towels, garbage bags, and a bucket of water and some bleach from the kitchen. He pulled on a pair of latex gloves, wiped Dewain's face off the books and the wall, and soaked up the blood pooled around his head. He pulled a plastic garbage bag over Dewain's head and tied it tightly around his neck. The pistol was still wedged in his hand. Perfect; he wouldn't have to touch the gun at all.

David went to the hall closet and pulled out his Ravens cap. It was a little dirty, the bill broken in from use—it would be the finishing touch. He turned Dewain's body over and tucked the folded hat into the back of his waistband.

He rolled Dewain up like a cigar in a waterproof tarp from the garage, securing both ends with rope. The cocaine and Oxy binge had poured strength into him; he dragged

Dewain through the kitchen, into the garage, and finally onto the back of David's truck.

The roads were quiet. A soft rain fell on the windshield. He drove over a bridge and made a sharp left turn onto a seldom-used service road that wound behind the shopping area, beyond the dilapidated bus shack and the old residential area. When he was a child, David's grandfather had taken him fishing at this "secret spot," the farthest northern point on the Eastport River. He found the overgrown trail, barely wide enough for his truck, stopped at what was left of the old dock, and parked the truck in the tree cover.

The bundle felt heavier coming out, one end bouncing like a bowling ball down to the ground. David pulled the tarp to the deserted dock and rolled Dewain into the river's swift current. The tarp floated, turning in the flow of the water, then slowly sank out of sight.

116

CHARLIE WAS A dream baby. He was a good sleeper, giving Annabelle the time she needed to rest and regain her strength. He rarely cried, and was content being held or swaddled. Annabelle swore he smiled at the sound of her voice and grabbed her fingers with his chubby hands, searching for her comforting touch.

With Annabelle occupied with Charlie, Jake spent more time getting back to his secret life and work. His clients didn't care about a baby. They were as strung out and demanding as ever. His suppliers and dealers kept up the pace, while Jake made excuses to Annabelle so he could make pickups and deliveries.

But something felt different. He found himself stopping by the nursery before or after his meetings. They were slowly becoming that family Jake and Annabelle vowed to create.

They had become a family of three—plus one. With Charlie's arrival, Madeline quickly pivoted from washing floors and changing bed linens to being Charlie's nanny, nurse, and protector. Annabelle grew to trust her as she would her own mother with Charlie's care.

"Look, Jake," Annabelle called. "He's doing it again." Jake stuck his head into the nursery, briefcase in hand.

"What is it this time, Annabelle? What is our brilliant son doing?"

"He's smiling at me!"

Jake studied his son's cherubic face—a perfect oval with big blue eyes, topped by a shock of dark curly hair. He searched for even a hint of a smile, but didn't see anything.

"Are you sure, Annabelle?" said Jake, laughing. "They say infants his age might make a facial expression that looks like a smile, but it's really gas."

Anabelle looked at Jake with a grin and held out her hand. He lifted it to his lips, and gave it a soft kiss. "Yes, dear, now that I look closely, I think I *do* see a smile."

Jake's phone buzzed. Another anxious client waiting impatiently for a delivery?

"Do you have to go out, Jake? After I feed Charlie, he'll be down for a few hours and we could have some time to ourselves."

Jake felt it again. A moment of hesitancy about leaving Annabelle and Charlie. And guilt over the secrets he kept from Annabelle. The affair with Darcy. His doubts about Annabelle's faithfulness. The danger he could be exposing them to with his association with the drug cartels, dealers, and clients. He had never worried about any of it before Charlie. He had only worried about how to widen his reach and gain more power, influence, and wealth. He reached over and held Charlie's leg, feeling the soft skin against his own.

His phone buzzed again. "I have to go, Annabelle." He bent down and kissed her forehead. She turned her face towards his, and he bent and pressed a soft kiss against her lips.

"I love you two," said Jake. "And I'm going to take care of you."

117

HIKERS FOUND THE body a few days later down the river, tangled in low water near some old wharf pilings. The river's current had loosened the rope on one end, enough for Dewain's left arm to escape the tarp, the middle of his remaining three fingers extended in a last defiant gesture.

Holt was at the morgue when they unzipped the body bag. There lay Dewain, who had been so slick and sure of himself. The left side of his face had been blown away; the other side had been deeply scratched and torn, clearly by an animal's claws. Then he had been rolled up like a piece of salt-water taffy and tossed into the river.

Since the councilman's body had been found on the side of the road, the media had hounded the mayor with questions about the spate of deaths and the possibility of a serial killer. First the councilman, then the CEO found with her throat cut in her high-rise office. The pressure was on to find who was responsible, and fast.

The evidence stacked against Dewain seemed to indicate an open-and-shut case.

The bartender reported that the guy who had driven away with the drunk councilman had worn a Ravens cap, had said his name was Dewain, and told her he worked at the hospital. The intern who discovered the CEO's body had seen a young guy wearing a Ravens cap coming from the elevator near Darcy's office on the night she was murdered. The wallet on the guy dumped in the river had Dewain's driver's license and hospital ID. And he had a Ravens cap tucked into his waistband.

Those details stuck in Holt's brain. Every description of the guy who had been on the bus and the ambulance had included a Ravens cap. The security cameras had showed the guy who was *with* Dewain had been wearing a Ravens cap. So was Dewain a Ravens fan, too? Or had the hat found on his body been a plant?

The mayor and the police chief couldn't be more pleased, believing the man in the river had murdered the councilman and the CEO. The hikers' discovery had taken the heat off everyone.

The ink was barely dry on the coroner's report when the mayor's office called a press conference. They had their guy. Holt stood behind the mayor with the police chief, a senior member of the city council, the captain, and the coroner. The CEO of East End Technologies and the young volunteer's sister Bianca stood to the side of the podium. When Holt was called to the podium for Q&A, he gave broad responses with enough truth to spackle the case together while covering up its gaping holes.

"We are confident that the man who was pulled from the river was the same Dewain Johnson who gave the councilman a ride home from the bar the night he went missing. We have his ID, the hospital ID, and a Ravens cap on his person matching the description from the bartender at the Anchor Inn. We believe that he also is responsible for the death of the CEO of East End Technologies. And given his known drug thefts at the hospital, he was also responsible for the death of a young volunteer." Mostly true, Holt knew. But no one else knew that he wasn't Dewain Johnson at all—a secret between him, the lab, and Dewain himself.

And dead men don't tell tales.

"Can you give us information on Mr. Johnson? There hasn't been a photo released or a description."

"The body was in the river for a couple of days. We are working with the hospital to secure a photo. We do have definitive evidence of his identity."

"We are still working on the cases with the CEO and the young hospital volunteer, but we have reason to believe the three murders were committed by the same person. It's an ongoing investigation, and we will release information as we can." Only Holt knew that the connections between Dewain and the deaths of the councilman and Darcy had more holes than Swiss cheese.

"Any idea how this Dewain Johnson ended up in the river?"

The mayor stepped to Holt's right at the podium and put his hand on his arm, pulling him away from the microphone.

"Thank you, Detective Holt, for your insights. Folks, the detective has a lot of work ahead of him with a series of such complicated crimes, and we best let him get to it. That's all for now. The public-affairs office will be issuing statements as the case progresses, and we will inform you of further press conferences. The most important message tonight is that the killer has been identified and is no longer a threat. Thank you all."

Holt scanned the crowd of reporters. He had been at this for a long time and saw by their expressions that not many bought the story. Nothing about the case fit together for Holt, except that they had a body that fit a very basic description.

No one had come forward to identify or claim Dewain's body. The hospital seemed to be dragging its feet and hadn't sent a photo or any information about Dewain. The hospital rumor mill was hot, but no one was talking to hospital officials or the police. The hospital administrators had had their own suspicions about Dewain that had gone unreported and not investigated. A killer had access to patients at their most vulnerable, and there was the unresolved, suspicious death of a high school volunteer who may have gotten the drugs that killed her from between the sheets in a hospital storage room.

There were enough unanswered questions for a nail-biting round of Double Jeopardy.

Dewain's death meant that Holt had another murder to solve, although for now his relief that Dewain was dead outweighed his curiosity about who had wanted him dead. Whoever killed him had relieved the town of another worthless criminal.

Holt knew how to give just enough information to satisfy the media. Dribble it out like a slow faucet, just enough to answer a few questions and satisfy their curiosity. They would soon enough lose interest and latch onto something more exciting, and he could work quietly behind the scenes.

Holt walked out of city hall to his car parked in the loading zone. He had swung open the door when he heard the mayor's voice.

"Holt! A word?" The mayor was just about down the stairs to the sidewalk. Holt slammed the door shut and walked over to the mayor. He could see him dismiss his entourage, leaving them alone on the street.

"Make this stick, Holt," said the mayor. He fixed his eyes on Holt and said it again. "This is our guy."

"Mr. Mayor. With all due respect, this is an ongoing investigation, and we're really only getting started. And Dewain Johnson's death is a homicide case. There is a lot of work—"

The mayor gripped Holt's arm, his gaze never shifting.

"Fuck the respect bullshit, Holt. Don't misplace who deserves your respect or your loyalties here. That piece of shit ending up dead is a gift. Make it stick. There's no trial for a dead man. No witnesses, no testimony, no judge, no jury. Case closed. Just make the pieces fit. This isn't a request, Holt."

As the mayor spoke, his grip tightened, his manicured nails pressing squarely into the sleeve of Holt's long-sleeved shirt. He was making a point—with just a hint of what kind of pain he could inflict if Holt wasn't compliant.

"I understand, sir," said Holt, returning his fixed gaze.

It didn't take a genius to figure this out. Ending the threat of a serial killer by making Dewain responsible for three murders would go a long way to gaining public confidence and securing a win in the upcoming mayoral election. Holt's stomach churned, and his neck muscles tightened. Scum rose to the top, and he loathed the scum he had to deal with to clean up their dirty messes. More than that, he hated being used.

The mayor slowly released Holt's arm and gave a nod, never breaking his gaze. Holt watched as the mayor and his entourage climbed into their black-and-silver town cars and sped away. He climbed into his car, rolled down the window, closed his eyes, and took a deep, slow breath. He sat for a minute until the pain from the mayor's grip began to fade. He looked down and saw his knuckles stretched tight on the steering wheel, white and bloodless.

Holt glanced at his cell phone on the passenger seat. The screen showed a text message from Veronica with a photo. He tapped the screen, enlarged the photo, and stared. He felt his hands relax, transferring the tension to another part of his body.

You are a bad girl, Veronica. And a bad girl is just what this detective needs right now.

118

DAVID WATCHED THE mayor's press conference from his living room couch through a haze of cocaine and bourbon. Thanks to Darcy, he stayed high. In the days since he had visited her office, the supply had started to dwindle, but the money and a new, eager dealer would keep him supplied for some time.

The room had a faint scent of bleach and Lysol, the aftereffects of Dewain's messy accident in the living room. David had long ago learned how to clean up messes. The damage to the books was unfortunate collateral damage. Some of the best of his collection, splattered with blood from Dewain's face, were now in the recycling center's shredding bin.

Stop crying, boy. Your mother isn't feeling well, so it's your job to take care of this mess. She should have done what she was supposed to do. You'll learn that women need to be handled; they get confused. Pour some bleach in that bucket of water and rub the red stains out of the carpet. Bleach for blood—remember that.

David watched Detective Holt at the podium during the conference, laying out the evidence that pinned Dewain to the councilman's murder. Behind him the mayor stood tall, an appropriate concerned look on his face; his mouth unable to control just a hint of an upturned corner. The mayor was pleased that the case was solved. And so was David. *The hat in the waistband was perfect.*

Hannah purred beside David, as if taking credit for the outcome, staring at the screen as well. Hannah's attack had made it that much harder for the coroner to take photos. Once the hospital's privacy policies had been satisfied, they'd release a photo of Dewain. Case closed. Everyone could relax.

David stroked Hannah from the top of her head to the end of her tail with a slow, gentle movement. Hannah responded to his touch, eyes closed, yielding slightly under his hand, stretching when David's stroke left the end of her tail.

He got up, went into the dining room, and pulled Annabelle's wallet from the drawer. He carried it into the living room, grabbed the bag filled with Darcy's money, and pulled out ten $100 bills. He stacked them face up and slid them into the wallet. He pulled Annabelle's phone from his pocket, got a large manilla envelope from the desk, dropped both the wallet and the phone inside, and sealed it.

Hannah sauntered over to David, jumping up to the chair and then the desktop. David tucked the envelope under his arm and reached down to stroke her back, staring ahead blankly.

"I've got one more bit of business to take care of, Hannah," he said.

This one will be painful.

119

CHERISE SAT MOTIONLESS on the couch. Empty beer bottles, a bag of tortilla chips, and a bowl of now-brown guacamole littered the coffee table in front of her. She was numb. The only sensation came through her fingertips, caressing the jacket Dewain had thrown over the couch before he left that night days ago. It held the scent of him.

The only voices in the room since he had left came from the television. She couldn't bear the silence. Dewain wasn't prince charming. He was loud and unpredictable, full of secrets, and a little dangerous. He had a past before she caught his eye at the hospital, and she had known she would be part of his past one day as well. He was sexy, brash, and fearless. She hated that she couldn't resist him and hated him even more for leaving her.

Her phone lit up again. The hospital had been calling twice a day. She couldn't bring herself to face anyone to discuss the rumors and questions. She was sure no one had seen her holding the bag of drugs that she and Dewain had removed from the storeroom; the bag now in the back of the bedroom closet. She sat, staring ahead, waiting for the ring tones to stop.

A headline flashed on the TV screen. NEWS ALERT! PHOTO RELEASED OF COUNCILMAN'S KILLER. Below that headline, Dewain stared, dressed in scrubs as if ready for his next shift. Next to the photo the mayor was speaking into a microphone.

"The hospital staff has confirmed the killer's identity. This murderer is off the streets, and the city is safe again."

Cherise walked to the television screen, and pressed her fingers to Dewain's image. She placed a kiss on her fingertips and pressed them against Dewain's lips.

She picked up her phone, turned it off, and picked up a half-empty vodka bottle. She cradled Dewain's jacket under her arm, walked into the bedroom, and opened the closet door.

120

"SON OF A bitch! There he is, the bastard! He looks like a killer!" The bar was filling up. The hospital day shift had ended an hour ago, and the overachievers were straggling in, thirsty for a beverage and some gossip. A news alert flashed over the two flat screens, igniting the crowd and sending up shouts, high-fives, and a string of profanities. "And I worked right next to that psychopath! Could have been me on the side of the road!"

Beatrice came out of the kitchen, balancing plates heaped with burgers, nachos, and onion rings. "Here you are, gentlemen," she said with a wink, dropping the plates in front of three doctors still in scrubs, working on their fourth happy-hour beers. "The cook got engaged last night, so he's generous with the helpings. I should pay his fiancée a salary just to keep him happy!"

"You played it right, Beatrice old girl." The voice gave the thumbs up.

She congratulated herself on her performance, playing the police and the press and taking advantage of the poor councilman's untimely death to promote the Anchor Inn. It had put the bar on the map. Pulling out an Anchor Inn cocktail napkin from a pocket or purse after a night at the bar was the thing at parties or in the break room. It was hard to get a bar seat or a table most any night, and happy hour was standing room only. The money was rolling in; tips had never been higher. The councilman might not have been worth shit when he was alive—but dead, he sure did raise her standard of living.

One of the regulars at the bar motioned to Beatrice, holding up his empty glass.

"What's your pleasure tonight, Jerry?" she said with a flirty grin.

"Did you see it?"

"See what? I just came out of the kitchen."

"The photo of the guy who killed the councilman. Dewain Johnson. The hospital finally released his picture. Creepy guy, too! Looks like a killer."

"On the news just now?" Beatrice grabbed the remote and started flipping channels.

"There . . . there it is!" Jerry pointed to the screen while Beatrice stared.

"Must be weird to see him again, eh, Beatrice? To think you were here with the killer and his victim that night. Thank God they got him! It could have been you dead on the side of the road!"

"Shut up, Jerry. I'm listening."

The reporter recapped the story of the councilman's death at the hands of Dewain Johnson while the split screen scrolled through shots of the road where the councilman's body had been found, the Anchor Inn's neon sign against the sky, and Beatrice, the woman who helped break the case. All the while, fixed on the screen, Dewain Johnson stared down.

Beatrice braced herself against the bar, her eyes fixed on the face of a man she had never seen. The photo on the screen wasn't the man in the bar that night. It might be someone named Dewain Johnson, but he sure wasn't the man who picked the councilman off the floor and marched him out to his death. The hair was all wrong. The man that night had fair skin and a few strands of dirty blond hair trailing under the hat's brim. The Dewain on the screen had dark hair and a ruddy complexion.

The reporter mentioned Dewain's missing fingers. Beatrice had seen both of the other man's hands when he sat drinking at the bar and grabbed the councilman to stop him from falling. This was not the same man. The killer was still out there somewhere.

"Hey, Beatrice, another round!" Someone shouted from the other end of the bar.

"Yeah, cool your jets." She reached in the cooler and pulled three longnecks out, popped the caps, and slid them down in the direction of the voices.

The news faded into a commercial break. The cook came out of the kitchen, carrying orders to the bar. "What the fuck, Beatrice? I got orders piling up in the kitchen and you're watching the goddamn TV?"

Beatrice grabbed the steaming plates from his hands. "I need a minute, Bernie," she said to the cook.

She took off her apron and walked through the kitchen to the coat rack by the back door. "I know it's here," she mumbled to herself, rifling through her coat pockets. She found a card, the corner bent, and a stain across the back. She pulled her phone from her back pocket and slipped out the back door, dialing as she walked into the parking lot. A voice answered, "Detective James Holt."

"Jimmy, it's Beatrice. You know, from the Anchor Inn. The dead councilman. I saw the photo of Dewain Johnson on the news tonight. Jimmy, it's not him. I mean, that's not the guy who was in the bar that night—the one who took the councilman away. Maybe he's Dewain Johnson, but he's not the killer. Whoever killed Eddie Ortese is still out there."

"Beatrice, are you sure?" Holt walked from his desk to an empty office along the side of the wardroom and closed the door.

"Listen to me, Beatrice," Holt spoke low and steadily. "Don't say anything to anyone. Not the press or the police or your boyfriend. This is between you and me. The killer thinks he's pulled off the perfect crime, and if he learns you blew his cover, he knows where to find you. No one knows his secret but you and me, and we need to keep it that way. Go back to work and play the hero for a little while longer. Be cool, Beatrice. Got it?"

121

HOLT HUNG UP the phone and slammed it on the desk.

"Sonofabitch!"

A couple of heads popped up in the wardroom over the cubicle walls. Holt held up his hand in an apologetic gesture.

The chief and the mayor had said make the story stick. Well, the story had just peeled off like a $10 hooker.

Holt's gut had been right. The pieces just hadn't fit. Dewain had been set up, and Holt's intuition said it had been the guy with the Ravens hat in the hospital security video. He flashed back to the gruesome memory of the morgue and the shredded flesh on Dewain's bloated, grey face.

He went back to his desk and pulled the councilman's file from the stack. Holt scoured the reports, the crime-scene photos, and Beatrice's statement, looking for what, he didn't know. He pulled out Dewain's file and combed through it. Nothing tied the councilman and Dewain together. There had to be something else. Holt thought that bad guys always leave something behind, a piece of evidence that gets overlooked the first or even the second time. Something so simple it remained hidden in plain view.

Holt unlocked his bottom drawer and pulled out a pint of Makers Mark whiskey. Just the thing to sharpen his senses. He poured some into the remains of his morning coffee. What was in these files that he couldn't see?

He read the coroner's report out loud this time. It was a technique the rookie Holt learned from an FBI agent when they had worked on an especially grisly kidnapping case years ago.

"Sometimes you can hear what you can't see," the agent said. "You got your eyes *and* ears working for you."

Holt read through the report, stacking the finished pages face down on the open file folder. Nothing. He picked up the last sheet in Ortese's file, labeled "Personal Effects." There were only a few lines on the report. You don't take much with you when you're thrown from a moving vehicle on a deserted road, Holt mused.

He read through the list of clothing. Size 42 pink silk boxers, pants, suit coat, white dress shirt, and tie. Cocktail napkin, Anchor Inn. The last line read "plastic water bottle (empty)."

He had read this report a dozen times. Plastic water bottle? It had to be a mistake—road trash that somehow got tangled up in clothing at the crime scene? Or some EMT tossing empties around in the back of the ambulance?

Holt dropped the page in the stack and called the coroner's office. After he had identified himself, the coroner boomed,

"Hey, Detective, Bill Kelly here. Nice work on the serial killer case."

There was something about a happy assistant coroner that didn't sit right.

"Yeah, thanks, Bill. I'm wrapping up the Ortese murder investigation and need to see a piece of evidence. The file listed a plastic water bottle in his personal effects. Is that right?"

"Yeah, detective. I worked that one myself. The EMTs at the scene said he had a grip on it like a vise, holding it against his chest. They found it when they rolled him over at the scene. The bottle was pretty flat, but since it was considered "on the body" and part of the scene, they catalogued and bagged it. It's in the evidence box ready to be sealed and shipped to the warehouse tomorrow."

"Ah, that's good," said Holt. "Hey, Bill. This case—well, you understand, it's sensitive. I don't see that the bottle was examined as evidence, and an oversight like that—my ass would be on the line, and so would your boss's. Just a little insurance for our future employment. I'll have Randy in forensics pick it up and do a once-over just to tie things up in a pretty bow. Then it can go to its final resting place."

"Well, I don't know. What if—"

"I'm sure the forensics lab can have it back before the evidence needs to be shipped off. Keep to the evidence protocols and sign on the dotted lines so everyone is happy. Thanks, Bill. I'm calling forensics now."

Randy picked up on the first ring. "No problemo, Detective Holt," he said. "I'm sick of blood and bodily fluids at the moment. A nice, clean fingerprint dusting is just what I need. But we're slammed right now, processing that grisly double murder down by the river last night. Multiple suspects and crime scenes. Those freaks must have been high on something— evidence markers on the river house, boats, vehicles! It may take a while to get this back—the mayor is freaked about another murder spree, and we've all been pulled on it. I'll pick it up from the coroner's office tomorrow morning. I'll phone you if I find anything

Holt sat back in his chair and rested his face in his hands. *Take some time?*

He was sitting on information that would blow the Dewain-Councilman story apart, with a killer still on the loose. And how long could he trust Beatrice to keep her mouth shut? The mayor and the chief would make him eat his badge in front of the press if these new double murders were connected to the murder of the council-man and the other killings. He still didn't have any hard evidence to save his ass. Better to let Dewain take the rap for a little while longer until the lab could come back with some results.

Here's hoping the real killer left something sweet behind.

122

ANNABELLE LEANED CLOSER to the mirror and brushed mascara onto her long eyelashes. She stepped back, pleased at the woman smiling back at her.

She turned around and smoothed her hands over her hips, snug in her pre-baby jeans topped with a loose, cotton knit sweater. Her co-workers were hosting a baby shower for her and Charlie in the office at four o'clock that afternoon. It had been almost two weeks since Charlie's dramatic entrance, and she wanted to show them that she hadn't turned into a frump in sweatpants and a t-shirt dribbled with spit-up. Did it always take this long to get dressed?

Jake had arranged his schedule to drop them off and then collect them afterwards at five-thirty on the Plaza.

Annabelle felt like a kid on the first day of school, or a prisoner who'd just been sprung. Little Charlie was a dream of course, and he was thriving. Jake called him the perfect baby. Well, he was for the few hours when Jake was home. Charlie could sometimes be a little nightmare until Jake walked into the nursery. She swore their baby boy was psychically connected to Jake's aura or voice, something that turned his tears into smiles. She loved dressing him up and watching him sleep. Even the bathing and changing could be fun. But two weeks of dirty diapers, piles of laundry, and two o'clock in the morning feedings left her exhausted and needing a change of scene.

Jake settled into his old routine and even had a few new clients. She never understood his hours or what took him away at night when she needed him, but it also kept him out of her way. A kind of peace had settled over the house. They were both trying to put the past behind them, and Annabelle made sure it would stay that way. The lab report was hidden away where Jake wouldn't find it.

"Miss Annabelle, would you like me to get Charlie dressed up for his party now?" Madeline walked into the nursery, holding a sky-blue romper and matching shirt.

"Thank you, Madeline. He will look so darling in that!" Annabelle walked to the crib where the baby was lying fresh from a bath, his arms and legs in motion.

"Madeline, can you change the crib sheet while we are gone? There's going to be more hair on the sheets than on his little head before we know it." She brushed the strands of dark hair clinging to the crib sheet, a natural shedding for a newborn. From the new strands at the nape of his neck, Charlie was transforming into a blond like his mother.

Annabelle took one last look in the full-length mirror and heard Jake come in the front door.

Madeline picked up the baby, stuffed more diapers into the carry bag, and headed to the door. Annabelle grabbed her lip gloss and put it into her Kate Spade bag, then spritzed Obsession on her neck.

Jake headed out the door. Annabelle pressed a handwritten note into Madeline's hand as she walked out the door. "This is where I'll be and the phone number in case you need anything. Or if someone needs to find me. You never know what might happen!"

123

ROGER HAD STAKED out Annabelle's house for a week, waiting for a glimpse of her backing out of the driveway or walking the baby down the street. The neighborhood was perfect for a little stalking. There were lots of trees and bushes, high enough to hide a car but low enough and spaced to allow for an unobstructed sight line to her front door.

He needed to get her alone. He had Jake's schedule down; he was out at seven-thirty in the morning. But for the past two weeks, Annabelle hadn't made an appearance—not even a goodbye kiss at the front door. So far, his efforts produced nothing, but he hoped that today would be different.

Roger was convinced that women loved to talk, or at least they will after a few margaritas. Roger didn't have many friends, but he had connections who did.

His client Christopher had a friend whose wife was friends with a woman who worked at the same company as Annabelle. Monica was divorced—again. She had struck out on a host of dating sites and had taken comfort in happy-hour half-price nachos and margaritas.

Christopher's sources said San Miguel near the Plaza was her hangout du jour, so a couple of nights ago Roger made his move. Christopher met him at the bar, pointed her out at a high top with a girlfriend, had a double Tito's on the rocks, and left. Roger sent over two signature "hot tub margaritas" to their table and waited while the waitress pointed him out as their generous benefactor.

Right on cue, they waved him over. One more margarita and he got all the information he needed. The baby shower would be held from four until five-thirty. He would confront her as she was leaving and show her the DNA report. What could she say? He had proof. He had no intention of breaking up her marriage, though what man could withstand such a blow? It was his son he wanted.

Roger checked the dashboard clock; it was three-fifteen. It took at least twenty minutes to get to the plaza and ten more to park. Hauling a baby could double that. He grabbed the report, now curled and crumpled after so many days waiting, ready to make his move.

Through the trees he saw the front door open. Instead of Anabelle, it was Jake with the baby in tow. Annabelle hesitated at the doorway, then followed. They climbed into Jake's BMW, backed out of the long driveway and sped out of sight.

Roger tapped the paper against the steering wheel in exasperation. He followed behind at a safe distance, anticipating the look on Annabelle's face when he showed her the DNA report.

124

DAVID SAT IN his dark living room, recalling his good for-tune. It had been a week since the photo of Dewain had flashed across the networks, announcing the councilman's killer. The mayor had announced the case closed. Darcy's drugs and money kept him satisfied and off the streets.

And they say you can't commit the perfect crime.

Annabelle's phone had gone silent. There had been no calls or texts from Jake since the botched meeting to get her phone.

David had options to deal with Jake. He could mail the phone to that detective from the news conference, along with a note that would tie Jake to the drugs that had killed the coun-cilman and to Darcy's death. But a trial with a slick defense lawyer and a light sentence was too paltry an outcome for what David had in mind. He could afford to be patient.

Hannah stirred when Annabelle's phone suddenly started to buzz. David picked it up and read the text message. "Reminder! Baby shower this afternoon for Annabelle in the executive conference room. Come celebrate Annabelle and sweet baby Charlie. Leticia."

He was sure Leticia didn't intend to invite him to the party. The baby shower could offer him the perfect oppor-tunity to meet up with Annabelle and—bonus—with the baby. David turned the phone over and over in his hand. All he needed was to find out what time the shower would be to set up a meeting. A little surprise party of his own, with her missing phone his shower gift.

David pulled Annabelle's driver's license from her wallet and put her name and address into a search app on his phone. The cell phone numbers that came up for her were blurred out, but a land line was listed. Land lines had answering machines or voicemail. He dialed the number and waited. Two, three, four rings, and then he heard a voice.

"Martin Residence. This is Madeline."

"Well, hello, Madeline. I was wondering if Annabelle was available. I understand that she lost her wallet and phone a couple of weeks ago. I was on the bus the night she went to the hospital. The EMTs thought I was with her so they gave her things to me to hang onto. I've been trying to get in touch with her to return them, and just stumbled on this number. Can I talk to her, please?"

"She has been frantic about those! You have them? What did you say your name was?"

"It's David. Yes, I can imagine how worried she must have been. Is she alright? And the baby?"

"Well, Mr. David, I know she would like to talk to you and hear your good news, but she's not here. She's gone out for the afternoon."

"Oh, that's wonderful. I'm sure she's enjoying a day out. And the baby? Is he with her? It's a beautiful day."

"Yes, they are at her office downtown. Her co-workers are giving her a baby shower. He's such a sweet little boy. The shower is over at five-thirty, so she should be back home after six o'clock. Should I tell her you called? How she can reach you?"

"Madeline, I'd really like to get her wallet and phone back to her. I'm going to be downtown myself later today. I could take it to her office."

"Well, Mr. David, you can call her cell phone. Wait, I have the number here; she left it just in case someone needed to get in touch with her, and here you are!"

"Yes, things seem to work out that way. The number, Madeline?"

She read it to him slowly, and he repeated it back.

"Thank you so much, Madeline. You've been really helpful."

"You're welcome, Mr. David."

"Baby showers are a waste of time and money." His father's words had crushed any hope of a celebration. Why would people who don't like you much spend money getting you cheap gifts? What's the fuss? And what if something happened? You'd be left with a lot of baby things and no baby to feed or to wear the stupid little outfits. Not in my house. Show me the baby first before I spend one dime on any celebration.

David punched the number on his phone. After a couple of rings, he heard Annabelle's voice against the background of laughter and music. "Who is this?" she yelled over the noise. "I don't recognize your number, and no one has this number."

"Is this Annabelle?"

"Yes, it is. Who is this? I can't talk now."

"My name is David. We met once, but you probably don't remember. Anyway, it was a couple of weeks ago on Bus 7."

Annabelle shuddered at the thought of that bus ride. "Why are you calling me? What is this about? How did you get my number?"

"Your housekeeper gave it to me when I called your house. The EMTs thought we were together that night on the bus. They gave me your phone and wallet to hold on to. I put them away for safekeeping and found them today when I was cleaning out a drawer. I would like to return them to you with the money and photos and stuff."

Annabelle thought about the photos. The blurry one of her and Roger, tucked in one of the pockets. The photos from the lake. Her phone—there'd been a rash of sexting and naughty photos after a few too many vodka collinses on a lonely night when her husband had been absent. And the frantic call to Roger to come to the hospital.

"You know there is a reward, don't you?" she asked. "You can turn them into the police."

"Oh, I'm not looking for a reward. I'm a little embarrassed that I've had them this long and forgot to return them. I'd rather just give them to you now instead of having to waste time answering questions—the police can be so suspicious of nothing, really."

He heard someone in the background calling, "Annabelle, we want to take a group photo with you and Charlie."

She turned back to the crowd in the breakroom. "A minute. Be right there."

David continued, "I'll be downtown at Market Square about the time your party is over. Your housekeeper said that would be around five-thirty? I can meet you in the square near the bus stop and give them to you there. You went into labor that night, and I'd love to see the baby. I had a baby brother, too."

The knot in Annabelle's gut tightened. That night was coming back. The guy on the bus who sat next to her had stared at her belly. He said something about a stepmother and a baby brother. How had he gotten her wallet and phone? He had gotten off the bus before she had gone into labor. Who was he, and why had he searched her out? He had let her know he's seen what's in the wallet. What about the phone?

She needed to get her phone back to delete photos and texts before Jake knew she had it. No one—not even that detective— needed to know it had been returned. Time to erase the past. Market Square would be crowded after five-thirty. and Jake would be there to pick them up this time. Nothing to fear.

"OK, David. I'll meet you on the plaza then. Thanks for keeping my things safe. How will I recognize you?"

"My pleasure," he replied. "I'll be wearing a blue blazer with a crest on the breast pocket. But don't worry. I can pick you out from a crowd. I'll be watching for you."

125

THE SQUAD ROOM was quiet. Every able body was down at the freeway overpass working a four-vehicle collision with multiple injuries. Holt checked his watch. No word from the lab all week on the water bottle found with the councilman's body. He reached for the phone to call the lab when it started to ring.

"Detective Holt? Randy here. Sorry it took me so long to get back to you. Seems that every low-life and junkie crawled out of the muck at once. I've been up to my neck all week in blood, body fluids, and puke. Anyway, I just dusted that bottle, and it was covered with prints. A lot of smears, and some good prints from the councilman. But there were some others that were pretty clear. I ran the prints on the database and got a hit. A David Westwood handled that bottle. He's about thirty and lives here in town. I'm sending the sheet from the database to your email. And now I'm out of here, amigo. There's a beer and a barstool waiting for me somewhere."

Holt printed off the FBI sheet that Randy sent. Who was David Westwood, and why did the councilman have his water bottle? Holt ran his name through the database.

This David didn't have a rap sheet, but a Google search turned up some newspaper stories linking him to some pretty freaky stuff. His father had been found stabbed to death in the family's home when David was twelve. David had been with his mother, who was pretty beaten up, crouched in the dark in the basement.

Mrs. Westwood had claimed that someone had broken into the house and attacked her husband. She tried to pull the intruder off, taking some hard blows herself. The house had been pretty messed up—broken chairs, blood smears on the floors and walls. The father's body had multiple stab wounds on his legs, arms, and torso. And his tongue had been cut out. They never found the intruder or any weapons.

Another article told the same story, with an update. The mother had refused to leave the basement, saying she wouldn't leave her baby alone down there. Officers thought she was talking about David until they found a baby no more than three months old, wrapped in a blanket in an old dresser drawer, hidden under the basement stairs. The child was dead.

The mother, Hannah, had a nervous breakdown and was subsequently committed to the county hospital. David went to live with relatives in Baltimore, Maryland. The article had photos from happier days, head shots of his father and mother, and one of David holding a kitten.

Holt scrolled down to a more recent news article showing a group photo of students from a local community college who had been awarded business internships. The interns stood in front with their sponsors behind them. The caption listed each intern and his or her sponsor. Holt counted across the faces to find David. It read, "David Westwood, intern, and Darcy Grover of West End Industries." David held a hat in his hand as if he had removed it for the photo, but the logo was clear. It was a bird with the word "Ravens" across the bill.

Son of a bitch. This David was the guy who rode in the ambulance with the woman who had gone into labor.

The same guy wearing the hat had met up with Dewain in the hallway. And he was most likely the guy wearing the Ravens cap coming off the elevator, headed for Darcy's office. His prints on the water bottle put him up close and personal with the dead councilman on the night he was murdered. And he likely set up Dewain to take the rap for the councilman's death, giving Beatrice a false name and planting his Ravens cap on Dewain's dead body.

But there was something else. Holt flipped the pages of his notebook until he found it. A call from Jake, husband of the woman they brought in that night off the bus. He had reported that she had lost a phone and wallet, and he wanted those back in the worst way. Meanwhile, the wife had made it clear that the police needed to return the wallet to her, not to anyone else. The wallet had concert tickets in it, and Holt had staked out the concert that night and ran into Dewain. Had Dewain been looking for David that night? Maybe David was the guy who sold the stolen concert tickets to the young couple. If David had the phone and wallet, why not collect the reward? Unless, for some reason, they were more valuable than the reward money.

He looked at his notes again. He had never followed up with the husband, Jake Martin. Holt's gut was twisting with dread. He couldn't shake the feeling that this David, Dewain, and Jake were connected somehow. Was this David the killer responsible for three—and maybe more—dead bodies? Were the phone and wallet worth enough to commit murder? Holt dialed Jake's number.

"Hello, Martin residence. Madeline speaking."

"Yes, Madeline. This is Detective James Holt from the Shepherdsville Police Department."

Holt heard a gasp.

"Oh, ma'am, nothing to worry about," he reassured her. "Sorry if I alarmed you. Jake Martin gave me this number.

I was working on an investigation about his wife's missing items, and just wanted to follow up. Is he there?"

"You must mean Miss Annabelle's wallet and phone. They have been looking for them for weeks. So terrible to think someone has your personal items. She has been very upset."

"Yes, I can imagine that she would be. I would really like to talk to Jake, Madeline. Is he available?"

"No, detective. He took Annabelle and the baby to her office for a baby shower, and they won't be back until after six. You could call back later if you want to speak to him. I'll leave a note. I will be leaving here myself at five-thirty."

"Thanks, Madeline. You've been very helpful."

"Oh, detective—I should have mentioned! I got some good news about her missing things. A young man called here just a while ago and said he found them and is going to give them back to her personally."

"What's that? A man said he has them? This could be very important. What exactly did he say?"

"He said he was on the bus with her the night Miss Annabelle went to the hospital. The EMTs gave those to him, and he wants to give them back. He was so nice. He asked how she was, and the baby, too. He said he had a little brother. I gave him her cell phone number. He really wanted to give them to her in person. He was going to be downtown today, so he is going to meet her there. Is everything alright? Did I do something wrong, detective? Sometimes I talk too much."

"No, Madeline, you did nothing wrong. Let me give you my phone number. You've been very helpful. Leave a note with my phone number for Jake. Ask him to call me."

126

ROGER SURVEYED THE plaza. He had been here before, waiting in the shadows, hoping to see Annabelle coming out of her building.

In fact, he had been there that night she had gone to the hospital. She hadn't seen him step through the back door onto Bus 7 just as it left the plaza. He saw the young man wearing a blazer sitting next to her and watched him put his arm up around the back of the seat to touch her shoulder as they were speaking.

Roger wanted to pull the fellow seated next to Annabelle off the bus and out of his way. Instead, he stood in the back, rode for a few more stops, and quietly got off the bus. He wandered through the streets until he found his way back to the plaza and drove home.

But not today. Today he had an important message to deliver to Annabelle. This was his big chance to put his life back on track. He patted the folded paper in his jacket pocket. It was five-fifteen, and the plaza was filling up. In a short time he'd see Annabelle and make his claim.

Charlie might be Annabelle's son, but he soon would be Sharon's son as well. His son.

127

DAVID PARKED THE truck behind the old warehouses now converted into pricy condos that flanked the plaza. He flipped open the glove compartment, pulled out a plastic bag, and took out an Oxy and a pint of bourbon. He stayed pleasantly high all the time, thanks to Darcy. This night called for a celebration, so he popped the pill in his mouth, followed by a long swallow of bourbon.

Something for you, and something for her, the voices sang in his head. *One sharp prick and it will all be over.*

The liquid burned as it pushed the hard tablet down David's throat.

He pushed the bottle and the plastic bag under his seat, out of sight. Annabelle's phone and wallet were in his pocket. The syringe with the drug cocktail originally meant for Dewain was tucked into another pocket. Way too much for such a small woman, but it seemed a shame to waste it. David locked the truck, walked around the buildings and into the plaza. It was almost five-thirty.

Perfect.

126

"PLEASE, I WANT to hold him just one more time!"

Annabelle sighed and handed Charlie over to Leticia, her assistant. He had done well and slept through most of the party, tucked away in her office. That was just fine with Annabelle. She was out!

She hadn't realized how much she missed just being with her friends—the gossip, the drama of the office, the client meetings, and projects and deadlines. She even missed getting dressed every morning, taking a swing through the coffee shops, and eating deli sandwiches with her colleagues in the plaza. Once the center of the office buzz, she felt like a disconnected outsider with nothing to contribute to the conversation.

She glanced at her office door, slightly ajar so she could hear any sounds from Charlie. He was her master now, and she was always on the alert for a summons. The laughter from the break room pulled her back.

The baby gifts were packed into boxes, stacked high in her old office. She looked at Charlie, tucked into his stroller. The diaper bag next to it overflowed with baby toys. A new teddy bear was stuffed in her leather bag.

Jake would have to come get the boxes another time. He should be waiting at the plaza soon, and little Charlie will be home just in time for his next feeding, a bath, and—with luck—a long sleep. Annabelle was surprised how happy that scenario made her feel. She was relaxing into this mother thing. Maybe it wasn't an either-or question.

Maybe she could have both—she could have it all.

She recalled the young man, David, who had her phone and wallet. Her sense of relief was followed by a wave of dread. She pulled out a $100 bill from her wallet and stuffed it into her jacket pocket. That should be a generous reward for his efforts.

"Ok, Leticia, hand him over. We've got to get out of here. Don't want to keep his daddy waiting!"

A streak of lightning suddenly pierced the darkening sky, followed by an earsplitting crack of thunder.

"Wow! That was close. When I was little, my dad always said thunder was the angels bowling up in heaven" said Leticia with a grin. "It scared the hell out of me, but the thought of those angels wearing bowling shirts and rolling those balls made me laugh."

Shards of lightning lit up the sky, followed by low rumbles and then a bang.

"Stee-rike," yelled Leticia, laughing. "Be sure that little guy is covered up, Annabelle. He's so sweet he might melt in a few drops of rain."

Annabelle picked up her purse and the diaper bag and slung them over her shoulder. She could feel her phone vibrate at the bottom of her bag. She fished out her phone; Jake was calling. She knew he didn't like to be kept waiting, but really, he should be more patient.

"Yes, Jake, what is it? We're just packing up. Are you here already?"

"No, Annabelle. Sorry, babe. I was just getting onto the bridge and a tractor-trailer and three cars collided about 500 yards ahead of me. All the lanes are blocked. The ambulances are taking people off the bridge, and the MedStar helicopter just took off. They are moving traffic in one lane, but there is no way I can make the plaza by five-thirty. Looks like there's a storm coming, and I don't want you and Charlie left standing in the rain. You should catch the bus at the Plaza after the shower and go to the end of the line as you have before. Leave any gifts and stuff at your office, and I'll pick them up later. I'll be parked in the turnaround at the end of the street. You know, in front of the flagpole."

"Yeah—Bus 7? Do you want me to relive that nightmare again, Jake? Really? With little Charlie? There's a storm coming."

"I know. I hate it too," said Jake. "But I can make it to the turnaround before the bus arrives."

Annabelle could hear sirens in the background.

"Who knows," Jake said with a chuckle, "it could be good therapy. I'll be waiting, I promise, and the ride will put Charlie to sleep. It's a short ride. You'll be fine."

129

HOLT'S THUMBS HAD turned into stumps as he misdialed Annabelle's phone number twice before he heard it ring. Damned phones! She probably won't even answer an unknown number. *Come on, come on, pick it up!* He heard a click as it went to voicemail.

"This is Annabelle. Leave me a message, short and sweet. I'll get back to you when I can."

"Annabelle, this is Detective James Holt with the Shepherdsville police department. Your housekeeper, Madeline, gave me your cellphone number. This is an urgent message about your missing phone and wallet. A man named David may be trying to contact you to return them to you. Do not, I repeat, *do not* make arrangements to meet him. His name is David Westwood, white male, about twenty-five, light hair. We have reason to believe he may be armed and extremely dangerous. Call me at this number immediately. Again, *do not* have any contact with this man. I am on my way to Market Square Plaza now. Please call!"

Holt felt for his service revolver in the shoulder holster under his jacket as he ran from the building to his vehicle. He activated the light bar as he tore at high speed down the road towards Market Plaza.

The bridge looked like bumper cars at a boardwalk arcade. He turned on the sirens and snaked up the bridge as cars parted ahead of him, making a narrow lane to the crash scene. The officers stopped traffic to the one open lane off the bridge and waved him through. He glanced anxiously at his phone, dark and silent on the passenger seat. Light up, he pleaded with the dark screen.

Annabelle, where are you?

130

DARK THUNDERHEADS CROWDED the sky above the plaza. In the distance, pops of lightening flashed a warning of an approaching storm. Charlie's stroller barely made it through the glass door as she left her building, catching on the diaper bag. Annabelle shifted her shoulder bag and grabbed the door when someone snatched it and held it open from the street side.

"Roger! What are you doing here?"

Annabelle thought her heart would stop. There was something intense about the way he was looking at her, and then at Charlie. Their last meeting in the hospital flashed across her mind.

"Thanks for catching the door, Roger. What a coincidence."

"Yes, isn't it." He seemed to be addressing Charlie. "Not really a coincidence, Annabelle. I had to find you, and I knew you would be here today. I've been waiting. I had to see you."

"Roger, you're scaring me. Have you been stalking me?" Annabelle looked at the crowd, moving nervously with the increasing cadence of the thunderclaps. Anger washed over her—Jake was leaving her to fend on her own again. She pushed forward.

"Just a minute, Annabelle." Roger's face hardened, framed by the dark, threatening clouds behind him. He pulled the crumpled DNA report out of his jacket pocket and thrust it towards her, his eyes blazing.

"He's mine, Annabelle. Mine and yours. This piece of paper proves it, and I plan to have him in my life. He's my son, and I'll be his father. Not that no-good husband of yours."

Annabelle pushed Roger's hand aside and pulled Charlie's stroller away from him. Roger stepped forward and grabbed the handle of the car seat clipped into the frame, nearly tipping it overboard. Annabelle shrieked.

From out of the crowd, a young man stepped between Annabelle and Roger.

"Is this man disturbing you?" he said to Annabelle, his arm extended, upraised hand inches away from Roger's chest.

Annabelle looked up to see a well-dressed young man wearing a crested blazer, shielding her from Roger. Her mind raced. She needed to make this quick. Get the phone and wallet, give him the money, and get on the bus. Months of lies and deceit were recorded on that phone.

"Yes, he was disturbing me," she replied. "I was so frightened. He started saying horrible things to me and my baby. I've never seen him before." Annabelle waited to see if her performance convinced her rescuer.

"Liar," Roger spat under his breath. "You can't get of rid of me like that, Annabelle."

Roger stepped closer. David turned to face him and put his hand on his shoulder, gripping tightly, his thumb pressing deep into Roger's neck.

Press harder. Break his neck!

"I believe the lady said you were frightening her," said David, his gaze straight and steady. "Back off and get out of here"

Roger winced and released his grip on the child's car seat. Annabelle repositioned the stroller behind David.

"We can let the police handle this," David continued. "They'd love to have another pervert to interrogate."

Annabelle's attention shifted from Roger to the man she assumed was David, who had her phone and wallet. His aggressive stance and the pain he so quickly inflicted on Roger frightened her more than Roger's threats.

"Know that your sin shall find you out." Her memories of Sunday school lessons flashed on her mind's screen. She had no time to ponder which sins were more damaging—the one on Roger's paper or those hidden in her phone and wallet.

Roger glared at Annabelle. She edged closer to David.

"This is not the end of it," Roger said, waving the crumpled paper in the air. He glared at David, turned, and disappeared into the crowd forming near the bus stop.

David turned to face Annabelle; his angry demeanor instantly fading away. "What a nasty guy. I hope you're all right. It's Annabelle, isn't it?"

Annabelle sized him up. He didn't fool her, whoever he was. Young, handsome, brash, and full of himself. He had stepped in, strong and commanding. Of the two, she could handle this one, even if she may have chosen the devil himself.

"Yes, I'm Annabelle, and I assume you're David?"

"Yes." As he spoke, lightning flashed overhead, followed in turn by a symphony of thunder, bathing the square in a queasy, unearthly light before darkening again. People pressed closer to the bus stop to get in position to duck out of the coming rainstorm. In the distance, moving towards the square, she could see pairs of headlights from buses making their way down the hill to the bus stop.

"David, you said you had something for me? My phone and wallet? I'm so relieved to get them back."

She reached into her pocket for the hundred-dollar bill, pushing Charlie along towards the bus stop, walking ahead of David. She turned and handed him the folded bill. "Here, I wanted to thank you for finding me and bringing them back."

David looked at the money in her hand, insulted and amused.

"I wouldn't think of taking any money from you. And your money is still in the wallet. Ten $100 bills. And the photos are there, too. There is one of you and your husband—I think it was your husband. Strange…the other photo was of you and a dark-haired man. He looked an awful lot like the man who just left. He's the same one who was in your room the night they brought you into the hospital."

Annabelle froze. David stared silently at her, his face taking on a knowing, satisfied look. She felt alone and exposed in his gaze; her feet unsteady. The sky lit up again, sending waves of thunder undulating above them.

Rain began to fall. Large drops splashed, covering the canopy shielding Charlie's head. The falling rain coated David's face, transforming it into a ghastly mask. Behind him, coming up to the bus stop, Annabelle saw Bus No. 7 queued up behind several others, disgorging passengers into the square, waiting to roll up to the boarding area.

"Give me the phone and wallet, David. I don't know who you are or what you think you know, but—"

With a crash of thunder, the rain started coming down in sheets. David grabbed Annabelle's arm with one hand, and the stroller handle with the other. He pushed his way through the crowd. "Woman with baby," he yelled out through the clamor, using the stroller as a wedge, shoving bodies aside, guiding her to the front of the queue.

The stroller rocked and pitched, jostled by the crowd. Charlie began to cry as the rain soaked the blanket covering his feet.

Once I get on the bus with all these people, I'll be safe. *Damn you, Jake!*

131

STOP. HISS!

Bus 7 rolled up to the boarding area and jerked to a stop. David leaned over Annabelle's shoulder and banged on the door.

"Open up! Open the goddamn doors!"

Through the rain-streaked doors, David saw the driver slowly pull the lever to open the doors.

David pushed Annabelle forward up the stairs. She stumbled around the driver and recognized him as Gus. She grabbed his arm and whispered as she passed by.

"I'm in danger, Gus. The man behind me is threatening me and my baby. Call 911! Please help me!"

Gus turned toward her while grabbing the front of Charlie's stroller. Annabelle gasped. He looked at her through cloudy eyes, his breath labored and face flushed.

"Sure, lady," he said, a slight whiff of bourbon with every word. "And you want me to stop at Starbucks, too?"

The crowd was getting restless, standing in the pouring rain. Charlie's stroller created a bottleneck. Someone was banging in frustration on the side of the bus. Those already seated inside shouted at Annabelle to get out of the way.

Gus pulled at the knot in his tie, stumbling forward, hoisting the stroller onto the bus. Annabelle detached

Charlie's car seat from the stroller and headed down the aisle. David folded the stroller just as the mob exploded through the doors.

David grabbed Annabelle's arm and guided her into an empty seat next to the window. He took the baby carrier and sat down beside her, the carrier balanced on his lap.

She squeezed herself as close to the window as she could, fearful as he pressed against her body. Annabelle looked out the window, searching for someone who could help her when she saw Roger in the crowd outside, working his way to the open back door. She caught his gaze, his eyes blazing with anger, and she mouthed "Help me!" through the rain-streaked window. He disappeared from her line of sight, seconds before she heard the back doors close.

Stop. Hiss.

The bus lurched forward and swung out into traffic. Every seat on the bus was full; the air was heavy with the smell of rain-soaked coats and leather. Rain dripped off parcels, backpacks, and umbrellas. Passengers crammed into every bit of standing room. Outside the storm raged on. The bus swerved and pitched, horn blasting an erratic staccato rhythm as the bus lurched its way through the downtown streets.

David pulled Annabelle's phone from his jacket and turned it on. He turned slightly towards her and spoke in a low voice.

"I was on the bus with you that night and took your phone and wallet off the floor. I also slipped your necklace off, the one you're wearing now. But I brought it back to your hospital room. Nobody saw me put it back into your bag."

David could feel his excitement building, fueled by the booze and drugs. He felt powerful.

Annabelle turned her face to the window, horrified. "You're lying, you bastard."

"No, Annabelle. It was me. I saw that dark-haired man leaving your hospital room, the same man who was on the plaza tonight. The one in the picture in your wallet."

Stop. Hiss.

The bus pulled to the curb to let off some passengers. The aisles were clearing. David put his knee balancing Charlie's car seat out into the aisle, out of Annabelle's reach.

She looked at David, searching her memory. There had been a man sitting beside her on the bus that night. Annabelle's throat tightened. "So, it's blackmail? What do you want, David?"

"There's more to this story, Annabelle. The other photo, the one I assume is your husband, leaning up against the BMW. The license plate is SOS J+A? Jake, your husband."

"So?" Annabelle turned to face David, her arms aching to grab hold of the car seat.

"Well, there's something I'd like you to see."

David held the phone out of Annabelle's reach, low and out of view of the other riders. He pulled up the video of Jake and Darcy at the concert, moving inside the BMW.

Annabelle felt faint at the sight played out on the phone. "Stop!" Her voice was low and ragged. She put her hand over her mouth. "I'm going to be sick! What do you want? Why are you doing this?"

Stop. Hiss.

A group of drenched teenagers boarded the bus, music blasting from their phones, filling the aisles again. Annabelle looked out the window. They were nearing the turn towards the end of the line. She had to get the baby carrier away from David before they pulled to the last stop.

"I'm not finished, Annabelle."

David leaned in so she could hear him above the racket. "You deserve to know everything. The woman in this video and your husband had a business dealing drugs together. I could have been his best customer until he tried to kill me with some Oxys laced with Fentanyl. Now that's *not* the kind of man to be a father to this sweet little boy." He gestured towards Charlie.

Annabelle's eyes widened, and she let out a shriek, grabbing for the carrier. David pushed her back against the window. Just then, Annabelle caught Roger's reflection in the windows across the aisle, slowly walking towards them from the back of the bus.

David leaned in closer, blocking her reach.

"My father was mean and said terrible things. I had a baby brother, and my father killed him. He tried to kill my mother and me, too. But I killed my father and shut him up forever. He was a bad man, just like Jake. Jake lied to me and tried to kill me, too. And I have the perfect solution for his treachery."

Annabelle couldn't think. Outside the windows, the street signs and trees were a blur against the wind and rain-streaked windows.

David rested Charlie's carrier on the empty seat across the aisle.

Rain pelted the bus from all sides at once. The wipers could barely keep up with the deluge, offering a blurry glimpse of the road ahead.

The bus slowed to make a left turn just as a bolt of lightning hit a transformer on a pole on the corner. The street lit up like daylight, plunging the bus into darkness. Screams pierced the air, competing against the deafening thunder. Annabelle strained to see through the bus' windshield for the shops lining the street at the end of the line.

The lightning struck again, illuminating the driver's seat. Gus was slumped over the steering wheel, arms dangling down, with his foot still on the gas. Committed to the turn, the bus rocketed around the corner, shifting Gus and the wheel back again. Bus 7 glided like a boogie board at the beach on the flooded street, headed for the fountain behind the flagpole and benches at the end of the street.

Annabelle lurched across David to grab the car seat. He stood and knocked her back against the window. She screamed, just as Roger grabbed David around the neck from behind. David swung around, fueled by the drugs coursing through his veins, grabbed Roger by the shoulder and shoved him, knocking him to the floor.

The bus gained speed as it approached its final stop. Passengers screamed as two teenagers crawled down the rocking aisle to wrestle Gus off the steering wheel just as the bus clipped a utility truck, knocking the three of them to the floor. The flower shop came into view. Annabelle thought she saw Jake's BMW.

Charlie howled in the dark, still strapped in his car seat. David pulled the syringe out of his right pocket, pulled the cap off with his teeth, leaned over and plunged the needle into Annabelle's thigh.

She grabbed at David's hands as he pushed the plunger down. Stunned, Annabelle gasped and slumped against the window, eyes wide, staring at the empty syringe protruding from her leg. David leaned in and whispered in her ear, "Jake is going to wish he were dead because in a few minutes *you* will be dead. Say goodbye to your baby, Annabelle."

The bus bounced like a pinball against cars parked along the road. The outline of the flagpole came closer. David crouched on the floor, braced himself and wrapped his body over Charlie in the car seat just as the bus hit the pole full force, spun around, and came to a halt.

132

THE PAIN STARTED low in his leg and went up his back, intensifying as he gained consciousness. Jake could hear deep, parting rumbles of thunder in the distance. Soft drops of rain splashed through the shattered windshield. The dark clouds parted, casting a soft light on the scene beyond the BMW's crumpled front end.

Bus 7 was twisted halfway around the bottom of the flag-pole, snapped in half by the impact. One turn signal, its cables dangling from the front headlight, flashed an SOS in the face of the stone cherub that once topped the fountain. The front door of the bus was open, a body tossed on the stairs, head suspended inches from the street.

Jake tried to get out of the car, but pain shot up his leg; he winced and closed his eyes and gripped the wheel. Clouds obscured the light; he could only see shadowy fig-ures dropping out of the door, falling, and getting up again, disappearing from sight. A woman. A man carrying some-thing in his arms. The woman staggered out of his sightline and into the night. Another man stumbled from the bus, moving in Jake's direction.

Jake felt a warm trickle down the side of his neck. His fin-gers found the sticky gash, the jagged edge of what felt like the rearview mirror imbedded above his left shoulder.

The figure came closer.

"Over here." Jake screamed at him through the broken windshield. "I'm over here. I can't move. Help me! Call 911! Help!"

Jake grabbed the door handle, but the mirror's edge pressed deeper into his neck. He watched, helpless, trapped. The man stumbled against his car and left a bloody handprint smeared on the glass. Jake stared at him through the cracked, rain-streaked rearview mirror. The man had stopped, steadied himself, then hoisted a baby's car seat up to Jake's window. Charlie's car seat? The man seemed to smile at him, turned, and walked away.

Jake banged on the glass "Stop, Stop! Bring him back! Charlie!"

His cries gave way to sobs. Imprisoned in the wreckage, Jake could only watch him walk away. He screamed into the now-deserted street and closed his eyes. Through his pain, before he lost consciousness, Jake heard the rain tapping metal, the diminishing thunder, and the low wail of sirens.

133

HOLT GOT THE call as he drove up to the Plaza. It was almost empty. A bus was idling at the loading point.

"Yeah, what is it?" Holt barked into his phone.

"Detective, we need you at the hospital immediately. There's been a mass casualty incident near the old shopping area, a bus bent in two like a beer can. Multiple fatalities. And we got a guy who had been trapped in his car when the bus spun into him, nearly taking off the front end of his car. He's screaming and raging in the ER, claiming somebody stole his wife and baby."

Stop. Hiss.

Holt looked up at the bus pulling away from the bus stop.

"What was the bus number, officer?"

"Let me see." Holt could hear the ruffle of notebook pages. "Here, I've got it. It was Bus 7. Not so lucky, eh detective?"

134

HOLT PULLED UP to the ER entrance. Through the lobby windows, he saw a bloodied man limping back and forth in front of the reception desk.

He walked first to a group of officers standing just inside the door and flashed his badge. "What do we have here?"

"Pretty bad accident. The bus driver was DOA, found him on the floor beside the driver's seat. A passenger at the bus door, partially ejected. A male passenger, about fifty, a businessman I'd say from his clothes, on the floor at the back of the bus. Unconscious but breathing. He's in the trauma unit, on his way to surgery. We're working to ID him. A female, about thirty-five, found in a seat in the middle of the bus. They thought she was dead when they found her. She's critical in ICU. Head trauma and some broken bones. A laundry list of drugs in her system. She's lucky to be alive.

"What about this guy?" Holt gestured to Jake.

"Collateral damage. He was injured when the bus collided with his car at the scene. He was treated there but insisted on coming to the hospital to find his wife and baby."

Holt recognized him as the man he met in the ER several weeks ago.

"Jake?" Holt walked up behind him and held up his badge.

Jake turned around, wincing with pain, a bloody bandage on his neck. He leaned up against the desk and grabbed Holt's arm.

"Detective Holt! My wife and baby—they don't know if Annabelle will make it. The baby wasn't there, but I know he had been on that bus. I saw a man come off the bus holding a car seat that looked just like Charlie's. You have to find him!"

Holt led Jake to the waiting area, motioning him to sit down.

"I'm sorry about your wife. She's in good hands." He paused, then continued. "You say someone took the baby? Maybe a survivor found him on the bus and took him to safety."

Jake stirred in the chair; his voice strained. "The baby carrier wasn't on the bus. I told Annabelle to take Charlie on the bus and meet me at the turnaround. Charlie was in a baby carrier on that bus with Annabelle. Oh God! Annabelle!" He covered his face, sobbing.

Holt saw a nurse walking towards them. She said, "I'll take care of Mr. Martin, detective. The EMTS gave him some meds en route. It will be a while before he can answer any questions."

"I have to leave," Holt told her. "But I'll be back as soon as I can." He bent down at eye-level and said to Jake, quieting his own fears. "We'll find your baby."

Holt dashed out the door, positioned the flasher on the hood, turned on the sirens, and headed towards David's house.

I'm not a praying man, God, but if you're listening, I'm praying now. Not for mercy, but for vengeance.

135

THE EMTS WERE in David's driveway when Holt arrived.

"What's up, detective? The call from the chief's office said to meet you here, that it was urgent."

"It may just be," said Holt. He pulled his Glock from the holster, holding it in ready position. "Wait here."

The door was open, as if someone was expecting him. He heard the disembodied sounds of a grandfather clock. Holt walked into the entryway and stopped, glancing into the ornate dining room. One small drawer of a breakfront was open and empty.

A hinged wooden swinging door stood at the end of a shallow hallway that split the first floor. Probably the kitchen door, Holt mused. These old houses all had the same footprint.

He looked to the left and walked into what would have been the drawing room in the old days. The room looked lived in. Cushions dented from use, pillows on the floor, coffee table smeared and littered with coffee cups. Holt detected a faint smell of bleach. He went through the kitchen, and then up the stairs to the bedrooms, clearing one after another. In the last bedroom, a dresser drawer was missing from a small wooden bureau. The other drawers were partly closed. What looked like a baby blanket was on the floor. Holt pulled out his phone and snapped a photo, descended the stairs. and went out the door.

He holstered his weapon.

"See anything? Bad guys or dead bodies, detective?

"No. You guys can go."

136

HOLT SAT DOWN on a wicker chair on the wide front porch and rested his head in his hands. *Bloody hell.* Where had David gone? He called the precinct to send forensics to secure the house and gather evidence.

He felt his phone vibrating and pulled it out of his pocket. It was the precinct.

"Yeah, what is it?"

"A photo just came in from the local station. It was sent to a reporter, with a message to give it to you. They also sent it to the chief, and he wants you in here *now*! You need to look at this before you see the chief. Sending it now."

The screen went black, then lit up with a message containing a photo. Holt enlarged it. There on the screen was a tiny baby wrapped in a blanket, lying in a dresser drawer. His eyes were wide open, wisps of dark hair sticking out from the edge of his knitted hat. A calico cat lay curled up beside the drawer as if on guard, ears up, eyes staring into the camera. A handwritten note was taped to the end of the drawer, just beyond the baby's feet.

"My baby brother is home safe now. No need to look for him. Hannah and I will take good care of him. No one will ever hurt him again."

About the Author

MARY J. NESTOR attended Marquette University in Wisconsin, and has a bachelor of Business Administration from Washington Adventist University. She has previously published a children's book, *Emily's Best Birthday Party Ever!* Her career as a manager, consultant, and human resources director inspired a second book, *Say It Now! Say It Right! How to Handle Tough and Tender Conversations*. Nestor enrolled in a writer's conference in 2016, resulting in *Bus No. 7*, a finalist in the Novel-In-Progress category of the 2020 William Faulkner Literary Competition.

Nestor lives in a waterfront villa a short walk from the ocean on Hilton Head Island, South Carolina. When she isn't writing, Mary can be found on the golf course, singing with the Hilton Head Symphony Orchestra Chorus and the Hilton Head Choral Society, or creating home furnishings with Sew So Chic, her custom fabrication business. She is at work on a sequel to *Bus No. 7*, and looking forward to her next adventure.

About Bold Story Press

BOLD STORY PRESS is a curated, woman-owned hybrid publishing company with a mission of publishing well-written stories by women. If your book is chosen for publication, our team of expert editors and designers will work with you to publish a professionally edited and designed book. Every woman has a story to tell. If you have written yours and want to explore publishing with Bold Story Press, contact us at https://boldstorypress.com.

The Bold Story Press logo, designed by Grace Arsenault, was inspired by the nom de plume, or pen name, a sad necessity at one time for female authors who wanted to publish. The woman's face hidden in the quill is the profile of Virginia Woolf, who, in addition to being an early feminist writer, founded and ran her own publishing company, Hogarth Press.